Dialogues on the Beach

D0003183

a novel by
John C. McLucas

DIALOGUES ON THE BEACH

Editor: Clarinda Harriss
Graphic design: Ace Kieffer
Cover art: Minas Konsolas
Author photo: Lauren Castellana/Kanji Takeno

BrickHouse Books, Inc. 2016
306 Suffolk Road
Baltimore, MD 21218

Distributor: Itasca Books, Inc.

ISBN: 978-1-938144-52-3

Printed in the United States of America

To my three beloved siblings: Pamela, Susan, and Roderick—
insightful, wise, and deeply kind readers
of books and of life.
Susan will read it on this planet; Pam and Rod from some loftier perch.
All three brighten my days.

Table of Contents

Chapter 1 – 1970-1993
College, Yale Graduate School, & home in Baltimore

Tony's wife Rachel and I had become good friends over time, in spite of the obvious: I was in love with Tony, my best friend at college, for years. Initially this was supposed to be a profound secret. Of course Walter caught on, virtually from the moment he and I became roommates in the middle of freshman year. Walter's gay radar was unmatched. No one else would have thought to call it love, though everyone knew that Tony and I were some sort of pair. Friends even joked about our being married. We were always together. If Tony or I was away for a weekend, the other got condolence calls, thoughtful invitations, kind distractions, from all over campus. Professors would give us each other's papers if one of us wasn't there when assignments were returned. I knew Tony's moods, his early-morning look and the look in class that said he knew the answer and the one that said he didn't. He knew me well, certainly. He was the all-time master of the butch straight-man bead-read: "I have my pride," I said once, and he said, "And several other people's too."

There was a girlfriend. I knew that, but at first I didn't worry about it much. Eventually, without rancor, that bond would succumb to distance and time. One day, our daily closeness, the shared books and midnight confidences, would become irreversible, and everyone would suddenly know that I came first with Tony.

But there was, fairly soon, a weekend, first of many, when Rachel came up from Vassar. She'd known him long before me, back to third grade I think. She knew his parents, his little brother, the famous family rabbi, the family dog, and Tony's best friend from home, whose very name made me jealous. She adored me at first sight: strictly Melanie and Scarlett. With real regret, with an actual weak sense of defeat, I liked her. She was sharply pretty in those years, smallish but nicely zaftig, dressed just as she should be in correct peasant blouses, old jeans, smocked dress for parties, her rich black hair pulled back into a thick braid or billowing pony tail, her jewelry, when there was jewelry, all beads and copper.

Her quick eyes rested on me at our first meeting and she said, "You're Jim – you're this wonderful Jim I've been hearing about. I feel like I love you already." Tony said hardly anything for hours, it seemed, as Rachel and I chirped brightly at each other about everything but Tony, dropping occasional familiar comments to show we knew all about him.

That night we all went with friends to a local pizzeria, where I got to show off my Italian by chatting with the owners, who with good commercial sense had learned by then to greet me as *signor Giacomo*. Rachel entranced the whole group, smart, funny, charming, hip. One was reminded sometimes, in college, that the kid in the Mexican blouse or torn Grateful Dead T-shirt was the offspring of Uptown shrinks or senior Foreign Service officers, and Rachel was like that: precociously a great lady, even with a leather strap stuck with a chopstick holding her hair off her forehead. I had a sense, as one friend after another yielded to Rachel's charm, of having lost a contest, though no one else present could have known it had occurred.

Hours later, after sitting around Tony's room drinking

Mateus with the hall mates, as the others one by one took their leave, I suddenly dimly realized that I had to go. This was not to be one of those nights when, at 3 a.m., Tony or I decided after all to crash on the other's sofa or floor; in the morning, it would not be me teasing Tony about his grouchiness; and in the interval someone, not I, would be annoyed, or not, by Tony's snoring. Of whatever else would happen, and of the fact that in any case it would not be the first time, I literally could not stand to think. There were good-byes of perfect friendliness, and then Tony's door was quietly and tactfully closed behind me and I strolled back to my room alone. To the extent that I let myself think anything, I thought She knows him better than I do.

Andreuccio – "Ootch" to his many friends – was barking frenzied high C's at the mailman, his tail wagging madly: he lived for this. I pulled him back from the front window. No one warned me (unless that was Ootch's message) that that day's mail would include my last note to Angel, returned as undeliverable. Angel had tyrannized my heart during my final years of grad school. He possessed a sweet self-deprecating hotness and, in response to my shy, gawkish courtship, gently insisted that sex would spoil our tender intellectual friendship. I had loved him absurdly, calling him "Beauty" in moments of ecstatic adulation and making jokes about "the flutter of little wings" when I heard him coming up my stairs. Looking back, it was incredible to me that I had ever felt that way or spoken such words – or that so much ridiculous passion on my part had not somehow bent the universe to my wishes or overridden Angel's fond, stubborn demurrals. Now he had apparently moved, and I no longer knew a soul who might know how to reach him. It was no big deal, of course. I hadn't laid eyes on Angel in nine years by now, and our friendship had been maintained mostly by my gentle persistence in calling and writing. He'd cycled through two or three lovers in the meantime and changed careers roughly as often, and always assured me affectionately that the men and the jobs were nothing compared to me and my work. Several times we'd been scheduled to meet: he would come to Baltimore; I would be up in Connecticut for a conference; we would get together at New York's Gay Pride Day. It always fell through. Now the cord was cut. It had taken ten or twelve years, but Angel – the longed-for, the elusive, the mournful-eyed, brooding beloved – had finally gotten away.

"Ehi, professore!" It was Dino on the phone: one of my pet students from the year before. Actually it might be more accurate to say I'd been his pet professor. He was the cute butch bouncy kind who always dropped by to chat during office hours and lingered after class, taking pride in being seen with me in the hall. He'd come by my house unannounced a couple of times since he graduated, once mildly drunk. He'd sprawled on the couch while I rather self-consciously offered him a Coke; he'd stripped off his lacrosse goalie padding and treated me to a clear glimpse of his humpy torso; he'd give me a sudden boozy embrace on leaving. I liked Dino: a lot. I had never imagined that he might be gay, or done anything to imply a more than mentorial interest. He had always been the initiator in our social contacts. Inevitably, being human and still having my virility, I had hoped – something. Now on the phone he was saying he

wanted to bring his new girlfriend by to meet me.

"Sure," I said, "great."

It was no big deal. We set a time and I hung up, mad at myself for being mildly disappointed.

I'd been seeing Peter for a few weeks. No big deal, of course. He was a nice man, my age, a professional, and clearly the marrying type. We had been bantering back and forth on one of our first dates, and he asked me if I thought we should go to bed. I said, completely spontaneously, my words taking me by surprise,

"I wouldn't want to go to bed with you unless we fell in love."

I hadn't even thought those words, much less spoken them, in years, but I meant them. Peter loved it, and laughed – we both laughed.

"Who knows?" he said. Then I was even a little proud of myself, for the unexpected naiveté I still had in me. We continued to see each other about once a week in this mutually negotiated bubble of romantic abstinence. Then one evening at a bar, a mutual friend asked if I'd met Peter's new boyfriend in Frederick. He wasn't intending to be catty; he just mentioned it because he knew I knew Peter and liked him and had been out with him a few times. And as I thought about it – while instinctively concealing from my informant any reaction I might have felt – I had no reason to be upset or angry with Peter. There was no commitment between us, and he was under no obligation to tell me anything he did, after all. I just liked him enough to be disappointed. He and I talked that night on the phone and I asked him about this other man; it registered with me that he wouldn't have raised the subject if I hadn't. No big deal, he said; there was no commitment yet there either. But he enjoyed this guy's company, and he would see what developed. He liked me a lot, and hoped we'd be friends. Of course, I said; How not? Wearily, I realized we probably would. Adulthood was awful.

"Hello, dear," said the answering machine, "it's Mother." It was a rather long, rambling message. Mom had caught on to answering machine technology and the chic of chatty, free-associative messages like the ones she'd heard me and Marie and Walter leave for each other. She had called me now to catch me up on her latest legislative project; she was lobbying in Richmond for more funding for social services. This whole busy breezy professional on-the-go side of Mom was wonderful, and I felt a little remorse at my irritation that she wasn't home baking cookies and acting like other kids' moms. My childhood friends in Connecticut, from grade school on, had unanimously adored my mother and delighted in her banter with them and the genuineness of her interest in their childish or adolescent concerns. Certainly I'd basked for years in her reputation as the neatest mom in town, and now, settled in Northern Virginia, she continued to enthrall Marie, Walter, Ricardo, Luellen – all of my friends. But there was a maternal archetype that I felt had bypassed me unfairly, a quiet lady with a soft voice and patient eyes and nothing to do all day but comfort and nurture… me. I'd gotten instead this kooky liberal do-gooder. I was a jerk for noticing the discrepancy. I called her back. Of course she wasn't home; she was the Woman of the Nineties and she was out and doing. I left her a long, rambling message.

"Hi, baby," said Ricardo. His voice always sounded deeper on the phone and, as had been happening a lot over the past couple of years, I found myself talking to him as to another adult. Of course, he was twenty-nine now and ran his own Dupont Circle florist shop and – amazingly – had been running Walter, rather efficiently, for over five years. He *was* an adult. I found myself telling him about my letter to Angel and Peter's new boyfriend.

"Oh, Jimmy," he said, "what a shame. I'm sorry." His sympathy was touching.

"It's no big deal," I said bravely.

"Yes it is," he said. "You loved Angel. You like Peter. That's a big deal." Then he called across the room to Walter: "Angel moved and Jimmy doesn't know where. Ungrateful little twerp." From the fact that he hadn't mentioned Peter, I gathered that they hadn't taken that relationship very seriously. Then he asked me, "So how's your mom?"

"O Son of God, Life-giver, joyful in Thine appearing!" the choir sang. It was the kind of grand British anthem you might hear at a royal wedding or as the credits rolled for "Masterpiece Theatre." It had been a favorite of mine to sing, years before when I was working my way through grad school as a paid singer in Connecticut churches. It was good, in a grown-up way, to sit in church now and hear the choir sing it without me. It was also poignant. I had considered trying to make music my career in those years, though I seldom had any regrets now about having chosen a secure academic path when the time came to choose, but occasionally a piece reminded me of how the younger me imagined a life in music. There was another dream too, not unrelated. "Life-giver – joyful in thine appearing!" There was a man who was supposed to come, back then, and somehow never had. Not Tony; not Angel – neither of them had materialized in this role. I could just make out the shape of this man, backlit, a glory around his golden head, white wings with a beating, a whirring, that thrilled and stunned as much as it comforted. Had I missed him somewhere along the way? Surely I would have recognized him. Maybe that was another dream not for this life.

"Great music," said Luellen at coffee hour. I told her how the life-giver had made me think of the lover I'd never met, even though the anthem was supposed to be about Jesus. She nodded her efficient comprehending medical nod and said, "God is love." I smiled. Luellen, a physician's assistant, ran the AIDS service at Hopkins Hospital with her own combination of Southern charm, offbeat Zen spirituality, and ironclad efficiency, and she never held back when it came to the meaning of life. "And Jimmy," she said, "it's coming. You know you've got a prayer committee working on this one that just scares God rigid."

She was right about that. Lydia Baldwin, tartar-tongued silver-haired doyenne of the Presbyterian Women, asked me almost every week if I'd met anyone. She was convinced, my frequent denials notwithstanding, that my close friend Robert and I had been a couple, and his sudden death five summers before had moved her to a passion of protective tenderness towards me that was still unabated.

"Is Bob the God in your life?" I asked Luellen. She eyed him narrowly, almost as though calculating how much she'd bid on him at auction. He smiled his conceited complacent genial handsome straight-man smile, fully conscious of his own similarities to the God Event in Luellen's world.

"Clearly," he said.

"*Sospira,*" I said.

"Hmm?" Luellen asked.

"It's what Beatrice says to the people of Florence when they all resolve to lead better, purer lives just because she's walked down the street."

"Roughly translated?" asked Bob.

"'Eat your pitiful hearts out,'" I said.

"How about this?" asked Andrea. "'O God, you knew us already in our mothers' wombs…'" Andrea was everyone's favorite progressive Anglican priest in Baltimore. She and her lover (she would say "life-partner") Sandra had raised or were raising a vast litter of children – their own, adoptees of several races and conditions, babies with AIDS, and God only knows who all else. I'd pretty much lost track since my last time at their house. One of their babies had died, and a bright-eyed Bolivian girl I'd never seen chased me around and around the coffee table, laughing, and the pumped-up boyfriend of a daughter home from college had yakked sociably on the sofa with me for half an hour before I realized he wasn't one of the brood. This was a mild let-down, because he'd been most charming and

I'd assumed he was one of their gay sons I'd heard about and never met. It had occurred to me that if we fell in love I'd have two delightful mothers-in-law who would give us no flak at all about Topic A. Well, life is full of disappointments and I tried to be happy for the lucky girl who presumably got to lick that smooth chest as much as she wanted.

Anyway, here was Andrea hosting a small meeting to develop a liturgy for an upcoming AIDS prayer service. Her Biblical reference suited her own lesbian hyper-maternalism and did honor to something truly Godlike about her chaotic home and others I knew like it. Somehow, the womb of God and the mothers' wombs wherein God already knew us and Andrea and Sandra managing their menagerie formed a single picture in my mind, and I liked it.

Then James spoke up, his voice acid as usual.

"That's heterosexist as hell," he said. I looked around the room. Hal, my minister, was too good a liberal to tell a charter member of ACT-UP/Baltimore that he was being an ass. Andrea didn't want to seem too defensive about her own draft prayer. It was up to me.

"We all come from wombs, James," I said. "Not only straight married people have children. Everybody wants to be loved by God from the beginning and with no conditions. I think it's OK." Get me out of here, I thought.

When summer came, Baltimore had the sense to slow down. I'd been tenured at my university the year before, my book on the *Decameron* had just come out, and my study of gender in Ariosto was still just a pile of notecards and some completely nonsensical jottings on my laptop. The state's ongoing fiscal woes had meant the fourth year in a row without a raise, with another increase in teaching load and administrative work. I had decided to take the summer off. There would be plenty of time for underpaid overachievement when classes started up again in the fall.

I let myself spend a lot of time daydreaming that summer as part of my vacation regimen, and refused to feel guilty about it. On the fifth anniversary of the day Robert died of a cardiac arrest during my summer party, I expected he would be much in my thoughts. Ootch was curled by the sofa after our afternoon walk in Patterson Park. He was six now and, though still the butchest and loudest dog of all time, occasionally napped quietly of an afternoon. I lay down myself and took off my glasses. For a moment I thought of Robert. He had been a dear, strange friend, and I missed him.

Then for no reason I found myself imagining a conversation with my recent boyfriend Peter. The guy in Frederick had started dating someone else, he said. Peter was disappointed and called me, ostensibly to share his disappointment with a friend – me – but actually, I could tell, intending to ask me out again. I told him No. I wasn't about to be anybody's second choice. He sounded ashamed, cowed, conciliatory. He tried to sweet-talk me for a bit, then hung up, still hoping I'd relent.

I imagined that I got a note from Angel. He hadn't written for a while because he wasn't sure where he'd settle after his last breakup. He was really sorry he'd missed our last rendez-vous in New York, but his mother had been ill, and I knew how demanding Cuban mothers were! When could he come to Baltimore? I sent him a short, correct note in response. It was great to hear from him; so glad he'd landed on his feet. He could come any time and I'd be delighted to see him. I wasn't holding my breath, of course, given his past record, and I wouldn't beg. From now on, our friendship, if there was to be one, would be strictly fifty-fifty.

I imagined that Tony called. He had left Rachel. I was actually sad for Rachel – less for Tony. He ought to have had the sense to become my lover back in early 1971. I'd lost count of how many times I'd whispered his name to my pillow, but it was too many. It should have been Tony himself, and it was hard to forgive him for the fact that it never had been. It was as though he had actually robbed me of a form of health and contentment that had been mine by right. It was his fault I'd grown to adulthood single, high-strung, repressed, and prickly. Now that he and Rachel were through, he turned to me, wanted to see me. He would probably get drunk, as he had that awful time in New Haven; I could probably, under guise of comforting him, take him to bed. It was too late now to imagine that I could be tender with him, but he would have to bear with that. It was his own fault and, deep down inside, he understood that.

The phone rang. Ootch gave a yelping bark, startling himself almost as me. The shrill sound cut into my unpleasant reveries like a nail scraped across a blackboard that was also, somehow, my diaphragm. It was Gene on the phone – acknowledged by all who knew him to be the Handsomest Man in Baltimore, who ruled in undisputed majesty over the city's gay social life. He'd remembered that it was the anniversary of Robert's death, and was calling to say he was thinking of me. I was touched, and we had a nice talk. I told him about Peter, but said quickly, "I'll get over it, I guess." I never liked to expose any of my vulnerabilities to Gene, the unruffled, hot, and glorious.

"Consider the alternative," he said.

"Going crazy, you mean, or having no life?"

"Thank you," he said. I could picture the regal nod. "You'll be just fine."

After we hung up, I looked inside for a moment and realized that I actually *was* fine. The turn my thoughts had been taking before Gene's phone call surprised me. They were unhappy vindictive thoughts, not like me, really, and anyway I'd expected to think of Robert. Well, thoughts of sex with Tony were right up Robert's alley. Robert, I'd sometimes thought, had died of grief at not being able to marry a straight man. There had been gay men who'd courted him quite assiduously, but he wasn't interested. "Straight-acting and –appearing" earned no points with Robert; the minute a man's cock plumped up for him, he was proven gay and thus unfascinating. Fanta-sex for Robert would have been kneeling in front of a man and blowing him, while the man, half-flaccid, called him a cocksucker and talked about his wife. Then somehow a miracle would happen and Robert would bring the man off, without the man's ever liking or wanting it – he thought. Robert would get up, smooth his hair, and go back to work, knowing he'd found a nervous spring at the base of the man's psyche, and/or penis, that no other man had ever touched or ever would again.

This was so clear an image that Robert was practically

there in front of me again, his ways provoking and sad. I missed him, and smiled. He had been unswervingly loyal and support-ive to me, and I hoped I had been as good to him, and we had truly loved each other – but I had always secretly known that he was way weirder and more neurotic than I was. This mem-ory of him made it less embarrassing to look at the pathetic far-ranging revenge-fantasies I'd just been indulging. Gene's call had helped, too. I do have a life, I realized, single or not; I won't go all twisted and nasty over this. If I'd had a turnip to brandish at Heaven, I would have done so, but even so, God was my witness.

"So what do you say?" Tony asked me. "Rachel says she won't go unless you can stay with us. We'll treat you royally." They wanted to get out of Chicago for a couple of weeks and somehow had lit on the idea of renting a beach house at Re-hoboth; it belonged to some business friends of his. Normally their vacations dazzled me – the first tour through China as it opened up, the last trek up to Machu Picchu before it was closed, kayaking in Alaska, pony trails and opera in Santa Fe. My modest forays to Europe seemed pretty pallid in compar-ison. Two weeks on the beach at Rehoboth were a whole dif-ferent matter, and I had trouble for a moment picturing them there, or myself with them.

Rehoboth was marked territory for Baltimore gays. We went to Rehoboth the way my grandparents went to Chautau-qua – reverently, religiously, every summer – though, generally speaking, we did not attend lectures on Theosophy while there. It was my gentle boast that, on my visit to Gene's house at

Rehoboth the summer before, I had scored with three men in three days, and then left in a cloud of glory, to the gratifying echoes of my friends' envy and astonishment. It would be tricky to manage Tony and Rachel along with the bevies of Baltimore boys we'd be meeting on the beach every day. Over the prospect of what Gene might say if he met me on the beach with Tony unprepared, I drew a chaste veil.

I'd never thought of myself as a real beach-person anyway: it was fun for a day or two of shrieking, but then I'd always get bored and restless. Taking the sun was not a big thing with me, and my waist, which took well enough to snappy Italian blazers, did less well in swim trunks. This consideration was very poignant at Rehoboth, where the beach was virtually an impromptu beauty pageant and one could easily spend every second gasping and slavering.

But Tony was pressing me to accept:

"Come on, Jimbo; it's been way too long. We need to catch up. I... there are some things I want to check out with you." His voice was almost wheedling. I loved that voice, and I said,

"OK; at least for part of the time. I'll bring my laptop and a car full of books; I may be totally antisocial. Maybe Walter and Ricardo can come up too, for a day or two, or Marie – Clare's taken the kids to Seattle on vacation and she's alone for the month. Is there room?"

"That'd be great," he said. "How is the little weasel?" This was his bizarre nickname for Ricardo, the most beautiful young man of our era.

"Flourishing," I said. "Should I ask them?"

"Absolutely," Tony answered. "The place is huge. Rachel's never met Marie or Ricardo, come to think of it, has she? *Make them come.*"

I had first laid eyes on Tony Neuberg during freshman orientation week in the fall of 1970. I was a nervous, closeted gay virgin at that age, surrounded by the exuberant funky hetero experimentation of the hippy Sexual Revolution. I knew what I wanted, but I tried to pass myself off as a very nice, modest, sensitive and artistic, old-fashioned but open-minded straight boy. I imagined deep chaste romantic attachments with certain kinds of friendly, humpy, butch but vulnerable guys, and privately indulged wild sexual fantasies about them – based on a complete ignorance of actual sex. When I first met Tony, the vital spirits about my heart gave me no warning that this was it; no thoughtful Hollywood director provided sudden closeups or heart-clenching harmonies, so that later, when the rocket took off, I was unprepared. He was a good-looking enough boy, with an open engaging manner, but in the excitement of so many new friends I didn't pay much attention to him at first. He was pretty heavily prelaw from the start, in defiance of the arty radical chic of the era, and I imagined we'd have little enough in common. I'd never seen a blond Jew before and that struck me at first, in my self-consciously tolerant garnering of new types and tales among my suddenly broadening acquaintance, as his main claim to interest.

Certainly his thick sleek body and simple smile made no strong initial impression on me. He had the darkish golden skin and curly sun-streaked hair of some lucky northern Italians, and from his first name I'd assumed that was what he was. But it turned out he was really Anton, and his father was the only survivor of a Prague ghetto family that had bribed prodigiously to get him to America before war broke out. This story, when I heard it sitting up late one September night on the hill outside our dorm, touched me deeply. It gave Tony a gently tragic glamor in my eyes. I began to see him as touched by sadness, the lone repository of the hopes of generations gone, a precious remnant, fragile in spite of all his exuberant health and high spirits. Within a couple of months we fell into habits of spending time together. By then I had developed a rather rote crush on my roommate, and my persistently sentimental view of Tony, history's victim, allowed no kindling of lust in me for some time. With Tony I felt wise, protective, almost maternal, a proto-Alan Alda sensibility that I firmly believed was too fond and disinterested to be sexual.

One day, late in the fall semester, we were teammates in a wild game of dodge ball in the hallway; something in his eyes, as we flattened ourselves against opposite walls and he grinned at me and panted and the ball flew between us like a meteor, stirred me unexpectedly. Then that night, as I sat at my desk reading a Pavese short story and he sat cross-legged on my bed tuning his guitar, I looked over and saw the lamplight shining on his hair. My spirits rose as though I'd just been awakened by sudden yellow sunshine in the window.

"*Capelli d'oro*," I said suddenly, shyly, surprising myself.

He looked up and smiled – "Huh?"

"Golden hair," I murmured. "*Capelli d'oro*." He repeated it after me, smiling as if I were teaching him a cool new Italian phrase and not telling him, and myself, that I loved him. From then on, in my most affectionate moments, I called him Doro. Our friends knew it was my pet name for him, but never knew why – except, again, for the inexorable Walter, who knew enough Italian, and enough Jim, to guess. When the others teased us about being married, we both smiled; and when they asked what Doro meant, I said nothing, and Tony said "He won't tell me" or "I forget" and smiled at me. Once he ran his fingers through his hair as he said it, to show me that he hadn't really forgotten. Another time I overheard Rachel ask him what it meant, and he just said "I don't know." For weeks after, the thought that he hadn't told her made me smile. He might never be only mine, but he kept some things just for me. He called me Jimbo and James and My Man McManus and My guy; and often when I picked up the phone I'd hear him say, "Hi, it's Doro" or "Hey, it's Dore"; if possible, even sweeter to hear that than, "Hi, it's me."

Chapter 2 – Monday
Rehoboth Beach, Delaware
(and flash-backs)

I got to Rehoboth Monday morning, the day after Tony and Rachel. This was part of my reluctant stance: let them get there first and set up and then I'd appear like a star stepping from a limousine. My drive down was lonely. I'd asked Marie to go with me, but she couldn't take off during the week. Gene was supposed to be at the beach already, but his best friend Jock – a gruff, portly, avuncular, and deeply wise older man whom I called the Mayor of Gay Baltimore – had told me the night before I left that Gene was having to come back to town for a couple of days to nail down some things at the office, so he wouldn't be there when I arrived. I had debated bringing Ootch with me. I decided that he would rather stay with the neighbors, whose teenaged son adored him, treating him exactly like a peer and exhausting him with endless games of Frisbee, than suffer with me through what I intended to be very slow lazy days of reading, writing, and talking. The boy's mother would step in every day, water plants, collect mail, and feed the cat Griselda. So I was alone, and conscious of being alone, for over three hours in the car. The roads were nicely clear; that just meant that no normal person would go to the beach on a Monday. I wasn't especially good company to myself. Furlough days and increased class sizes at work; Peter's pusillanimity and the gay grapevine's implacable efficiency in dashing one's illusions; the unceremonious end to what felt like one of the great tragic loves of my life distilled in the "Addressee Unknown" stamp on my last letter to Angel; and embittered gay activists… it felt good to be driving away from all of that. At the same time I was a little scared of being so long with Tony and Rachel. This vacation was to be my escape from the world of ego deflation and burnout, but there was no point in denying that there would be tensions there too. Tony and I hadn't been two weeks together since college; Tony and Rachel and I, never. I'd brought enough books that, if things got awkward, I could retreat into my studies.

Tony had given me the address, and as I pulled up I realized it was just a few doors up from a house Gene and Jock and Jock's stolid dull sedate lover Larry had taken two or three years earlier. That house I was surprised to see still standing; surely the carryings-on of that summer should have compromised its structural integrity. There had been more men through it that weekend than perhaps in any like period in its whole tacky history. I remembered taking, amid shrieks, what seemed like the longest roll of pictures ever made, of Gene dressed in a black sequined sheath gown and flipflops, perched with pertly crossed legs on the edge of a grumpy Jock's bed at 3:00 am, slinking down the stairs, wrapping his arms around a partially amused Larry, leaning over the porch rail puckering like Marilyn, humping the poor young bartender he'd picked up at the Strand and who, at first, had taken him for an idol of butchness. Because God is merciful, the camera, the next morning, proved to be empty. I had been busily working a Costa Rican waiter from DC most of that weekend, and had barely noticed the new white pile that faced on the beach at the top of our street, though we must have walked past it several times a day. This was the house Tony and Rachel had taken.

It hardly fit my image of a beach house. It was a deep-porched two-story number with a Cape Cod saltbox silhouette which the builder, not understanding, had chosen to do in white brick, with green shutters. Squinting, I could make it look a bit like Selznick's Tara, a kind of squat patted-together hybrid of North and South that only Delaware or Maryland would think made any sense at all. I remembered years before, when a French teenager visiting my family in Connecticut had demanded to be shown houses like the ones in *"Autant en emporte le vent,"* and wouldn't buy our embarrassed explanations that Georgia was a thousand miles to the south. Finally we were able to quiet her with a drive up the Old Post Road in Fairfield, where staunch abolitionists and Unionists whose faces Mrs. Merriwether would have paid money to spit in had raised white-porticoed Greek Revival mansions which, to this deluded French child, were indistinguishable from Twelve Oaks itself. She might have gone for this one too.

There was a note on the front door in Rachel's rapid Italic, telling me where to find the keys; Tony and Rachel were running errands. I was to make myself at home. They'd taken the master suite and I should pick a room for myself – maybe the studio over the garage. The house was furnished with unimaginable splendor and in spite of myself I liked it. Everything that white leather, teak, brass, and twelve-over-twelve windows could do for it had been done. There was a complete new stereo system and I wished I'd thought to bring CD's: a quick glance at the storage rack showed a tedious yuppie selection of New Age, Motown, and Pachebel. There was a beautifully refinished

Victorian upright grand in the living room. I checked it quickly and found it well kept and in tune. It's hard enough to keep a piano in tune in Baltimore and I wondered how many humidifiers and dehumidifiers and visits from the tuner its gracious presence here on the beach front represented: What money can buy, I thought. The dining room had a huge halogen chandelier. The kitchen, with its terra cotta tiles and triple sink and Vulcan stove festooned with Calphalon pans, staggered me. I couldn't imagine that anyone with that much money would spend it on a beach house, and tried, for my own amusement, to visualize their primary residence. I half-expected from moment to moment to see Woody Allen and Dianne Wiest lounge into the room, sipping Vouvray and doing Bergman more tastefully than Bergman had ever thought to do.

The bedrooms were upstairs under the eaves. Tony and Rachel were about half-unpacked in the front room, which had two dormer window-seats facing the ocean, a majestic bath, and an actual canopy of blue and white ticking over the large bed. The other rooms, with perfect striped wallpapers accentuating the hips in the ceiling, sleigh beds and cast iron camp beds and futons to die for, made me wonder what Rachel could have meant about studios over garages – I don't think so! I thought. Then, to indulge her, to be nice, I went outside, up the stairs by the garage door, and into the studio.

Well, OK, it was heaven. There was a long sofa, upholstered in slick green cotton with white piping; it would fold out into a king-size bed. In the closet, sure of my choice, Rachel had already put white cotton sheets and vast white cotton bath towels and a robe of slick white Egyptian cotton that reached to my ankles. The large main room was a story and a half high and was lit with a high slanting studio skylight facing the ocean and big-paned windows on all four sides. Below the wall of skylight a sliding door led to a small balcony over the boardwalk. There was a good compact stereo system and I realized that, with the equipment so handy, I'd be forced to go buy a few desert-island disks to make it through the visit. Was there any chance a store in Rehoboth would carry Berganza retrospectives on CD? There were large bookshelves, sleek Scandinavian furniture, and a kitchenette considerably better appointed than my own kitchen in Baltimore. Separating it from the main room was a glass-brick counter exactly like the one I'd been thinking of putting in at home, except that this one, about ten minutes trendier than me, had brilliant red and teal grouting between the bricks. The glass doors of the cupboards showed that Rachel had already laid in some groceries. The bathroom, also lit by a skylight which could hinge open, was as large as the kitchen and had a bidet. I longed to meet the yuppie queen who had put this place together, and shuddered at the thought of what it was costing Tony. The kitchenette and bath backed up to the main house; that was the only corner of the studio without windows. Looking out the front, I saw the main building to my right and realized that the kitchen wall adjoined Tony and Rachel's bedroom. Privacy would be one big plus of staying here; assuming I ever managed to score, I could sneak the guy up the stairs and back down without their having to meet, approve, or disapprove him. But I rapped the party wall, hard, to test it. It would do no good to bring a screamer upstairs, thinking the place was private, if the wall separating us from Rachel and Tony's headboard turned out to be just a slice or two of sheetrock. Gratifyingly, I hurt my knuckles knocking on it.

Within half an hour I had unpacked my books onto the shelves and my clothes into the closet and dresser. I was sitting on my balcony sipping Campari, watching a lot of cute ditzy gay boys who were convinced they were macho spontaneous jocks because they were playing bad volleyball. They kept punching their fists in the air and giving each other high five and saying "Hey!" and "Yeah!" and "YeeAH!" Why be gay at all, I wondered, if it just means you have to act like a clueless frat boy who'd beat you up for two cents? Of course, Madonna seemed to think that was the main goal of life on the planet, and these boys worshiped her to a man and followed her every slightest cue; I was still recovering from their vogueing phase. Fortunately they were for the most part superbly pretty, though not, alas, especially butch. Occasionally, delightfully, one would forget that gay was normal now, and shriek.

I heard Rachel and Tony's rental car pull into the drive. I put my drink down on the rail and hurried to the back and out onto the entry landing over the driveway, waving as though I were welcoming them to my place. The car was a sporty little blue American convertible, quite of a piece with the house.

"You found it!" called Rachel, waving up at me and smiling delightedly as she got out of the car. She'd been driving: the Nineties, I thought.

"*You* found it," I said. "I love it. I want you to buy me this studio for my birthday."

"Hey," said Tony, running up the steps. He was wearing khaki shorts, Docksiders, and a crisp yellow broadcloth shirt, sleeves rolled up, which cast a bright buttery reflection up onto his face. His eyes looked bluer than the ocean and his curly blond hair, noticeably silver around his ears now, was shining in the sun. His arms and legs, as they always had been, were thick and comfortably rounded with muscle; his waist and neck had taken on the strong columnar gravity of a naturally athletic man of forty. It wasn't quite right to say he hadn't changed a bit since that first day I knew I loved him, back in 1970. One could have said instead that the years had made him bigger, dearer, and sexier. He looked more like a J. Crew model, bounding up the steps to me, than anyone in their catalogue. Yet I knew for a fact that he didn't work out and never thought twice about what he wore. Damn him, I thought, as he put his arm around my shoulder and kissed me on the cheek.

"Doro," I said, my arm around his waist.

"Hey, you," he said. "Come downstairs and let's get a drink." There was real urgency in his racing up to hug me like this, in his kiss, in his eyes. He does have something to talk to me about, I thought; something on his mind. And all I can tell him – or maybe can't – is that, after all these years, I still adore him.

"I've got one inside," I said. "Wait a second." I ran in to get it, nervous, almost shaken at seeing him again. It took me a second alone on the balcony to compose myself. I looked with a kind of weak longing at the bogus athletes on the beach. In a way it would be easier to leap down onto the sand and join them than to go back and face Tony; their attitude and silliness were completely predictable to me by now and at least a couple of them could probably push every single button of mine that the weary routine of Baltimore bars and parties had accustomed me to. Tony took me back to something else. It was what my letdowns over Angel and Peter had reminded me of: old dreams of love and happiness. The ritual puncturing of those dreams over the years had taught me for a long time just not to dream them anymore. They were coming back to me now, and they scared me. Something scared Tony too, at least a little, apparently. He'd been very moved to see me, even a bit shy. This was crazy: He's my best friend, I thought. There's nothing to be nervous about – picture being nervous with Walter, with Marie! Knowing full well it wasn't at all the same thing, I went back out to join him and his wife.

Rachel too was getting more beautiful with time. In our college days she was bright and birdlike and charming, but the years had given her stature. At some point soon after she started working, she decided it wasn't suitable for a grown woman to wear her hair down; quite a nineteenth century scruple, but terribly becoming to her. Her thick black hair stood out from her face in a demure pompadour even when pulled straight back into her simple everyday chignon. Her ears were usually covered, and she favored heavy dangling earrings, museum reproductions or lavish ethnic beads, gold coins and spangles, as though she were a shtetl bride wearing her dowry. I once accused her of studying pictures of Chléo de Mérode and the Comtesse de Castiglione, but she denied it, laughing, knowing exactly what I meant. With her sharp, slightly aquiline Mediterranean profile, this whole look gave her the stateliness of a Roman noblewoman or a goddess on a gold Syracusan stater. Her figure was fuller now too, swelling far beyond the bounds of fashionable anorexia, a proud indictment of the very concept of fashion, healthy, heavy, maternal, archetypal – even to me, extremely sexy. Her plain sea-blue cotton shirtdress flattered her without affectation, rising to follow the curves of hip and breast and hanging in natural flutings and drapings over the hollows of her narrow waist. She hugged and kissed me too.

"Oh!" she said, "it is so – good – to see you! Don't you look just beautiful!" She pulled back, her hands still on my waist, and looked at me with real joy, as though she were my mother and couldn't believe how tall I'd grown. Then, glancing over my shoulder and seeing Tony already stepping into the house with bags of groceries, she said more softly, "I think it will do Anton so much good to see you and talk with you." A few years earlier she had taken to calling Tony by his real name, believing it gave him more dignity; certainly it gave her a great deal. "He's been…" She frowned slightly and looked back at the car; maybe the car would tell her how he had been. "Well," she smiled after an instant, briskly, shaking her head, "you can just see for yourself. Imagine! Two whole weeks! Oh, it's so wonderful to have you here." She took my arm, put her head on my shoulder for a moment, and walked with me into the kitchen.

"Jim," called Rachel from the living room. Tony and I were in the kitchen making a seafood salad to her exact specifications for lunch. "You have got to go buy us some decent CD's. Solstice-this and Yanni-that... who are these people – Linda Evans?" A moment later we heard her start to roll chords on the piano and then launch into a little program of Bach and Mozart, interrupting herself rather frequently with a murmured "No, that's not right" and "Or something like that." I could picture her furrowed brow. She always played nicely, but because she did so many other things so brilliantly, music by comparison made her seem like charming determined underachiever.

"She sounds happy," I said.

"Yeah," Tony nodded. "You through with that knife?" He started julienning some kind of Asian vegetable I'd never seen and that Rachel, somehow, had procured in Delaware.

"This is fun," I said after a minute, pinching *herbes de Provence* into the olive oil and balsamic vinegar and feeling like an outtake from "ThirtySomething." Any moment Tony and I would start shooting hoops.

"Way fun," Tony said, looking up and smiling without quite meeting my eye. Then he caught himself and looked up again, more directly. "This is going to be great, Jim. We're really glad you could do this." I nodded, a little embarrassed that their underwriting my stay in that astonishing gilt-edged studio was to be construed as my having done them some enormous favor. "You've been good, no?" he asked. "You look great, by the way."

"I've been fine," I said. "The usual, I guess; not ecstasy, but…" I considered telling him about Angel or about Peter, but could picture myself babbling like a fool for half an hour and boring him to death.

"Hey," he said brightly, after a pause, "we've got a great bottle of champagne for after dinner tonight. Check the fridge. We haven't officially celebrated your tenure yet."

"Champagne?" I said, putting my hand to the door of the cavernous space age refrigerator. "You know I practically never drink champagne."

"Right," Tony grinned, because he in fact knew the exact opposite. If I were God, I would do nothing but drink champagne all day long. There on the top shelf was a bottle of Billecart-Salmon. I gave a little yelp.

"You're serious!" I said.

"You're our guy," said Tony, shrugging. Then, to my surprise, he asked without looking up, "You seeing anybody?"

"Nobody special," I said, off-hand. "I got dumped recently; that's the 'not ecstasy' part, I guess." Typically, over the years, Tony had responded to news like this with something like 'Then he wasn't good enough for you' or 'I can't picture anybody turning you down' or even once 'Men are jerks.' This time he said,

"Hey, count your blessings." Then he suddenly started hunting for plastic wrap to cover the salad bowl, opening silky silent drawers and cupboards.

"What?" I asked. He turned his head partway over his shoulder to answer, not quite far enough for our eyes to meet.

"Nothing," he said, with a little dismissive laugh.

Again, after dinner, he and I were alone in the kitchen. He had insisted on doing the dishes.

"He has a guilty conscience," Rachel said to me darkly. "I know this trick."

"He wants something from you," I said. "I read him like a book."

"Hey!" he said. We all laughed and Rachel consented to go sit on the porch till the dishes were done and we would open the champagne. The dishes went fast. I noticed he knew exactly how to load the dishwasher, which pans to soap and which to oil; I couldn't have trained him better myself, I thought. He asked me to tell him about the guy who had dumped me. I gave him the most rigorously abridged version I could, keeping it light: Peter was a super-nice guy; it was no big deal; and – the carefullest part of the package – I thought it was a good sign I'd been drawn to someone who was the marrying type.

"Hey," he said, "there's nothing wrong with being single, you know. You've got a great life. You're your own man."

"I know that," I said. "Nobody's better at being single than I am. And like they say, single guys always wish we weren't, and coupled guys always wish they were. But I feel like I've pretty much mastered this set of problems and challenges; I'd like to try some new ones for a change. It's kind of skitzy too, because on the one hand I've succeeded at everything in life and everybody worships me, but on the other hand when it comes to settling down, nobody wants me – like there's something wrong with me." That was starting to sound maudlin, and I'd already talked too long. "But I'm fine," I concluded. He smiled, gruffly, wishing he knew what to say, I thought.

"So what do you want from Rachel?" I asked, teasing him.

"Don't start," he said, irritably. "It's what she wants from me. I just want her to lay off." I was mortified; I'd been joking. But I kept my face blank. He kept scrubbing the counter, and I, the last of the pans dried, finally flicked his shoulder with my dishtowel.

"Spill your guts," I said.

"Hear that ticking?" he said, after a minute. I listened for a second, thrown off, before I caught the expression in his face – he was being witty. After a moment, I got it. "Rachel wants a child?" I asked. He turned back to the counter again and didn't answer. Well of course Rachel wanted a child, come to think of it. She had worked for years around the country as a consultant on education; some of her programs in Chicago had become national models. She had more publications than I did and had appeared occasionally on highbrow talk shows, talking about the rights of disadvantaged children especially. She worked with Hillary Clinton on national boards long before any of the rest of us had heard of her, and did some fairly high-profile campaigning with her in Illinois. Moreover, she was turning into an earth mother before our very eyes. It occurred to me, from the mild queasiness I was feeling, that I'd always been glad Tony had no children; part of me would never think of him as really Rachel's until there was a child. But for the first time I could feel the tug at Rachel's heart too and couldn't untangle my loyalties. I stepped up next to Tony and asked,

"Don't you? Doro. You'd be the most wonderful father in the world."

"Yeah," he said, nodding, smiling down at the counter. "I guess. There's more to it than that." He turned suddenly to face me, changing the subject, and the look of excitement in his eye was exactly what it had been twenty-three years before when we played dodge ball together. "Let's open that bottle!"

As he stood at the porch rail, leaning back and aiming the bottle as though he were about to strafe the beach, I couldn't help smiling. He was showing off for us, of course, goofing, still in so many ways the sunny bouncing kid he'd always been.

"Tony's fun," I said fondly to Rachel.

"Jim," she said to me, shaking her head, but smiling too, "we're almost forty-one." Then, louder, so he could hear, "Here, dear; I've got the glasses." He poured and we all leaned forward to slurp the prodigal foam he'd let spill over the flutes. The bottle was so big for the three of us we didn't need to fuss about wasting a little fizz. Then Tony held his glass up.

"To Professor M'Man," he said.

"Yes," Rachel said warmly, and we sipped. "To dear old friends," she added, and we sipped again.

"The future," I said, lifting my glass. "Whatever it brings… " Rachel met my eye, still smiling, but serious. She could tell he'd told me. She leaned across the little iron table to clink her glass against mine.

"Whatever it brings," she said. We all three sipped again.

1980 – New Haven

Tony blew into town with barely a day's notice.

"I need to talk to you," he'd said on the phone. He was flying into Hartford and I offered to meet his plane. Then my damn VW Bug wouldn't start and I had to have him paged with the bad news as he arrived at the airport. I found this embarrassing, as though I were guilty of incompetence as well as graduate-school poverty, and I imagined I heard a trace of annoyance in his voice on the phone. Within moments, however, he'd figured out the limo schedule and arrived barely ninety minutes later by cab from the limo terminal in New Haven. This quick fix involved an amount of money – it might have been thirty dollars – which struck me as incredible. I was living then on a lean teaching stipend and routinely walked the mile and a half into campus, and back, two or three times a day, just to save the seventy-five cents bus fare. Anyway I ran down to meet him at the curb. It was mid-evening and he was still in his suit, having left Chicago directly from work. I very seldom saw him dressed for work and found him almost intimidating, wonderful as he looked. I was in my usual corduroys and wrinkled cotton shirt: good old Jim.

"Tony," I said, grinning like a fool.

"Hey, Jimbo," he said. He showed an amazing ease in paying the cabbie, mentally computing a big tip while greeting me, deftly slipping the change into his wallet without dropping his bag.

My apartment, which passed for stylish among other grad students, looked suddenly cramped and tatty as this young corporate dynamo came up the stairs. He glanced around as he set his bag down and I imagined he must be looking for the king-size bed, the phone to call room service, the controls for the air conditioning and the big-screen TV. I hugged him a little hesitantly. I was surprised to catch a whiff of some cologne, an old-fashioned one – I pictured a big green bottle covered with testimonials from Second Empire divas and monarchs. It was strange how a cologne could carry so distinct a message of heterosexuality, of the locker room at the corporate gym: of men suiting themselves up for women. Tony might as well have screamed, Rachel bought me this! in my ear. I became self-conscious for a moment about my Aramis. It was a scent I normally loved, proof of my ability to function in the daunting gay world of bars and disco and dating, but in hugging Tony I wondered if I smelled too fey to him.

I hung his garment bag in the living room closet and offered him a seat on the sofa, where he'd be sleeping, and a beer. He sat and looked around, his energy still racing. The room felt small with him in it. I didn't know if I should sit, and if so if I should sit by him on the couch, or if I should putter, make him at home. I mentioned the beer a second time.

"Hey," he said, fidgeting, as though he hadn't heard, "it's late. Let me take you to dinner." He feels claustrophobic in my space, I thought. His life is too big for mine.

Dinner at one of the Wooster Square Italian restaurants ended predictably with a flash of Tony's Gold Card and a ladylike moue on my part.

"Reunions!" Tony said, and clinked his glass against mine. There was just enough wine left in the bottle for us to toast with. "You realize it's been ten years this fall since we met?"

I smiled.

"How's Rachel?" I asked.

"She's great," he said. "She's great." He was looking at his empty plate. Then he looked up. It occurred to me, from the sentimental look in his eyes, that he was feeling the wine a little. Of course, he was jet-lagged and had worked a full day before travelling; the wine would hit him harder than me. "Ten years," he repeated. He didn't want to talk about Rachel, but about him and me.

"Amazing," I smiled, holding his eye.

"Hey," he said, suddenly looking around, busy, energized,

very Let's-get-the- waiter-over-here. "You want some cognac... some sambuca, maybe?" He had stretched a little to remember one of my vices, and again I smiled. I had been smiling a lot that evening.

"I've got some at home," I said. "You look beat." He nodded, giving in. I sensed he had been postponing going back to my apartment. Here in this larger outside world of credit cards, expense accounts, and airport limos, Tony knew his way around. This was a comfortable place for him. But he had asked to visit me, the narrow rooms full of my bookish life, and if that made him feel a little confined, it was by his own choice. So we went back to the apartment.

We sat together on the sofa, talking about his work and mine, neither fully getting what the other said. His corporate legal work, with its brutal hours and staggering pay scale, mystified me, but he seemed to find it exhilarating. He got very excited about the fact that I was teaching now, while writing my dissertation, and talked a lot about how much my students must adore me. He reminisced about how I'd idolized my Italian professor in college and touched me quite a lot by suggesting that I was already starting to create the same kind of impression on the kids who studied with me now.

I remember too that he asked me about my love life. I had no love life then to speak of. There were guys I was hot for, but I hadn't gotten very good at casual sex yet and wouldn't have liked to tell him about it if I had. I put some quick thought into how to respond.

My mind inevitably flashed back to the time I had shyly come out to him, two or three years after we graduated and before I had ever slept with anyone. We were back on campus for some reason – maybe Homecoming – and we walked past the building where my Italian professor had had his office. Tony didn't have to name him, because, smitten as I was, I'd always referred to him simply as "the Professor" or *il professore* to my friends, and they normally called him that as well in speaking to me. We all knew he had gotten a job at Cornell and moved away a year after we graduated. Tony pointed at his office window and asked if I'd heard from him. This was his polite acknowledgement of the bond which my idol and I had actually shared – an edgy, secret, uncomfortable crush on my part and, I believed in hindsight, a gently forbearing recognition on his part that his brightest student childishly thought himself to be in love with him.

Now somehow I heard my own voice saying to Tony, "No… but you know senior year he and I actually talked about maybe sleeping together." This was completely untrue and I was astonished at myself for saying it. It must have been my idea of how to raise the topic of homosexuality with Tony in a way that made me sound worldly and implied that other men had discussed it with me. I may have hoped at some level that he would react with jealousy. At the very least, we were now talking explicitly about the fact that men theoretically might sleep together.

"Huh," he said. "No, I didn't know that. But I guess that didn't happen?"

"No, it didn't," I said. "And now I'll never see him again." Tony looked a little confused – sympathetic, respectful, embarrassed. He understood what I was saying about myself, but this was 1976; even cool young men friends didn't use the word "gay" much. "Gay Lib," as we called it, had been a very small, very eccentric, radical faery fringe element at our resolutely gendered lefty school. After a moment, Tony rallied with a smile.

"I'm jealous," he said. "I don't have any other friends named Jim." For a second, I didn't understand him. Then it hit me: the professor's first name was Antonio and Tony's real name was Anton. This comment was his kind, loyal straight boy way of telling me it was OK with him that I was gay and that he was himself so hetero that he could jokingly pretend to be worried about competing for my affection with a man I loved. It was actually very sweet, and deeply disappointing.

Now when Tony asked about my love life, I also realized that we never had talked, and never would talk, about the night I'd lost my virginity. How could we? It was right after a phone call from Tony during which I'd heard Rachel singing in the background while they were cooking dinner one night. She and I had already had our brief, cordial Hello, and Tony and I were doing a quick catch-up, and somehow the domestic sound of her happy enjoyment of his company filled me with desperate sorrow. After we hung up, I played Linda Ronstadt singing "Long, Long Time" three or four times in a row and succumbed to a wave of appalling self-pity. I knew that he and I would never be together.

I was already in grad school at Yale by then, starting cautiously to dabble in campus gay politics, attending consciousness-raising sessions sponsored by the Graduate Student Association, and trying to position myself as an erotically aware, articulate, sensitive, aesthetic, monogamy-oriented new activist. I knew that my secret virginity made this stance a bit inauthentic. One or two of my new friends knew about my on-going attachment to Tony, but I allowed them to assume that there had been at least some dalliance involved in that friendship. Now that I had convinced myself – with some help from Linda – that he was permanently out of reach, I had a fierce, despairing impulse to find my lover-for-life, pronto.

There was an out gay guy in one of my grad school classes – handsome, smart, cultured, and terribly sophisticated in my eyes because I knew he had had affairs with a few older men. I had spoken with him enough to be sure he was kind as well as elegant. The next time I saw him, I asked him out for coffee and he agreed, offering to make it at his apartment. We started looking at books and playing records and before we knew it, it was late. He was subtle, amused, and experienced; eventually and quite naturally we were in bed. I had almost no physical attraction to him, but the presence of a man's warm naked body awakened a primal response in my long-frustrated nerves. Somehow I rolled onto him and somewhat roughly had my awkward way, and he was gentlemanly enough to permit it. None of it felt as I'd imagined. He was not tight or muscular or passionate; rather, he was gentle and accommodating with someone he knew was a beginner. I knew simultaneously that we would be together forever – because I had waited so long and had always intended to have only one lover for life – and that we would never sleep together again (as indeed we never did), because in spite of my determination to move on from Tony, I was still thinking of him every instant I was with this nice man who was supposed to make me forget him. The fact that I had had sex without love and almost without desire meant that I was suddenly exiled from Eden, aware of my nakedness, a man of the brave new gay world. I felt arid, old, and free.

So that whole story wouldn't do as a response to Tony's friendly question about my love life. I also couldn't imagine telling Tony now about the one disastrous date I'd had recently with a guy I liked only because, in dim bar light and from certain angles, he looked a bit like Tony. He too was a blond Jewish man, mildly hunky, with light blue eyes (nothing like as sparkly as Tony's) and the vocabulary of a ninth-grader. He sold tires; I don't think I'd ever met a blue-collar Jew before, and that was anthropologically intriguing. For a few days I thought he might be deeply kind and gentle but, when I eventually persuaded myself to go out with him, I found him doltish and boring – probably not a fair assessment, in truth. Somehow, still hoping that his passing resemblance to Tony was proof that the universe had picked him to make up for what Tony could never be in my life, I did end up in bed with him, and found that his hairy back and stammering attempts at hot banter made the idea of sex with him completely repellent. In those heady post-Stonewall days, part of me felt guilty for not being able to mate at will with a dozen men a day if the opportunity presented itself, but my fantasies of Tony's sweet, energizing brilliance and glowing sexiness made any connection with this affable mediocrity impossible. In the face of my obvious lack of response, he said resentfully, "You smart queens are all so stuck up." I'd just been reproaching myself for not living up to my marginalized community's ideal of the erotic picaroon, and it turned out I was just an etiolated snob.

And so that was another story I couldn't tell when Tony asked about my love life. I became aware that his arm was up on the back of the sofa behind me, and his hand probably only an inch or so from my shoulder. I said there was "no one special" – thinking, Except you. He said that was because nobody was good enough for me.

Tony talked more about his life in Chicago, which I'd briefly glimpsed during a weekend visit the year before. He had a sleek modern apartment in a high rise on the Lake. It was furnished in authentic Straight Man – there were big square modern tweed chairs, usually with baseball gloves and empty beer cans tossed on them, an expensive stereo sitting on the living room floor among dust balls and tangles of wire, and a big platform bed that his mother (or Rachel, I knew, but he didn't say this) had to remind him to change the sheets on. There were some big ferns that he often forgot to water, and big museum posters on the walls, which I had to straighten before I could settle down to talk to him. He hung out with some other young attorneys, played racquet ball with them, went to games at Wrigley Field. During my visit, we met some of these guys and went out to a pub and ate burgers and watched some sports event on the TV in the bar. Rachel was away that weekend and much was made of how it was like old times, just Jim and Tony – and, I thought, this bunch of thickening jockish workaholics I had essentially nothing to say to. The sociologist in me noticed that Tony didn't have much to say to them, either. They commented beerily on the game we were watching, and talked in precisely the same tone about cases they were handling. As usual, the presence of more than a couple of straight men made me self-conscious. I kept up with their conversation by the familiar stratagems of careful mimicry, diplomatic feigning of interest, and suppression of impulse. Tony, because he was dear, accomplished a delicate shift of gears on our way back to his place after dinner, asking about my mother, telling me about how his mother was adjusting to widowhood, mentioning the latest book he'd read and deferring to my opinion on it, congratulating me on my accounts of musical successes and, as always, sounding solicitous about my happiness. He'd put me up on his ample sofa and made me cappuccino in the morning. It had been a nice weekend, but it showed how different our adult worlds were. We had become close at college, where neutral territory and long strings of lazy days allowed very disparate friendships to grow; we met now, always with limited time, on one person's territory or the other's. Rachel, I thought, often served as a kind of interpreter for us, and I was almost sorry she'd been out of town. It was actually a relief to get back to my little uncensored society of singers and academics in Connecticut.

Now a year later Tony was in my city, in my apartment, and again it was a little awkward. He was telling me something about Rachel. She had her own place in a frame house in a renovated neighborhood near his apartment, but most nights they were together, usually at his place because it was closer to work for both of them. His mother lived nearby too, in the suburb where they'd grown up, and it took all his diplomacy to keep her from cooking all his meals. Rachel's mother was even worse, he said, and had taken to calling his place in the early morning, ostensibly to say hello but in fact hoping to catch Rachel there. She knew they'd been sleeping together since high school and practically living together since they both moved back to town three years before, but in some matriarchal masochistic way she seemed to enjoy harrowing her nerves about it. She loved Tony, of course, and made elaborate gestures of ritual adoption, bragging about him to everyone she knew as though she considered him part of the family already. But she still made those morning calls; one day, he thought, Rachel would carelessly answer the phone and her mother would yell, "A-HAH!" Somehow she succeeded in making them both feel massively guilty. Here he gave a self-deprecating roll of the eyes. People like me, mere Scottish-Americans (Presbyterians mind you!), knew nothing of guilt, I gathered; apparently Abraham established some kind of patent.

He broke off here and asked for more sambuca. He was sounding distinctly lit. I poured, and asked him about some of the guys we'd had dinner with that night in Chicago. He looked confused for a second, as though he had trouble placing their names.

"We're not really all that tight," he said. "They're just guys I hang out with." Then he looked sentimental again. "They're nothing like you. There's something about old friends. I mean, somebody who knows you well, for a long time. Nothing takes the place of that." At this point, he finally patted my shoulder. I smiled, sitting rather primly beside him.

"Sometimes I feel like I barely know you now, Doro," I said suddenly, not having meant to. He looked surprised and slightly wounded. "I mean, our lives are very different now. You've got your career and you're making a lot of money, and you're…"

"Hey, Jimbo – none of that matters, not to you and me. We're still the guys we always were." He was looking at me rather hard, through a haze of fatigue and sweet liquor. "Come on; I'd hate it if… if I thought we weren't still… I mean, you're still my guy, right?"

"Right," I said. "Naturally. I hope so. Tony. But. Not really; I… I'm your – guy, I guess, but you're…" I couldn't think of a word for this that wouldn't make me sad.

"I'm what?" he prompted me.

"Well, I'm single," I said. He didn't say anything for a long moment.

"I don't get that," he said at last. "I never have."

"That I'm gay?" I said, tightly.

"No! Give me some credit! That you're single. You're the greatest guy I know. They ought to be fighting over you." Then he stopped. He knew what I was thinking: If I was so great, why didn't HE fight over me? Of course that wasn't fair, but it was what I was thinking. "Rachel…" He said her name gently, for my sake, knowing it might not be the name I wanted to hear. "She says the same thing; she always wonders why you don't find someone. Why somebody doesn't find you."

"She knows it would be – a man, right?"

"Of course she does. She knew it before I did… before –" Again, he stopped, remembering that that wasn't true. Maybe she had put it into words before he had, but he'd known it from the moment I looked at his blond hair and called him Doro.

"She likes you so much, you know."

"I know," I said. "She's great."

He started to get up and found it harder than he'd thought. On his second try, laughing at himself, he got vertical, pulled his loosened tie off, and headed for the bathroom. I heard some extravagant splashing as he washed up, and smiled; getting Tony clean usually involved drenching every surface in the bathroom. On his way back, swaying through the kitchen, he pulled two beers out of the refrigerator. "I'm buzzed," he said happily, and cracked one. He took a sip, made wine-tasting smacks with his mouth, and handed me the can with a stiff little bow.

"Our very best year, monsieur," he said. "The slight hint of oak has attracted favorable comment." Then he opened the other can, drank from it, and sat back down beside me. I laughed; I always laughed at Tony's little jokes.

"You are the weirdest man I know," I said. I put my arm around his shoulder. "So we need to talk about...? Or you came from Chicago to buy me dinner."

"Hmm," he said, closing his eyes. Without looking, he took another pull on his beer. In a minute or two, he slackened all over, and I realized he had dozed off. With my free hand, I turned off the lamp beside me to keep its glare out of his eyes. The room was still gently lit by the lights from the kitchen and hallway. Being an infatuated young man, I couldn't help feeling that some of the dim golden light came from inside my Doro himself. The slight pressure of his weight on my arm, leaning back on the sofa, was comfortable and familiar. I allowed myself the luxury of watching his face closely for a few minutes, feeling that I was stealing every instant. Of course, his features were more than familiar to me. In my mind, I had traced every line of his face a thousand times. For years I had sometimes found myself doodling pictures of him in my notebooks, and they were usually fairly exact likenesses: not because I was any kind of artist, but because my fingers followed my mind which knew his face by heart. God knew, most people would consider him a very good-looking man, but that wasn't what I was watching now, what made these moments so privately thrilling. He was giving himself up to me, giving me the chance to re-memorize him. I was dimly aware that he was conscious, not fast asleep. Somewhere in there, among those familiar lines and contours, behind the companionable swell of his shoulders and the well-recalled rhythm of his resting breath, my best friend Tony was watching me watch him. I felt that I could proudly kill anyone who touched him that minute, that the greatest joy of my life would be to kill someone who tried to hurt him. I felt an ache in my chest, a pride and an exaltation that he would trust himself to my keeping like this. It occurred to me that, after all, I was OK in Tony's eyes. It might even be that I would be safe if he were the one watching, I the one sleeping. I closed my eyes and, for a few minutes, I dozed too.

I stirred awake and realized how late it was. I had to go to bed. I pulled my arm off his shoulder and, still warm with trust and happiness, I kissed the top of his head so lightly I was sure he might barely dream he was standing in bright sunshine. As I stood, he stirred too, and took my arm.

"Stay here," he said, his eyes closed.

I stared at him, too startled to breathe. He was practically asleep and I couldn't be sure I'd heard him right. He barely shifted his weight, enough to kick off his shoes, slip his pants down, toss his shirt. He lay down on his side on the sofa, in his undershirt and shorts and socks. He patted the sofa in front of him and said again, "Stay here." So, with my heart pounding and my mouth dry, I took off my shoes and shirt and pants, got a blanket from the cupboard, turned the lights off around the apartment, and lay rather stiffly beside him. He put his arm over my shoulder, made a few grumbling yawning sounds, and fell asleep again.

What is this? I wondered. I tried to recover the warmth and safety I'd felt a few minutes earlier. It confused me that he was asleep. I wanted to know what his assumptions and expectations were. If I was supposed to go for it, for example, it would be nice to know. Maybe I was supposed to know without being told; maybe that was why he'd let me hold him a minute before. Maybe love was supposed to make these things clear. I knew I loved Tony, but that had always involved a lot of confusion and frustration. Now the frustration began to settle in the pouch of my shorts.

Tentatively I put a hand on his waist and pulled myself a little closer. Something a little firm in my shorts rubbed against something soft in his. He sighed and pressed back. Very gently, scared to death, I moved my hand from his hip to the contact point between us at the front of his pants. His hand moved quickly to mine and I stopped breathing; but then he released my hand and let me rub the backs of my knuckles right where he wasn't getting hard. I leaned into his face, moving by millimeters, and barely brushed his mouth with mine.

"Mmm," he said, sounding drunk and dubious, and puckered a bit, and made the tiniest of smooching motions once or twice. Then he shivered, and his face turned up, just slightly, away. I felt my throat start to clutch with a sense of miserable mortification and failure.

He sighed again, hard, and opened his eyes.

"I'm sorry," he said, slurring. "I thought I could. I tried to; I mean I wanted to. I can't." I sat up and turned my back to him. The moment there was a particle of strength in my legs, I would lurch off the couch and get to my room. This was an unimagined disaster. The sun had not set; it had crashed. I was scorched with a humiliation and disappointment so deep I couldn't tell them from heartbreak. Tony propped himself up on one elbow, his other hand over his eyes, though the room was dark now, lit only by the streetlamp outside. "God," he said, "I'm such a jerk."

"I don't get you, Tony," I said, thinking I could talk without my voice shaking. "What was that all about?" There was a squeak in my voice that gave me away and I wished I never had to look at Tony again.

"I don't know," he said. His voice was weak too, full of weariness and self-reproach. "I wanted to feel like... you to know that we're still..."

"Best buddies," I said. "Pals. I'll see you in the morning." I got up, shaking.

"Jim," he said, "I'm really sorry." He put the pillow over his head for a second and then made a cringing face when he pulled it back off. I smiled at his little theatrical pretense of self-loathing.

"It's no big deal," I said.

Breakfast was pretty horrible, as you'd expect. It would be bad enough when, as we were assured often happened, they put out like Persian harem boys all night long and then said gruffly in the morning, "Boy, was I drunk last night!" (What pornographer dreamed up that scenario, I wondered? And how could so many seasoned queens corroborate it, quoting the identical lines – they couldn't all be lying? And, if it was true, who taught the straight boys what to say? Or were they born already knowing?) The apologies continued, lacerating my nerves, until I suggested we just drop the whole thing. Tony agreed.

We made a little small talk. Then I asked, "So was there really something you wanted to talk about – I mean, other than... was there something?"

"Yeah," he said. He was back in his suit, laundered shirt – the uniformed stranger. His eyes were puffy. He looked stressed: of course, he'd slept badly, and he had a plane to catch. He looked down; he looked up.

"Rachel and I are getting married." He smiled. "In three weeks. We decided kind of suddenly, a few days ago. Her grandfather will be visiting from Israel, so we thought – and we were actually hoping you might come and..." He stopped. I had made some kind of strangling sound. "I know, Jim. But she just likes you so much. She wants you there." I was staring at the table.

"I like her very much," I said steadily. "You know that." He waited. Suddenly I felt my hands shake. "What if – we'd...

You came here to tell me this. Then, last night, we almost...
What if – we'd – ? This morning, you still would have told me:
this." I looked up at him. I felt a stinging horror over all the
surfaces of my body. "I don't get you, Tony."

"I don't get myself either," he said. "You've got to believe
me, buddy. It was because I care about you. I wanted to tell you
in person. And I wanted you to know that..."

"That I'm still your guy," I said, direly sarcastic, hurting
myself and only hoping I could hurt him a bit too.

"That marrying her doesn't mean I don't care about you,"
he said hoarsely. "Damn it, Jim. You know that's what I mean.
But I messed up. I was stupid. I should have just said that and
not... Because now you're upset." He was making incompetent
shuffling motions in the air with his hands.

"I'm not 'upset,'" I said, all acid, thinking I was being
strong. "I'm so angry I'm about to hyperventilate. I don't think
you've been honest with me. I don't think you've been fair."
Tony was a Libra and hated being called unfair.

"Look," he said, heating up. "I can only say I'm sorry so
many times. I came here to tell you, in person, because I cared
that much. I haven't been fair. Sue me."

"How can I sue you?" I shouted furiously, jumping up,
rattling the dishes on the table. "I don't know any honest law-
yers! I don't think there are any!" He actually laughed, at my
joke. Sick with myself, I laughed too. He got up and put his
arms around me, but I broke away. I went to the wall phone
and called a cab.

"You're hurt," he said.

"I'm fine," I said. "You need to leave soon to catch your

plane."

Half an hour later, he was gone. I didn't go to the wedding after all. Rachel called to ask me again, but she didn't push me. This made me think she knew, at least generally, why I couldn't go. Then they called me during the reception. I congratulated them, and I meant it. After Rachel had said good-bye, Tony asked me shyly if we were still friends.

"Doro," I said, gently, and he said, "Thanks."

Then a few months later I met Angel.

Chapter 3 – Tuesday

Tuesday morning we met for breakfast in the kitchen of the main house. It was a slow-starting day and by the time we'd finished the cold tortellini salad and passed the sections of the newspaper around and loaded the dishwasher it was almost eleven. Then Rachel said she needed to finish some paperwork or she wouldn't enjoy herself for the rest of the vacation. She set up a work space on the glass top table on the porch, where she could see the ocean, and sent Tony and me – "you boys," she called us – to the beach without her.

The house stood about where the straight and gay sections of beach met. There was no actual line in the sand, but there might as well have been. "Poodle Beach," as it was called, was the southernmost stretch of shore in Rehoboth. There the gay boys and girls stretched out with their boom boxes and their *Prince of Tides* and their day-glow sunglasses and their "Sylvia" beach towels. Just a few yards away swarmed the American Family, the fathers harassed and, often, tattooed; the children skinny and ribald; the mothers in their halter tops looking as though vacations were an even worse affliction than daily life in the subdivision. It was an odd juxtaposition. Many of these straight people would cheerfully have burned the Capitol to the ground to keep homosexuals from teaching their children. Yet they came to Rehoboth and lolled, mesmerized, mere yards from gay volleyball orgies. There was no lack of furtive glances back and forth across the border; the fact was that we were fascinated by each other, like it or not. About the third time some austere fashion queen stared over the top of his sunglasses at the straight beach, then turned back with arched eyebrows to say, "That woman's bathing suit – I DON'T think so!" you began to wonder why he kept looking. A mother of six who had, acting under no external compulsion, planted her brood within easy shrieking distance of a thousand riotous gays, shook her head and pursed her lips at a falsetto outburst or a jockish tussle that ended with a wet kiss; then she cocked her ear, enthralled, for more. "Can't we all just get along?" Rodney King asked. Strangely, warily, at Rehoboth, we seemed to.

There were incidents, of course. Two summers before this, I was at the Blue Moon just before closing one morning when a bunch of redneck boys got out of a pickup with a baseball bat. Usually this type of thug sought out lone gays in darkened streets, and then we all read about the outcome – or, more usually, didn't – in the papers. But these kids, with stolid macho stupidity, had chosen to posture and swagger in front of a large crowd of milling barflies, those who hadn't yet headed for home or for gritty embraces under the boardwalk. Yet all of us, cowed by memories of times we'd had to face such little lynch parties on our own, kept our mouths shut and looked at each other in uneasy silence, scorn and fear mingling in our expressions. The rednecks circled, smirking, calling us names. Then in an instant, with the quick savage grace of a cat, the humpy bar back Billy jumped up on the patio rail facing them.

"Yeah, we're faggots!" he yelled, taunting them. "You want me to tell you about how I sucked on my lover's dick last night? You want to hear how good it tasted?" He made a low throaty growl of lust, aimed at the wannabe bashers like a Patriot missile. He was incredible: a *tricoteuse*, a Luddite, a Fury.

My face prickled red at his brazen bravery. How did he know they wouldn't shoot at him as he leaned out towards them, one hand on the corner pillar, a rampant tigress, Outness Leading the People? His words seemed to sicken them; they were turning green, ugly, nasty. In a moment they might strike. "You got about fifty cocksuckers up here who'd be more than happy to ream your little redneck butts out," Billy screamed. "And you got one cocksucker who's already called the police. But you're all so butch, you don't care, right?"

"Yeah, FAG!" one of them yelled, wavering. "I bet you LIKE sucking cock, yeah!" The idiot child didn't seem to realize that Billy had just boasted of this very thing.

"No shit," said Billy, offhanded, jumping back down lightly as the police car pulled up. "You ought to try it some time. You'd like it too." The kid lunged, fangs bared, and an officer getting out of the cruiser deftly caught him by the arm – Rehoboth didn't want to lose its gay dollars. Billy vaulted over the bar and went back to dishing with a regular customer. I felt like I'd just seen a Queer Nation remake of "High Noon."

Anyway, Tony and I found ourselves right at the affectional-preference divide in the beach. He asked where I thought we should sit, and I shifted us slightly to the left, into straight territory. The beach wasn't terribly crowded, but I wanted to be able to reconnoiter a little bit before exposing Tony to the southern crowd; there was no telling who might be there, or what they might think or say or do seeing me with him. We found a place near the water, some distance from the nearest towel, and set our stuff down. Then Tony pulled his T-shirt off and headed into the water. I joined him for just a few minutes, enough to get wet and feel like I'd been in. The current was a little too strong for me to do any real swimming. We rode some waves, but the third or fourth one tumbled me too hard to be fun and I didn't like the idea of Tony seeing me staggering and spluttering in the surf. After rinsing as much sand out of my jock as I could by jumping and swishing in shallow water, I went back and sat on the shore and watched him for a while. He was a stronger swimmer than me. He did the equivalent of a few laps, just out beyond the breakers, and then came in too, hopping comically for my benefit as the waves tumbled around his knees and ankles, and smiling at me. He had a smile that said he knew I liked him, and I could never resist smiling back. He shook his head; released from the water's weight, his hair bounced back into its curls, darkened by the water but so brightly lit by the vertical sun that it seemed almost metallic. The hair on his body looked darker too, and it stood out with brilliant droplets of water, giving a strange three-dimensional look to his skin. He was still fair from the Chicago winter, but the sun gave him a glow. He's superb to look at, I thought, the apotheosis of the regular guy. He heaved himself down heavily on the towel next to me and lay on his back, hands behind his head. Almost immediately, he sat up again and looked around at the few distant family groups.

"You know," he said, smiling, "all those people are going to think we're together." He liked being racy and cool about it.

"No," I said, "the gay beach is down to the right. They'll probably think we're best friends from college." He cocked his head back: Yeah.

"You remember how everybody said we were married back then?" he asked, smiling as though it were his most wholesome memory of youth.

"They didn't know what they were saying," I said.

"Yes they did," Tony said. "They knew we... we were best buddies. We cared about each other. Like now, still, right?" Of course that was true. I sensed what Tony was trying to do, and I respected him for it. Certainly I'd never had the courage to raise this subject since his visit to New Haven thirteen years earlier. Over the years, we had never really made that awful night right between us, though we'd managed to edge gingerly around it. My visits to their stunning house in Glencoe, their visits to my – I believe – charming and choice little one in Baltimore, had always been fun: not just civil, but really wonderful. Time heals all wounds, I supposed. The dreadful crisis of my friend Robert's sudden death in 1988 had brought out the best in Tony. He'd cleared his schedule so that he could come for a couple of days around the funeral, and with my defenses leveled to the ground by shock and sadness, I'd been able to see and take comfort in his genuine concern. It had also been very touching to see him connect with my Baltimore friends: Walter, whom he'd known since college of course, but also Ricardo, Marie, Bob and Luellen... they had unanimously adored him.

"Sure," I said. "Just like always." I was fussing with a nub in the towel by my ankle and wasn't looking at him. I felt suddenly parched. I'd never quite said it to Tony; he knew, of course, but I'd never absolutely said it. "But what I meant... when I said they didn't know what they were saying... was – Doro..."

"Why did you always call me that?" he interrupted. I felt a quick chill, knowing he knew. He might as well have told me to back off. But I hadn't said anything yet.

"'*Capelli d'oro,*'" I said. "'Golden hair.' You remember."

"Oh, right," he said, quickly. I reached over and pulled one of his curls.

"Don't be provoking," I said.

"Yow!" he smiled, and then grimaced as though I'd hurt him, which I hadn't. He took a deep breath and faced me. "So you were saying... ?"

"I was just saying – Doro... that to me we were: more than best buddies. You know what I mean. I wished we really were – married – or whatever." He didn't say anything, so I said, "I was in love with you, Tony, all those years."

"I know," he said harshly, as though he were angry with himself. He was looking out at the water and, finding a little pebble on his towel, he tossed it towards the waves with a hard gesture of frustration; but he wasn't mad at me. "Remember when I came to New Haven that time?" I nodded, hoping he couldn't tell that every instant of that visit had been worn smooth in my memory. "I screwed up. I know," he said. I had an impulse to apologize to *him*, take the guilt myself. But he was right. He'd baffled and hurt me, and I'd never admitted it to him, and he owed me this. I was staring at my knee. My face and neck burned as though I'd been in the sun for hours. I was barely breathing.

"Jimbo," Tony was saying: "what do you do when there's somebody you just like so much, so *much*?" He gestured with both hands, grasping vaguely in front of him. "He... holds you up; he believes in you, and you count on that to get you through – lots of things; more than you remember sometimes. You'd do anything for this guy. But there's something he wants from you, and it's just not possible. Once you even... you get drunk, and you try it, or you *try* to try it – because he's your best, best buddy, and you're about to tell him something that will hurt him. But it's not right, for either of you. He gets hurt even worse, and you feel like a jerk. But you can't change it. And you still – he's still... What do you do in that situation?" I didn't say anything for a minute. I was very moved and was afraid to look at him, but I could feel him looking at me. His presence, a few inches to my left, was as palpable as if a scent or a sound of him surrounded me.

Finally I spoke, not sure if any voice would come.

"You do exactly what you're doing now," I said, barely phonating. "That means a lot to me. It does. You're my Doro. We get one per lifetime, and you're it."

Tony put his arm around my shoulder and said,

"You're my guy." I put my arm around his waist. "You're not sad, are you?" he asked after a minute, because my breath was a little uneven.

"No," I said, exhaling hard. "I'm happy, I guess." I felt like there was a lot to say, but really the best had just been said. This was a moment I would go back to a lot in the future, a moment I had waited for and hoped for and dreaded, and I should just be still and live it. I could feel that my chin was shaking slightly, but I wasn't sad. It was good to sit next to Tony after so long, and just to enjoy the fact that we were still best buddies. I was too old to make myself miserable over things that couldn't be changed. Finally I straightened up and took my arm off his waist. "You're right," I said, nodding at the others on the beach. "They'll think we're together."

"Who gives a fuck?" he said, and rocked me back and forth a couple of times.

About half an hour later, I asked him: "So, Rachel is... what? slightly bummed? medium to very bummed? about the baby idea." He chewed for a minute on his lower lip.

"You know," he said, "I'm not sure. She's hard to read on this one. Rachel is..."

"She's a goddess," I said.

"Yeah, whatever that means," he said. "Her life is very full, you know. She's a star in Illinois. She hotdogs around and does studies and gives recommendations and people fawn all over her. Like even in our congregation; she grew up in it, you know – old ladies always patting her cheek and saying 'I knew you when you were just a little girl' – and..."

"What's your point? We know people adore Rachel and it would be very strange if they didn't. She's possibly worried about not being a mother. Connect A to B, please." Tony laughed. He always laughed at that sharp marmish tone, on the rare occasions when I forgot to filter it out for his benefit.

"She doesn't need children," he said. "Kids are complicated, messy. Whereas Rachel kind of glides through life with this... this perfection thing she does. I mean, you've seen her: my God! Everything she touches – our house, the temple, her work, our friends..."

"Herself," I said. "Do you see how she gets more beautiful all the time?"

"Oh no, Jim, I hadn't noticed." He was being arch again, turning up one eyebrow and one corner of his mouth for my appreciation. I became serious, though, suddenly identifying with Rachel in a way I hadn't seen coming.

"People think my life is full, too," I said. "'Jim doesn't need a relationship; he's perfect the way he is...' But it's not fair. It's like being single is my punishment for being well-adjusted. Maybe Rachel feels like she'll never get a child just because she's obviously the greatest mother in the world. She may save half the kids in Chicago, but it's still the other women who have the kids, not her. That's not fair."

"Maybe," Tony shrugged. "You should talk to her about it."

"Well call me Ann Landers," I said, "but it occurs to me that maybe *you* should talk to her about it."

"Don't think we haven't," he said. "Now we just kind of sulk about it. Like there's something I know she wants, and I can't give it to her."

"'Can't'?" I asked.

"Certain things have to happen before you can have a baby," he said, looking out across the water again. Men! I thought. He was doing that dreamy loner Captains Courageous thing, Don't Fence Me In, rolling stone... it was so sexy that, exasperated, I wanted to knock him back on the towel and have him, that second. That was the thing about men, though; you couldn't have us. The second you tried, we'd gaze inscrutably out to sea and your mouth would go dry.

"Plain English, Tony," I said. "It's not something

physical?"

"No," he said. "It's the expectation. Every time, you wonder: Is she thinking about the baby – or me – ? I didn't marry a mother. Rachel and I were – friends." It occurred to me that this was part of Tony's rock-solid OKness, what I had always perceived as his amazing freedom from neurosis. He had not married his mother, as so many men unthinkingly do; he and his wife were – friends. "We always had a good sex life because she was my friend. I was OK with her; she wanted me, I wanted her – I was grateful, I trusted her." Here I admit I felt a little stab inside. This was exactly what loving Tony had denied me. Maybe if there had been someone like that for me, I would be the simple happy lovable man Tony was.

"So what are you saying?" I asked. "Never? You just don't have sex now?"

"Practically never. She told me she wasn't going to do anything to keep from getting pregnant, and I kind of... lost interest, I guess." He was looking down unhappily at his big strong feet as he spoke. No, I admitted to myself, on second thought; no amount of being securely loved would have made me be like Tony. Maybe it was actually part of my physical makeup to be highstrung and skittish, part of his to be stable and strong. I thought, looking at his feet, that if he were my husband I would force sex out of him – tickle and caress and lick his feet until he was screaming with lust, if need be. He could not refuse. But then I remembered how, on the couch in New Haven, he hadn't gotten hard. There was nothing you could say to that. Miss Otis simply Regrets She's uninterested in fucking Today, Madam. Rachel and I had both been there.

"Anyway, like I say, what does she need children for? Her life is full. She doesn't need anything."

"That's her call, don't you think?" I was aware of a small satisfaction at the idea that Tony and Rachel were practically never having sex. But really it did me no good; it wasn't like he was saving himself for *me*. And Rachel was my friend too.

"Mmm," he said, as though he wished this talk were over. "Are you ganging up on me now?" Suddenly I heard something in what he'd said – 'She doesn't need anything' – that filled me with a compassion for him that almost hurt. I wanted to embrace him and tell him things would be OK. This was something I hadn't felt for him in years, since he'd sat on my couch and dozed under my watchful gaze. But I covered my expression and smiled.

"I sincerely hope St. Peter is writing this all down," I said. "It's surrealistic that I am encouraging you to have more sex with Rachel, and I ought to be canonized during my own lifetime."

"I thought Presbyterians didn't have saints," Tony said, smiling slyly.

"OK, Tony," I said, "here's the deal. I'm going to tell you something that is actually going to hurt me." I put my hand out to shake his as though we were about to close a deal; puzzled, his brow furrowed, he shook it. "You're a straight man, Doro. You get hard for women – not for men, not for me. So Rachel got you, and I didn't, and that's fine. Now, one reason – one of the reasons – Nature makes straight men get hard for women is to make children. So at some level, your ending up with Rachel represents some kind of opting for that possibility. Rachel must think she's got a right to you – that way: to sex with you, to a child from you. And I'm afraid I agree with her. If you're not going to have sex with Rachel, I might as well have gotten you, for God's sake." I hardly recognized my own voice – a kind of gay Zorba the Greek spouting earthy wisdom about love and sex. I'd never dreamed of talking that way to anyone, let alone Tony. It was so out of character that he seemed stunned at first, looking at me with the blank defiance of Ootch when I scolded him. But what he said next sounded submissive and unhappy, not defiant.

"Sex is supposed to be about two people together," he said, "not three: not babies." Then, "Rachel doesn't need anything," he repeated. He meant, Rachel doesn't need me. That was what touched me: Tony's thinking he wasn't needed. Tony had been for so many years the very pole of need around which my universe revolved, the Most Wanted Man of all time, that I couldn't imagine he'd ever felt the sorrow of not being needed.

"She does," I said. "She needs you. For two reasons. Because you're the nicest man she knows and she loves you. And because even Rachel can't make a baby without a man to help her."

"You make it sound like I'm being put out to stud," he said.

"I make it sound like you're a good loving husband, and maybe a good loving father," I said. "Tony, you can't string this one out. Rachel's forty." He nodded slowly, three or four times. Then,

"I'm going back in the water," he said, jumping up. "Come with me."

It was a long slow day. Rachel, by moral and aesthetic conviction opposed to any kind of wretched excess, offered a light simple lunch this time, and we split up for the afternoon. I got a fair amount of work done up in my studio: that is, I wrote and deleted several pages on Ariosto and, skipping like a grasshopper from book to book, read whole paragraphs at a time before my eye drifted out to the beach and ocean. By four I was restless enough to go out and sit on the gay beach. There I ran into two or three acquaintances, traded uninteresting dish on which bars had the cheapest happy hours and cutest bartenders, and finally, as they headed off to do further research on the topic, went back to my room for a nap. A nap already on the second day at the beach, I thought: how dull am I, really? Before six I got up and drifted downstairs to stir something up. I found Rachel reading on the porch and was told that Anton was horizontal upstairs. Looking again, I saw that the book in Rachel's lap was my own. I took a chair and put my feet up on the rail.

"I've decided the most impressive words in the language are 'All translations my own unless otherwise indicated,'" Rachel said, pointing at one of my first footnotes. "I've been trying to get to this ever since you sent it to us, and then I thought, What better time than when Jim is right there to explain everything? So I brought it with us."

"'Explain'... " I said dubiously. "I'm flattered you're reading it at all; I just thought you could use it as a doorstop or something." She made a swatting motion and clicked her tongue at me.

"I was very moved by your introduction," she said. "That

kind of connection – the Black Death then, AIDS now... I think it's very brave of you."

"Not really," I said. "It would be very cowardly not to do it. I'm not brave. I just do what I have to do. One thing you *have* to do when you write criticism is take the author's vocation seriously. Nobody put a gun to Boccaccio's head and forced him to write a book full of... civility, good humor and human solidarity, pointing the way out of despair and chaos. That was his gift to humanity. To us today. A critic who dodges that – who just writes one of those I-am-a-hot-trendy-critic pieces, with requisite jargon and sly winks at the promotion and tenure committee – isn't keeping faith with the author." I realized I had just delivered an uninvited mini-lecture; we college professors had a tendency to think in fifty-minute sentences. Rachel didn't seem to think I was being pompous, though I sounded a bit preachy to myself. She just nodded and smiled. "Anyway, thanks," I said. We didn't speak for a moment, looking out at the rhythmic grey surf. Then I asked, "How's your work going?"

"Oh," she said, "it's never enough, you know. It's hard in a new way, now, when for once we hope we'll get Head Start fully funded, for instance, and societal priorities finally seem to be more in line with my pet programs and policies. But it's still not enough. Look at the big picture and you may see some improvement; but look at the kids on a street corner in Chicago and you realize, Some of these kids we won't reach – they're lost, it's too late. Even with the best systems you could dream of – and we're a long way from them – we'll still have people slipping through."

"So you do what you can," I said. "You're my hero."

"I do what I have to, as you were just saying. There's no choice."

"That's not true. Lots of people don't feel they have to do anything; they make the choice of staying uninvolved. That's one way we got into this mess to begin with."

"Oh Jim," she sighed, "it's always 'this mess.' We responded badly to the plague in 1348, and we responded badly to the plague in 1982. 'Children's rights,' we say now – but when have children ever had 'rights,' really? When will we learn?" She squinted at the horizon, weariness and sadness in her eyes: it was what I thought of as her Jewish-saint expression.

"Hey," I said, "let's call Peter Paul & Mary – I think there's a song in that." She smiled at me.

"That's exactly the kind of thing Anton would say. Make me smile; change the subject. I used to think it was denial, but now I realize it's his way of affirming life, fighting back the demons and dragons. I think it's very dear, and I've gotten to count on it a lot. You're just like him, that way."

That was a new idea.

"I always thought he just did that with *me*," I said, "when I got too serious. I always felt like I was the one who needed to be reassured and told to lighten up."

"No," Rachel said. "I think he does it with all of us. And you do the same thing. Maybe you've learned his techniques; or else you taught them to him. No, come to think of it, he was always like that. Not the class clown, exactly, but just someone who always made you happy." I was reminded she'd known him ten or more years longer than I had.

"Does he make you happy now, Rachel?" I asked quietly.

In her utter stillness I could tell that she knew exactly what I was asking, about the baby. Her gaze didn't falter, as though she hadn't heard me, but during the long pause I knew that she was weighing, pondering in her heart. She seemed to be scanning the horizon for an answer: maybe a ship or a blimp or a biplane trailing a banner would suddenly appear, and tell us if Anton made her happy. Then a breeze brushed me, and I felt a shiver, as though all the hairs on my arms had decided to shift one follicle to the left at the same time. She wasn't looking out to the ocean, I realized; the ocean was inside her, and she was checking there. A dense mystery enveloped me. It was a moment to be savored: for once, I understood what straight men meant when they said, Women!

Rachel's eyes were very soft, tender, as though she might cry. I thought she would cry, and say that she wasn't happy. The part of Tony that withholds, I thought – the part of him that we all want, and no one can have – it breaks hearts: hers, mine. That was what I was thinking.

"So happy," she said at last. "So happy. There's no one else in the world I'd want to be married to." Her voice was tremulous but strong; of course she loved Tony, and there was no weakness in saying so. She turned to face me with her wise kind eyes. "Jim, dear. I'd be ashamed to say that to you, because I know how much you've always – cared about him too, and I wouldn't hurt you for anything in the world. But I know he's brought great joy into your life as well as mine; far more joy than sorrow. So you understand what I'm saying, and you won't begrudge it to me. It's one of Anton's gifts, that he makes people happy. There may be things he feels he can't give. But neither of us would choose to be without him. Am I right?"

I was very surprised by what she'd said. Was she right? I glanced out at the sand, which clouded and darkened the rough surf. It took me a moment to be sure, but, amazingly, I was neither jealous nor hurt. And then there was a flood of faces: not only Doro's face over the years, listening, laughing, coaxing me to laugh, but my own face too, young, trusting, grateful, and happy.

"You're right," I said, smiling at her.

After dinner, there was some talk about what to do. There was the option of walking on the beach; renting a video ("On the Beach"?); reading aloud to each other in the foolishly rich living room. Tony favored doing nothing. It was nearly eleven, and the idea had some appeal. Then Rachel said, "Jim, you've been here before – what do you DO on a Tuesday night?" The implication was that Rehoboth had a magical night life that only I, the raffish boulevardier, could initiate them into – "Oh, Tuesday nights there are those candlelight-and-champagne prom concerts at the Palais Garnier; then onion soup at Les Halles, of course, in the wee hours, and a pub-crawl through Pigalle." In fact, it was pretty much dancing at the Renegade, period. So that was what I suggested.

"Dancing," said Tony, as though I'd suggested we swim to Portugal. Rachel looked at him as he sprawled back on the sofa in a pose of burlesque exhaustion.

"'I won't dance,'" she sang.

"'Don't ask me,'" he answered.

"Anton is worn out," she said to me. "The law is a harsh

mistress." Then she asked him, "Would you mind if Jim and I went? You'll have to promise to come out later in the week." Tony on the dance floor was an image I treasured and pulled out, to smile and croon over, whenever I was feeling blue. He was always a perfectly respectable cruise-dancer: that is, dancing with girls in college, he had the moves, the attitude. But he was also master of a *hoch* Klesmer male-bonding kind of dance that was new to me when I first knew him and that flattered and delighted me more than almost any other aspect of our young friendship. I never understood where it came from till, years after, I saw the groom and the father of the bride dance together at a Jewish wedding, exactly as Tony danced with me – spinning with linked hands or elbows, kicking, stamping, laughing, clapping hands and snapping fingers over their heads, showing off for each other and, at the same time, promising each other a lifetime of affection and respect.

"Promise," I said. He rolled his eyes, a martyr to his public's demands: OK, OK!

"What should I wear?" Rachel asked me. I was afraid for a minute we'd have one of those straight woman/gay man fashion consults right out of a trying-to-be-hip sitcom – talk about pink suede miniskirts and spike heels and vampirish lipstick and hair raked back over one ear and frizzed out over the other. Rachel was way too classy to get into that drop-dead look.

"Actually you're perfect just like that," I said. She was wearing a wide-gored denim skirt and red silk blouse, with one of her Third World sash belts. "I'm just going to put on long pants, and we can go."

"These shoes won't work," Rachel said, looking at her

espadrilles. "I'll meet you in two minutes."

"My dancing fools," Tony said, as she ran upstairs and I headed for the back door.

The crowd at the Renegade was moderate that evening. The lights were, perhaps for that reason, not too perverse: none of those mannerist distorting displays which held you in perplexity for quarter hours at a time wondering if the boy in the blue tank-top was an extraordinary beauty or the very refuse of the trailer park.

"What fun," Rachel said as we entered, as Queen Mum might say "What fun" at a tribal dance. Sometimes I forgot Rachel and I were the same age. There was a great-lady side to Rachel which made her seem older – ageless – the age of your mother in old memories: you realized consciously that she was no older than you were now, but in your memory she still seemed large, wise, beyond you, and without beginning or end. I got myself a Corona and Rachel a glass of white wine and we stood for a while and watched the boys twirling. The younger ones were doing what they did in those days: they swished and stomped from one end of the floor to the other with flailing arms and splayed feet, or waved their hands over their eyes like odalisques, squatting at times, all elbows and knees, while their skinny boyfriends seized them from behind for some merciless X-rated hip-grinding. Some in their late twenties had kept faith with vogueing, or even with the punk intransigence of the mid-80's: no beat at all, just a sullen black lurching. Men with thin hair and the remains of pecs were loyally resurrecting disco spins and earning smug tolerant glances from the slim big-haired stompers and humpers. The music had a beat that came up through the ankles more than in through the ears. The melodies consisted of a single shouted high note or sentence fragments uttered with glacial disdain by bulimic girls in hard leather hats. One favorite song earned screams of recognition from the crowd, who swarmed onto the floor with bold flouncings to lip-synch and twirl and snarl and snap their fingers in imitation of the enormous drag queen who recorded it. It was too loud to talk, and so Rachel and I sipped and pointed and smiled until, with one hand up to smooth her hair, she pulled me onto the floor.

I wasn't sure when I'd last seen Rachel dance. She began just as one should, slowly. Keeping her elbows near her waist, she snapped her fingers to left and right, her hips swaying, her feet barely moving. We'd been dancing for less than a minute when a shrill thin boy in ACT-UP boots and short shorts flounced up to her and, leaning forward from the waist with a blinding shimmy of shoulders, shrieked in her face, "Oh WORK it, girlfriend!" She closed her eyes, smiled, and tossed her head, her earrings tinkling. The boy stood with legs spread, knees bent, and seemed about to try some kind of lurid lombada motion with her, his hands reaching out for her waist to bring her closer. He kept throwing his head back and giving piercing cries that carried painfully even above the thudding music; his smile was terrifying. I moved a step closer to him and tapped him on the shoulder, pointing first at him and then at a distant corner of the bar: Walk away. He gave me a quick sneer and then, flinging an invisible mane over his shoulder with a snap of the head, disappeared. Rachel smiled at me and shook her head. I wasn't sure why I'd felt the need to protect her from a mere dancing child, but I was as pleased with myself as if I'd routed a Philistine army.

Within a few minutes her response to the music was picking up, and she had her arms out, waving from the shoulders in sinuous temple-dancer poses. She did a slow turn, feet together, shifting her hips in a hypnotic, graceful motion. Her wide skirt spread and rocked as she turned, making her waist and ankles and feet seem tiny. Her eyes were closed, her face upturned and striped by the pulsing lights. For a moment I was in a temple square in Mesopotamia; the priestess was dancing, marshaling the forces of fertility in crop and womb, and the men who watched her, rapt, bewildered, felt surges of divinity in their loins. I was on the threshing floor at the Palace at Knossos, and the Queen spun and lifted her arms and stamped her feet, as the Goddess, her Mother, smiled and listened and the people stood proudly entranced. Then, thank God, I was back at the Renegade with Rachel. She was really a good dancer, in a personal womanly way. There was nothing exactly sexy about her dancing, certainly not when seen beside the manic thrustings and flauntings of flesh and joint that surrounded us. Curiously ladylike, like Giulietta Masina, genially responsive to the odd encouragements and tributes of the rag-tail mob around her, she nodded and smiled at the many boys and men who were drawn to bump a hip or shake a shoulder with her. It was almost subversive at a gay men's bar; almost recruitment. The integrity of her gender identity – I am a woman – and the simplicity of her movements made her absolutely the most magnetic person on the dance floor. All the men who brushed against her then followed her with their eyes, as though aching for her notice or approval. They spun for her, clapped their hands and yelled for her attention, looked suspiciously at me – Who's that queen? with her? – and seemed all taken by the same dream: to dance with Rachel. I wondered how many of these men would go home and call, for the first time in years, their old girlfriends, their sisters, their mothers. Rachel seemed to offer everything anyone could ever wish for in the way of affirmation from a beautiful woman: not sex, really, but the knowledge that in the eyes of the one from whom your being flowed, you were OK.

She actually seemed to be dancing mostly with herself, withdrawn into that inner ocean, her smiles to the others and to me courteous and kind and detached. At length, she tired of the way so many men were approaching her, and she moved closer to me and put her arms around my neck. Her touch was cool and comfortable. Rachel doesn't have a brother, I thought inconsequently. My role, I sensed, was to protect her reverie. By dancing with me like this, she wasn't inviting a greater warmth or confidence; she was getting the space to keep dancing with herself, away from the needs and demands of the energetic crowd. It had been many years since I'd danced this closely with a woman. I remembered dances in high school, when I'd felt the swelling of a girl's shallow breasts against me, the softness below the waist where her young hips, for all that they might be called boyish, were so palpably unlike my hips, a boy's. I had watched myself coldly in those days, and hoped that, at last, I would respond "normally" – remember "normal"? – to these anatomical prompts. This self-monitoring, waiting for a response that didn't come, had blocked me from noticing that the sensation of dancing with a body unlike my own was enjoyable strictly for its own sake. Rachel, her rich figure lightly pressed against me, seemed to my body like the Venus of Willendorf, pillowy, blooming, burgeoning in breast and belly and thigh. I half expected to see that she had suddenly become obese, but no: it was just that hand and torso receive the contours of the body differently from the eye. I made a mental note to mention this to Walter, the eternally curious art historian. Those Stone Age artists weren't necessarily doing sculptures of fat sedentary women. Maybe they were just giving visual expression to the sensation I was having now, that a healthy woman's large lovely breasts feel greater than the tide, the earthquake, the cataract when they rub against you. For a moment I felt for Tony. You could go into such a billowing force of nature when quite sure you were welcome and loved; but then what if there were suddenly some little third one in the very midst of your adventure, a stranger, a homunculus, hers, not yours? Had he always been there, before you, waiting, watching you, bound to her in complete solidarity while you bobbed and dodged, a twig on the torrent? God, I thought, I've learned more about heterosexuality in the past fourteen seconds than I've ever wanted to know.

A bit after one o'clock, we drove back to the house, hardly speaking most of the way. "Jim, you drive," she'd said in the parking lot, pulling the convertible keys from her skirt pocket. The night was beautiful, the air salty and cool. Along the highway, the lights were at least as bright as on the dance floor, and glancing over at Rachel, I saw her distractedly watching the lights of oncoming cars, the rows of closed stores, bobbing her head a little to accompany some song in her head, barely smiling to herself. Sentimentally, I imagined she was humming a silent lullaby.

"What are you thinking?" I asked.

"Mmm," she said, drowsily. "Just that it's fun to dance."

"Do you two ever have time to go out at home?"

"Sometimes," she said. "We make time. We're pretty good about that." After riding another block or two without speaking, she turned to me suddenly.

"Do you ever get sudden feelings? Premonitions, or just knowing what's coming? I know you do; you're the type."

"Oh thanks!" I laughed. "Now just let me get my dolls and pins and chicken entrails."

"No, silly; I mean you're a very spiritual person. You're in touch with things like that. I had a feeling about you, tonight, while we were dancing. While we were dancing close." She paused. If she had been just a standard-issue yuppie woman, it would have been a pause for effect. With Rachel, though, I took it more seriously. This woman has oceans inside her, I thought; she dances to heal psychic wounds and draw the powers of god down to earth. "Jim. I think you're going to meet someone."

"Really?" I asked politely, my eyebrows going up: maybe slightly overdoing the intrigued reaction.

"Soon," she said. "There was a tension in your body tonight that said, I'm ready. I half-thought there was someone there, in the bar, but all those people coming up to us: it wasn't any of them. You know, I don't think you and I have ever been that close physically for so long, but I felt as though we'd danced like that a thousand times. Because you remind me of

Anton, as I was saying this afternoon; I feel that easy with you. And yet all these years, I've thought you two were opposites."

"Me too," I said. "Everyone has always said that, even back in school. They'd see we were friends, and they'd say, Opposites attract."

"I know. But you're not. You have the same gift, Jim. You make people happy; you have generous hearts. And if... even if – things were different, you two wouldn't have... well, you might not..."

"Mate?" I suggested, fascinated.

"Yes," she nodded. "You're too alike. You were put on earth to be brothers, partners, comrades." While part of me balanced this new idea and found a surprising amount of truth in it, part of me noticed that she was neatly desexualizing my relations with her husband – not that he hadn't done a pretty superb job of that himself over the years. "Anyway, that's not what I was mostly thinking," she went on. "I was thinking of you and this new person, whoever he is. The difference between you and Anton is that the world, the way it is now, has made it easier for him to find his way to being happy. You've both given happiness, but it's been harder for you to receive it. But there's such a fullness in your heart now: all that you've given over the years is ready to come back home now. Happiness given and happiness received – they finally balance out."

"Who are you?" I asked, laughing. "The Dalai Lama? Shirley MacLaine?"

"I know," she giggled. "This is what happens on vacations, I guess." She was animated now, as though we were in the midst of a good adolescent heart-to-heart. It was like sitting up half the night with your friends in eleventh grade, going "Wow" about the meaning of life. She'd turned to face me, one leg curled under. "So about Mr. X: my hunch is it's going to be someone who's nothing like you, at least on the outside. Nothing like Anton."

"Well that leaves just about everybody," I said. "There's nobody like either of us, mercifully."

"And be careful how you deal with him," she said, laughing. "You'll find him very difficult, because he's so different." She was half-joking now, talking as though this were already settled.

"So help me out," I said. "Tell me if I'm screwing up. Give me the high sign."

"Count on it," she said. By now we were on the back streets of the residential area, nearing the house. The streets were dark and her face was shaded.

"Rachel," I asked. "Speaking of Tony. How about this baby business? I hope you don't mind him telling me."

"Of course not. I wanted you two to talk about it."

"So is it going to happen?" We pulled into the dark drive and I turned off the motor. She sighed. Across the black sand, we could hear the waves.

"Time will tell," she said finally. Then, "Actually, I guess it will have to tell, fairly soon, won't it?" She made a dim little sad face. Then she spoke more firmly. "But I can't ruin my marriage for a child. And I'm afraid some things just can't be forced."

"'You can't hurry love,'" I sang, and she smiled at me as she had on the porch. "Well, either way, Rachel, you're a wonderful mother. You know that." We got out of the car.

"Dear Jim," she said, as she let herself into the kitchen. "Good night."

Chapter 4 – Wednesday

The next morning, Wednesday, I was up early in spite of my intention to be lazy. I'd slept with the windows open and by morning was glad to have the cotton blanket to pull up and wrap myself in, in the indolent wasteful spaces of the enormous bed. The room was drenched in amber sunlight from dawn and I had even, for a few minutes, been stirred to sit up and put on my glasses and enjoy the sunrise over the water. I lay back down afterwards but couldn't sleep past seven. So I got up, showered, had some coffee, and took a stack of books out to the beach. Since I was alone, I headed directly to the gay section, though its gayness at that hour was strictly conceptual; there was scarcely a soul out but me.

I had brought several classic Italian novels with me, planning to mark passages I could use in language classes to illustrate grammar points or to build vocabulary. The wind and sun were too exciting for that, though. I surveyed the spines and felt no sympathy for Lombard peasants barred from marriage by overbearing dons; for Sicilian princes forced to sell their lovely nephews in marriage to impossibly lush and vulgar heiresses; for the plucky loyal inhabitants of a poor Florentine neighborhood I knew I'd rather die than reside in for ten minutes. With a shudder of recognition, I also tossed aside a book I'd loved for years, about a cranky school teacher vacationing at the beach with his best friend and the friend's wife. Finally, giving in to my low motivation, I turned to a birthday gift from a colleague who taught Italian in Atlanta: *Via col vento – Gone With the Wind* in Italian. She had quite rightly said that she was the only person who could give it to me, and I was the only person she could give it to. The fact that Scarlett was "Rossella" in Italian had always made me laugh (though hadn't Mitchell herself called her "Pansy" right through to the last draft?). This summer, I had found too that India became "Lydia," Honey "Gioia," Archie "Baldo," and Bonnie "Diletta" in the same mass conversion. Rhett and Ashley and a few other lucky ones kept their names intact: Ellen was decently "Elena," though my blood froze every time Scarlett called her *mamma*, as though she were a big-chested gnarly-knuckled woman stirring a pot of polenta. Scarlett owned property at *i Cinque Punti* and built her garish house on *via dell'Albero di Pesco* and remembered with nostalgia the time when she dreamed of marrying Ashley and becoming the mistress of *le Dodici Querce*. Of course, none of this could diminish my interest in the story, the rise and fall and rise and fall and rise of that unbelievable Irish girl with her swaying hoops and slanting green eyes. The absolute certainty that she would get Rhett back had gotten me through more crises than I liked to admit, and I frankly wouldn't have given a damn if they'd changed her name to Ortenzia, Adeltraut, or Barbara Bush. No, I had not read *Scarlett*, and I didn't plan to – not until I'd finished my own drafts for *Dante: The Next Thirty-five Years* and *Aeneas: The Epic Continues*.

Anyway I had been amusing myself fairly well for a good while when I looked up and saw a man swimming alone in the heavy morning surf. Occasionally a wave would toss him free of the water and offer a glimpse of a glistening torso dense with muscle. From time to time he shook the water out of his hair, which showered generous arcs in all directions and fell into a mass of close curls. His body said he was a man, not a boy, but his hair was as thick as a sixteen-year-old's. I decided that he must be Italian, and that I liked him. Despite his imposing mature body, there was something touchingly young in the way he breasted the waves, wavering before their force but stubbornly and optimistically turning back to face them, and in the way he bounced in the rising water and shook his hair and splashed with his hands and feet. I imagined that meeting him in a bar I might find him rather scary, with his muscles and his curls. But playing in the waves which dwarfed him, rolled him over and over, left him staggering or lying prone in their retreating foam, laughing and shaking himself dry like a dog, he was distinctly endearing. I sentimentally hoped he had a lover, someone who loved him a great deal, because everything about him said We won't be young forever. He was already not precisely young, and it was good that someone should hold and cherish him now, before it was too late. Good grief, I thought suddenly, any minute I'll start humming "Hello, young lovers." Why shouldn't I be the one? He's here alone. Maybe he's single; he may be one of those shy under-socialized guys who don't know they're attractive...

Then I went back to Rossella.

Some time later I looked up again and saw that he was coming out of the water. It wasn't much past eight, and the beach was still mostly deserted. Yet he seemed to be walking towards me, with the whole blank stretch of sand to choose from. He stopped to pick up a towel and some shoes and sunglasses and lotion which he had left near the edge of the waves. I noted in his favor that he was wearing short baggy trunks of a faded green, comfortable and functional, not one of these repellent lycra fuck-me thongs that some hot boys wore just to ruin the peace of other men on the sand. He had a sexy walk, rocking weightily from side to side as some muscular men do, and still seeming to falter slightly from the pummeling the waves had given him and from his uncertain footing in the sand. His hair was already lighter than it had looked in the water, not blond at all but the light flat brown with no highlights from the sun that a lot of Romans have. He was shorter than I'd thought, probably no taller than me, but packed strongly into his five-nine or ten. His heavy shoulder muscles shifted beautifully as he wrapped his towel around his back. He had a slightly self-conscious rightness of movement and proportion that showed he worked out, yet no one could say it wasn't worth it in his case. He had stopped short of overdoing it. There was a softness to his contours, none of that icky icy definition we were invited to admire in too many muscle queens. In a very charitable mood, one might have said that his musculature looked natural. The sun was behind him still, and I couldn't see his face clearly, but any man with his easy rolling gait and thick body would have to be attractive.

A second look a moment later confirmed that he was actually walking up to me. Maybe he mistook me for someone; maybe he was going to ask me what time it was; maybe God had told him that he would marry the next man he saw on the beach. I looked up and shaded my eyes as he got within speaking distance.

"Jim?" he asked. "Jim McManus, right?"

"Yeah," I said.

"Joe Andreoli," he said. "You remember me?"

Dear God, yes. I could feel a sudden thump in my chest. This was not possible. Joe Andreoli was a boy I had lusted after years earlier, when I was in grad school. I'd heard him sing a big solo with one of the undergraduate singing groups, and not only I but virtually the entire audience had fallen in love with him: not that he sang all that well, but that, in his tux, with a torrent of curls to his shoulders, he glowed with such satisfaction at his own cuteness and belted high notes. You just wanted to run up onstage and squeeze some of that self-enjoyment out of him, can it, and save it for your next crisis of confidence. It turned out he was taking Italian with one of my classmates that term, and I met him at a conversation circle soon after the concert. He wasn't a super-handsome kid, but he was the next-best thing: humpy and cocky. He was active in music and theater groups around campus. Seeing him perform several times, I was never able to think he was quite as good as he clearly thought he was, yet his delight in his own passable skills was incredibly magnetic. He gave and gave when he performed, but you always felt he got more back than he gave. It wasn't coarse conceit, really. You loved to hear him sing or act just because you thought, for once, Here's somebody who knows he's OK.

Then during his senior year a dove descended from Heaven and, in defiance of his hulking Italian papa back in Brooklyn, he came out. I half expected the *Yale Daily* to run a front page article about it, with maybe an editorial: it was absolutely the biggest news in New Haven that month. Strangers embraced on the street. Jodie Foster, the most famous undergraduate on campus at the time, had been in the same section of Italian 101 as Joe; she reputedly said she'd always thought he was gay. And Jim McManus lay awake panting for a week.

I was in love with Angel at the time, had been rebuffed, and was engaged in the exhausting attempt to maintain a friendship with a man I loved desperately. This meant good-night kisses that left me weak, stiff, and slightly sick, horrid phone calls when he asked my advice about other men, and a manic masturbatory life. I tried briefly taking refuge in promiscuity. Unfortunately, or not, I turned out to be only minimally functional sexually when not engaged emotionally. Maybe men sensed that, or maybe I was being shielded without knowing it: sex was far more dangerous than we knew in those years. In any case I found it perplexingly hard to score. As the frustration level rose, I found myself fastening on surrogate fantasies and, for periods of a few weeks or more, riding them to death in my mind. There was usually some frail hook: I actually knew these guys as a rule, a little, and liked them some. But mostly they provided a phantasm of sexuality that distracted my howling nerves from their longing for Angel.

Joe Andreoli was one of these. He had the easy affability of an average butch kid who knew he was popular and attractive. We hung out some. We attended a gay dance together at one of the residential colleges, and I lived for weeks on the screams of envy that greeted our entrance. We went dancing at Partners. I'd go looking for him in the crowded bar and find him seated on a stool, engrossed in the videos – "It's Raining Men," "Gloria" – it was those days. Just to see him watch those videos made me smile; his whole self was given to the generous collegial appreciation of what the singers were doing. He knew this was art, and he knew one day he'd be making it himself, and the respectful fusion between him and the screen was lovely to see.

Once at a keg party, the cups ran out and, on a daring impulse, I suggested we take turns squirting beer into each other's mouths from the hose. To my surprise, he accepted, sucking nicely on my fingers as I served him and then, as I was sucking on his, saying dreamily, "This is kind of sexual when you think about it."

Another time we were at a party, and he came over and said, "This is beat," and suggested we slip out for a drink at the bar.

This kind of overture elated me and make me hope certain things might happen. Then I realized that he merely hated arriving or leaving or standing alone, having the natural star's instinct for appearances. This realization did nothing to moderate my lust. In my mind, I rode his compact body a hundred times, tangling my fingers in his tossing curls; in reality, I got a number of rather sweet, rigidly puckered kisses. When given in public places, these did marvels for my ego and reputation, and I was always grateful for that, even when he made it clear that he wanted our relationship to be strictly platonic – he used those words, as if consulting a manual. Joe was completely enthralled by pale frosty preppy boys named things like Skip and Alden, and had, that year, most of the ones available. He told me, "I'm not into older guys, Jim." I was twenty-eight. That stuck in my craw for years.

Here I was, forty-one now, looking up at Joe Andreoli

again. A moment before I'd been hoping that by some miracle the man in the surf was approaching me. But Joe had never wanted me.

"Hey, yeah," I said, putting my hand up and sucking my waist in. "Joe, how have you been?" I was trying to sound casual, but realized it was stupid to make no reference to the strangeness of this meeting. "I... what are you doing in Rehoboth? I can't remember what you've been up to all these years."

"Can I join you a minute?" he asked. He shook his towel out and flopped down beside me. He looked magnificent, leaning on one elbow like a river god on the Campidoglio. Maturation and hours at the gym had given him real shoulders and a real chest. His face, which I could see now, was cheerful and manly. He'd been getting too much sun for years; especially around his eyes, you could see the leather setting in. But it was a good look. I tried to remember his face at Yale, but got no clear memory of anything but his shallow chest held up proudly, and his round meaty butt. There had been a kind of scruffiness about his face, I recalled, as though something hadn't set yet. His nose was a little crooked maybe, a little big for his face, something like that. Certainly we'd all liked his face, his smile, his squinty eyes, but he'd never looked as good as this. His features were better on a man than on a boy: that was it.

While I was taking in his looks and he was settling on his towel, I tried to remember things I'd heard about him over the years. He'd gone out to LA to make it in show business, I was sure of that. As far as I knew he hadn't gotten much work in that line. He was working as a waiter when a mutual friend saw him, and hanging out with an exclusive crowd of desperately sexy actor/singer/model/waiters who went to trendy clubs and slept with each other and hoped, through continual working of the cute-boy scene, to break into the professional networks; surely those networks couldn't be any harder to break into than the one these boys formed themselves. I had seen one picture of Joe in a magazine. It was an arty underwear ad, a kind of homage to Cocteau I guess, with boys in trendy drawers standing in slack caryatid poses holding empty gilt picture frames and the detached cabriole legs of chairs. Joe was the one on the left, lit dramatically from one side, his face in profile, looking down, his back to the camera. The lighting threw the muscles of his back and buttocks into thrilling relief, probably the reason he had been picked. I remembered looking at the picture with a mixture of lust, which was clearly the photographer's intention, and sadness. Joe's face was sad in the shot. There was recognizably the same sense of his own greatness as I'd seen at Yale when he threw back his head for a high note, never the ghost of a fear that he would miss it. But in this picture that inner knowledge was subjected to someone else's sense that what was important about him was his curvy butt and curly hair. There was a kind of weariness or submissiveness in the way he looked down in the picture; he'd always had that swaggery way of looking up. Now he looked simply bought and paid for. Clearly, people were noticing his curves; I had an unhappy sense that someone who'd ridden them recommended him for this job. I had heard, around the time I saw the ad, that Joe was getting sick of that life, and in the ad it showed. He was over it: competitive glamor-tricking and breaks that weren't breaks and nowhere jobs waiting tables, hoping to be cast in some nowhere role – maybe as the cute boy who screamed as a lesbian serial killer slashed his leg off with her stiletto heel, just before the real star turned her into Betty Crocker by savagely raping her. I could picture Joe finally saying, This is beat.

"Weren't you living out in LA?" I asked.

"Still am," he said. "I had two weeks off and I came out here with some guys I work with back on the Coast; one of them is from here. We just got here Monday."

"Me too," I said. "What kind of work are you doing these days?"

"Waiting tables," he said. "It's an OK job. Hey, it beats peddling your ass, right?"

"Right," I laughed, hoping he hadn't just been reading my mind as I remembered his fashion shot.

"How about you?" Joe asked. "Still teaching?"

"Yeah," I said. "I'm in Baltimore. I got tenured this year, by the way. So things are good. And Baltimore's a great town; I never expected to stay, but here I am, nine years later." He gave the smile everyone gave when you said that Baltimore was a great town. Usually they then said something condescending about how good the Inner Harbor and the new ballpark were for the city, and about how Baltimore was so "real." I couldn't think of what else to say, so I said, "I had a book published a few months ago…" His eyebrows went up, a genuine I'm impressed look, as though I'd sold a screenplay to MGM. "Well, just literary criticism," I said quickly; "the *Decameron*, you remember? Did you read any of that in class? I forget which courses you took."

"Wo," he said: stoked. "I've never known anyone who's

had a book published. You're really doing something with your life. That's pretty great." I would have fallen down in a faint if I hadn't already been firmly seated.

"I could show you a copy," I said brazenly, with a sense of tempting providence; how much could Joe Andreoli possibly care about my book? "I've got one with me at the house." He asked where I was staying, and I pointed. He whistled, and I laughed. "No," I said, "it's not mine. Some rich friends of mine are staying there and they invited me down."

"I'm at a guest house about a mile out of town," Joe said. "My buddies and I were out dancing last night and we got seriously wasted. They're all sleeping. But I took my bike and came into town. I needed to swim it off, clear my head out." He sat up and held his knees, looking out to sea. "You see me last night?"

"No," I said, "but of course I wasn't looking for you."

"I saw you there, dancing with that beautiful lady. She's... are you married?"

"Good grief, no, Joe; you know I'm a homosexual. I would have married *you* if you hadn't laughed in my face."

"I never laughed at you," he said, smiling. "But when I saw you last night, I just thought... there have been a lot of changes in the gay world since I saw you last. Lots of guys I know have gone straight – like I'm so sure, right?" He shook his head, trying to knock some water out of one ear. "But you were always the marrying kind, you know. I figured maybe you got tired of waiting for Mr. Right and you went for her. It would make sense in a way. I mean, your life is set: you've got your career, your book... That's the kind of person who settles into a really strong relationship – marriage, family or whatever. So who is she?"

"That's Rachel," I said. "Her husband was my best friend in college. In fact I was in love with Tony for years. But we're all real close friends, and they're the ones who took this house."

"You see a lot of them?"

"Not usually; they live in Chicago. We just got here a couple of days ago, and we'll be staying till next Sunday. That's longer than we've gotten to visit in years."

"You still have it for Tony?" Joe asked. "Talk about changes; half those married men in LA can't keep their hands off the waiters, I'll tell you. Anything can happen, right?"

"No," I said. "I mean, with an old friend, over time you stop expecting some things. You accept your relationship for what it is." I thought about Tony's arm around my shoulder when he ran up the steps to greet me, about our talk on the beach when he said, "You're my guy." I guess my expression changed. "But you always love the men you've really loved, one way or another."

"You're such a romantic," Joe said, studying me. "That's why I never got involved with you. I liked you, but I didn't want to be tied down. You looked like you'd glom on and never let go." I laughed, but I was slightly put off. I seemed like kind of a sweet young man to myself in retrospect, and it wasn't my fault if I'd had an affectionate nature and some bad disappointments. I didn't like him making me sound like some tar pit. "No, you did!" he said, responding to my look. "Woo! Scare me. But I liked you a lot."

"I thought you were about the hunkiest kid in town," I

said. He laughed, turning his eyes away.

"Gee, thanks," he said.

"That's a compliment, Joe," I insisted. He didn't say anything for a minute, watching a little girl and her father trying to launch a kite down the beach. Then he turned back to me and tapped my shoulder with his fist.

"Hey," he said, "this is pretty incredible running into you like this. I want to see your book."

"Now?" I asked. Even after twelve years, it was exciting to have had his attention for so long – ten minutes by now! – and here he was accepting my proposal to prolong the contact.

"Whenever," he said. "I'll be here two weeks, just like you." Then he laughed at me. "OK; now," he said. "I hate to see you look like that." I didn't know how I'd looked. "Besides," he went on, "my buddies will be here by lunchtime and I'll have to hang with them. Yeah: now."

Back in the studio, he showered while I set out some Danish and laid my book on the table. He came out of the bathroom toweling his hair, and glanced at the plate of pastry.

"None for me," he said. "I've got to watch my waist these days. I'm thirty-three now and it doesn't take care of itself anymore." He flicked the towel at my waist and said, "But you have some if you want." He was teasing me and his point was clear. But I said,

"You never cared about my looks anyway. You weren't into older guys. And I'm forty-one now. So why should I worry about my waist for your sake, thank you very much Mr. Gold's Gym?"

"I liked your looks fine," he said, when he finished laughing. "You still look great. No way do you look forty-one. I'm just into eating healthy, that's all. Everyone should be."

"Don't start," I said. Then, realizing I'd rather slit my wrists than eat a cheese Danish in front of Joe now, I put the plate back in the refrigerator and scowled at him. Joe looked as though I'd unjustly accused him of a murder. Then he dropped it.

"Do me a favor?" he asked. "Rub this lotion on my back. I'm getting a little freaked out about the ozone and stuff. And you know how California is; we're all permanently roasted." He handed me the bottle of sunscreen lotion and turned his back to me. I put the bottle down and said,

"Kiss me first. It's nice to see you again."

"Wo," he said, turning back to face me, smiling. "You've gotten *real* smooth." He took my face in his hands and kissed me slowly, gently, his parted lips grazing and nibbling mine very lightly. It was perfectly clear that this kiss was mere mechanics; he could do this with his buddies, his tricks, his boss, his vixen costar on a soap opera if his break ever came. Nevertheless it felt wonderful. I put my hands on his waist and would have gone on kissing him for hours, but he pulled back after a few long seconds. He turned around again.

"Now rub the lotion on my back," he said. I rubbed some onto my palms and then started on his shoulders. He swayed slightly, with his eyes closed, and made soft contented sounds as I spread lotion all across his broad ripply back. He hadn't asked me to massage him and I resisted the urge, keeping my touch light and discreet. His lower back had wonderful vertical ridges leading my hand down towards his trunks and I made him turn slightly to the side so that the flat of my hand could negotiate those valleys of muscle. His eyes were still closed, and I kissed him on the cheek, growling slightly. He smiled without opening his eyes.

"Tiger," he murmured. Then I patted him on the small of the back, to indicate that the anointing was over. On impulse, just as he opened his eyes, I pulled the elastic band on his trunks as far as it would go in back, looking down on his bare pale ass. He turned to me with a silent open-mouthed face of mock outrage, and then smiled. His turn had freed his trunks from my hand, and the waistband snapped back. "You're wild," he said, a kind of rote tribute which, in its flat lack of urgency, showed he considered me no kind of sexual menace at all.

"I've always wanted to see your bum," I said.

"Now you have," he said. "So this is your book?" He sat at the table and patted the chair beside him.

For about twenty minutes, he flipped through the book, starting at the table of contents, asking me specific questions about the chapter titles and themes, reconnecting forgotten fragments of knowledge from years before. I wasn't sure how much he'd ever actually known about the *Decameron*: he'd had only two years of Italian at Yale, as far as I could recall, and what he had learned about Boccaccio would have depended entirely on his instructors' initiative in bringing historical and literary material into class to supplement the textbooks. He was a good faker if nothing else, and had a plausible way of saying, "Oh, right" and nodding his head quickly upward when I answered questions like "What plague?" and "This is before or after the

Renaissance?" I answered his questions casually, staying cool, assuming from moment to moment that he would tire of this polite display of interest and return to the beach in search of his waiter friends.

Yet he stayed. He glanced at the back cover and saw my picture, an informal shot Marie had taken in front of the bookcase in my study.

"Cute," he said, whistling and jabbing me lightly in the ribs with his elbow. He started to stir in his seat and I resigned myself: this was where he'd leave, and I'd be lucky to get so much as a wave on the beach from him for the rest of our stay. But, to my amazement, he asked instead if he could stay a while longer and if I had a T-shirt he could borrow. My heart pounding, I rummaged in a drawer and found him one, a faded blue I thought would look right with his trunks. It bore the logo of the Lyric Opera of Chicago; it was a gift from Tony several years earlier. Joe pulled it on. With regret I saw his lovely chest and stomach disappear. Then he took the book to the sofa.

"May I?" he asked, before sitting in the massive crook of one of its corners, tucking one leg under him like an earnest studious kid. "You go ahead and do whatever you were going to do."

Self-consciously, wishing I could sit by him on the sofa and run my hands up and down him, I opened up the laptop computer on the table where we had been sitting and started to work. Within a minute or two, though, I was feeling happy and cozy. There was a friendly ease about having him in the room and feeling safe in taking my eyes off him: he was settled on the sofa and had said he would stay. In fact I found that my writing went faster and better with him – with someone – there. He asked me what I was writing, and said "Ariosto: Renaissance – so... how many years after...?" Then, as I wrote and he read, he would stop me with questions – "What's 'liminal'? What's 'specularity' mean? What's 'Lacanian'? What's 'ludic'?" After several of these, I realized he was reading the first chapter.

"Did you skip the introduction?" I asked.

"Yeah," he said, being fresh, "isn't that just fluff?" I made an Italian scolding gesture at him, threatening him with chopping motions of my right hand, and he laughed:

"Just like my mom," he said.

"Well show Mamma some respect," I said. "I think the dedication and acknowledgements and intro will interest you." He flipped back to the very first pages.

"'To Robert (1953-1988),'" he read aloud. "'Some stories for the eleventh day. We'll talk soon.' Who's Robert?"

"He was my best friend in Baltimore," I said; "a friend from church. He just keeled over one night five years ago – a heart attack, no warning."

"Jeez," said Joe, shaking his head. "Life is scary, no?" He looked as though he were about to say something profound and then realized he couldn't think of anything. So he read the epigraph below the dedication: "'Ashes, ashes; we all fall down. Silence = Death.' Yay, Jim." He paused. "Everyone must think Robert died of AIDS, reading this," he said.

I shrugged: "We all have AIDS now, Joe, whether we've got the disease or not." He nodded and put his fist in the air. Then he glanced through the acknowledgements.

"Who's Walter?" he asked. And "Professor Who? Oh, I

remember him, from Yale. Here's Tony and Rachel: what did they have to do with it? Who are all these people: Marie; Luellen; Cheryl and Zack; Gene; Mark; Ricardo... your 'baby'? What's a *lieta brigata*?" He listened to my answers with his head to one side. He thought a moment. "God, Jim, how many best friends do you have?"

His steady stream of questions, each one making me turn my head to answer, finally gave me a fair excuse to take the laptop and a book and join him on the couch. The sofa was so long that I knew it looked rather pointed that I sat right beside him, but it made sense if I was to look over his shoulder to point things out or look at words he asked about. As we read in silence for a few minutes, he allowed his leg to rest against mine, and I was emboldened to put my arm up behind him:

"May I?" I asked, patting his far shoulder. A few minutes later, he said,

"I don't think I've ever done this."

"Done what?" I asked.

"Read with somebody."

This whole thing was so unexpected and so pleasant that I found the nerve to ask him,

"Isn't this kind of... beat – for you? I never pictured you taking an interest in this stuff."

"Right," he said. "I was the hunkiest kid in town. How could I be interested in books, is that what you're saying?"

"Well," I stammered, surprised by his pique, "usually cute hunky kids give me a big yawn. You almost have to apologize in gay bars if you're not a flight attendant or a lifeguard. My career always seems to bore people. It always seemed to bore you, in fact; you just liked those snobby blond boys. Now you're hanging out with all these drop-dead gorgeous LA surfer-waiters. Those guys are not my biggest fans as a rule."

"Who have you been talking to?" he asked suspiciously. "You don't know anything about my life in LA." His eyes were a little furtive and I sensed, though he wouldn't admit it, some diffuse dissatisfaction with himself. "We're not just bar boys... We talk." He hesitated, then made a partial confession. "Well – not a lot of my friends in LA went to college," he conceded. "They'd never read this kind of book. They read *Sex*, or books about... I don't know: Princess Di."

It occurred to me that Joe was something of a rarity in the world of underachieving gay pretty boys: he had a Yale BA. I doubted he'd been challenging himself very heavily in the reading department, but still: what would he and his disco-buddies talk about, when they were through talking about their tricks and drugs and show biz connections? It was a window on Joe's disappointment, and much as I enjoyed having my little revenge on that class of men, I wanted to spare his feelings. He had dreamed of being wonderful; in fact he had been quite sure he was. His charisma had gained him entry into a scary competitive world in which he had invested his energy and his dreams and which, after ten or more years, proved not to be as exciting or rewarding as he'd hoped. It wasn't his fault. I patted his shoulder and even presumed to squeeze it gently.

"Well," I said, "you're welcome to any of the books I've got here. We can read together like this any time you want."

"Yeah," he nodded. "That'd be great." He looked at my book again and frowned. "Do you have it here? I mean the

Decameron?"

"Yes," I said. "But I wonder if you'd rather read a modern book, to get back into it – it would be more like the language you learned at school. You could work up to the *Trecento*."

"You're the teacher," he said. Even to me, that sounded too submissive, as though he were still a kid at school, not the adult he clearly wanted me to think him. I could almost hear his mind looking for a demonstration of his new maturity and experience. "Plus I think I might be able to teach you some things, too."

"I don't doubt it," I said. "What did you have in mind, precisely?" He turned to face me directly, his back against the arm of the sofa, his legs pulled up in front of him.

"I'm going to teach you to come on to guys without scaring them to death," he said.

"Have I scared you?" I asked, surprised, feeling oafish and clumsy, but trying to sound cool.

"Nobody scares me anymore," he laughed, with a toss of his head. "You know what it is about you: you act like you expect to fail. It makes you kind of sneaky and grabby and weird. There's no reason you would fail; I bet you could pick up anybody you wanted, if you just believed in yourself a little more." I opened my eyes wide, adjusting to the bead-read, not sure if I was hurt by it or not. He didn't seem to mean to hurt me; he was just sharing something he knew a lot about. He took my hand from the back of the sofa and put it on his knee. "There," he said. "You can touch me; you don't have to steal it."

I was groping for something racy to say, but then I decided to risk saying something honest.

"It's nice of you to want to help me out, Joe. But at this point in my life I'd rather concentrate on meeting somebody to get serious about than on picking up boys."

"Hey," he said, meeting my eye frankly, "it's a lot of the same skills."

"But I don't want to be stroking your knee if you're just being polite, giving me a little cruising practice. Meanwhile you're going back to LA in two weeks and we'll never see each other again."

"You didn't mind pulling my shorts down a few minutes ago," Joe said, "and I was going back to LA then too. What's different now is, we're talking about it." He had a point. I rubbed his knee for a few seconds, as though it were Buddha's belly.

"Have you ever had a lover?" I asked.

"No," he said.

"Neither have I," I said.

"You were in love with Angel."

"How did you know that?" I asked, stung. "I didn't know you knew him."

"I didn't. Somebody pointed him out to me once. Everybody knew you were in love with him. He was famous for it."

"Anyway," I said, "he didn't love me; or he didn't... I don't know. It never happened." Joe looked at me appraisingly. He had a funny brand of kindness; there was no rudeness in his hard dispassionate gaze.

"You know what's wrong with you, Jim?"

"You barely know me, Joe; go a little easy on this 'what's wrong with me' bit."

"OK," he said, shrugging. "Not 'wrong with you.' I mean,

I can tell what your problem has been, with men. You've been in love. You loved this friend of yours, Tony, and you loved Angel; and then you tried scoring when your heart wasn't in it. You didn't really care about going out with me, for instance; you just wanted to make up for Angel."

"I haven't been in love with either Tony or Angel for years," I said.

"Maybe not," he said, "but they're your pattern – guys who let you down, don't come through for you. You expect to fail."

"Well thank you Dr. Joyce Brothers," I said. "So... would I fail with you?" I wanted to know. "If you were going to be around, if it were feasible; would you give me a chance?"

"To be your dream-trick or your lover?" he asked back. "I'm not sure you know what you want." He sounded offended, as though I'd suggested he was only capable of tricking. I'd thought it, I suppose, but I hadn't said it. He must have heard my thought, though: every gay man in America said, I'm not sure you know what you want, when what we meant was, You just hurt my feelings.

"Hey," I said, "you said on the beach that you didn't want to get involved with me in school because you were afraid I'd tie you down. So would you give me a chance now?" He looked a little shifty, unsure of himself.

"You haven't answered my question," he said. "Trick or lover?"

"You just told me they were the same skills," I said. "I guess if you're avoiding answering, it means you wouldn't be interested." Little as it mattered, I felt let down.

"You're confusing me," he said, after a beat or two. I looked him in the eye and realized it had cost him something to say that.

"Put your feet here," I said, putting the computer aside and patting my lap. I was surprised at how kind and fond my voice sounded. He heard it too, I guess, because he stretched his legs out and laid his feet gently in my lap. I liked Joe and enjoyed the fact that years of change and letdown for both of us had made this contact possible. I started to stroke his feet, not looking at his face. He sighed finally, and I looked over to see that he had leaned his head all the way back so that it hung over the arm of the sofa. I lifted his feet and kissed them. He heaved himself back up and looked at me with a sleepy sexy look, as though the tenderness of my touch had exhausted, undone him.

"Hmm," he said, "that feels so nice... you doing that."

"I'm not doing too badly?" I asked. "You're not scared off?"

"You've got a point to prove, haven't you?" he said, more awake than a second before.

"Yes," I said, leaning over his knees, to kiss his mouth. "My point is, I want to kiss you." He frowned, even as he gave me a tight peck.

"You're too smooth," he said. "You're stealing now. When you kissed my feet, you really liked me for a second." He was right, and I was embarrassed. I straightened up; so did he, putting his feet back on the floor.

"I'm sorry," I said.

"I said I was going to teach you something," he said. I'd

messed up, and now he would leave.

But he didn't leave. He took the book again, and opened it. I remembered him saying, You expect to fail. He was right; I had just this second expected him to leave after my misstep. Looking sideways at him, I couldn't help feeling grateful to him for staying.

"Thanks," I said. He smiled without looking up, and leaned against me for a moment, gently, casually.

"Hey," he said.

Sometime around noon, Rachel and Tony knocked on my door. As they stepped in, Tony asked if I wanted to join them for lunch downstairs. In mid-sentence, he saw Joe on the sofa. He barely stole a glance at me before putting his hand out.

"Tony Neuberg," he said. Joe stood up and shook his hand, looking him up and down. He rocked on his feet and swelled his chest, almost belligerently, in shaking Tony's hand. It pleased my vanity for Joe to see how handsome Tony was.

"I'm Rachel Fleischer-Neuberg," Rachel said, maybe even more cordially than was necessary. Joe put his hand out to her.

"I saw you last night, dancing with Jim," he said. She smiled at me, and I almost shivered, remembering how she had said she thought Mr. X might be right there at the bar. Clearly that was what she was thinking: chalk one more up to the Eternal Feminine, women's intuition, whatever. She didn't realize that Joe couldn't possibly be the one.

He hadn't told them his name yet.

"Tony, Rachel," I said, "this is Joe Andreoli. We knew

each other years ago at Yale, and we just bumped into each other this morning on the beach."

"Well how nice!" Rachel said. "Joe, you've got to come too; for lunch. There's plenty." Joe stood, his arms hanging, his feet apart, looking as though he might start stammering. I wasn't sure what the big deal was: to look at him, you'd have thought that Tony and Rachel had just swept in in full evening dress and asked him to the opera, in his trunks. Then I recalled what he'd said that morning, and tried to get him off the hook.

"Didn't you say you had to meet your other friends around lunchtime?" I asked, putting my hand on his elbow. He looked at me with a strange expression of disappointment; apparently I'd said something wrong. He turned away from them, towards the front of the house, and motioned me to turn too.

"You trying to get rid of me?" he asked under his breath.

"Joe!" I said. "Of course not. I just thought you said – "

"Am I OK like this?" he asked.

"You're fabulous," I said. "This is the beach, Joe. And they're very cool." When we turned back around, I could tell that our little whispered conference had struck Tony and Rachel as rather intimate. In a kind of defiant way I enjoyed their thinking that I'd managed to pick someone up so quickly; at the same time it embarrassed me.

They'd had the politeness to talk to each other while Joe and I huddled, but now Rachel said,

"Joe, do come with us. Unless you have definite plans. You can meet your friends on the beach later, can't you?"

"Sure," he said. "Thanks." The four of us stood there, exchanging uncertain smiles of good will.

"So..." I said. "Are we ready? Should I bring anything?" Tony was looking at Joe.

"Jim has a shirt just like that, don't you, Jim?" he said. He was teasing me; he recognized it. In another minute he would be winking at me and saying, Quick work. Joe took some kind of obscure offense, though.

"This is Jim's shirt," he said, with a stalwart tuck of the chin. "I didn't bring one into town, for the beach. So he loaned me this one." Tony was about to explain, but decided it was too much trouble.

"So what do you do, Joe?" he asked. Joe held his eye, not at ease yet. I'd told him that Tony made a lot of money.

"How about yourself?" he asked.

"Lawyer," Tony said.

"I'm... in the restaurant business," Joe said.

"How interesting," said Rachel. "Are you from around here?"

"LA," he said.

"And you – what? you have a restaurant out there?" asked Tony, hanging back to talk with Joe as we stepped out onto the landing over the driveway. Joe looked over at me as though I could help him out.

"... No," he said, part way down the stairs. "I wait tables at a grill. I make good money; it's a very trendy place."

"I love LA," said Rachel quickly. She was ahead of us a few steps, opening the kitchen door. "Such a fascinating city – so much happening, all that talent, that diversity, so much style."

"Those riots," said Tony.

As we all trailed in after Rachel, she was asking, "Are you involved in the arts scene at all, Joe?"

"Yeah," he answered, more happily. "I went out there for theater. That was my major in school. I've done a little showcase work, commercials, some modeling. It's not a real easy way to make a living. A lot of plastic people out there." Rachel was making some understanding reply to this, and Tony caught my eye. He smiled and raised his eyebrows tolerantly. He knew exactly what Joe was saying and he clearly thought I could do better.

"Beer, Joe?" he asked, standing at the open refrigerator. "Jim?" He handed me a bottle, and slid one across the kitchen island at Joe. It practically flew on the slick counter surface and Joe fumbled it at the other end. It fell on its side and rolled for a second before he got a grip on it, so that when he twisted the lid off, it fizzed and spilled. "Sorry," Tony said. "My fault." He tossed Joe the hand towel from the refrigerator handle. Rachel gave Tony a quick look, which he didn't see.

"Jim," she said, "set another place, please. Joe, would you be sweet and help me serve out here? Anton, get out from under foot. Go talk to Jim or something." So Tony and I went out into the dining room together while Rachel and Joe bonded.

"She's a wonder," I said to Tony as we loitered around the table for a moment.

"*You're* a wonder," he answered. He glanced at his watch and then laughed at me.

"Joe's not interested in me," I said. "He never was. It's no big deal. He was the undergraduate sex symbol at Yale years ago, but he never had time for me. We just met on the beach and he's latched onto me. Maybe he thinks he can reclaim his literate past with me. I have a feeling his life in California is starting to bore him."

"It would bore a hedgehog," Tony said. Then he added, under his breath, "Maybe Joe is a hedgehog." I stared at him, though he missed it as he straightened a placemat absent-mindedly. I couldn't recall ever having heard Tony say anything catty, and he hadn't known Joe for ten minutes.

"Do you two have any kids?" Joe asked at the table.

"No," said Rachel.

"Did you ever think about it?" Joe pursued, looking from one to the other.

Tony put his fork down rather hard and didn't say anything, so Rachel said,

"Oh, I suppose you always *think* about it."

"I like kids," Joe said, smiling at Rachel.

"Oh," she said, "do you have any... I mean, nieces or nephews or... ?"

"A bunch," he said. "You know Italian families, right? My sisters and brothers all live east though; I don't see them all that often. I don't see many kids in LA either. I miss that."

"Cheer up," Tony said. "There'll be about a million kids on the beach this afternoon. Maybe you can steal one; I doubt the parents would notice." Joe looked at him, and then turned back to Rachel.

"You'd be a great mom," he said. She nodded her head.

"Well thank you, Joe," she said generously.

"I saw your names in Jim's book," Joe said. He was trying to make conversation.

"Oh, you're reading it too!" Rachel said. "Isn't it fascinating?"

"Well," he said, "I just gave it half an hour this morning, before you came up. It's fairly slow going for me. I ask Jim about every other word."

"That's our guy," said Tony. "Always the teacher. He got me through college, you know. He'd give me this real patient smile and tell me what something was, and I could just hear him thinking, What an idiot!" He smiled at me a little gruffly.

"Tony!" I said. "When I think you're an idiot, I say so out loud. You know that." He tossed his head back: Yeah. Then he turned to Joe, motioning with his fork.

"Watch out, Joe," he said. "He's a tough grader."

"No he isn't," Joe said. "Everybody at Yale knew he was a wuss. Tell him your cat had a headache and he'd let you make up the quiz." He grinned at me. I was still surprised that Joe either knew or claimed to know much of anything about me in those days, when he'd given me so little of his active attention.

"Everybody at Yale didn't know him like I do," said Tony darkly. "Sure he comes off like a tender-hearted softie; but you cross his lines and see what happens…" Again, he made a menacing gesture, this time tracing circles in the air with the blade of his knife. He looked suddenly like a patriarch at the head of the table, blustering at his beloved brood. "There's that fierce McManus intelligence to be reckoned with; that unflinching integrity. Watch out, Joe."

"You're making Jim sound perfectly horrible, Anton,"

said Rachel. "Don't let him scare you, Joe. He's just being awful."

"I'm not scared of Jim," Joe said, trying to smile, trying to hold my eye.

Joe helped Rachel clear between courses.

"He really doesn't like me, does he?" Tony asked me as we sat alone at the table.

"How should I know?" I asked him. "He's barely met you. Why wouldn't he like you?"

"He's crazy about Rachel. He probably thinks I'm mean to her."

"Tony," I said, "when did you develop this bizarre paranoiac imagination?"

"Oh right," he said. "I'm the dull practical type. Not sensitive. I forgot."

"Doro!" I said, provoked. "Stop it!" Just as I spoke, Joe came through the swinging door and looked, confused, for another person at the table. Then he realized who Doro was, and frowned slightly.

Rachel and I stood at the sink, rinsing dishes.

"He's very sweet," she said.

"What's going on with him and Tony?" I asked her. I didn't want to talk about Joe's sweetness; I didn't want her to think this was a bigger deal than it was.

"Jim," she said patiently, as though this were the simplest and most obvious thing in the world, "he's jealous."

"Who?" I said. "Of whom?"

"Joe. Of Anton. He knows you two are close old friends,

of course. But every time Anton says anything that shows he knows you well, Joe's hackles go up."

"Why should he care? He isn't interested in me; he likes glamorous busboys and surfing fools."

"We'll just see about that," said Rachel with a superior smile, as she backed through the door into the dining room with the coffee tray. She hadn't noticed, or at least hadn't mentioned, that Tony seemed a little edgy with Joe too. Of course, she hadn't heard Tony call Joe a hedgehog.

Joe and Tony were sitting in silence when we joined them.

"Isn't this fun?" said Rachel, pouring coffee. "Joe: it's so nice you could join us." Tony gave her a quick look – Go easy, OK? Joe just said,

"Thanks."

Joe went back to the studio with me after lunch, to collect his things for the beach. I liked that he had my shirt and would have to bring it back. I wouldn't let him take any of my books out onto the sand, though. I said it wasn't him, but it was: what waiter would I trust with my Ariosto at Rehoboth? Coconut oil, water, sweat, KY... he got the implication, unfortunately. Again, he looked mildly hurt. It was annoying how sensitive he was to any sign that I didn't see him as a peer. When had he ever seen me as a peer? I was too old for him; not cute enough; too beat. But I was supposed to respect him and entrust things to him which I prized and which he couldn't possibly understand.

"You want to come meet the guys?" he asked me.

"They're... fairly fun. I think you'd like them."

"Maybe tomorrow," I said. "I'm going to try to do a little more writing this afternoon. Then Tony and Rachel and I will probably go out. Maybe we'll see you." He looked slighted: I chose to spend time with dear old friends, and not with the disco-bunny pals of a boy who'd washed up at my feet after giving me nothing but attitude for years. He tucked his chin in again, in that OK, I don't care gesture I'd seen him use before.

But, "Hey," I said, "this has been really great, Joe. It's wonderful to see you again. Why don't you come by for lunch tomorrow, and we can read together again – if you want... Plus it's fun you got to meet Rachel and Tony. They liked you."

He nodded curtly. "They're both big fans of yours," he said, as though I might not know that. He was standing uncertainly, shifting his weight, making up his mind to go. I couldn't tell what he wanted.

"Can I kiss you?" I asked.

"Sure," he said noncommittally. I kissed him, little kisses, soft, lips barely apart: five or six of them.

"I'm not stealing?" I asked him, feeling surprisingly shy.

"No," he said, eyes closed. "I'm giving, now." He opened his eyes. "*A domani*," he said, rather proudly, and left.

Chapter 5 – Thursday into Friday morning

Thursday morning, I made breakfast for Rachel and Tony and we sat on the front porch talking until after ten. It struck me that Joe's name didn't come up, as it hadn't at dinner the night before. I wondered if this represented scrupulous discretion on their part, or deep disapproval, or complete lack of interest. As I stood, finally, to go back to my quarters, I mentioned that Joe was coming by for lunch and asked if they wanted to meet us on the beach afterwards. "Sure," said Tony, "why not?" The lack of enthusiasm in his voice was so obvious that I noticed Rachel slip him a Be good look. Then, stretching and looking around the room restlessly, he asked if he could come up with me for the morning.

"Sure," I said, "why not?"

The balcony in the studio was just big enough for one lounge chair and one director's chair. Tony lay back in the lounge chair, and I sat next to him with my feet up on the rail. He had brought a couple of newspapers with him and commented to me on things I would never otherwise have noticed: financial news about corporations his firm had worked for; the International Monetary Fund. There was a story about the Vatican's involvement (or non-involvement, depending on whom you believed) in Italy's latest banking scandal, and Tony was surprised I didn't know more about it. Groping for a connection, I told him about a story I'd read on a trip to Rome not long before, about how the government had had to step in, over protests from the Church, to regulate the manufacture of light-up St. Anthony of Padua statuettes, because a number of the faithful had been electrocuted by faulty ones. He laughed. This was vintage Tony-and-Jim: he talked man-of-the-world business savvy, and I offered an amusing anecdote, a human-interest story. It reminded me a little of talking with my father when I was fifteen.

After a while he got bored reading. He took his shirt off and lay back to take the sun. With his eyes closed, I had a chance to look at him, my book folded in my lap. It was an old forbidden pleasure to ogle Tony, and I offered it to myself frankly. But I found that the fascination, at least for that day, was gone. Our talk on the beach had drained some of the hot tension of his presence for me. I looked at him and just saw my old friend Tony.

Sleeping people naturally look a little slack and passive. It had been a long time since I'd seen Tony this way, minus all his galvanizing charm and high spirits. I remembered he had just told me two days before that he and Rachel practically never had sex anymore. I knew myself well enough to admit that, in a way, this knowledge pleased me. If the hotness had gone out of their marriage, then really Tony was no more Rachel's than mine. By sitting companionably beside him and sharing his reading I was enjoying as full an intimacy with him as anyone. But at the same time this abstinence made him seem less himself, less dynamic, less thrilling. People who don't have sex don't seem sexy: maybe that was it. That meant that his neglect of Rachel left me bereft too. I shook my head. I was getting as bad as Robert, for whom the very thought of another man's heterosexuality was enough to make him lather. What did Tony look like to Rachel now, I wondered – did she see him as I did, just this comfortable homey presence? God, what a comedown, after holding that supple crackling tree-trunk of a man in your arms for twenty-five years.

There was a brisk sea-breeze, but I became aware of the heat of the sun and looked again at Tony. He was just starting to take on some color and this near-noon light would be too harsh for him. With his eyes closed, he looked defenseless. 'Married white male,' I thought, 'blond/blue, attractive, 40, solar passive.' Better ask him, I thought.

"Doro, did you put on any lotion? This sun is pretty hot." He sat up instantly, sleepy-eyed.

"Good thinking," he said. His movement had been so sudden it startled me; how could he spring so fast from such torpor? He reached into the pocket of his sweatshirt and found a tube of some European lotion he rubbed on his arms and chest and legs. Then he lay on his stomach and asked me to put it on his back. This was a rather austere test of my new-found freedom from sexual passion for him. Only the day before, with Joe, I had been unable to restrain myself from pulling his pants out in back after performing this same friendly task. But as I rubbed up and down Tony's strong soft back, I found that indeed there was no lust in the gesture. Mainly I felt responsible to protect him from burning. His skin was already hot to the touch, from the sun, and I could sense how the light strengthened and energized him as it soaked in. I could almost hear the regeneration of cells as his pale skin gave itself up to the sun; that was how he had bounced up so fast a moment before. Tony wasn't worn out; he was just recharging.

"Tony," I said, after a few minutes. "You're going to have

this baby, you know." He didn't say anything, but he frowned and kicked his feet up and down a couple of times in a kind of silent tantrum: Leave me alone. So I went back to what I was reading. Maybe ten minutes later, he rolled over abruptly, sat up, and reached for the lotion.

"You should put some of this on too," he said. "You're whiter than I am." He was right. I rubbed some on my face and up and down my arms and legs, and he said, "Come on, take your shirt off. Let's pretend we're at a Robert Bly retreat." I turned around and he rubbed the cream on my shoulders and back. When he'd finished, he held me hard by the shoulders, as though I were driving a motorcycle and he were holding on for dear life.

"And you're going to end up with your hedgehog waiter," he said. This was a fairly amazing leap and I didn't know what to say. It was far from decided even that Joe and I would spend the afternoon together, let alone our lives. But after a few sheepish Uhs, I asked,

"Would you mind that?" Tony was still gripping my shoulders. I couldn't see his face, of course.

"I have no right to mind," he said. "That's what Rachel said last night." So she *had* noticed that Tony didn't like Joe; she just hadn't admitted it to me. Then Tony added, "I don't hate Joe. He's a nice enough guy. It's just..." I turned around.

"What?" I asked.

"Nobody's good enough for you," he said, smiling, knowing he was being unfair, stupid. He'd never wanted me for himself, and so he – as Rachel had said – had no right to pass judgement on those who might. I faintly resented his little display of possessiveness; it was just getting in my way. But I also treasured it. Tony who was not sleeping with his wife; Tony who was jealous of the men I met; that Tony, in a way, was still my Tony. I knew that part of my heart would never get tired of that.

"Doro," I said, smiling too; "I don't get you." He shrugged.

"Anton Neuberg," he said, "man of mystery." He lay back down and closed his eyes.

Around twelve thirty, we heard Joe's bike on the gravel out back. Tony stirred, and I went to let Joe in. Joe came up the steps with a diffident swagger. He smiled and showed me two books he'd brought: a first-year Italian language text, and a bilingual dictionary. Both were used, heavily marked and underlined. He'd found them in a second-hand book store on the road outside of town and acted as though they were worth a lot more than the fifty cents each he'd paid for them. I gave him a pale smile over them; I couldn't pretend I thought they were exciting or valuable.

He said, "I can ask you stuff, right?"

I cocked my head to one side and shrugged and said "Yeah" without enthusiasm. Spending my vacation reminding Joe of what a verb was and then watching him go after twenty-five-year-old blond waiters with wispy goatees: what fun.

Tony stepped in from the balcony. He and Joe nodded at each other without smiling or speaking. I felt as though I'd been caught cheating. This was genuinely annoying, since I'd never had the least lay from either of them.

"I've got to get downstairs," Tony said to me, pulling his

shirt on. "You guys be good. We'll see you out on the beach?"

"Right," I said. "We'll see." He gave me some kind of jockish cuff on the upper arm and left.

After lunch, Joe sat at the table with a collection of modern short stories, and started reading. He'd come to a word he didn't understand, and he'd look it up and then, if he couldn't find it or if what he found didn't make sense, he'd ask me about it. I'd point him to a chapter in his grammar book or a conjugation table, and he'd nod and say he remembered. I was sitting across from him, reading *Orlando furioso*, following my marginal notes from canto to canto and making occasional notes on my diskette. If I had been suddenly swept out to sea, future scholars would have found my notes obscure enough that I might have become the fountainhead of a new trendy school of cryptic criticism:

- 1, 11 – Rin after Ang = peasant chasing *palio*: cfr. *Inf* xv, 121-3 (sodomites).
- Falanto descr w/ floral imagery 20, 13; band of boys '*fior di Grecia*' 20,
- 16: discourse of floral male beauty/valor.
- *Pazzia* scene 23, 129: rhyme *dramma/fiamma* (*Purg* xxx) – Orl's recog of Ang's defection = Dante's recog of Beatrice's arrival? (See also Segre note *ad loc.* on Petr's use of same rhymes.)
- 28 – AstB's incredible vanity, lust to see Iocondo (so handsome): again, oddly aesthetic attitude to men [cfr. *Dec 'Io son sí vaga della mia bellezza'*?].
- Senapo's liber'n by Ast's horn – comedy, not epic. Ast's 'hu-

bristic' journey to Underworld = quest for which Senapo is punished. License of Poet? Astolfo *figura poetae* – Ariosto's link to Dante?

- 46, 114 – Brad's plea to Rugg (unlike Andromache, Doralice): let HER fight in his place.

I was getting nowhere – a headache. I'd forgotten Joe was there for a minute when he asked,

"What is this story about, really?"

"What all modern Italian stories are about," I said distractedly. I couldn't remember which story he was reading. "It's a critique of bourgeois materialism, or a protest against the alienation of the individual in an impersonal and mechanistic society, or nostalgia for the mythical past – land, Italy, religion, family. Take your pick." He smiled.

"You don't like this stuff much, do you?"

"I don't hate it," I said. "It's my bread and butter. But this guy…" I slapped the screen lightly with the backs of my fingers and rocked on the back legs of my chair.

"Ariosto, you mean?" he asked, proud of remembering the name, and I nodded. He stood and came around the table to read over my shoulder.

"Show me," he said. "Tell me about it." I was about to put him off with a shrug or Let's not talk about work on vacation. Then I realized I had never once had an attractive man ask me to tell him about Ariosto. Joe seemed interested and there was no reason I shouldn't try.

"Do you ever read science fiction?" I asked him. He shook his head. "Neither do I," I said. "I just watch the new 'Star Trek.'

But I think good science fiction must be something like this. He writes about knights and dragons and magic, sorcerers and trips to the Moon – fantasy stuff – but he uses that imagery to look at real issues. He asks questions like What is beauty, and why do we care? or How do we understand mystery, God, in this new modern world? And he makes his characters out of pure formula: damsel in distress, noble but inexperienced warrior – nothing like what we would call character development in the modern sense. But then he adds two little weird details, and suddenly we care about them. He provides space for our own projections, I think; since there's really no Ruggiero, and Ariosto does practically nothing to make him a rounded-out person, we just put all of our own dreams onto him, and we love him. It's fabulous."

"Look at you," he said. "You're practically shaking." He sat down beside me. "Maybe I should read him."

"You can't," I said. "I mean, he's hard – 1532, it came out in its final form."

"I want to read something you haven't figured out," he said. I looked at him, struck by his unusual request. His broad Italo face was set, stubborn, dumb-looking. He wanted to learn from me, but he didn't want me to think of him as a kid. And, absurdly, he wanted to teach me too. That was a challenge, since I was used to being the teacher, and I taught young people, people who didn't know as much as me. But Joe had good sense, and he wanted to try this. I got up and went to the shelf.

"If you can make sense of this," I said, pulling a book down, "*you* can write a book."

"Do you like it?" he asked me.

"Yes," I said; "I don't get it, but I like it. It's a modern rephrasing of ancient myths – scary myths, human sacrifice, all of it. It's from when novelists all read *The Golden Bough* and yearned for the primitive. But it's still wide open. It's a mess."

"Could I read it?" he asked.

"Yes. It's written in this pseudo-American, speechy style, very fluid and casual, even though it's Hercules and Apollo talking. See what you think."

"Cool," Joe said. I stepped back to the table to hand it to him.

A while after this, I looked over at him from my seat. He had his head down and he hadn't asked a question in several minutes.

"Joe, what's all this about? What's going on? Why are you here?"

"Because I like it? I like you, maybe?"

"No," I said – I didn't believe that. "Why?" He looked out the window.

"Do you ever watch 'Blossom'?" he asked when he looked back. I shook my head.

"My students talk about it," I said.

"A couple of weeks ago, one of the stars came by the grill. Limo; people wanted his autograph – everything: the real star-treatment. Jim – he's seventeen. I'm thirty-three. I'm almost twice his age. What's going to happen to me? I've waited tables for twelve years. I... missed it."

"So, now... what? You're going to become an Italian teacher?"

"Now, I just want to look at other people's lives a little.

People who do things; people whose lives are together. I never learned anything but waiting tables, because I didn't need to: I was going to be a star. I didn't want a job. I wanted to be... great." He smiled apologetically.

"You're great, Joe, in your own way."

"I get a lot of compliments," he shrugged. "That proves nothing, except that men are hot for me. I know that." I felt a little confused. Joe wasn't that important to me; I had no real reason to flatter him. On the other hand, it bothered me for him to feel disappointed in himself. The memory of his local legend, from years before, was still strong in me: the cocky happy boy who had exhilarated the whole campus with his sureness of success to come. It depressed me to think he'd failed or, worse, that he thought he had. His dream of stardom was only a little more recent than mine, too, come to think of it. It was only a few weeks since the anthem in church had reminded me of when I expected to be a professional singer, to make a mark as an artist, to sing at Covent Garden and La Scala – not so as to be famous and rich (though that would happen), but to do justice to the *holde Kunst*, the *heilige Kunst*, the *recondita armonia*. The memory was seldom a source of grief to me now. I sang around town; I still had my little paddle in the stream of art. But of course, unlike Joe, I also had a career that brought its own, different, joys and rewards.

"Joe," I said. "You've devoted yourself to the theater, to music, and you've loved it. Think of the courage it took to go out to LA and pursue that dream – dozens of kids in your college class, thousands around the country, had the same dream, but they let go of it. Whereas you've done it, you've gone after it, you've gotten some work... That's success, Joe. I think you should be very proud of yourself."

"What's the point, when you never get anywhere?"

"Nothing is ever lost," I said. "You did some good work at Yale; you've probably done more good work out there. So it hasn't made you a star – think of the people who saw you, heard you. I'll bet a lot of them still remember songs you sang, plays they saw you in, even though they may not remember your name. You changed their memories, their lives. You kept faith with the art. That's what an artist does." This was strictly for myself, and I hoped not to be struck by lightning for calling Joe an artist – at least, not before I got into his pants, as I deserved to for this. But my words had their own sincerity and their own logic, and they carried me.

"I guess," he said, looking distinctly un-consoled.

"Did you ever think of what it was like for actors and singers before there was any way of recording their work?" I asked him. It had always made me feel a little sad and guilty that I, with my reedy serviceable voice and dewy artistry, could play and replay tapes of my modest triumphs, while Faustina and Pacchierotti and Tamburini and Viardot went to their graves without ever getting back more than the acoustical reverb of their lavish gifts. It had always been one of my firmest beliefs about Heaven that there, not only would I be able to hear them but, more gloriously, they would be able to hear themselves. Joe's face showed me he'd never thought about this. "There were big stars back then, Joe," I said, "and I'll bet you don't even know their names; practically no one does now. But they sang, and they acted, and they did the best they knew how, to do honor to something that you've honored too. They scaled the heights; they wrestled with angels, and they scored triumphs that lived for generations in people's memories – Grandad telling how, when he was a boy, he heard la Banti, and how Malibran couldn't touch her; literal riots over Forrest's Hamlet or Macready's, for God's sake... That was what these people left behind them. Just like you have. They never asked if it was worth it, What's the point... they knew what the point was." Joe was amazed; staring at me.

"How do you know all this?" he asked.

"I was supposed to be a star too, remember? I was going to be an opera star."

"That's right," he said. "I forgot that. Who was it who heard you once... my roommate, maybe. He said you were amazing."

"See?" I said. "The legend lives on. Joe: I remember the first time I saw you, with the Alley Cats, singing 'Ride the Chariot' – do you remember? With your head thrown back on the high note; I wanted to jump on the chariot that second, and: Go! Ride!" I made a whooshing gesture with my hand. "We all did. You must have felt it."

"Yeah," he said, smiling freely. "I can still feel it."

"Come sit on the sofa," I said, after a moment of enjoying his smile, as he remembered. He agreed, and I put my arm around him when we were seated. "Let me kiss you, my great big star," I said. His eyes were down, shy and grateful.

"OK," he said.

I think I went into a trance, kissing Joe. After a moment I was numb: I didn't remember who he was, where we were.

We found ourselves lying on the sofa, hunched over awkward-ly, faint and murmuring. I was feeling something too deep for lust, vague, flaccid, impersonal, and tender. His eyes, when they finally opened, were as blurred as mine.

"Wo," he said. It felt as if, logically, we should do some-thing definitive: have sex, call a clergyman, sing a big duet, something. "Guess what?" he said, stirring.

"What?" I whispered.

"Beach time," he said.

We did not stop downstairs to tell Rachel and Tony we were going. On the boardwalk, Joe headed directly for the gay beach, to meet his friends. I had turned down the chance to meet them the day before, and now he was determined.

There were four of them: Bobby, Dennis, Chris, and Michael. Bobby, Dennis, and Chris were younger than Joe, mid- to late- twenties; Michael was more like my age, and the others called him Mother. He was very heavy and had frizzy brownish hair. He wore an unbecoming beard and a quantity of heavy gold jewelry. His skin was bitterly tanned to the line of his very brief red Speedos. His four boys, as he called them, allowed him extravagant kisses and fondlings, but the brittle possessive smiles he gave them struck me as rather angry.

The three other boys were prettier than Joe. Bobby was the poufiest, a svelte blond with big graceful gestures. Every time someone or something caught his eye, he would roll his hands at the wrist and point, palms up, fingers loosely curled, and the other four would laugh riotously, Chris and Dennis burying their faces in their towels, Michael shaking his head, shrieking with one hand over his eyes, Joe tossing his head back and avoiding my eye. I realized, with some prompting from Joe, that Bobby's gestures were copied from Vanna White.

I asked him what he did in LA, and he said,

"Honey, I'm ALL waitron... that's my MEDIUM, girlfriends!" He held one hand palm up over his shoulder, balancing an invisible tray, then made a swatting motion and collapsed backwards, laughing brazenly at the others, as if he'd just brilliantly dissed me. But the 'medium' was a clear dig at their artistic pretensions, so I pressed on: were they all waiters?

Michael gave me a manly complicit nod, since we were the two adults in the group:

"I have my own business," he said, serious and modest. It was a record store selling twelve-inch dance remixes. He had met Joe and Bobby when the grill where they worked catered a party for him at the store. Chris and Dennis worked for Michael.

Chris, dark and slim, with a blinding smile, pale blue eyes and curly black hair, was a video artist. He was working on a piece about the dance scene in LA, boys in their underwear bouncing on speakers, proving something too about death – I didn't get it. He wore a rather elaborate gold cross on a chain around his neck. It wasn't quite big and garish enough to be Madonna dress-up, but it was much flashier than the usual Catholic school crucifix a lot of bar-boys wore. It might be some kind of California trend I hadn't seen yet.

Dennis, ruddy and blond and muscled, his hair buzz-cut, had the sharp precise generic features of an American soldier on a recruitment poster. I guessed he was the oldest, except Joe, of Michael's boys. He wore beach jewelry – a narrow woven bracelet on one ankle, a string of tiny beads around his neck – and a pair of billowing trunks which bunched intriguingly around his crotch. He and Michael were the only ones in the group whose eyes had actually met mine as Joe introduced me. Michael had looked edgy, shy, protective of his turf, his pattings and shriekings with his boys. Dennis held my glance briefly, with frank appraisal and a challenging smile. Even my eggshell ego registered, with astonishment, the import of that smile.

He sat cross-legged facing me, and asked Joe, who was beside me, "How was *lunch*?"

"Lunch was great," said Joe, declining to pick up on Dennis' suggestion. His chin was tucked and he sounded rather guarded, considering this was supposed to be one of his best friends. Dennis looked right at me again, smiling – square jaw, dimples, crinkling blue eyes: fabulous.

"Joe's a big eater," he said.

"You know him well," I said, evenly I hoped. It had suddenly occurred to me that Dennis knew Joe very – very – well. Of course: Joe always went for those hyper-wholesome American types. Glancing sideways at Joe, I caught him glancing sideways at me. I was right.

"Joe's all excited because you're an intellectual," said Dennis. "I don't think I've ever met a real intelLECtual before." He smiled disarmingly at me and I wasn't sure if this was a crack or a compliment. I looked at Joe.

"What have you been telling them?" I asked him. "You make me sound so boring."

"He told me you were going to READ," said Dennis,

swaying his head back and forth, eyes wide open.

"Be still my *heart*!" Bobby laughed and made a heart-shaped gesture with both hands, rolling his eyes. Chris threw his head back and gave one full-throated HA! while Michael yipped, hand to mouth. The way they all laughed at Bobby seemed rather forced to me, and I wondered if they were acting strange because I was there. If they had to spend their whole vacation laughing at his every banal little humorism, they'd go home exhausted. They were being conspicuously rude, when you thought about it: laughing at me, maybe, or in any case laughing at Joe's enthusiasm. But they must have seen dozens of Joe's affairs. Whatever Joe had told them about me probably didn't seem at all serious to them. Not that it mattered to me, of course: Joe was just a cute boy from years before, an under-achiever showing signs of wear now, getting crow's feet. Except that kissing him on the sofa had slipped me into a ten-minute state of grace.

"Which one of you guys is from around here?" I asked.

"I am," said Michael, the nice-guy voice masking sus-picion; part of him clearly wished I'd go away. It was nothing personal. The kind of adjustment that went into an ugly man becoming the center of a cute-boy coterie was very costly to the ugly man. He gained a sense of élite clannish connection, the right to be seen among the stared-at. But he must con-stantly walk a line between bonding and groping, risking an instantaneous drop if the boys ever felt he'd gone too far. He gave too, of course. He gave them sheltered space to flaunt their attractiveness without risk, to laugh in public, to hug and giggle, to be seen to have friendships based on something other than looks: all critical components of their cruising strategy. It was a very fraught symbiosis, and the ugly man was naturally reluctant to have new characters introduced who might upset the balance.

"How long have you been on the West Coast?" I asked him.

"Honey since NOAH!" said Bobby, hands up over his head in Vanna's *Voilà!* gesture. The others screamed.

"No," I said, smiling, man-to-man. "How old are you, Michael?"

"Thirty-eight," he said apologetically.

"You're a baby," I said. He smiled gratefully, still not without suspicion. It cost me nothing; he'd been ugly at twenty and he'd be ugly at ninety. He was younger than me, though, and that would pass for a compliment on my part.

"Jim is forty-one," Joe said, looking at Dennis. Michael looked sick as Dennis said, "No way!"

"Are you an artist too, Dennis?" I asked.

"*Artiste!*" said Bobby, and Chris howled.

"Like Joe," he said. "I'm an actor and a singer. Just like Joe." He looked at Joe with frank rivalry. "Except I get more work." Dennis' pretty-boy looks might account for most of that, if it was true, but it was still unkind to Joe. I risked.

"Nobody's just like Joe," I said, and, putting my arm around his waist, I kissed his cheek. Dennis put his eyebrows up and said to Joe,

"Today's special is…" Then he turned away from us to face the water. For a while we all sat like that, Michael and I exchanging civilities, the boys cackling among themselves, Joe and Dennis ignoring each other. Chris eventually stood and said he was going in the water. He asked if anyone wanted to go with him, and I was the only one who said Yes. I'd expected the whole group to go and was uncomfortable going off without Joe. But Chris took me by the arm and we started towards the waves.

"You sure know a lot of people here," I said, as one man after another called out, "Hey, Chris!" or tossed a beach ball at him or whistled and called him Sweetheart or Baby. I exchanged greetings with a few men I knew from Baltimore, but none of them whistled at me. "Have you been here before?"

"Just since Monday," he said. "We've played volleyball a couple of times; plus we meet guys out, you know." Then he had the politeness to say, "You seem to know half the beach."

Just then a man I recognized from the DC bars, a notably built-up banker my age or older, came running up and grabbed Chris around the waist, spinning him a half turn. Chris had his feet planted and mildly resisted the spin, though he laughed engagingly and said, "Wild man!" The DC man looked at me, questioning whether he should acknowledge that he recognized me to gain points with Chris. Then – rudely, I thought, since he didn't know that Chris and I weren't together – he just asked,

"You going out tonight?"

"Probably," said Chris; "maybe we'll see you there." That "we" might have meant Chris and his friends, or Chris and me. The man let go of Chris' waist and, looking confused, watched us step down the sandy incline into the water.

"I would have introduced you," Chris said, "but I've got no idea who he is." When we were bouncing in the breakers, he asked me, "So you just met Joe?"

I was disappointed Chris didn't know. Maybe Joe hadn't spoken much about me after all, or maybe only to Dennis, or maybe only Dennis had noticed what he said.

"No," I said, "we knew each other at Yale, twelve or thirteen years ago. He was in college and I was in grad school."

"Wow, that's right," Chris said, shaking water out of his hair. "Joe went to Yale." He took a few strokes and then said reflectively, "Super nice guy." Then he winked at me. "Hot, too. I mean, BEER can." I felt a physical clutch of jealousy in my stomach. Joe had slept with all of them, apparently; then he brought me books and complimented me on having my life together. There was a game being played, and I was losing. I put my hand out to the back of Chris' neck and pulled him close enough to kiss his forehead.

"You're so pretty you give me a headache," I said. He smiled at me.

"You're sweet," he said. That was gay for You don't exist. He rode a wave in to shore, and I followed him.

Some time later, Joe decided to go swim. He didn't ask me to join him; Dennis hopped up and went with him. As they went, I could see some of the same excitement in the crowd as had greeted Chris on our walk to the water. Sitting next to Michael, while Chris and Bobby lay back voluptuously to sun, I was mad at Joe for leaving me. In fact, he'd been fairly unforthcoming since we came out on the beach. Now Michael started to make wary conversation.

"Joe's a sweetheart," he said. I nodded, and he ventured further. "He's a mess, of course."

"Indeed?" I said, uninterested in his opinion.

"He doesn't know what he wants," Michael explained. "One day he wants to settle down; the next day he's out tricking like mad. One day he gets all excited about some big break; then he wants to get out of show business and be... God knows what." He gestured helplessly, and paused, giving me a watery comradely smile. He apparently believed I would take his words as indicating a deep caring bond between him and Joe. "Nobody knows Joe like his Mother," he concluded.

"Did you two ever go out?" I asked, cruelly.

"No," Michael said, unabashed, ready. "We decided it would ruin our friendship." Right, I thought. "You?" he asked me.

"No," I said. "He wouldn't give me the time of day when we knew each other before. He was after the pretty blond boys." Michael nodded.

"He and Dennis are good together, don't you think?" he asked me. "They've had their ups and downs, of course, but I've got a feeling..." He smiled at me again, as though we were Joe's fond parents, caring only about his happiness.

"What?" I asked, not returning his smile.

"I just think they're right for each other. They'll figure it out sooner or later."

"How long have they been involved?" I asked.

"Oh, off and on for a couple of years, I guess. It's a very difficult relationship. They're both stubborn. Joe needs someone to take him in hand, but he hates it when somebody tries. He hates to be criticized..." He went on for a while like this, psychoanalyzing Joe for me. I wasn't listening. It gave Michael some kind of thrill to know all about Joe, to explain him to me in this wise friendly voice. His message wasn't especially friendly, though: he made Joe sound immature, crude, foolish, dumb. He also was obviously at pains to make me understand that Joe was not for me – didn't like men like me, wasn't ready for a relationship, was involved with Dennis. I resented Michael strongly. At the same time, I kept thinking *He's right; he knows Joe a lot better than I do.*

When Joe and Dennis came back from the water with their arms around each other's necks, I felt suddenly tired of being there. Dennis sat next to me this time. Again, he gave me that look of appreciation, and leaning against me he asked,

"What's Joe's secret, huh? How does he get all the hot men?" As I returned the pressure of his shoulder against mine, I wondered if Joe had told him he had "gotten" me, or that he wanted to. I also wondered if Dennis actually found me attractive; maybe his attentions were just gestures of provocation towards Joe.

Joe was sitting shifty-eyed and constrained just a few feet away, and I was disoriented, so I got up and said,

"I'm going back inside. This is enough sun for me." Michael looked relieved.

"You have to?" he asked, waving.

"Joe," I said, "you want to come with me?" Joe looked around the group.

"Sure," he said, and got up. Dennis looked up at him, then at me, and smiled his lovely smile.

"You're not asking the rest of us, I notice," he said. Why ever would he want to come – for me, for Joe, to be annoying?

I hesitated; No, I certainly wasn't asking the rest of them, but that sounded rude.

"Lovebirds!" said Bobby, placing his hands over his heart and then making a fluttering gesture. Chris smacked his arm and giggled while Joe smirked without looking at me. It was perplexing that, with Joe and me so vague about what was between us, his three young friends seemed convinced we were an item. So had Tony and Rachel: Tony had even said we'd end up together. Maybe he was right; but then of course, maybe Michael was.

Back at the studio, things were vaguer than before. Joe drifted around, picked things up and put them back down, sat and stood and sat again. I tried to read and couldn't.

"Michael seems like a nice guy," I said.

"Yeah – Mother," he said, smiling smugly and nodding.

"He said you've been seeing Dennis for a couple of years."

"He says too goddamn much," Joe said with sudden heat.

"Well it's nothing to get mad about," I said. "Dennis is a great guy, and he's very attractive."

"I like Dennis." He paused. "Everybody's hot for Dennis. He's all up for you, obviously." My ego was grateful; Joe thought Dennis' flirtation was real. But I had a strategy going – I was after Joe.

"No he's not. He just wants to work your nerves. I think he was jealous of my being there; like Michael." He wagged his head slightly, without interest – You may be right. I ventured further. "Dennis is nothing like as attractive as you are, Joe. He looks like a model; you look like a person. Much hotter – *I* think." He looked at me cagily, not fooled. Right: Joe was used to compliments on his looks. So I tried another way. "And he obviously has no interest in the kind of thing we talked about after lunch. He practically made fun of us for knowing how to read."

"That's true." He almost flinched: I'd scored a bull's-eye, dishing his chosen companions. To cover his embarrassment, he walked to the balcony door and looked out over the water. "He's a great fuck, though," he mused, facing away from me – *his* bull's-eye, not innocent. He turned back. "Hey," he said, "I've got to split. I'm going back to the guest house to crash."

"You can crash here if you want," I said, sensing him slip through my fingers.

"No… " He gathered up his things, his books. "Hey," he said, facing me, his legs planted stubbornly. He hesitated. "Thanks for lunch," he said after a moment; that wasn't what he'd wanted to say. He looked as confused as I felt.

"That's it?" I asked. "'Thanks for lunch?'" He stepped closer to me, and I was able to put my hands on his waist.

"I'm not for you," he said. Then, illogically, he kissed me gently and said, "Mmm."

"We don't know that," I said. "Maybe yes; maybe no." I tried to kiss him back, but he pulled his head away.

"You want two different things," he said. "You want to get married; but I can't do that – I live in LA."

"You just said this afternoon your life there wasn't…"

"No I didn't," he said. "I just said I didn't know where

it was going. I'm not moving to Baltimore, Jim." I dropped my hands.

"What's the other thing I want, Dr. Freud?" I asked him.

"You want to score me," he said, "but we both know your heart's not in it. That creeps me out." I wanted to make some cutting sophisticated retort, but I said,

"That's the kind of thing you said you'd teach me about. You already have, some. I do like you, Joe; I'm just kind of unclear about what to do about it." He squinted, evaluating me.

"That's honest," he said. I thought, Yes, it is; he can tell. Joe's smart in his own way.

"Let me see you again today," I said. "You want to meet after dinner? Get a drink or something? Chris said you all might be out."

"You want to meet up with those guys again?" He looked surprised.

"They're your friends; I like them," I lied. He considered.

"OK," he said, "whatever. The Moon; ten o'clock?" Then he challenged me: "You want to bring your friends too? Ask them." I felt a moment's queaziness at the idea of Tony and Michael talking, and hoped it didn't show in my face.

"I'll ask them," I said. "I'm not sure they're old enough." He smiled.

"See you there," he said, slinging his bag over his shoulder and stepping to the door. Again, he turned, hesitating, his hand on the knob. I was supposed to say or do something.

"One more?" I asked, moving to kiss him.

"Mmm," he said, consenting. Then, "That's so nice. Sometimes you're so... nice. I don't get you."

"Jim McManus," I said, "is notoriously hard to get."

In the event, mercifully, Tony and Rachel declined my tepid invitation to the bar, though Rachel encouraged me to bring Joe by the following day for lunch or dinner if I wanted. So I walked over to the Blue Moon by myself a bit after ten. Naturally, Joe and his friends weren't there yet: silly me. I got a glass of club soda and talked for a while to a veterinarian I knew from home and a truck driver down from Philadelphia who introduced himself. The truck driver, a rather hunky man with a tattoo on his forearm, offered to buy me a glass of "whatever that stuff is you're drinking" and had his hand up on the wall by my head and was leaning rather close when Joe came in. I had my eye on the door and saw him before he saw me. He had his little group trailing behind him and looked impatient, as though he'd been hurrying them. He scanned the crowd and saw me with my truck driver. His expression didn't change, but his eyes flickered away from us. I put my hand up and motioned him to come over. I nodded at his friends as they headed for the bar. Dennis and Joe spoke a few words before Joe broke from the group and joined me. As he walked, he continued to look left and right, and did not meet my eye even when he stood beside me and I put my hand on his shoulder. The truck driver, a gentleman, smiled and moved on after a moment. But Joe was still on edge. He returned the nods and smiles of several men who cruised past: "How you doing?" "Hey, man" and "What's up?" He stayed with me, though from his fidgetings I expected him from one instant to the next to slouch off after one of his other admirers.

Finally, catching some of his restlessness, I said, "I'm going to walk around. You're a million miles away."

"No," he said quickly, "I'll come with you."

We ambled around, talked to friends and acquaintances of his and mine, tentatively touched and patted each other, even briefly kissed against a wall. But the whole time he was distracted and nervous. I noticed and frankly encouraged his steady downing of beer, though he bought most rounds: like most waiters, he carried more cash than a millionaire. He was drinking almost conscientiously, as though on a program, bracing himself for something. Latish in the evening, he took a long hit off his beer and then put his arm around my waist:

"So how you doing?" he asked, flirtatiously, eyes hooded. I understood now what he was bracing himself for. The implication was not flattering, but I felt quickly hard, resolute, and cunning. He wasn't sure he liked me, or how: fine. In honesty, I had to admit I felt the same way. The dream of love, the Angel-dream, the Tony-dream, revived and again discarded for Peter – they were dreams that were not for or about Joe Andreoli. I'd never imagined loving Joe; I'd imagined scoring him, and dozens of men like him, hundreds of times over the years. Now was my chance. Kissing him on the sofa was some kind of aberration. What was important was the hotness he – they all – had always withheld from me. For some reason, following the perverse and capricious groin-logic of cute boys everywhere, Joe had decided we would get it on this evening. Well, let it be. I would enjoy it, even if he had to drink himself into a stupor to go through with it.

"I'm good," I said. "I've got more of that" (I pointed to

his beer) "back at my place; nightcap?"

"Hey," he said, "I'm easy." He pressed his crotch firmly to mine and swayed at the hips, still holding me by the waist. He put his head back, eyes closed, and hummed. When he looked at me, there was an odd mix in his eyes. He barely recognized me, could barely focus: the beer, his nerves. But below that, there was another expression. He watched me, knew me, and was scared of something.

"I was supposed to teach you something, wasn't I?" he asked, smiling and confused.

"Let's go," I said.

"I need to say goodnight to the other guys," he said.

"No," I said. "They know exactly where you're going. You'll see them tomorrow." I put my hand on the small of his back and pushed.

"OK," he said, with a slight stumble in his step.

I sat with him on the sofa, carefully watching him get drunker. Eventually, my arm around his shoulder, I asked him to bed. I didn't ask if he wanted to "crash here" tonight; I said, "You want to come to bed?"

"Yeah, OK," he said, and we stood and opened the sofa out. The crisp white sheets looked cool and stylish, with their foam-green cotton blanket, against the bright green upholstery, and Joe commented sleepily on what a classy place this was. Aware of his stumble, aware that I was exploiting his drunkenness and generally being a sleaze, I pushed him, not un-gently, onto the bed. He let me undress him, rolling and shifting when necessary to free an item of clothing from his weight. His eyes were closed and he seemed barely to notice as I touched and stroked and fondled; he gave an occasional grunt or hum that seemed to indicate consent, even sleepy pleasure.

It was plain conquest on my part, and revenge. There was no illusion of tenderness; I didn't particularly care about being romantic or showing that I respected him. All the hot boys in the world lay there, drunk, shopworn, and unresisting. Everyone who'd ever driven me mad with redundant praises and unasked-for respect, everyone who'd ever then lavished his embraces on men who were merely cute and sexy, was suddenly in my power. He lay back on the bed, his eyes closed, his cock large but slack against his belly. He was ready for whatever would happen; he'd been through this kind of drunken lay a million times. His level of interest seemed only moderate. He made chewing motions, groggily smacking his lips like someone who will be asleep in a moment. Being with me was no big deal for Joe, apparently, but he was easy.

I lay on him and he kissed me inattentively. His hands in my hair seemed to be trying to push my head down to his crotch. I ducked free of him and started to roll him over instead. He understood instantly.

"Wild man," he said, without opening his eyes. "So hot..." He was barely awake. An urgency came over me, vicarious or voyeuristic: these were a few of the words, imperfectly recalled, he'd exchanged over the years with Dennis, with other waiters, International Male models, lifeguards, porno starlets, flight attendants. This was the forbidden world of cute boy fanta-sex that he'd reveled in, and tired of, while I'd gotten barely a glimpse through the harem keyhole.

"Suck me first," he said, his voice unexpectedly clear and sober. I looked up at him and saw that his eyes were still closed.

"No," I said.

"Suck me," he said, even as he let me roll him face-down.

"No," I said. He reached back to tug listlessly on his rising cock. He wasn't going to get what he wanted; sometimes it went like that.

"Yeah," he sighed. "Big guy gonna fuck that ass, OK." That came straight from video: "that ass," they always said, meaning their own. The voice was barely his; it was the impersonal undifferentiated voice of Southern California sex. Then, as he felt the cool lube, his eyes opened with a sharp, alert look. In his own voice he said, "Is that the stuff?" I held up the tube, and read the small print:

"Nonoxynol 9." Then I showed it to him.

"You got the rubber?" he asked. I showed him the package and he glanced at the label and nodded, closing his eyes. He's wide awake, I realized. This is theater. "Yeah," he muttered sleepily, "... big old cock of yours... want you inside me." I came into him, selfishly, not caring if he was quite ready or not. He grimaced and exhaled hard: "Hoo!" Again. It might have been "Whoa" but I didn't care. After twelve years Joe Andreoli was giving it up and all I cared about was taking it. He kept up his Lamaze exhalations, twisting the sheet in his fists, raising his head, then burying it in the pillow. He was slick and strong, nervous twitchings like the flank of a cop's horse. My hands wandered and he lolled carelessly, rising at times when I growled in his ear, flopping back down when I released him.

I looked at his muscular back. I laughed privately at the

memory of Joe watching music videos at the bar in New Haven, like the TV-loving puppy in a Disney film, his back turned to me, a study in dreamy butch gay boy contentment. He felt so good that I actually laughed out loud.

"Joe," I said, half-gasping. Something in the sound of his name set him off and he started to whimper. He clutched a bit and for the first time I had to struggle to stay with him, holding on to him roughly. Then he relaxed.

"Oh man," he said, chuckling. "Great fuck. Oh man." He took a minute for his praise to sink in, and then started to pull away.

"No," I said.

"I can't," he said. "You have to stop. I've shot."

"I haven't," I said. I went on for a moment and he groaned with a drunken gagging sound, as though he might throw up.

"Come on," he said. "Stop. I'm sorry. Stop." I felt myself going down. I didn't want to stop; I wanted to carry him around on my cock for a week. But he'd said to stop.

"In the morning," he said, "… again. I make it up to you. … Tiger." He shifted up onto his elbows and started to twist at the waist. Suddenly I grabbed him by the hips, pushed hard, and shot. I hadn't meant to do that.

"Yow!" he said, squirming, his face twisting. Apparently it hurt, with his own erection gone. My haze of sex was clearing and I was sorry if he hurt, but I couldn't let go till it was over. That was too bad, because he would be angry. He had every right; I'd taken something he wasn't giving. That wasn't like me.

Joe reached back to stroke his butt consolingly as we pulled apart. He made a frowning face. Then he flopped over onto his side, facing me. I was ashamed and didn't want to look at him, to face the anger and withdrawal, the slammed door. I reached for a Kleenex and pulled the condom off, putting all my attention into tossing the crumpled little bundle into the wastebasket a few feet away. Without looking at him, I handed him the box.

He chuckled while he cleaned himself off. For the first time I ventured to look him in the face. He winked at me.

"Wo," he said. "Sex bandit. Butt pirate... " He reached to grab my hair and pulled my face to his chest. His arm went around my neck and he was rocking me, crooning and humming. In a moment or two he was asleep.

I lay awake for a while wondering what had just happened, pressing him to me, kissing him, looking for a response of some kind. There was none: no withdrawal, no approach. Was he happy? Did he like me? Was I a good fuck, really? It could be a very good sign that he'd gone right to sleep, or a very bad one. He'd done this with some of the most beautiful men in LA, I assumed; they were probably better than me. Dennis, Chris – they were daunting samples of his conquests: clearly far hotter than good old Jim. But his breath on my neck was sweet and comfortable, and my racing thoughts suddenly clicked off and I slept too.

Chapter 6 – Friday

A few hours later the sun was up and I felt a tongue brush my ear. Joe was holding me from behind and I worried that his arms around my waist would feel more tum than they liked. In a moment he would realize he was holding a soft-waisted man in his early forties; he'd jump out of bed to seek hard young steroidal beauties on the beach. And if I rolled over to face him, there would be my breath to worry about.

"How's our macho man?" he asked me. I just smiled and stirred. "Quite a ride you had last night, Tiger," he said. "You owe me." He was rubbing his cock against my leg and chuckling to himself. I had never in my life awakened to such a conversation.

"You want to do it again?" I asked.

"Mm," he said. He shifted behind me and the sheets tangled. Then his rough chin was grazing my stomach and I realized with some detachment that he was lining us up without preamble for a little morning tumble. Without my moving, his cock was suddenly there in front of me. It was a nice thing to look at first thing in the morning. In the slanting sunlight I admired the soft curves of muscle in his lower belly and groin. My hands reached up and around him. He tasted and smelled fresh, even after a night of boozy sweaty embraces. There was a warm scent to him that was fleshly and sweetly salty, a bit like what my mother called "good clean dirt," the rich topsoil she used in gardening. I was reminded of steamy days in Rome, when I stood on a crowded bus packed in among people glowing, oily, holding handkerchiefs to their streaming foreheads, and smelled only this kind of bracing air that could be the beach or the garden. That was Joe's gene pool. He was a captive legionnaire in my arms; Cola di Rienzo, caught between his ideals and his squalid greed; a loyal beloved ungrammatical footman in the household of Tommaso de' Cavalieri; Pasolini's hottest *borgata* boy toy. I was suddenly deeply happy to be making it with him. He felt my warning convulsions just in time to pull his mouth off me and spatter his face and neck with a serious smile. With a few pulls on himself, he wet me too, and lay with his head between my legs, shuddering. He flopped and rubbed gently on me a few times, his whole body pressed to mine, enjoying the sucky sound of our friction.

"Get back up here," I said. He did.

"Do you still respect me?" he asked, smiling.

"I've never respected you," I said lightly. That was the way hot men talked. He laughed. His eyes squinted at me in the new sunlight. "You have green eyes," I said. "Like Scarlett O'Hara." The back of the green sofa behind his face brought the color up sharply in his eyes. The sun lit them as though from behind, and they seemed miles deep, a dark piney green especially where his lashes shaded them. I was Rhett for a moment, my mouth dry at the wonderful beauty of this infuriating young person. But as I looked into the green eyes I saw, I was sure, sadness at what I'd said. I had slipped up, trying to be hip. It was scary: he could get away from me that fast. I tried again. "Of course I respect you, Joe. You scare me to death." I kissed him but he pulled away in a second. Apparently that wasn't right either.

"I need to clean up." He got up and headed for the

bathroom.

"I said that wrong," I said. I jumped up and ran to put my arms around his waist before he could close the door. "I do like you, you know; I've had a great time tonight with you. Thanks." He looked at me coolly. Again I felt that he had the advantage. Good sex was easy for him to get, whereas if I didn't sleep with him again I would have to drown myself.

"Let's talk when I'm clean," he said. He pulled away.

"OK," I said quickly. He mustn't see that I was afraid of his rejection. I turned away to get my robe out of the closet, and walked towards the kitchenette. I wouldn't beg him. I ground some coffee and poured water into the machine. I could hear the toilet flush, barely: This house is really well built, I thought, the bathroom walls as thick as though they held the roof up. Then the water started running in the shower, seeming surprisingly close and loud. With a sudden grateful smile, I realized he had opened the door.

After about a minute, he called me to join him.

He brooded over coffee. He sat there, one of Rachel's pristine white bath sheets wrapped around his waist and draping nicely on the chair and floor. The glass brick counter behind him, the sunlight sailing through the large windows and soaking the white walls in brilliant squares, Joe's easy masculine presence, his big legs comfortably sprawled, his arm over the back of the Conran's chair, half-Récamier, half-Costner — it was like a cologne ad, or the first shot of one of those "Big Chill" rip-off TV spots. A bright-eyed woman in a bathrobe, toweling her hair, would come up behind him now, kiss the top of his head, and ask him if her Colombian decaf was ready; he'd say they were out, and offer her something else, and she'd toss him his jeans; he'd try to kiss her, and she'd say, No, not till he ran to the store and brought her her Colombian decaf – she couldn't kiss a man who wouldn't support her Colombian decaf habit! Then the Motown sounds would swell as she blew him a kiss on his way out the door.

He was lovely to look at in the morning, handsomer than I'd seen him. There were distinct lines around his eyes now, though: he was thirty-three, not a kid anymore. The lines were signs of manhood. They were supposed to mean he'd lived and grown and achieved. The thought that he'd been drifting from one low-level service job to another for years gave me a sudden warm feeling of protectiveness towards him. He hadn't achieved, really; he'd dreamed and yearned and discoed and screwed around and been, to some extent, screwed over.

It had been sweet of him to ask me into the shower. He had shared himself with me even though he wasn't sure I respected him. Actually, I wasn't sure either. Rubbing his back, slick with soap, licking the splashing water off his neck, feeling the light slap and sting of his soaked curls on my face when he tossed his head to clear his eyes: that felt so interesting and important to me that respect had nothing to do with it.

He'd managed to make the simple process of showering together into a kind of sweet hot bonding, though neither of us was fully up for sex. I had tried screwing in the shower once at home, with a nice young man, and it had been a fairly major flop – the tub too narrow, its angles too hard, the muscular effort too great, the four legs too much to choreograph. Somehow, even without sex, this shower with Joe was a success, a full contact. Joe seemed to think that the point was just to be naked together, to touch each other: he smiled, for instance, as he soaped his cock and mine, a smile of indulgence and fondness even though neither of them was standing. I was impressed with his tact, as if he'd shown off an unsuspected technical skill of some kind.

Then an unpleasant thought crept in. If Joe was this good at handling nervous numbers like me, it was because he'd handled a lot of them: he was what you might call an expert at scoring. It was exactly what he'd promised he could teach me about. Maybe this wasn't really a bonding moment; it was a little laboratory demo by my new cruising instructor. I felt suddenly defensive, subject to unfair comparisons. Dennis, Chris – God only knew who all – they didn't need these lessons. Joe didn't have to pat them gently with encouraging little That's OK smiles; he didn't have to be patient and supportive about their lagging erections. They were just hot by nature, and naturally he preferred them. He was that type: the hot scorer, the bar-star, the cute guy with no life. He must have sensed what I was thinking, because we had hardly stepped out of the shower when he began to sulk. We dried each other off, and he put my robe on me and the towel around his own waist, in silence. It was as if he knew I expected him to be good at sexual etiquette, but little else.

By the instant, now, at the breakfast table, I could feel myself losing patience with his sulking, with his pretense that I owed him something more than the abject adulation my body had paid him all night.

"You want to come over this afternoon?" I asked.

"I notice you're not asking me to spend the day," he said.

"Well of course you're welcome to; I just thought you'd want to hang out with your friends," I said. "Stay here. Please. We'll... I've got a couple of new pages I want you to read."

"So you still remember I can read. Thanks."

"Joe!" I slapped the table, exasperated. "Do whatever you want. I don't care."

"No, you don't. I knew that." He got up. I waited for the sounds of him dressing, not looking. After a moment I saw he hadn't moved, but was standing just a step or two away, his back to me.

"After last night I shouldn't have to prove I like you," I said. "Come on, Joe." He turned to me, looking harassed.

"That's not liking," he said. "Every guy I meet wants to do me that way. I thought we could talk." I reached out to take his wrist and tried to pull him closer. He resisted and I let go; it was obvious he was stronger than me, and we risked having a grotesque little scuffle if I pulled too hard.

"Joe," I said. "Joe." He looked sad, which wasn't fair. I was the one who should be sad; I was losing. He would disappear, taking all his sure easy fuckiness with him, and I would go back to my books and chilly memories.

"Besides," Joe said, his eyes wide, candid with outrage, "you need to see *your* friends. You talk to *them*. They don't want me around." I got up.

"Who cares what they want?" I said, feeling disloyal, but fierce in my stratagems. I was beginning to panic at the prospect of what I'd feel if Joe didn't stay. I stepped up to face him and put my hands on his shoulders, hoping he wouldn't shake me off. "Joe: every man *I* meet wants to talk to me. Everybody thinks I'm the nicest smartest guy they know, and they want me to be their best friend and big sister. You've shared something else with me. Maybe you don't think that's as important as I do. I *want* you to stay with me today. Please, Joe. I'll be miserable if you go." I could feel his shoulders soften under my hands.

"OK," he said. "I'm going to run back to my room and bring some clothes back. Then maybe we can hit the beach." I kissed him. Relief was flooding my system and the softness of his lips to mine, sleek and tender as cellophane at the center of his sandpaper chin and cheek, was wonderful. He had splashed himself generously with my *Impériale*, the right scent for a day one didn't shave. Implausibly, I felt a stir below the waist; it hadn't been half an hour since we'd last made it, and normally I'm not that much of a morning-person. Truly Joe was a miracle.

"'Thou art the Spring,'" I murmured, on pitch, my mouth straying to the back of his neck, as he stretched and turned his head like a cat. He laughed, deep in his throat.

"Hey," he said, "be good."

"This is as good as I know how to be," I said, breathless.

"Let's try something new, Tiger," he said. "How about a day with no nookie?"

"In what sense is that new?" I asked, chilled. I was sure he didn't mean a day; he was telling me it was over. "How is that different from practically every other day of my life?"

"I need it," he said.

"Right," I said, trying to be casual but sounding bitter even to my own ears. "You're going to go for someone else before the day is over. I'll never hold you again." He stepped back, stung.

"That's what you think, isn't it?" he asked – offended virtue.

"That's what your entire life for the past ten or twelve years has proven," I said.

"Fuck you," he said. He walked around the bed, picking up the clothes I'd taken off him the night before, muttering. The flash of his nakedness, as he dropped the towel and stepped into his shorts, made me ache. He was furious, slapping his socks rightside out, whipping his tank-top to air it, yanking the straps on his sneakers as if they'd just insulted him. I was mad too. I wasn't going to apologize for telling the truth. Joe and other boys like him cared about nothing but screwing each other; then they called the rest of us dirty old men.

When he was dressed, he looked up at me. His eyes were pale now, barely colored at all, blank and frightened behind their anger.

"Look," he said, "I know I've slept around a lot. I'm a hot guy. Guys dig me. I've done exactly what you would have done if guys dug you the same way. You've got no right to call me a tramp."

He was a ridiculous kid, even at thirty-three. It occurred to the nasty part of me that I could let him go, having slept with him once. There were plenty of people who'd heard about Joe Andreoli years and years ago and would be thrilled to hear I'd scored with him at the beach. I had my story now. In a way, that could be enough. I didn't care about his anger. But to my own surprise and annoyance, I found that I did care about his fear and his hurt feelings. It bothered me that he would think I hadn't been fair to him, hadn't been nice to him, and that he would think that meant there was something wrong with him. Of course, I was the real loser here; I should get the pathos points. He could frustrate and elude and intimidate me, and still get the sympathy – even from me. It wasn't fair, but he had me. I sat by him on the bed and kissed his cheek.

"Truce," I said. "OK? Let's go back three minutes. You're going back to your room to get a few things. Then we're going to the beach. Then we'll come back here for lunch and you'll read my new pages and tell me what you think. I won't lay a hand on you again if you don't want me to, and we'll still be friends at happy hour. And if you don't promise to sleep here tonight – sex or no sex – I'll jump off the speakers at the Strand and let the crowd stomp me to death."

He pushed me back onto the bed and lay on top of me, holding me down by the wrists. He kissed me, hard, till I thought my cock would suddenly spring from my robe and torque him against the ceiling.

"Help me out here, Joe," I said, groaning. "You're not making this any easier."

He reached down with one hand to stroke and hold me.

"I don't want you waving this at any other men today," he said.

"OK," I gasped. "Like a lot of other guys want it, right?"

"Guys will be hitting on you today," Joe said. "You just got laid; it always happens."

"Well, then, they'll be hitting on you, too," I said.

"That's normal."

"But I'm not allowed to touch you?" I asked.

"Just one day," he said, and hopped up. "I need to see if a man can go a day without it and still like me."

"I like you," I said. "I'll still like you in twenty-four hours. Kiss me good-bye." He did, with surprising gentleness.

"I'll be back in half an hour," he said, getting up. He turned at the door and pointed at my crotch, making a pistol-shooting gesture with thumb and forefinger. "Dude," he said, with a little frowning "Whoo!" and a shake of the head. It was cute; I wasn't used to being teased by sex symbols about how hot and naughty I was. Then he was out the door.

I lay there for a minute wondering what to do with this exuberant hard-on. It seemed stupid to jack off, and I hated to resort to the cold-shower trick; it was the wrong message to send to my nerve endings, which deserved some kind of rich reward for acting so satisfactorily young and randy. So I got up and went back to my cooling coffee. There were some doughnuts in the fridge which I'd been ashamed to get out for gym-maniac Joe. Just the thing for a man who wanted to be good to himself and who would never, no matter how hard Mammy pulled at his stays, fit into his college jeans again.

Tony came in on me a few minutes later. I was wrapped around a coffee-dunked doughnut like Claudette Colbert herself, humming my nastiest imitation of Horne's *"Mon coeur s'ouvre à ta voix"* – nasty enough in itself, God knew. Something about her Roller Derby slamming of registers, her belchy chest tones and tonsilly high notes – the very antithesis of everything French opera was about – satisfied me that morning. The day had dawned breezy, clear, nicely hot. I loved the absurd yuppie cleanness, brightness, and spareness of the studio. The sheets were still twisted on the bed. I had screwed and blown the night away and still felt a comfortable thickness ready to leap or subside, depending, in my lap. So Dalila had nothing on Jimmy McManus, just then.

But the sight of Tony suddenly made me feel guilty and foolish. My life wasn't really about hot sex with feckless good-hearted actor/singer/model/waiters. It was about this smiling wonderful man who had been in my heart for more than half my life. He was smiling his simple generous male-bonding smile.

"So somebody got laid last night," he said. I could feel myself blushing, as though he'd caught me cheating on him.

"These walls are too damn thin," I said, knowing that wasn't it, standing up and putting the doughnuts away, my back to him.

"No, Jimbo; I just saw him leave. So... ?"

"So what?"

"So it was OK?" he asked. I shrugged, as though Joe weren't important. I wasn't sure he was. Something about having Tony there made the night with Joe seem tawdry or juvenile.

"How's Rachel?" I asked. "Are you all going out to the beach this morning?"

"Who knows how Rachel is?" Tony said. Seeing my face, he amended that with, "She's still asleep. Do you have any more coffee?" I didn't, so I started to make some more. I was aware of avoiding Tony's eye, and as mine wandered the room, I saw the big white towel lying by the bed where Joe had shed it. I went and picked it up, shaking it out and folding it in half. It released a smell of soap and water and cologne. If it had been soaked in pheromones for a month, it couldn't have brought Joe back more vividly. Suddenly I felt divided, distracted. There was Tony, dearer than habit itself; and there, wrapping me in his scent, already familiar after one night, was Joe. The coffee maker was dripping steadily now, and, draping the folded towel over the back of a chair to air out, I went back into the kitchenette.

As I passed behind Tony, who had taken Joe's chair, I put a hand on his shoulder companionably. I had a weird perception in my fingertips at touching him: for an instant, I could tell exactly what it would feel like to have sex with him – if he were into it, I mean. This was odd, because I had certainly imagined it often enough, but I think my imagination had been both too reticent and too lurid. I had at times made myself believe that sex with Tony would be purely sentimental and romantic, and at times allowed fantasies that were surreally wild, disembodied. What had changed, I knew instantly, was Joe. My mental humping of Joe had never been like the reality, the softness and the slippery gripping strength. Now I knew the adjustments between fantasy and truth, and I could apply them to Tony too. It was uncanny and rather disturbing, an abuse of a friendly touch. I stepped past Tony and poured us both some coffee.

"So what's the verdict so far?" I asked him. "Are we having a good vacation?"

"Yes," he said. "It's relaxing just to get away from the phone." He looked at me over his coffee mug. "And it takes me back to see this much of you."

"Mutual," I said, hoping he couldn't read my lewd imaginings of the past minute.

"Assuming we *will* see this much of you," he added. "Now, I mean."

"For crying out loud," I said. "I'm not marrying Joe." He put his hands up defensively.

"Far be it from me to push you into it," he said. "Anyway, marriage is for losers." He laughed: Just kidding! "Say, you want to go swimming after this?" He pointed at his coffee.

"I can't," I said; "at least, not right away. Joe's coming back…"

"Oh," he said, arching his eyebrows – Very interesting. "And… refresh my memory – how come you didn't come by yesterday afternoon?" He was pressing me, leading the witness.

"I had to go to the beach and meet Joe's horrible friends."

"'I'm not marrying Joe!'" Tony quoted, smiling triumphantly, dishing me to my face.

"Come on, Tony," I whined. "We're allowed to date in the Nineties, aren't we? This hasn't happened to me in a thousand years. It's just a coincidence that it's happening now, under your prurient gaze."

"So how was it?" he asked, laughing at me. "Last night; come on. How was it?"

"It was fine," I said. "Nice. It's just that nothing will come of it. He lives in LA; plus we've got nothing in common."

"Well," Tony said, looking at me intently, "he sure put a smile on your face. You should have seen yourself, when I came in just now. I like that. Even if he is a…"

"Don't call him a hedgehog," I said.

"You just told me nothing would come of it," he said. "Now I'm not allowed to call him a hedgehog. Which is it, buddy?" He looked thoughtful. "You don't think he looks kind of like one?"

"I think *you* are perfectly infuriating," I said. He smiled; this was clearly the reaction he'd been angling for. "No, to be frank, I think Joe is incredibly attractive. It was: OK, it was more than nice. It was the lay of a lifetime. The earth didn't just move; it heaved. Whatever."

"This is a good thing," he said, speaking slowly, trying to get my point. "I mean, most guys would say – no?" He looked at me closely; I suppose I was scowling or something. "Of course," he went on, "I'm sure there's some reason it's really a *bad* thing, and I'm missing it because I'm a block of stone and don't speak Italian."

I laughed. When Tony read beads, he read savagely, from left to right.

"He's put me on a twenty-four hour vow of chastity," I said, sighing. "He claims it's to test me, because most men only like him for his body. I think it's because he means to drive me mad and then run off with some lifeguard by happy hour."

"He seems like an honest enough guy," Tony said. "Why not assume he means just what he says? Just pretend you're Sir What's-His-Name and you've just been ordered to go sit in a bog for a year to prove your love."

"You're right," I said, amused. "And it's only a day. Plus it's really no big deal either way – Joe, me; I don't know. I mean – where's the future in it?"

"Who knows? The important thing is, our boy Jim got his rocks off big time. That sounds pretty good to me." He slurped his coffee and looked up through the skylights over the ocean. "I wonder if I'll ever have an affair," he said speculatively.

My blood chilled. I had a sudden horrid image of bimbos drooling over Tony, and it occurred to me with great vividness that they probably already did: secretaries, receptionists, smart nympho paralegals with glasses, all talking at their coffee breaks about what a hunk Mr. Neuberg was. It wouldn't take more than a word or a whistle from him before those panties came down with a crash. Sharing Tony with Rachel was bad enough; I was used to that. Tony having an affair, or affairs, was a simple horror.

"Tony!" I said. "That's disgusting." He looked at me cannily.

"Little double standard here?" he asked. "Jim thinks it's disgusting for me to have an affair. How many affairs have you had in the past fifteen years, Jim? I've lost count."

"I'm not married," I said. Our eyes were locked for an instant; then he looked away.

"Well, I'm not having an affair either," he said, relaxing. "I'm just daydreaming."

"I guess this is one of those Grass is always greener moments," I said, still nervous. "Having affairs is beat, Tony. Having someone at home who knows you and cares about you: I can't even imagine how nice that would be."

"Having someone at home who's always watching you and expecting stuff from you," he said. "Yeah – great."

"You're such a ramblin' rose," I said.

A few minutes later we both heard Joe's bicycle wheels on the gravel and his step on the iron stairs. Tony looked up at me, one eyebrow cocked, when I jumped up at the sound. Joe came in without knocking. He was wearing an extravagantly skimpy green tank-top and some hot baggy flowered shorts, all yellow and pink and turquoise, pulled down just far enough that the waistband of his underpants was clearly visible: flashy, teen-sexy clothes that would have been silly on a man his age, except that he looked so good in them. His eyes met Tony's before they met mine and he came to sit next to Tony at the table. "How you doing?" he asked, exactly as if Tony were a man at the bar for whom he either felt or feigned indifference. Tony nodded. Joe's eyes were still casting around the room, ill at ease, but I saw Tony make a decision and look closely at Joe's profile.

"Hey, Joe," he said, "you see yourself staying in your present line of work?" God help me, I thought: Tony is screening Joe for me.

"Has Jim been talking to you?" Joe asked suspiciously. He looked at me and I shook my head. I knew better than to try to get Tony to back off.

"He's just told me you're a nice person and he likes you," Tony answered. "I'm just looking out for my guy."

"What does that have to do with whether or not Joe keeps on doing what he's doing?" I said. I was still standing, and they seemed far away. Joe didn't thank me for my help. Instead, he admitted something to Tony.

"I don't know what I'll do," he said. "I don't expect I'll keep on like this. I wanted to be an actor, I guess I told you. When that doesn't pan out, it's not obvious what you do next." He smiled, trying to ingratiate himself with Tony. "Maybe I'll be a lawyer," he said.

"Hey," Tony said, "I wouldn't wish that on you." He smiled too and patted Joe's leg. But he pulled his hand back rather sharply, as if scorched by the casual manly touch: the feel of Joe's flesh seemed to make him uncomfortable. He looked at me for a second, his eyes naked and alarmed. He looked as though he had just noticed that his old friend Jim was an alien, a different species, a man for whom Joe's thigh, with its twitching muscle and fine springy hair, was an object of lust. It didn't precisely disgust him, but it threw him off – Who are you, really? My eye faltered before his, a vestigial bit of bad conscience. Immediately, though, I looked back. Joe had been surprisingly good, accepting, and generous to me for three days now. He had not withdrawn any of the several times I'd expected him to, whereas Tony's withdrawals were one of the organizing thematic principles of my whole life. Before I could start singing "I am what I am" or waving my fist in the air, Tony got my message. And he was trying, he really was.

"Joe," he said, "I asked Jim before if he wanted to go swimming, and he said he had to wait for you. How about we all three go?"

"I'm there," Joe nodded. "You want to ask your wife?"

"She was still sleeping half an hour ago," Tony said. "Let's just leave her a note." It was almost eleven by now and I couldn't imagine Rachel sleeping this late. Maybe this was her vacation behavior, a remission from relentless overachievement. Joe said he'd better "hit the can" before we went, and when he'd closed the bathroom door, Tony said to me, "She's actually up, but she... kind of kicked me out for the morning." I looked at him questioningly. "She's mad," he explained. "OK, we had a fight last night."

"You two never fight," I said. "I've never seen you fight."

"Well, we always have, a little," he said. "But now she's giving me the silent treatment. It's the same issue; kid, no kid... Anyway, don't let Joe ask her to come. Maybe she'll cool off by afternoon."

"You've been giving her the silent treatment too, Doro, in your own way," I said. Something about this conflict with Rachel made him seem scared and small to me. It was like when a child was afraid of the dark: the peril always seemed very real to him, and your heart clutched a little in sympathy even as you crooned and cradled and said There, there. "I know how that feels to her," I went on; "trust me, I know." He looked up and – positively – blushed. He was remembering the feel of Joe's leg, and wondering maybe what I felt when I touched him. This thought had a new clarity for him now, rather as the thought of sex with him had for me.

"Yeah," he said, looking away. Then, as Joe came out of the bathroom, he put his finger up to his lips to signal me: Shh. What? I wondered, and remembered – Don't let Joe ask Rachel to come. So we went without her.

It hadn't occurred to me to wonder which beach we would go to. We walked three abreast, Tony to my left and Joe to my right. I looked from one to the other and back as we walked down the steps onto the sand. The beach was crowded on both sides. Since neither of the others was leading, I made a symbolic decision and led us right down the invisible divide. There was an empty spot quite close to the water, surging gays on the right, darting children on the left. We put our stuff down and went directly into the water.

We didn't say much, scudding from wave to wave. The surf was stirring and the sunlight powerful. Tony was in a playful mood and got fairly involved in splashing and grinning and acting like a fool, showing off. That behavior never failed to make me smile, and he enjoyed that and worked it wildly when the mood struck. Joe was a bit more stand-offish and I didn't want to press him, given our agreement. He swam more seriously than Tony or I, just beyond the crashing surf, with strong strokes and bright dripping flashes of arm and shoulder. He'd be gone for a few minutes at a time, going down towards the gay set and swimming back against the current; then he'd stand panting for a moment or two to talk, and go again. I looked over at one point and saw him talking to someone in the water. A second glance showed it was Dennis, whom I hadn't recognized at first: his short blond hair somehow looked very dark when wet. He was laughing, and tossed his head back and put his arm around Joe's neck. Then he caught my eye and waved.

"Who's that?" Tony asked me, seeing Joe with Dennis.

"Old friend of Joe's," I said; "old boyfriend, actually." Tony did something prim with his eyebrows or the tilt of his chin that conveyed strong disapproval but, alas, no surprise: that Madame Etiquette thing that straight men occasionally did.

Joe was back a few minutes later.

"Dennis says Hi," he said.

"I saw him," I nodded. I mustn't seem jealous, I thought, so I gave a cordial smile to suggest that I was genuinely fascinated by Dennis and hopeful for his happiness. I wanted to hug Joe myself, as Dennis had been allowed to, but I restrained myself: twenty-four hours. Then I turned, because Tony had started splashing again, but the moment my back was to Joe, he put his arms around my waist, under the surface. He tried to kiss me, but I squirmed. I was distinctly embarrassed to have Tony witness this.

"What?" Joe asked.

"I'm trying to be good," I said. So Joe swam off on another of his long laps.

I looked over in a minute and saw Dennis' arm again around Joe's neck. Dennis looked a little different, I couldn't quite say how, but that could just be the sun or the water. Again he waved at me, with a great show of excitement, and I waved back without much energy. Then to my surprise he started swimming over, leaving Joe standing alone in water up to his chest. A few strokes after Dennis, he started back too.

"Dear Heart!" Dennis called to my astonishment, righting himself to stand in the choppy high water a few steps from me. Dear Heart! I thought, smiling falsely, partly excited by this flirty greeting, partly jealous of his easy touch with Joe. Then with a shock I saw that he wasn't Dennis.

"Precious one!" I said, happy to see Gene, really, though my mind was buzzing distractedly around the image of him embracing Joe in the surf a moment before. Gene: Baltimore; Joe: Yale/Los Angeles – they didn't know each other, that I knew of. Gene didn't in fact even seem aware that Joe was following him. He staggered the last step or two up to me and we kissed each other on both cheeks. Tony was standing by me, about to introduce himself, but Gene, merely flashing him a quick appreciative smile, was already yakking.

"Aren't you just the sweetest piece," he said to me. "Jocko told me he spoke to you, *shrieks* at the office the past couple of days, and she said – you know Mindy; that hand on that hip, and those RED lips, and that HAIR, and I... DON'T think so, I said, and here we are, dear, so VERY flattered to be among you!" He laughed. Gene got pretty wired at times and it could be hard to keep up. "Just this morning; I mean, Cybil said, 'I like to be driven,' and I said, 'Honey we all *know* you're a driven woman!' and we just decided: Beach! or Die! so we did; and here... men for days here – and THAT one... !" He gestured over his shoulder, almost hitting Joe who was right behind him by now. "Well here you are, you pretty thing," he said graciously, showing no surprise that Joe had followed him. He put his arm around Joe's shoulder again. Joe smiled uncertainly and nodded at me. "This is our darling Dr. McManus," Gene said, "and this is... now just what IS your name, dear?"

"Jim and I have met," Joe said stolidly.

"Well I'm just sure you have," Gene said, and dropped his hold on Joe without the slightest flicker in his rhythm. Tony was looking frankly amazed by now and I laughed. The whole thing was so fast and strange: boundaries blurred, and not a thing I could do about it.

"Gene Townsend," I said, nodding around the little circle as I introduced people, "one of my very dearest in Baltimore. And this is Tony Neuberg, my best friend from college..."

"Competition for our Walter?" Gene said, a smiling generous tribute to Tony's good looks. Gene could afford to be gracious on that score. Giving Tony a cool measuring look, balancing him against the absent Walter, he said, "Oh, it's just Hugo Boss vs. Land's End; I get it."

"Just stop," I said, shying from Gene's shameless verbalizing of my years-old fascination with Tony's appearance. "You would have met Tony years ago, but you missed Robert's funeral, you know. Anyway, Tony and Walter and I go back just forever. And this is Joe Andreoli, my... well, a... an old friend."

"From school," Joe said, standing behind me, his hands on my shoulders.

"From school," said Gene, nodding; "indeed! Those hallowed halls! And how the good doctor works them." Then, suddenly bluff and manly, he put his hand out to Tony and Joe in turn. He winked at me. "My appreciation of your work has never been higher," he said. The assumption he was making about me and Joe was weakly reassuring; about me and Tony, both embarrassing and titillating. Switching again, he went on. "Now you've just GOT to... Cybil will be beside himself: PROmise me, Dear Heart; we'll be pining. Over there?" he asked, pointing. "And *don't* keep us waiting – you KNOW how she gets!" I couldn't remember who Cybil was – one of his matronly caftanned gay mentors, or this week's cute trick. He gave Tony and Joe a bright honest smile and brushed my cheek again with his own. Then we glimpsed his shining brown muscular back as he rode in on the next wave.

"Let me catch my breath," said Tony.

"Great guy," said Joe. On impulse, I turned around to face him. I didn't care about Tony being there; I wanted to kiss Joe, just a simple little smooch, that second. He turned his face away, smiling.

"Be good," he said.

The three of us sat on the beach and talked. Joe kept scanning over to the right, and my paranoia told me he was looking for Dennis or, worse, Gene. The years had brought me some slim wisdom, but I was still in envious awe of Gene's ease in picking up desirable men. He could probably snap his fingers and have Joe; indeed, it would hardly have surprised me to find him tightly clasping Tony himself. While Joe's eye wandered, Tony kept up his insistent interrogation about Joe's plans for the future. Joe answered in monosyllables. His grudging tone reflected, I thought, not resentment of Tony's questions, but the nervous dissatisfaction with his own life I had noticed the first day we talked in the studio. Tony might regretfully inform him, at the end of the interview, that the committee had decided he wasn't qualified to be Jim's new boyfriend, and Joe would just shake his head and say, I know; thanks anyway. They would work it out between themselves, man to man, without any need for what Joe would call Word One from me. Then Joe would spend the rest of his vacation with Gene and my life would go back to normal.

No, I decided. I had already done more in the way of going for it with Joe than was usual for me: I'd admitted confusion, worked through some misunderstandings, apologized, strategized, flattered, stroked, and risked. I'd given up and then hoped again, several times already in a few days. I'd felt myself genuinely touched by his irritating needs and weaknesses, and by his sudden bodily kindness and honesty. I'd also had a night of transfiguring sex, of course. For a few moments, there was a lull in Joe's and Tony's talk, and as they sat in silence, I watched the surf a few yards in front of us, puzzled by the strange acoustic that made its rhythmic roar seem so distant. I soaked my mind in the churning sandy water where shore and wave met. The sand we sat on felt soft under the towel, comfortable, yielding, almost like living flesh. I realized I liked the beach after all – I liked scuttling along that border of water and land and feeling their attributes shift and exchange. Joe was sitting less than a foot from me, and again I was grateful for his presence. It didn't matter that there was no future in this, that he was perplexing and perverse. This might well end at the end of the next week – so be it. For now, Joe was here.

"Tony," I said, pointing far to the left with exaggerated excitement, "look!" He knew exactly what I was doing, and gamely craned his neck and stared at nothing, gawking like a rube, while I turned to Joe and put my arms around his neck for a second.

I kissed Joe's ear and whispered, "I want to talk to you alone. Come up with me for a minute." He was still looking off to the right, where boom-boxes played premature Paul Lekakis retrospectives for lounging boys in thongs. He turned his head barely enough for his eyes to meet mine, crinkling with gruff amusement – I was hassling him, but that was cute.

"In a while, Tiger," he said. He started to turn his gaze back to the gay beach, but first, catching himself, he kissed the tip of one forefinger and touched it to my lips. Then he said, over his shoulder, "So tell me about your friend Gene."

"Where's Rachel?" he asked Tony a while later. "Do you think she's coming out?" Tony shrugged. "Should we go get her?"

"She'll come out if she wants," Tony said. "She's a grown woman." Joe looked at him rather hard.

"She's a real nice lady," he said. Tony nodded. This was where I wanted him to say something – something appreciative of Rachel, something at least polite about Joe's tribute to her. Instead, he sat without speaking, watching the waves. I remembered how he had predicted Joe would think he wasn't nice to Rachel. He wasn't doing much to change that. I wondered if he just really didn't care what Joe thought of him. Or maybe he was too proud to defend himself to Joe, unwilling to let Joe share in or judge his family dynamic. Perhaps he was irritated with me for bringing Joe into the circle.

Rachel did come out soon after, not as expected. We had been sitting in silence for a while when she stepped out of the water a short distance to our left. Joe was the first to notice her.

"Wo," he said, and pointed. "Where did she come from?" Tony and I looked over and I was barely aware of Tony's slight unease at seeing her. Rachel was standing with the surf still slapping around her ankles, seeming to smile to herself. I'd never seen Rachel in a bathing suit, and it had been years since I'd seen her with her hair down. Her lush body was sleek and gleaming as a seal's in her wet black suit. There was a slight soft shake in her rounded arms and thighs, and her breasts were as high-arched as the waves behind her. Her hair hung down almost to her waist, its dense curls bending her head back with their drenched weight. She ran one hand behind her neck, gathering her hair forward over one shoulder to wring it out, and torrents scattered from it as it swung. Still absorbed comfortably in herself, her gaze gentle and abstract, she squeezed her hair partly dry and then tossed it, an amazing cascade, behind her. Who is Rachel, what is she? I hummed to myself, smiling, knowing: we had all seen her rising from the sea before. I had an awestruck impulse to applaud, as though Berganza had just sung *"Pensa alla patria"* or Björling *"Nessun dorma."* I felt actually proud of Rachel, proud to know her.

Glancing at Tony, I couldn't tell much about what seeing her did to him, beyond his minor nervousness at taking up their fight again sooner than planned. Joe was staring at Rachel like a pilgrim at Cnidos. She was looking at no one, standing like a fountain sculpture, feet together, her weight on one leg, her hands in her hair at her neck, taking the sun for a grateful still moment. Then a child's beach ball struck her knees and she turned to smile at a pair of mortified apologetic kids who came to retrieve it. She patted the smaller child's head and tossed the ball for them, waving up the beach to where, I assumed, their parents had caught her eye. Then she stepped out of the shallow water and walked, a strong, purposeful, prowling walk, with a supple rolling of hips, up to wherever she had left her things. Joe was going to wave to her, but since she hadn't seen us, I made good on my promise to Tony and put my hand on his arm.

"We'll see her up at the house," I said.

"She's incredible," he said, after a moment, looking with puzzlement at Tony's bland uncommunicative face.

Tony trailed along with Joe and me when we went back to the studio for lunch. The two of them were polite to each other through the meal. When the dishes were cleared, Tony knew he had to go face Rachel. The three of us stood at the door and Tony, looking a little constrained at the thought of the conversation he was about to have downstairs, looked back and forth between us.

"Wish me luck," he said quietly to me. I wondered if he'd have preferred saying that to me alone, but, turning to Joe, he said, "Jimbo will explain." Joe tossed his head back slightly: Yeah, OK. Tony hesitated another moment. I sensed he was thinking about me and Joe, and what we might do after he left. I wanted to remind him about the no-nookie deal I'd made with Joe, just to reassure him, but that was a stupid idea. It would be rude and disloyal to Joe, and not all that reassuring to a man who was on his way to engage in some close sexual negotiation with his wife. It was going to be a rather chilly night at this house, come to think of it – no nookie for anyone, apparently.

Then Tony surprised me.

"Hey, Joe," he said and, rather tentatively, he patted Joe's shoulder. "Good to be with you today." He caught Joe's eye and nodded once, smiling just a bit.

It wasn't much, but it was everything, irreversible. Joe had been received by Mrs. Astor; Tony had withdrawn his black mark. Now it was up to Joe and me to decide what came next. I had a sudden rush of gratitude to Tony.

"Thanks," I said.

"No," he said, smiling down at the floor, "thank *you*. For lunch." Then he went down the steps, bouncing, swaying slightly from side to side, like a kid. Joe watched him go.

"He's an OK guy," he said, turning back into the room.

"I love Tony," I said.

"I know," he said. "I don't get why he's so weird with his wife. She's such a great person."

"Other people's relationships are impossible to understand," I said. He stepped to the window over the ocean, then turned to face me.

"So?" he asked. He wondered what I'd wanted to tell him on the beach; it delighted me that he'd remembered, all through lunch.

"Are you having a good time?" I asked. He nodded vaguely. "I sure am," I continued. "I – like being with you. Even with no... you know." Again, he nodded, meeting and then avoiding my eye.

"I don't know," he said. "I don't know if I can go all day. No – " he smiled, seeing my reaction: I'd made a joking gesture to open up the sofa. "I mean, like your friend Gene, before I knew you knew him; even old Dennis. On a normal day, I'd pick up Gene, or I'd call Dennis, or something. I miss that." I'd just told Joe I liked him; I didn't deserve this.

"It's been, what – seven hours?" I asked sarcastically, heating up instantly. "This is just what I predicted."

"I'm just being honest," he said.

"When I was honest this morning, you practically took my head off," I said. "I said this would happen, and you were furious." He looked unhappy.

"You're right," he admitted. He was looking at the floor, my knees, the walls. "Maybe I wondered if I could do it, not just if you could do it. Maybe I can't." I turned away.

"Clearly this is where I'm supposed to thank you for sharing," I said. "For being honest. Then I tell you No hard feelings. Well I'm terribly sorry. You think you can jerk me around and get my hopes up and then go fuck every man with a pulse, and I'll still congratulate you for your honesty. No." He put his hand on my shoulder and turned me back to face him, not very gently.

"Hey," he said, "I don't jerk people around. You got your own hopes up. You know I'm splitting at the end of next week and we may never see each other again." His eyes were flashing – that jerk-around thing hit his self-image right on a nerve. But I was right. I was about to yell at him, something angry: we were only one step from arguing. I was actually drawing breath to shout. But, avoiding his eye, I happened to look right over his head, just an inch or two, and saw a glow of refracted light on the window. It distracted me from my anger just for a second. Don't fight him, I told myself; talk to his spirit.

"I didn't just get my own hopes up," I coaxed. "I got yours up, too. You've enjoyed this as much as I have, even though we're both obviously freaked out by it. Think about it, Joe. Think how nice this has been – reading, talking, meeting each other's friends. OK; so we don't know what will come of it. It's nice just for its own sake, just for now. Don't run away from it." He was looking straight at me with his stubborn confused look. I smiled and kneeled in front of him. I put my arms around his knees. "Don't run away."

"You're something," he said after a while. I looked up and saw his face, touched but uncertain. I stood and put my arms around his waist. He didn't squirm or resist. At last, I was winning.

"You made me promise to go twenty-four hours without jumping your bones," I pressed. "Now you promise me: for twenty-four hours, don't think about scoring Gene or picking up on Dennis one more time. Think about being good to a nice man who really likes you." I was rocking him gently and he consented to be rocked, bobbing his head back and forth in rhythm with our motion.

"Dennis is nice," he said, "and he really likes me." He was smiling sullenly, teasing me, pretending to stay distant, hating to give in. But he was giving in. "Let me go," he said after a moment. "I'm going out by myself now. Let me take that book you gave me yesterday."

"Are you going to be good?" I asked. He took my arms from his waist.

"I'm not sure," he said. "But I'm not jerking you around. I'm sleeping here tonight, whatever happens. Meanwhile you've got to just risk it."

"This is my big happy ending?" I wasn't sure if I was happy or not.

"Tell me if it's not enough and I'll just split." I glanced quickly out the window at the surf. Each small foaming wave, just as you thought it had spent itself, sent a sudden broad silver sheen shooting out ahead of itself across the sand. Something in the sight made me optimistic. For some reason it struck me as fairly likely that Joe would be good. It also occurred to me that it would be fun, once or twice, to be good about his being bad.

"OK," I said. "I'm cool."

All afternoon, while I tried to read, I told myself it was OK that I didn't know what Joe was doing or when he'd come back, if he came back. I would have paced if I weren't too proud; certainly my thoughts paced.

Dinner in the main house was quiet. Whatever Tony and Rachel had talked about after lunch was smoothed over by the time I came downstairs. I watched for signs of strain: nervous courtesy, repressed rage – nothing. The good cheer seemed unforced, though the energy was maybe a little low. These two really like each other, I thought, in spite of everything; they get along. Rachel asked politely about Joe, and I said, hoping my nerves didn't show, that he might be by later.

We had barely finished dinner when Joe knocked at the kitchen door, where he saw the light on. I looked at my watch: 10:30. This was still very early for him to leave his friends at the bar. I knew that Gene would never be seen leaving at this unfashionable hour, even to score. I felt a coolness of relief over my whole body. Joe had been good.

Tony got up to open the door, and Rachel, looking at me across the table, smiled. She couldn't possibly understand the details of Gay Standard Time, but she could tell I was happy about something, about Joe.

"Yes," she said, hissing the "s" excitedly, like a teen cheerleader. Then, very quietly,

"Yes."

Chapter 7 – Saturday into Sunday morning

The next morning I was awake very early. Joe and I had held to our pact and lain beside each other as chastely as two good little Cub Scouts. It was pleasant to lie in bed chatting and shyly smiling at each other at midnight. It might be something like this to lie beside your lover of twenty years: nothing to prove, and the happy certainty that he was there. I went to sleep very comfortably. Then I awoke around five in a flaming rage of lust. In porno, he would have been lying there waiting, erect, his eyes glimmering like wicked emeralds. But he was not just asleep; he was sunk in an altered state of being. His chest rose with each breath and was held, expanded and motionless, for a long second or two. I half-expected to see him float off the bed with each inhalation, like an inflating balloon. The sound of his breathing was deep as a bellows. He frowned slightly at whatever it was that made his closed eyes flick back and forth. He looked something better than handsome; he looked good, and he looked real. I would have kissed him, but in my state I was afraid to touch him. I had a bureaucratic scruple about our agreement – three hours or more to go. A single touch might undo all my resolve: I would roll over onto him and start humping him ferociously, like a dog. So instead, I let my eyes embrace and thank him. He didn't have to be there, but he was. His heavy body had warmed the bed and, even without a touch, that was a generous gift.

"Joe," I whispered, hoping he might hear me and open his eyes. Maybe he did hear. He rolled onto his side, facing me, and pulled a pillow over his head. I looked down his belly and saw, in the pouch of his boxers, that his dream was not a dream of passion. My chest was starting to tighten with liking Joe. It would be good to lie next to him like this – but with lust stilled – morning after morning, to wait for his awakening, to ask him what he'd dreamed, to get up to make his coffee or lie slack and warm while he made mine. I lay back down and tried to sleep a little more, wishing he'd wake up, wishing it were eight already.

Then I heard the water running in the outdoor shower below my balcony. I checked my watch, wondering if I had maybe dozed off without knowing it, but I was right: it was still barely five a.m. I got up stealthily and stepped out onto the balcony. I couldn't quite see the shower over the rail, but I could see wild splashes surging over the top of the little stall. That was Tony – Ootch himself didn't splash as much in his bath as Tony. I leaned on the rail and waited for him to finish.

"Doro," I called when the water stopped, as quietly as I could, and he stepped into view, wrapping his towel around his waist and looking up smiling. I was reminded suddenly and urgently that I'd had a raging hard-on a few moments before.

"Hey," he said. "What are you doing up at this hour?"

"Monitoring your every move," I said. "Joe's still sleep-ing. You going out on the beach?"

"Yes," he said. "Come with me?"

"For a minute," I said, glancing over my shoulder to be sure Joe wasn't stirring.

Inside, I looked for a couple of seconds at him, sleeping with his head covered. Then I wrote a note in conspicuous red magic marker and left it on my pillow beside him. "J: on beach with Tony. Don't you dare move. Back by 6. XOXO (Remember?) J. 5:10" Out front a moment later, Tony asked me if I wasn't going to shower. "After the ocean," I said. "It's a whole primal element thing. Plus: I don't want to wake up Sleeping Beauty."

"Did I wake you? I didn't think you'd hear me," Tony said.

"I probably wouldn't have," I said, "but I was already awake."

"Gazing... ?" he asked. I just smiled, and we went down to the water.

Tony didn't want to swim, so he sat and watched while I jumped in.

"Don't go in too deep," he said, protective for no reason. There was something intensely wholesome about swimming in the ocean at dawn and I felt happy at that and at Tony's noodgy watchfulness. My arousal subsided in the cool water in a nice natural way, as though sex were completely integrated into my general physical well-being. When I came out, I was exhilarated enough to knock Tony back on the towel with my arm around his neck and tousle his hair.

"Hey," he said, sitting back up immediately. "Somebody's in a very good mood this morning."

"Yes," I said.

"Joe?" he asked.

"I like him, I've decided." I sat up. I wasn't looking at Tony; I was looking at the grey waves shot with pink and yellow sunshine, and wishing I were a painter.

"That's good," Tony said. "He makes you happy. That's good." He nodded in his Old World patriarch way.

"Did you and Rachel ever make up?" I asked. "You seemed OK together last night."

"We always make up. This isn't as big as maybe I made it sound." He sounded a bit sly and I wasn't completely convinced. He squinted at the rising red sun. Something in the sun seemed to make him happy, because he smiled. It was inconsequent – his smile had nothing to do with what he was saying to me. Maybe the sun is talking to him, I thought; maybe they swap little jokes and oneliners and crack each other up. Then I saw that he wasn't exactly smiling; it was just that the squint-lines in his face looked like smile lines. Most people frowned or grimaced when they looked at the sun, but Tony smiled. It was endearing, of course. It was also maddening.

I adjusted my shorts with one hand to conceal something: Damn it, I thought. I tried for a minute to think of Joe, who I devoutly hoped was still sleeping. In the back of my mind I feared that he might wake up, find me gone, and blow me off. But while Tony smiled at the sun, a million miles from me, I would have sacrificed Joe twenty times, just to keep watching Tony's face. In fact, for a moment I couldn't picture Joe at all. I tried. I called up things I knew were true: his brown curly hair, his thick forearms, his odd big features. Tony kept slipping between my images of Joe.

"What are you looking at?" Tony asked me, noticing me looking at him.

"Just you in all your amazingness," I said. "This whole gaze-out-to-sea number you do when you don't know what to say. Were you put on earth to drive us all mad?" He shook his head. A second later he laughed.

"You're too much," he said. I didn't say anything. After a moment he began to seem embarrassed. "Jim," he said. Then, after another pause, "Jim. I want to talk about this thing with you, but I don't want you to think I'm a jerk. This kind of stuff always makes the guy look bad, and you'll side with Rachel. I know you will. You already have. You think I'm just holding out on her. You think she's a goddess." Joe would say That's honest, I thought. I waited before I answered. My right hand was off the towel, in the sand, and I felt with a surreal clarity how the sand was warming on the surface, still wet and chilled just below.

"I don't think I've ever thought you were a jerk," I said.

"Not ever?" he said. He was talking about his visit to New Haven. I would have pretended not to understand what he meant, but he was being honest.

"You disappointed me," I said. "I was sad. Some things were – mishandled, or miscommunicated. But we were much younger. You were doing your best; you meant well. You weren't a jerk." I scanned again. I didn't want to make a speech; I wanted to be right with Tony. "Anyway, that was then. We're big kids now, and we're talking about you and Rachel, and babies. You are really OK with me either way," I said.

"You're a loyal person," Tony said thoughtfully. "What would I do without you?"

"It's doubtful you'll ever have to find out," I said.

"I don't know," he said, trying to start. "It's being tied down."

"Fear of commitment," I said; "it's a cliché." He looked irritated.

"I'm not afraid of commitment. You sound like Phil Donohue. I've been married to Rachel for over thirteen years, and we were together for a long time before that."

"And you're happy in your marriage."

"Yes," he said, but he had to take a moment to consider it. So had Rachel, I remembered.

He tried again. "Grown-ups have children," he said. "People who know what to do."

It would have been easy to say that Tony was a grown-up and knew what to do. Something kept me from saying it. As I inventoried my favorite impressions and memories of Tony, I saw mostly his wonderful sunny easiness, his vitality, his spirit of fun and exhilaration. They weren't precisely grown-up qualities. He saw me hesitate and raised his eyebrows at me: A-hah, you know I'm right.

"Rachel's grown-up," I said. "She knows what to do."

"So where do I fit in?" he asked. "I could just – what? pay the bills? Watch Rachel being amazing at one more thing? You don't leave me much pride."

"You don't need pride," I said. "Everyone knows you're the greatest guy in the whole world."

"Yeah, right," he said, shrugging, and looked back at the sun. Clearly my attempt at a compliment didn't really register. Then he went on, almost shyly. "I always wanted you to think I was OK, to be proud of me," he said. "It was always one of my favorite things about myself, that you liked me."

This was so surprising I didn't say anything. I couldn't even look at him; I just looked down and smiled at the towel between my legs. I was so gratified at the idea that he needed my approval that I was afraid to talk about it, so after a second or two I said,

"Look, Tony," I said. "I don't care if you have a child or not. I just..."

"Want me to be happy," he finished. "I know that." He turned back to face me. "Maybe you should have a child. Who says 'I just want you to be happy'? A father. You'd be great at that stuff." He smiled. "You know, sometimes you remind me of my father. Not like you're a father-figure, exactly, but you're steady and patient like he was, gentle and approving."

I remembered Tony's father for a moment. It was impossible that a man who, at fourteen, had lost every loved one of his childhood to the gas chambers should not carry deep grief within himself, yet I never saw him without a smile on his face. He was too good a man, and too wise, to be simply in denial. Rather, I sensed that he knew the cost, the preciousness, of every moment's happiness. He was happy with his American wife, his two handsome healthy sons, his honest prosperity: so... he smiled. Was I like him, really?

"When Dad died," Tony was saying, "... I mean, of course you came to the funeral, of course you said the things people say – and you always seem to know exactly how to do all that stuff – but it was more than that. You were the man I needed to be there, more than my brother even. A guy who's smart and strong and thinks I'm OK... Since Dad died, you're who I've got in my life who sees me that way, treats me that way. That's why I say you'd be a great father."

"I've thought about having a kid," I said. "Not if I'm single; but if I found somebody, I might." He looked genuinely interested in this, and perhaps he would have liked to change the subject from his own life, but I felt we were getting off topic. "You know why *you*'d be a good father?" I asked. "Because you make people happy. People want their fathers to make them happy. And that's your specialty."

"You got that from Rachel," he said. "She tells me that." He was looking down. "I haven't made you happy, Jimbo. You're not happy."

"Well," I said, "you're not my father. It's not your job to make me happy."

"Come on," he said. "Don't act tough. You're not happy. I feel bad about that. I mean, sometimes." I didn't say anything, so he went on. "And Rachel, these days. Look at her. People depend on me, or care about me, and I let them down. What if I did that to a kid?"

I wondered if I was happy or not. It wasn't just for me now, but for Tony, for Rachel, for a child who might be born. Tony thought there was something wrong with him. I knew he'd picked that up from me over the years, from my hurt feelings and cool proud blame. Certainly there had been years when the absence of Tony, or Angel, or anybody, had felt like grief. Unhappiness, or the lack of happiness, had pretty much defined my personality for years. Friends in grad school always thought of me as deep and sensitive and caring, even at times as funny; never as happy. I felt a breath of that old persona, and it saddened me for the sake of the younger man I remembered being. Tony saw that in my face, because he put his hand on my shoulder. His hand was as hot as the sun-warmed sand I'd been stroking.

"I'm OK," I said. "I've always been afraid you'd go away, I guess. You; everybody: all of you. That would be the real sadness. But you're here. I'm OK."

"Really?"

"You do make me happy, Doro. When you're like this. When you're here like this."

"You can hold me to that," he said.

"Yes," I said. "I will." I patted his hand and he took it off my shoulder. "Like – well, speaking of funerals… when you came east for Robert's. All my friends were there, but nobody else could have done what you… you're just so nice, Tony. So loyal… such a great friend." I wanted to say something else, but an old protective habit kept me from saying it. Then I thought of all that had been said over the past few days, and discarded the habit. We were being honest now.

"You're someone that people love, Tony," I said. "It's a burden sometimes, I suppose, but it's just who you are." I took a deep breath. "You know I've always loved you. I've never regretted it, either."

We didn't look at each other. I could feel that he was as moved as I was, and as relieved. Something was draining away through the sand: fear. Tony and I no longer feared each other. There was no need to say anything.

His watch caught my eye. Suddenly I remembered:

"I am awaited," I said, and added, "I hope." Tony hadn't referred to Joe when he worried aloud about my unhappiness, and I honestly hadn't thought about him either. He was not really part of the old melancholy pattern and I wasn't sure yet what he was. But I did feel a tiny new lift inside, just at the idea that I was going back to Joe. I got up. Tony opted to stay a while longer. The beach was still deserted.

"Don't go in the water by yourself," I said.

"OK, pop," he said, and smiled at me as I headed back to the house.

I took my shoes off before climbing the iron steps, and let myself into the studio as silently as I could. As I opened the door, I heard a slight commotion of footsteps and bedsprings and billowing covers, and was just in time to see Joe rolling onto the mattress and pulling the pillow over his head again.

"Good morning," I said, kneeling next to him on the bed and pulling the pillow off him. He smiled and said,

"Buon giorno, professore." His eyes were authentically sleepy. I could hear the toilet running.

"What's all the frenzy?" I asked. "Jumping back in bed like this?"

"You told me not to move," he said. "In your note." I had to smile.

"You're too cute to be real," I said. "I don't deserve you."

"Guess what?" he asked. Before I could guess, he said, "Nobody does." Feeling bolder, I pulled the sheet off him and put my hand to his crotch. Things were stirring now, and I gave him a few pats and strokes through his shorts, meeting his eye after a moment or two. He winked at me and said, "Hoo."

"Do you need these?" I asked, popping the elastic in his waistband. He shook his head. Then, when his pants were off, he glanced at his watch and said, "We made it twenty-two hours. That'll have to do, I guess."

"I think we've been awfully good," I said. "I'm proud of us." He nodded. Then he squinted at me.

"You're still dressed," he complained. "Come on." That was quickly taken care of. When I was lying next to him, he said, "I'm still sleepy, I think."

I was sinking in his sweet green eyes and I just said, "Yes." He put an arm around me and pulled me till we were pressed chest to chest and boner to boner.

"Can you sleep like this?" I asked him, panting.

"No," he said. He started kissing me, murmuring gently. He hooked one leg over mine and clamped us together at waist and crotch, humping slowly. He was a strong man and his touch was firm and unapologetic. It confirmed what I'd let myself hope while I watched him still sleeping: Joe was there, as he'd said he would be; he wasn't running, he wasn't jerking me around. I was safe with Joe, to the limit of what he promised. I was kissing him back, sleepily, with none of the hotness I'd felt earlier, but just because I liked him and we were together. I could feel defenses melting away, walls crumbling and citadels yielding, and through my haze, after a few minutes more of his rhythmic soft humping, I could barely feel something warm and amniotic surge quietly out of me to sweeten our friction. A moment later, there was an answering flow from inside him. He was laughing quietly, his lips still loosely laid to mine.

Then he said, "But I can sleep like this."

When we were both awake later, he sat up and looked at me in the bright midmorning sun.

"You're not my type," he said. "But we have nice sex."

This seemed to perplex him.

"You've had your type," I said, still lying down, "and it didn't make you happy." He smiled.

"That's true," he said. Then he gave me a wicked sidelong smile. "Well, not for more than half an hour or so."

"We've all been there," I said. "Ritual frustrations of fantasy on the one hand, and on the other the bitter lesson that fantasy-fulfillment bestows no lasting spiritual peace. It's in the literature."

"Yeah," he said, still being bad, "but I'm your type. You're all hot for me. Your fantasies aren't being frustrated."

"You've been indulging your fantasies since the minute you came out," I said. "I've only been indulging mine since Thursday night. And they probably won't last anyway."

"Meaning you'll get tired of me now that you've had sex with me," he said without bitterness, pursuing what he saw as a very simple logic. "Guys always do – they get their fantasy rocks off, and then they move on. Because then it's work."

"What I meant was that you'd get tired of me," I said, reaching to put my arms around his waist. "I meant you'd go on to some new hotness project. But if you're worried I'll run when it gets to be work, you're in luck. I'm a Presbyterian. We love work. Anything that isn't just a wretched dull grind makes us feel guilty. Life is supposed to be labor and misery; the grimmer it gets, the better we like it."

Joe was smiling at this. I was wide awake now and I realized he'd been saying he wasn't all that attracted to me. It was a good and funny sign that I hadn't risen to that bait sooner. Now I took a pillow and flogged his back.

"How dare you say I'm not your type?" I said. "What about that unflagging hard-on you've been sporting?"

"That," he said, "just happens. It's the way I am: boing." He made a priapic gesture, uncoiling one forefinger to point up. I had to laugh.

"My indefatigable little sex god," I said. "There's a clear solution: I will never leave your side."

"You're in an awfully good mood this morning," he said, the second man to notice.

"So are you." He laughed out loud.

"I am," he said, as if he hadn't realized it until I told him. So I insisted on a sore point, for my ego's sake.

"You think I'm moderately cute, don't you?" I asked. "Otherwise you wouldn't keep sleeping with me." He shrugged, nodding: emphasis on the Moderately.

"I sleep with you because you're nice," he said. "Then I get hot because you're there." Suddenly he lay back down and looked urgently at me. "But that's really good, isn't it?" He sounded excited. "That's good." He lay on his back to look at the ceiling, his eyes darting. "Maybe that's how people do it, when they're together." Then he turned back to me, scanning my face dispassionately. "Actually you are cute," he said. "Not cute; you're nice-looking. You're not hot like... like porno-hot. But I like you – I like it with you."

"Thank you," I said. Part of me missed a certain kind of ringing affirmation: it would have been nice, for instance, if Joe had said that he loved me desperately, or that I had the biggest cock he'd ever seen. But neither of those things would have been true, and I knew it. It was fine this way. He was saying things he meant, and they were good things. I sat up.

"Coffee time," I said.

"No," he said. "Shower time." He stood up and walked to the bathroom door. He turned when he saw I wasn't following him. "Tiger," he reminded me, and I did.

"There's a boy," I told Walter. Joe had gone out to meet Michael and Dennis and Bobby and Chris. I was going to meet them later, but I'd stayed back to make some calls. I'd called Walter to insist he and Ricardo come out from Washington for the last weekend at least, if not earlier.

He made a courteous "Hmm?" at my announcement and I asked, "Do you remember Joe Andreoli, from Yale?"

"Do I remember Joan, from Arc?" he said. There were two or three seconds of silence. He was waiting for me to explain the way in which the new man reminded me of Joe. Then, from my silence, he got it, and then he screamed.

"No!" he said. "Jimmy McManus, Star Fucker of the Nineties! Tell!" He was laughing happily. So I told. I could hear Ricardo say, "What?" in the background, and Walter turned from the phone to tell him, "Himself has scored the principal peninsular fantasy of his troubled adolescence. Joe Andreoli." He groaned lustfully, and Ricardo giggled.

"Way to go, honey," he called into the receiver. Then they huddled for a minute, and Walter said they'd definitely be up to inspect, by Friday.

"There's a boy," I said. Marie didn't know about Joe – Yale was before we knew each other – so I gave her some background. Then I tried to explain what was happening now. I told her about Dennis, running into Gene, Tony not liking Joe at first; I felt I was rambling, not getting my point across. Marie was making polite noises, sounding unconvinced. Then I told her about Joe jumping back in bed and calling me *professore* and Tiger; about his hanging around even when he was mad; about his Italian books; what he'd taught me about stealing; and she said, "I like him."

She agreed to call Walter and Ricardo; maybe they could carpool up for the weekend if she could get out of some minor commitments. She didn't require a lot of persuading. Marie had moved down to Washington two years before, partly for her job and mostly for Clare. Clare was an ex-hippy, a gentle and pretty early-music expert whose recorders and sackbuts sometimes bored me, as did her profound belief that authenticity was the same thing as artistry. This seemed to have obscure political ramifications: vibrato was counter-revolutionary, apparently, indicative of some deep complicity in consumerism, militarism – whatever. But she was a dear person who had done worlds for Marie. She had two small children, a boy and a girl, and unlike many lesbian mothers I knew had remained good friends with her ex-husband. I had taken to calling Marie the Little Princess of Co-Parenting. She had thrown herself into the role of second mommy, helped by the fact that Josquin and Hildegard were fun kids. Clare had taken them to Seattle for the month to visit their father, so the house on Capitol Hill must have felt a little echoing and empty. Marie admitted she could do with some amusing.

"Finally I meet Rachel," she said. "And Joe, of course."

"I've been seeing someone here," I told Mom; "someone I knew when he was in college at Yale, but he's thirty-three now." Mom worried that in my line of work I spent too much time with very young men.

"Well tell me all about it," she said, and listened while I gave her a rigorously bowdlerized account of the past several days. "How nice," she'd say, or "Oh, I like the sound of that"; and by the time we hung up I was very happy.

Mom had also asked rather closely after Tony and Rachel. Tony had been her pet among my friends since the summer of 1971, when he first came to visit us at home for a week. She hadn't known I was gay at that time, at least not officially, but her intuition was considerable. At the very least, she'd understood that he was very important to me and that we were close.

Tony had always brought out something almost annoyingly maternal in Mom. She'd always fretted when she heard he'd had any kind of reversal or disappointment. This was ridiculous; Tony was in every way more competent and successful than practically anyone I knew – certainly, I'd often thought, far more than myself. Why wasn't Mom lavishing this maternal concern on me?

I asked her about it once. She said,

"You've always been very resilient, because you've had to be. But I just can't bear it when anything goes wrong for someone as – happy – as Tony." She'd always been devoted to Rachel. Rachel was Tony's bulwark, as she saw it: Rachel was the woman who took care of Tony, and Mom was grateful to her for doing it so well.

I couldn't really tell her what was going on between them. Strictly speaking, it wasn't her business, so I put her off with vague answers.

Then she said, "I wonder sometimes why they've never had children. Rachel would be such a wonderful mother." I stammered a bit and admitted in confidence that it was under discussion. She brightened up and said, "Well, keep me posted on that. And do give them both my love. Now, what were you saying about... Joe, is it?"

I found Joe with his little party on the beach. He got up to greet me with a quick hug, as though I were just home from the office – as though we'd been together for a thousand years. This time Michael had brought along a beach umbrella with a Keith Haring knock-off graphic in red and black. It cast a lurid red light on his already lurid form, but, as he explained,

"Mother's not as young as she used to be; we have to be careful about the sun now, don't we?" He patted the towel he was sitting on, inviting me to join him in the shade: we were both so old, you see.

I was feeling cheery enough that I took his challenge and sat beside him. I had never been good at baking in the sun, and my age had nothing to do with it.

"Those of us with aristocratic complexions will shelter here," I said, settling on the towel, "while the peasantry crispens."

The group laughed exactly as though Bobby had just done Vanna, and I had a sudden enjoyable sense of fitting in with them and their canned gay laughter. Joe, who had been sitting with Dennis when I got there, came and stretched out beside me under Michael's spreading canopy, his color in the shade as pretty as if he'd been under a great rose window in a cathedral. I put my hand on his shoulder, glad that he had moved out of the sun to be next to me. Dennis didn't seem to be watching, but Chris and Bobby smiled tolerantly, as though Joe and I were two mushy old lovers whose behavior in public had tried their friendly patience for years.

A little later, I saw Gene walk past on his way towards the water and I called out to him.

"Dear Heart!" he said, waving, and came over to join us. I introduced him to the others; he gave Joe a bland smile of recognition to which Joe responded with a reserved nod. "And that blond thing?" Gene asked me, looking around for someone. "Mad for him!"

"Tony," I said severely. "You can't have him."

"Never say that to me," he answered, smiling brazenly. "You're saving him for your own use, you mean thing? We'll just see."

"He's married," Joe explained. "Plus Jim has loved him since... when, exactly?"

"The very beginnings of life on the planet," I said. I reached to stroke Joe's hair. Gene lifted his eyebrow slightly.

"And how long has *this* been going on, exactly?" he asked with a smile.

"Whole days," I said. He'd seen us in the water together the day before; maybe he hadn't believed anything was really going on between us. Of course, I hadn't been sure myself. Just before he gave me a congratulatory smile, he slipped a look at

Joe. I was quite sure I understood it. I had looked at Joe that way myself many times in years past.

"Well good for you both," he said graciously. "Joe: Dr. McManus is just one of our very favorites, you know. You've got to be awfully good to him." Joe took a moment to answer. He gave Gene a little smile, not sure he was getting all of his meanings.

"I'm doing my best," he said, with a tone of surprising meekness.

Chris and Bobby had been more or less staring at Gene since he joined us. I was so used to Gene after our several years of friendship that I sometimes forgot what a powerful first impression he made. Chris looked actually shy.

"What do you do, Gene?" he asked. There was a lack of ease in his voice which suggested that he was unused to making the first gambit. Boys like Chris needed normally do nothing more than respond to other men's timid approaches.

"Sales," Gene answered distractedly, pulling his eyes away from Joe without quite focusing on Chris. "Insurance."

"Wow," Chris said, nodding and smiling superbly. Gene dipped his head slightly to acknowledge the tribute.

"Chris is a video artist," I said after a moment of silence.

"How marvelous," Gene answered.

"You were going in the water, weren't you?" Chris asked Gene after another few beats. "When Jim called you over. Want to go in? I could... go with you." That was fairly brave of him, gambling that Gene would take the offer as a favor. His courage slipped a bit and he fumbled in the sand with one hand, his eyes falling. Gene was an act of God: he had toppled Chris from his citadel of beauty in a matter of instants. He smiled at me as though he had just been paged by the office, and turned to Chris kindly.

"Sure, dear," he said, and got up with some show of reluctance. "Catch you all later," he said to the group. Chris was flushed as he scrambled to his feet, frisking and fawning as he followed Gene down to the water.

Dennis, who had barely spoken since I arrived and had seemed to doze through Chris' conversation with Gene, now smiled broadly and shook his head at the others, amused at the quick capitulation. Then he moved closer to Michael's umbrella. He came and lolled on his stomach next to me, propping himself on his elbows, kicking the sand indolently and favoring me with a number of crinkly smiles. Despite Joe on my other side, I was tempted to brush off the sand that powdered the seat of Dennis' brief orange trunks. The movements of his legs as he kicked gave outrageous ripples to his curves. Joe was looking at Dennis too. I wasn't sure which one of us the show was for. I hoped pointlessly that Dennis was coming on to me, and that Joe was jealous. There was no clue for me in Joe's expression: jealousy, lust, boredom? I chatted with Dennis, liking him a bit for the sake of his apparent attraction to me, and wondering what it would be like to go after him if Joe weren't in the picture. It was exasperating that someone like Dennis should for once show an interest in me just as I was getting involved with Joe. Gene often said to me wisely, "When it rains, it pours." Where he gained this wisdom, no one would ever know, since in his universe it was always raining men. I recalled Joe's reluctance about settling down, missing out on these unexpected bonanzas. In spite of my better nature, I understood a little. Flirting with men like Dennis could be habitforming.

I had to go back to my studio in time to change for dinner at the house. The beach crowd and I had agreed to go dancing that night and my assignment was to get Tony and Rachel to join us. When I stood up and stepped out from under Michael's umbrella, Dennis got up and gave me a good-bye kiss, before Joe did. This was my first kiss from Dennis. For an instant I felt like a hot clone with a high scoring record and hundreds of sexy friends: in fact, I felt like Gene, or like Joe. I liked the feeling. Then, as I stepped away from the group, I saw Dennis sit down next to Joe and put his arm around him. It should have made me jealous, but I could feel how Dennis' flirtatiousness, his kiss, had bought me off. You could forgive a great deal for that.

Rachel and I talked on the porch before dinner. It was a windy evening, almost chilly in the shade, the water lit up in an opaque Tiffany green as the slanting sun struck it. Rachel wore a blue and green paisley shawl and the strong wind lifted a few strands of hair out from under it to slap photogenically across her face.

"Did you always think you'd end up with Tony?" I asked her at one point. "Even back in grade school?"

"No, not really," she said, smiling: it was an unusual and distant memory for her. "No; he wasn't my type, I guess you'd say." After a pause she added, "I always was... fond of Anton. Back in – oh, fifth or sixth grade, when boys and girls don't get along, you know – he and I already got along. I thought of us as friends before it even occurred to me that I didn't like boys."

"You didn't like boys?" I asked. Then suddenly I could picture it. "I'll bet you were cootie-captain," I said.

"Kind of," she nodded. "Of course, there were no boys in my family. I wasn't used to boys. I had an idea I'd like a boy who was... shy, needy – someone I could boss around, and take care of. When I was in nursery school, a boy joined my class in the middle of the year, because his family had fled Hungary. I don't remember his name; just a skinny boy with a big head and the most enormous eyes, and of course he didn't speak English. He just stood around looking knobby-kneed and sad. For years, I was fascinated by that memory. I imagined him growing up, how we'd meet again, and he'd still be the gentle sad boy who needed someone to stand up for him. But I never actually knew any boys like that. Boys made a lot of noise, and broke things."

"Except Tony," I suggested.

"No, he was like that too, in school. He was a big show-off, always fooling around, boisterous. Terribly smart, of course, which was irritating. But I liked him anyway. But I never thought of him as a potential boyfriend; not until we were sixteen or so. And I did go out with other boys, at first, even after he and I had connected. In high school some – even a few times in college."

I remembered, for the first time in years, that there had been a few brief periods in college when Tony and Rachel were, as he said at the time, "cooling it." I couldn't help getting my hopes up a bit each time this happened. Tony as a free agent, however – Tony out on the prowl, Tony checking out women we passed on the street, Tony introducing me to girls who seemed bewildered that he'd wanted them to meet me and resentful of the time I was with them – that Tony was so alarming to me that I was actually relieved when he and Rachel sorted things out and got back together.

"It took me a while to be sure Anton was the one," she said. "I think I wanted to meet that boy from Hungary again."

"That's interesting," I said. "When I first knew Tony in college I was haunted by the story of how his father had had to leave Czechoslovakia. It made Tony seem very – well, the word is overworked and I hate it, but: vulnerable. Almost accidental; he almost wasn't born. I mean, if his father hadn't made it out of Europe... " Rachel raised her eyebrows, considering my point. "Maybe a little like your boy from Hungary."

"I've never thought of him that way," she said. "He's never struck me as needy, really. It seemed like a big change when I found myself attracted to him, to someone so... bouncy. He's always looked pretty sturdy to me. Of course, he's a gentle person, sensitive; I know that. I like that about him. But not... not tragic or pathetic."

"Of course not," I said. I wasn't sure if I should go on. "He is troubled by this whole discussion about family, though," I said. "It's bringing out his not-sturdy side, I think. He's afraid of failing in some way, and he's not used to failing."

"Lots of people have children, Jim." She sounded a little impatient. "It makes everyone nervous, but they do it. You don't need a PhD or a Nobel Prize to do it."

"But lots of people don't think about the implications of it," I said. "They just stumble into parenthood through brute procreative instinct. You and Tony aren't like that; you're not ignorant breeders. So he thinks about it, and it scares him."

"I guess," she said, looking out at the water dubiously.

"Why do you want a child, Rachel?" I asked. "It's a dumb question, I know, and it's none of my business." She shook her head seriously, allowing me to ask, admitting my right to be involved. So I went on. "A lot of people would say your life is complete as it is. What would it mean to have a child?"

Rachel was looking at the water, but no immediate answer came to her.

"This whole child/family rhetoric these days frightens me," I went on. "People say they love their children, but half of the time it's just self-promotion. What they really want is to project their own selfishness into the future: use their child as an excuse to step on someone else's rights; make sure the world is never without someone just like them. 'Sure I love my kids: that's why I'm throwing this bomb at YOUR kids, to keep them out of MY kids' school.' But that's not you." She smiled regretfully as I spoke. Her work brought her up against all kinds of parental pathology and she acknowledged my point with a nod and a sigh. Then she tried to answer.

"The world doesn't need another child, I know. There's nothing magic about a child of mine and Anton's, really. And I don't need to have some little clone of myself to feel that I've had a valuable life. But..." She didn't finish, and apparently hoped I would understand without her speaking.

"You need to tell me what you mean," I coaxed her. "These are things I can't guess. I haven't been through this." Rachel looked over suddenly and said,

"Anton told me you have considered adopting." I

shrugged.

"Purely preliminary speculation at this point," I said dismissively. She realized I still meant to talk about her and Tony, not myself.

"The world is very troubled," she said. "I'm a good person; Anton is a good person. We should have some say in the future, and some commitment to it. Of course, a person doesn't need to have a child for that. You're a good person, you care about the future, and you have no children. But a child is one way for married people to commit; something irrevocable, a statement. We commit ourselves that life will go on, that good people will go on."

"'Children are life renewing itself, Captain Butler,'" I said.

"Something like that," she said, smiling. I wondered irrelevantly if she remembered who Captain Butler was. "It's frustrating to me that Anton doesn't want that."

"I think he does, Rachel," I said. "I mean, maybe the specific concept of fatherhood is difficult for him, but he wants Life to go on. He's definitely working on the side of Life."

"But you've noticed that he's afraid," she said.

"I think he's afraid of two things. He's afraid of looking like a fool. Everyone says what a great mother you'd make, whereas Tony is the eternal boy in some ways. He thinks he'd be an incompetent father, or at best just a witness to you doing your maternal overdrive thing. That embarrasses him."

She was looking at the waves again, distractedly. She seemed to be confused: these were harder questions than whether or not she loved Tony. After a moment she turned to me and said,

"That's one." She pointed to her thumb, counting. I'd said he was afraid of two things.

"He's also afraid of being superfluous," I said. "To you. You'd have the baby and you wouldn't need him anymore." She gestured impatiently. Her reaction was so swift I knew that she had been aware of this before I said it.

"That's ridiculous," she said. "We'd *both* have the baby. People think that mothers go off and form perverse little committees of two with their children. It's some weird patriarchal paranoia – that women suddenly forget men when they become mothers. As if men didn't get enough attention from women already. As if Anton could possibly think I don't care about him. I wouldn't banish Anton from my life just because we'd had a child." She was sputtering. I didn't remember ever hearing her lose her cool like this and it made me smile. She saw that and deflated. "You're right," she said quietly. "I know he thinks that. It's very hard to argue with someone's paranoia."

"It's what you wanted in grade school, though," I said. "A boy who was needy and had secret sorrows. You just never thought he'd come in the form of Tony." After a longish pause, she gave a defeated little smile and a shrug.

"Is that what you call a bead-read?" she asked. I laughed.

"It's partly my fault," I said. "He's thought I blamed him for... for things that weren't right, years ago. He's had a theory that he hurts people who care about him. If I'd been a nicer person I would have let him off that hook a long time ago. I think that colors how he pictures himself as a father."

"That could be," she nodded. "He's always had some bad

conscience about you, I think. I'm glad you've been able to talk." She paused and looked back at me. "So your advice for me is… ?"

"I don't have any advice for you," I said. "Just a few observations." I stretched. Suddenly I was feeling restless. "One of which is that you and Tony are great together, children or not. You two will work it all out and it will be just fine, either way. I'm sure of that."

"Now that you mention it," she said, "I am too." In my mind I heard the Countess, when the beat suddenly picked up at the very end of *"Dove sono"* and, though her words were still mournful, the music said: I know I will be happy again. We heard Tony come down the stairs and start puttering in the kitchen. It was a homey sound and we both smiled, happy to have him in the house in spite of everything we'd just been discussing.

"Campari time?" Rachel asked me, and we stood and went inside.

I made an elaborate gesture of paying Tony and Rachel's way into the Strand. It was barely eleven and there weren't many people there yet. Two lesbians, younger than I had ever been or would ever be, were gyrating on the speakers in leather bras and huge black boots and impossibly short cutoffs. They held their hands over their heads with wrists crossed and thrust their hips at each other. One of them, prettier than any girl on "90210," had long blond hair which she swept off her shoulders with rhythmic tossings of the head, incongruously reminiscent of Gene on the dance floor. They were behaving exactly like the hippest young ACT-UP fashion mavens and I mused privately on this new gender equality among the young. Once it had seemed, in the early days of AIDS, when community trauma was bringing men and women together again, that parity would come about by gay men becoming as earnest, nurturing, and in touch as lesbians. Now it appeared instead that baby dykes aspired to the condition of disco queens.

The dance floor had been redone since my last visit and both Rachel and Tony were impressed by its trendiness. I felt a certain responsibility as their official gay friend to make sure that they knew what was going on on the arty fringe. The sleek industrial look of the space, especially noticeable now when it was still uncrowded, seemed to be satisfyingly novel to them.

Tony asked if we should dance, and my usual reluctance to be among the first on the floor was made sharper by the idea of being seen dancing with the only straight people in the room. I was relieved when Joe led his group in after a few minutes. I had noticed before in Joe's favor that he did not insist on being late just to prove he was gay. Rachel embraced him and kissed him on both cheeks. He looked happy and flattered at this, and he smiled proudly as he introduced everyone. It was too loud for easy talk.

Joe's friends seemed fascinated by Tony and Rachel. Tony looked especially engaging that evening. He had on a deep blue linen shirt that showed off his eyes even in the darkened flashing bar. When I asked Chris if Gene would be coming, he took a moment to take his eyes off Tony, and Bobby just kept frankly staring. Chris said vaguely that he wasn't sure what Gene's plans were and I saw that Gene had given him fairly little hope. It was good for Chris to sample this side of gay life for once and I didn't feel especially sorry for him.

"Gene thinks the world of you, by the way," he told me, touching my elbow: clearly I had become visible to Chris, for Gene's sake if not for Joe's or my own.

Michael stood with his arm around Joe's waist, making a show of whispering something to him and then laughing. Joe nodded at Michael's comment and laughed too, politely. He glanced my way, but Michael gripped him and spoke privately to him again. I realized he was signaling me that he had known Joe first. To my own surprise, I was touched by this, not irritated. I would have to make sure that Joe's time with me didn't take away from his established friendships. This had always been Rachel's line where Tony and I were concerned: she had always encouraged Tony to spend time with me, made herself scarce to allow us private talk, reminded him about my birthday. I appreciated that. I also liked the irreproachable majesty of it. That was how I would handle Michael.

Meanwhile Dennis came up and kissed my cheek familiarly. He had an eager intense expression, his eyes almost feverishly pale and glittery in his dark face. He looked a little sunburned, something I didn't think ever happened to boys from LA. I asked him about it and he admitted he'd underestimated the rays that day.

"Does it hurt?" I asked, stroking his neck lightly under the collar of his bright Hawaiian shirt. He patted my unshaven cheek and said,

"Only when some big man rubs his beard against it." Even though I'd known I was flirting when I touched him, I was surprised and pleased at this immediate hot rejoinder.

"Do you feel like dancing?" I asked him.

"No," he said, "I want to dance with the lady. We saw you two together the other night, at the Renegade. It's my turn."

He stepped over to Rachel and asked her to dance, with an unexpected courtesy. Soon they were doing a graceful improvised twostep/jitterbug, with Dennis very lightly and respectfully leading. Where did he learn that? I wondered. His smile to her made me almost jealous of her: there was nothing nasty in it, no hint of that buffed cruise-missile I'd seen on the beach. There was a glimpse of someone actually very nice, a gentleman almost. He's an actor, I reminded myself.

Joe and I were walking around together. It was hard for me to be sure how together we were supposed to be: a little sex, a little abstinence, a few heart-to-hearts, and now here we were in a gay bar designed for cruising. Maybe we were headed for an open relationship, or no relationship. Maybe we were friendly fuck-buddies and would have a good time out in public, cruising in synch, encouraging and applauding each other's scores, and then occasionally sharing a tumble or two. Maybe that was Joe's expectation: it was the Nineties; Joe was from LA.

Someone I barely knew from home, an aggressively handsome broker who'd given me a fair amount of attitude over the years, came over at one point and pretended we were old friends. His brazen "Hi!" with its matching smile crudely interrupted me in the middle of a sentence, but I didn't quite have the nerve to blow him off. After all, Joe might actually prefer to talk to him.

I couldn't remember his name, so I told him, "This is

Joe," giving him the chance to put his hand out and introduce himself.

"Curt," he said. Then he hovered between Joe and me, laughing vivaciously and patting my arm in the intervals of his closer and closer approaches to Joe. Pretending he needed to lean close in to hear what Joe was saying, he slipped a hand around to his lower back.

It was clear theft. I could tell that Curt knew that I knew this, but it was perfectly in line with everything I knew about him, and since he was a lot hotter than I was he had every right to assume Joe would drop me in his favor. I wondered if I should just take a hint and make myself scarce. Joe was smiling and being rather charming with Curt. I wished Curt would just back off long enough for me to ask Joe if he wanted me to leave them together. Then to my amazement, when Curt moved his hand so that his arm was around Joe's waist, Joe said, very politely and very clearly,

"I'm here with Jim."

I had never heard those words spoken, by anyone or to anyone or of anyone, in a gay bar. It was so surprising that Curt literally didn't know how to react. He kept smiling and didn't move his hand, afraid to acknowledge that he'd been put down. Joe smiled too and stepped sideways, twisting slightly, so that Curt's hand dangled in midair. Joe put one hand on my shoulder and said to Curt, "Good talking to you." Then he asked me, "Want to walk around?" The smile dying on Curt's face gave me a feeling of revenge more perfect and thrilling than if I'd cut him to pieces with a meat axe.

"So?" Joe asked me. "Dance?" I looked at Tony, standing

nearby and watching the dancers. Joe immediately went around me and asked Tony, "Join us?" Tony nodded and we stepped onto the floor. Joe was always a very cute dancer, and though he had picked up a lot of new steps since Yale, I still recognized some of his cocky self-sufficient moves from those days. He closed his eyes and, with his feet widely planted, tossed his whole weight bluntly from one foot to the other in a sexy lurching motion. He made little punching motions and shook his head. He rarely caught my eye. He was dancing mostly to please himself, enjoying his own cuteness. Dancing at the Moon two nights before, he'd held me a few times for some lewd Nineties hip-slamming, but tonight he had the tact to avoid it.

In fact Tony was touching me more than Joe was. After a few moments I saw that he wanted to do his ethnic wedding-dance, for old times' sake. I felt shy about it for some reason: Not here, Tony. But I went along with it; it was always hard for me to say No to Tony. At first Joe tried to join in, putting his arm around Tony's waist as though we were all going to do a horah. But Tony wasn't really encouraging him, and soon Joe just stepped back and watched and clapped.

Within moments I was aware of how people were making room for us, nodding, smiling for the most part. There was something a little weird and free about Tony tonight, very manlike. It hadn't occurred to him not to do this for the sake of other people's reactions. He did as he wanted, and people made room. Some of that sense of entitlement started to rub off on me; I enjoyed the fact that we were taking up room, being guys together, tossing our energy around in people's faces, getting attention. There was exhilaration and potency in Tony, and apparently I could have it too. I barely caught glimpses of the others – Chris watching Tony admiringly, Rachel laughing and clapping, Dennis restless at this interruption of his dance with her, and a few dozen gay people I didn't know looking at Tony's freedom and wondering where he got it. As I took in their looks and smiles, I reflected that the most attention I'd gotten on dance floors in years came from dancing with Rachel at the Renegade and now with Tony. Straight people, I thought: don't leave home without one.

We were standing on the sidewalk at one-thirty, Michael's group breaking off to go back to the guest house. Tony had his hand on Michael's shoulder, a picture of comradeliness, when a red Camaro pulled by. It had flames painted all over its hood and was packed with teen beer-swillers.

For some reason, one of them yelled, "FUCK gays in the military, and FUCK Bill Clinton!" The car slowed, as if they were hoping this provocation would give them an excuse to beat us up. The one who had yelled leaned out of the window now, cords distended on his neck, his shag-cut blond hair matted horribly on his dopey forehead. "And FUCK you faggots!" he screamed.

The whole scene was surreal. It was barely a moment since we'd been saying private and civilized good-byes. I don't think anyone was actually frightened, but we all froze, startled and uncertain how to react. I was glad that Tony was there. He would know how to handle macho bashers: he had the credentials. He would do something virile, practical, and forceful.

He dropped his hand from Michael's shoulder, looking alert. Then he smiled disarmingly at the boy.

"You know, you're kind of *cute* when you're mad," he said. The boy's face turned a sick puce color and he writhed, held back by unseen peers inside the car. The car took off, wheels spinning, several beery voices calling ugly names.

The situation was handled: yes. But I hadn't expected Tony to resort to this kind of campy strategic ditziness. Michael turned to Tony as though he had just slain a giant.

"There's a police car just down the block," Tony shrugged. "I knew they weren't going to try anything." This explanation merely increased the awe of Michael, Chris, Bobby. Clearly they had a new favorite straight man – not just handsome, but an OK guy. I was proud of him. Rachel put her arm through Tony's.

"My Charles Bronson," she said.

As the group divided, Joe came and took my hand. I gave his a squeeze and glanced at Michael, to whom I'd just said a cordial goodnight.

"Do you want to go back with the others?" I asked him, whispering. "I don't want to steal you from them."

"Do you want me to go back?" he asked me. I looked at him. His eyes were veiling defensively. Incredibly, he wasn't sure I wanted him with me; maybe he thought this was my way of telling him to back off. Or was I making that up? We were on the brink of a spiral of second-guessing, and I quickly said, "No, Joe. I want you to come with me. I just don't want to break up your group if..."

"They're OK with this," he said. "That's nice of you.

Maybe tomorrow I'll have lunch with Mother." He smiled at me, looking relieved. He kept surprising me with this touching groundless fear of rejection. I felt a pleasant swell of trust.

"But you'll have breakfast with me," I said.

"Deal," he nodded. So we strolled back through the warm dark streets with Rachel and Tony. I looked over at them at one point and was surprised to see them holding hands and whispering. It was the first time I'd noticed a close physical contact between them all week.

Chapter 8 – Sunday

The sky was still dark; it was the middle of the night. I was only half awake. Joe was next to me, his eyes barely open in the moonlight that rained through the skylight.

"I was dreaming about you," I said; "you were painting." I was still in the dream, really. He was holding a palette. The oils were thick and wet-looking, in plain bright colors, red and yellow and blue and a lot of green. Something about the colors and the fat generous way they were squeezed onto the palette made you happy to look at them. Joe nodded without expression when I told him about my dream, and closed his eyes.

Hours later, I awoke again. He was facing me and seemed to be asleep, his forehead almost touching mine.

"I dreamed about you before," I whispered, "but I forget what you were doing." Without opening his eyes, he took his hand from my shoulder and made dabbing motions in front of my face. "That's right," I murmured. "You were painting."

The sun was up the next time I opened my eyes. Joe's back was to me and I propped myself up to look over his shoulder. He was awake, and smiled at me. His smile triggered no hot passions in me. He was lax and easy as a sunning cat, and rolled over to put an arm around me. I put my hand to his cock and felt it soft as mine; it warmed my hand for a minute while we looked at each other's eyes from an inch away.

"It's still sleeping," I said. "It's cute." He smiled.

"You have pretty eyes," he said. "Pretty blue eyes like a baby's."

A moment later I said, "What happens if we fall in love?" He shrugged and said,

"We deal."

I waited a minute to be sure; then I sighed and said,

"That may be now." He didn't say anything, though his eyes didn't waver from mine. "I mean, for me," I said. He nodded. I would have liked him to say something, but even so his eyes, frankly searching mine, gave me courage. So I pressed it. "How about you?" I asked. He paused for a long time, still looking at me, smiling slightly.

"Getting there," he said finally.

I was so happy I said, "I love you." I hadn't said that to anyone since Angel – nine years now.

He smiled and said, "Thank you."

My mind noticed with distinctness that he hadn't said he loved me, but the thought didn't trouble me. He would not say more than he was sure of.

Rachel tapped discreetly on the door mid-morning.

"Anton's off running errands," she said. "What are you two up to?" I was lying on the sofa with my feet propped on the arm, reading aloud to Joe from his book. He was pinching and watering plants. It would have been pointless to pretend we were real busy.

"Waiting for you to propose something amusing," I said.

She sat at the table and asked for some coffee.

"It's a lovely day," she said. "I was hoping you'd feel like going down to the beach." I glanced at Joe, but without looking at me he said,

"Sure."

Scanning the beach, Joe didn't see Michael's garish red umbrella. His friends apparently hadn't come out yet. Rachel suggested we go sit in the gay section, in case they came looking for him later. As soon as we'd spread out towels, she said she was going swimming.

Joe started to go with her, but she said, "No, no. I'm fine by myself. You stay here and keep Jim company. Save my place." She seemed very happy this morning: untroubled, confident, independent. I don't think it was my imagination that men's eyes, not just mine and Joe's, followed her as she walked down to the water alone.

"Who's that guy you've been seeing recently in Baltimore?" Joe asked me suddenly.

"I haven't been seeing anybody," I said. "I told you, I can't buy a date."

"Who's Peter? You said something about a Peter the other day." I remembered: I'd mentioned something perfectly neutral about Peter's hair color or some remark he'd made. Joe had apparently noticed something in my tone or look. I was impressed by his close reading, but I tried to downplay Peter. He was still a rather tender subject.

"Oh," I said, "we went out a few times. He's a super-nice guy. It was no big deal. He – met someone else."

"Someone you know?" Joe asked.

"No; someone from out of town. I heard about it from a mutual friend before Peter mentioned it."

"Piss you off?"

"No," I said reasonably. "Peter doesn't have to tell me everything he does."

"How long had he been seeing this guy when you found out about it?"

"I don't know; a few weeks, maybe."

"Your mutual friend, who told you – he wasn't dating Peter too, was he?"

"No."

"But Peter told him he'd met someone before he told you. That's fucked up. He should tell a man he's been dating."

"Come on, Joe," I said. "We're adults. There was no commitment there. I still think of Peter as a friend."

"I think of Peter as a creep," Joe said. "And so do you; you just don't admit it. He must have known you liked him – you're not super hard to read on that subject. He should have told you himself. Instead he tells the rest of gay Baltimore and lets you find out on the grapevine." He squinted at the water, following Rachel with his eyes. I put my arm around his shoulders.

"I think it's really sweet of you to be mad about this," I said.

"I'm not mad," he said. "I don't care about Peter either way; I don't know Peter. But he jerked you around. That explains some stuff. He wasn't honest with you."

He was still looking out at the water and, despite his denial, he looked mad. I was pleased that he was angered by an injustice to me. I also realized he was right: Peter hadn't been honest with me, and I had some bad feelings about that.

"He's nice enough, in a namby-pamby way," I said. "He doesn't have to be brave or honest. He's cute and he has a pretty smile. He calls people 'Honey' and hugs everybody; everybody says how nice he is. That's all it takes, I guess." Joe nodded without looking at me. "I told him I'd only want to sleep with him if we fell in love," I said.

"You were honest," he said. Then, for the first time since he'd raised this subject, he smiled and turned to me. "But you fucked me just for the fuck of it? Thanks." He threw his head back and closed his eyes: "'Oh Peter; oh romance!'" he said. Then he made a wanking gesture and opened his eyes a lustful slit. "'Gonna fuck you, Joe, yeah!'" he growled. "Thanks a lot, man." Fortunately, he was laughing.

"I was honest," I said. I laughed too, enjoying his laughter. Then, stroking the nap on the towel, I said, "This morning I was honest again. I told you... something."

"I know," he said. He didn't speak for a while. Then he said, "There are things I'd have to give up. To feel like you do. Like..."

"Tricking?" I asked. "And acting like a sleazy starlet?"

"Yeah," he nodded, refusing to be stung. "Maybe I'll give it up; maybe I'll want to. I don't know. You know I like you, Studly." I smiled at the name.

"Ooh," I said. "I just felt my penis increase in size." He rubbed the seat of his shorts and grimaced: Ouch. It would be hard to describe how gratifying this little joke of his was to me. "Sex came first with you," I continued seriously. "The order was reversed in your case. But I had to know you'd give me that; I don't know why."

"That's what I was gambling on," he said.

"'Gambling'?" I asked. "You mean, you were hoping I'd

fall in love with you eventually? The first night I figured you just wanted to get your rocks off, and for some reason you picked me."

"If I'd just wanted to get my rocks off, I would have done Dennis, or picked somebody up at the bar. I've known you were hot for me for years. But this time around I was gambling you might get to feel more than that." I couldn't stop smiling; Joe had liked me all along. But of course, he'd said that. I just didn't know at first that he always meant what he said.

"Well you've won your point," I said. "Now you know I like you a lot. Now what? You fly away and leave me with a broken heart." I was smiling, joking; somehow the broken heart didn't seem like a real danger.

"Nobody's heart is going to get broken," he said. "We've both won something. We've both gotten something we didn't think we could get." He looked at me and suddenly his face turned modest; his imperturbable coolness, his superior hotness, left him for a moment. "Anyway, I have."

"Joe," I said. I was very touched. "That's nice for me to hear. I... I'm OK about your going back to LA, you know, if you... Of course I wish we lived in the same time zone, but you have your whole life there. You have to go. I know that."

"There's still a week before I go back," he said. "Then there's... there's time after next week too. I mean, you never can tell. Anything can happen. Nobody knows." He blushed suddenly and stopped talking.

"Do you have a kiss for your biggest fan?" I asked him.

"For my Tiger: always."

"Break it up, you two," said Rachel. She was standing over us, wringing her hair and smiling, and we had been absorbed enough not to notice her approach. We smiled up at her, embarrassed, and she sat next to us. "The water's nice today," she said; "almost too warm, though. You should go in." Joe said he wanted to, and I started to get up too. But Rachel put a hand on my arm and asked me to stay. Her smile to Joe was very sweet, an unmistakable dismissal. He said he'd be right back, and headed down to the waves with a little parting salute.

"He's lovely," Rachel said when he was gone. "I like him for you, even more than I thought at first."

"No," I said, "you had him picked out at the bar, even before you saw him; remember?" She was sitting with her knees drawn up to her chin, and threw her head back smiling.

"That's right," she said. "I did, didn't I? But when I first met him I thought he was just a nice sexy man, he'd make you feel better for a while. Now I think he's really very very dear."

"He *is* nice," I said. "I like him. I wish I knew what will happen when he has to go back to LA."

"You've got a week to figure it out," she said. "What does he say?"

"He says he doesn't know."

"That's fair; how could he know?"

"Right," I said. I paused. "This morning I told him I loved him. The words just popped out."

"Good for you," she said, with a sudden proud smile. "Very brave. As usual. What did he say?"

"He said, 'Thank you.'"

"He's so polite," Rachel laughed. "That was it?"

"He said he might be getting there. He's worried about what he'd have to give up; his independence, some of his wildness, I guess." Rachel was nodding. "He didn't say he loved me," I said, testing myself to see if I was disappointed. It had seemed OK at the time, but maybe Rachel would say it was a problem. She would know. Her head was turned towards me, but her eyes went out to sea for a moment.

"Lots of people say 'I love you,' Jim," she said, "and we all know how much it's worth. I'm sure you've heard kind words that didn't mean anything – Let's be friends; You're very special; I'll call you... even: I love you. Joe is telling you something honest and sincere. He's not sure. He's telling you what's true. I think that's very – wonderful." She was right. Angel always said he loved me; Peter always said he'd call.

"Honesty is our theme," I said. "He prides himself on being honest. I'm getting to like that." I smiled again. "He told me he liked me just now. Just before you walked up, he said he's liked me all along."

"Well of course he has. I could see that when he came to lunch the first day. Not to mention when I came out of the water just now and saw you two... well. And he – watches you, you know. He follows you with his eyes. Not exactly that he idolizes you; I don't think he does, actually. But he knows you're there. He takes an interest. You always have his attention. He likes you very much."

We looked and saw Joe walking back up the beach to join us. The sun was still behind him, and his wet skin looked dark and shaggy, except for an outline of blinding Mylar where the light struck his hair and shoulders. His baggy trunks were a rich wet green.

"And, Jim," Rachel added, smiling darkly, her hand on her neck, "he's so attractive."

She smiled at Joe as he approached, then took my book out of her bag and opened it to a page about half way through. She put on her sunglasses to break the glare of the page. She adjusted her towel in such a way that she moved a couple of feet away from me, and at least pretended to get caught up in reading. The surf was very loud. She was giving Joe and me privacy.

After Joe had dried off, he sat behind me, his knees to either side of me. He put his arms around my waist and pulled me back against him. He felt as solid as a brick wall, and I relaxed and let myself lean back and rest on him. I was conscious of his hands on my stomach and wished it were tighter. Maybe he read my mind because he gave me a couple of proprietary pats and made a faint private growling noise in my ear, imitating me – his tiger. If a little slackness in my waist didn't bother Joe, I supposed it shouldn't bother me either. My old instincts made me wonder for a moment if this rather intimate scene was embarrassing Rachel. Of course I'd sat next to her and Tony often enough while they held hands or embraced, and never once called the vice squad on them. With no reason in the world to think she disapproved or felt uncomfortable, I still felt that Joe was outing me, and in a way I liked the feeling. I felt like a gay militant staging a kiss-in on the White House lawn. When I glanced over at Rachel, she just looked up from her reading and gave us a fond motherly smile.

"*Sei il mio ragazzo?*" I asked Joe, leaning back to whisper.

He frowned.

"No," he said. "*Ragazzo* is going around breaking things and killing together."

"It just means 'boy' or 'boyfriend,'" I said, surprised. "You're my boy, aren't you?"

"Read the book," he answered. "Every time two guys are *ragazzi* together, they're being ignorant jocks, getting violent, showing off for each other. It's the kind of male bonding stuff you hate and make fun of." This was startling. He was right, in that book at least. Hot Italian boys always had their arms around each other in public. Like most gay Anglo observers, I nurtured choice fantasies that they were hotly engaged in private too, though the sociologist in me knew that Latin male bonding was both highly passionate and fervently homophobic. Still I'd always liked to indulge my fantasy in Joe's book, and think of all the *ragazzi* in it as boyfriends, crypto-homos. Joe's reading was far more accurate.

"You got me," I said. "You're right."

"Now I can write my book," he said. He left a little time and then went on. "I think part of you wants to be *ragazzi* with Tony. He's your whole normal-boy fantasy. You want to hang out with him and have him think you're one of the boys. I don't think you really want him to be your boyfriend." I felt a slight shiver from a sudden gust of wind across my sun-hot skin. I mildly resented Joe's suggested psychoanalysis, but he was at least part right. Rachel too, I remembered, had maintained that Tony and I would not be well-matched as lovers. I didn't say anything.

After a moment, Joe gave me a sudden shake.

"And no, I'm not your *boy*," he said. I could hear the smile in his voice. He had his arms tight around me, and rocked me rather fiercely once or twice, tussling nicely. He started to say something, and hesitated, sorting words out in his mind. "*Sono il tuo uomo,*" he brought out after a moment. His voice was shy and slightly higher than usual with the hesitancy of speaking a foreign language.

"My MAN!" I said, laughing. "Scared of YOU!" I twisted to smile at him.

"*Non devi avere paura di me,*" he said. "*Perché...*" He paused. "How do you say it?" he asked. "Not '*Ti amo.*' That's too poetic, I remember." My face prickled. I squirmed enough that he released me and let me turn to face him.

"You can say *ti amo,*" I said. "Or sometimes they say *ti voglio bene.* 'I care for you,' something like that. It's kind of borderline family/friend/lover talk." He cocked his head back and smiled.

"That's right," he said. "That's what my parents say. '*Te vojo bene assai.*'" I took his hands and looked down at the towel between us. I didn't want to have to ask him to say it again, to be sure he was saying it to me. He pulled my hands up to his chest and spoke into my ear. "*Ti voglio bene assai.*"

I wondered what to say. I could feel my face turning hot, my breath suddenly very shallow. Something was going on inside me that was totally private, a little storm of feeling that I couldn't define, that was more like flustered nervousness than joy. Yet I knew it was joy. I couldn't remember ever feeling it before, but I recognized it. I said, "*Grazie.*" I turned around again and he put his arms back around me. Even looking at Joe seemed too dangerous for the new fragile feeling I had.

Joe called out to Rachel over my shoulder.

"Rachel," he said, "I just told Jim I love him." I laughed incredulously and felt completely foolish. That was an absurd thing for him to say, an intrusion on Rachel, a violation of my pride and of our privacy. Yet Joe's voice was distinctly proud, and after my first shock of embarrassment I knew I was proud too. Rachel turned to us and lifted her sunglasses. I hoped she wouldn't say anything too sentimental. Her face expressed plain acknowledgement, no surprise. I wondered what I had been afraid of in her reaction.

"You'd be very foolish not to," she said to Joe. "Good. Now that's settled." Then she put her glasses back and looked down at the book again.

By lunch time the others from the guest house had joined us, and I encouraged Joe to go off with Michael for a sandwich in town. Rachel and I met up with Tony at the house and I made pesto for lunch. Rachel told Tony about Joe's little declaration on the beach, smiling knowingly and enjoying making me blush. There was something very freeing about the whole conversation. Certain kinds of validation could only come from straight people, apparently. Rachel and Tony's thirteen-year marriage gave a kind of legitimacy to this new attachment of mine. They'd often shown a polite interest in my dates over the years, but this was more gratifying. Even their teasing and needling was pleasant – I knew it was the way they teased and needled friends who got engaged, friends they fixed up together, whatever. I could imagine taking Joe home to Mom when the time came, based on the easy approving banter Tony and Rachel were lavishing on me now. So by mid-afternoon, not having heard anything from Joe, I went looking for him. I felt very grown-up and very secure.

On the beach I found Chris and Bobby. I laughed at Bobby's baggy T-shirt, inscribed, "You're an actor? Which restaurant?" I asked where the others were. Michael had gone off with his family, they said, after his lunch with Joe. They thought Joe might have gone back to the guest house to crash; Dennis they'd lost track of. He might be off tricking, Bobby thought. A boy had been hitting on him that morning.

"Have you seen Gene today?" Chris asked me casually. I shook my head.

"He may have made plans with his friend Cybil," I said. I hadn't actually seen Cybil yet and still wasn't sure who he was, but Chris said he'd seen Cybil by herself a few minutes before, eager to show his familiarity with Gene's friends. "Then I have no clue," I said. "He could be here; he could be there. Gene is a law unto himself." At the very back of my mind, I noticed the ghost of an apprehension that Gene and Joe were unaccounted for at the same time. Chris was about to ask me something. He put a casual expression on his face in preparation and I assumed he wanted to pump me about Gene.

Just then two boys came bouncing up. One of them, a slight youth with blunt-cut blond hair, hurled himself on Bobby, knocking him back on the towel, kissing him and shrieking, then in a flash sat up frostily and turned his back to him.

Bobby smiled, a surprising butch smile, and said, "Where you been GIRL!" while the boy tossed his head coldly. I looked at Chris, hoping for an explanation, but he was engaged in talk with the other boy, a whitish redhead, bearded like a Trotskyite, in beach sandals and a tight knee-length striped suit with shoulder straps. The boy suddenly stuck his tongue into Chris' mouth in mid-sentence, then just as suddenly swooned across Chris' lap, lolling like Cleopatra. A moment more and he was sitting up, suggesting in businesslike tones that they all go swimming. The flirtations of the young were becoming increasingly difficult for me to decipher. I found now that I wasn't all that interested either. So I got Chris' grudging attention just long enough to get the address of the guest house, and walked back to the driveway to get my car. All these days, I realized, I hadn't even asked to see where Joe and his friends were staying. I should show a friendly interest in his life: he'd certainly been more than generous in finding ways to fit into mine. And I liked the idea of surprising him during his nap.

The guest house was an elderly white clapboard building with six apartments on three floors, just off the main strip leading out of town. It was identified by a cracked glass sign pointing from the highway down the side street to the driveway, and stood in a dusty lot with a few depressed bushes trying to grow in the sand. I'd expected a cute little cottage and was disappointed. It was fairly creepy – not quite the motel in *Psycho*, but a few years behind on maintenance. It wasn't hard to picture local redneck children bringing their dates here for quick bangs during the off-season. I wondered if Michael's family had booked it for him; I couldn't imagine a chic coterie of LA trend queens taking it on purpose. Maybe economics had something to do with the choice, I thought more fairly. I'd almost forgotten about money, staying with Tony and Rachel. Air conditioners were running crankily in a couple of windows. The ocean breeze didn't carry this far, and it was noticeably hotter than on the beach. No wonder Joe preferred staying with me. I went up the outdoor stairs and knocked at a second-floor apartment.

Joe took a minute to answer.

"Hey," he said smiling when he opened, and stepped out to join me on the balcony. He was sweating freely in spite of the stale cool draft that came with him out of the air-conditioned apartment. He was wearing only his trunks. They were bunched a little awkwardly, clinging to his damp legs as though he'd just pulled them on. He put his arms around me, and it pleased me to notice that I recognized his scent and felt welcomed by it. It was that slight trace of salt and soil, nothing musky about it, that I'd noticed when we first had sex.

"Show me the place," I said after we kissed.

"Can't, yet," he said. "Hey: Tiger." He sounded nervous, stalling. "Dennis is in there." I felt an absurd relief that Gene wasn't with him.

"Oh; Bobby and Chris thought he was off tricking with some boy in town."

"No, he's been here," Joe said.

"So shouldn't I say Hi?" I asked. He looked down; he looked up.

"He's nude," he said. I laughed at the word.

"So were you, until a second ago," I said, tugging on the twisted waistband of his trunks. I was smiling. He shrugged, smiling too, relieved.

"Sex happens," he said.

Incredibly, until that moment, I hadn't understood what he was saying. I must have had some picture of two naked buddies napping together dormitory-style in a kind of Herb Ritts *faux* innocence. Now there was a sudden heat in my face and I turned away instantly so he couldn't see it. I looked down at my car as though there were something interesting about seeing it from above. I heard Joe shuffle behind me. He put his hand tentatively on my back.

"It wasn't all that," he said. "It just happened. Dennis and me... it's like that. You're not upset." That should have been a question, but it was a statement. Apparently Joe was sure I wasn't upset.

"No!" I said, trying a laugh. "Maybe I'll see you tonight." I was still looking away from him. I started down the stairs.

"Where are you going?" he asked, sounding surprised. "You just got here. Don't you want to see the place? You want to hang out?"

"You're busy," I said. "I'll come back some other time." I didn't recognize my own voice: I sounded like a hip cold modern socialite, Pat Buckley or someone like that. "Call me." I still hadn't looked at Joe and I was afraid that my face was still red. Hopefully he'd just go back inside and wouldn't notice. The stairs seemed very steep now and I put my hand on the wooden railing as I went down. There was some slimy condensation on it and I got a green smear on my hand and quickly rubbed it off on my old chinos. I was standing at my car door fumbling to get the key in the lock when I forced myself to look up at the balcony; I thought I could manage a quick nod or wave. Joe was halfway down the stairs, bouncing from side to side with each heavy step. He wasn't running and didn't seem to mean to catch up with me; he was just trailing after me looking confused.

"You're going," he said. "You don't want a Coke or something." Still his voice was flat and declarative. I didn't want a Coke. I was going.

"No thanks," I said, smiling cheerfully. "Really. Uh – call me some time." That sounded like a blow-off. "Tonight. Whenever. I can come back."

"You're really doing this," he said, sounding dazed. "You're just standing there lying, and then you're going to drive away." I still hadn't managed to get the key in the lock. Now I was angry.

"'Lying'? I am lying?" I repeated, amazed at his nerve. I took the whole keychain and threw it at him, hard, across the roof of the car. It hit him in the chest and fell. He flinched slightly, not hurt, and just looked at me.

"There," he said.

I turned away from him and leaned against the car door. I felt like an idiot. I had no way to get into the car now and get away without talking to him. After a few moments I heard the keys jingle. He must have stooped to pick them up. Turning, I saw him coming around to me, mincing slightly on the bits of sharp gravel scattered in the hot sand lot.

"You can go if you want to," he said, holding my keys out to me. Again I barely caught his scent, and it desolated me in an instant. I wasn't sure I could stand, let alone drive. I didn't say anything, so he reached forward gently and put the keys in my pants pocket. Then he leaned next to me, close but not touching, waiting for me to speak. The apartment door opened behind us and we turned automatically to face it.

Dennis was standing there, leaning around the door-frame from inside to hide his nakedness. He seemed surprised to see me.

"Hey guy," he said, waving casually with his usual lovely smile.

"Hi Dennis," I said, my voice surreal to my own ears. "What's up?"

"Not a whole hell of a lot," he answered pleasantly. "Joe, you taking off?" Joe glanced at me uncertainly.

"Not sure," he called up to Dennis over his shoulder. Then, "Yeah," he said. "Jim. Give me two minutes to get my shoes and a shirt. I'll come with you. Don't just go." I didn't answer. "Two minutes," he said. "Please."

I put my head down, unable to look at him. He backed away, one hand out, making a Quiet gesture as though I were a child he was afraid of waking. "Two minutes," he repeated, and went up the stairs. I didn't look, but I could barely hear Dennis hiss "Shit, man" to him, and a quick concerned exchange of whispers, before the door closed.

I hadn't moved when he came back; I'm not sure I'd breathed. He had been very quick and I appreciated that. He stood at the passenger door waiting for me to get in and unlock it for him.

"Hey," he said, reminding me. I looked up and he saw that I was crying. "No," he said sadly, and came around to me. "No," he said, sounding incompetent, "you're not crying." He put both arms around my shoulders. My arms were dangling

224

and it was awkward. He was kissing my forehead and my hair and kept repeating that I wasn't crying. This went on for a while. I felt his arms and smelled him and heard him, but made no move to embrace him.

"Take it inside, OK?" came an irritated voice from one of the first floor apartments. "We got kids in here."

"Why don't you just pull the shades like a normal person?" Joe shouted, furious and stubborn. I could feel the vibration of his shout in his arms. "This is important." There was muttering from inside and the sound of venetian blinds dropping. "I'll drive, OK?" Joe asked me, his voice oddly crooning. I nodded and handed him the keys without meeting his eye.

When we were in the car, I said,

"Careful shifting into third." Then I looked out the window and didn't say anything till we were in town.

On the main street a few blocks before our turn-off, we saw Gene walking with someone. I recognized Patrick, an older friend of his who did interior decorating. He was slim and elegant and had fits of madcap Cole Porter charm. Cybil, I thought: I'd never connected the name with Patrick. Joe slowed down enough to honk, and we all waved. Gene gave us a beck-on, but I rolled down the window and called,

"Can't stop, dear. On a mission." He nodded, held one fist to his ear, and pointed to his watch: Call me later. With a sick chuckle, I remembered that I'd been afraid earlier that Joe might be off with Gene.

"I'm scared of *you*, now," Joe said as I rolled the window back up. "You're the smoothest liar I've ever heard. You sounded perfectly natural with him just now."

"I *was* perfectly natural," I said. "If you thought I wouldn't be I'm not sure why you honked. Maybe you think it would be more honest if I cried in front of my friends and made a scene." My voice in the car was low and deadly. It took an incredible amount of energy just to get sound out. There'd been a quick surge of adrenalin to get through the brief interchange with Gene, but it was used up.

"That's not fair," he said.

"Sue me," I said. I looked out the window again in silence until we got to the house. We got out of the car and Joe let us into the studio without speaking. I went and stood by the balcony door, looking out at the water. The day had turned grey, almost a welcome respite from the steady sun we'd had all week. The waves were high and dark.

"I'm putting your keys here on the counter," he said politely from the kitchenette. Then I heard him open the refrigerator and pop a beer can open. "Come here," he said, sitting in his usual spot in the crook of the sofa's arm and patting the seat beside him. He put the can of beer on the floor by his feet. I sat and he put his arm around my shoulder. He pulled me closer and I laid my head against his chest while he kissed my hair and made funny mournful humming noises I hadn't heard before. His shirt was open in front. I had one hand on his chest, tugging absently at his hair. He smelled good and his skin was warm against my face. Against my will I began to feel something for the first time since I'd understood that he'd been having sex with Dennis. It was a safe feeling, a feeling of reassurance. I'd have preferred to feel rage and follow it up with hatred, but that wasn't happening.

"I hurt your feelings," he said. "I'm sorry I hurt your feelings." My eyes started to get wet again. I couldn't hold on to Joe; he could get away in a moment, his wonderful warm chest pressed to someone else, a stranger, a friend.

"Have you... ?" I asked him. I stopped because I wasn't sure what question I meant to ask. I didn't know what words to put to the shapeless doubts I felt.

"Have I what?" he asked. I remembered him saying "*Ti voglio bene assai*" on the beach and I felt cold, but I said,

"Nothing."

After a while he said,

"I thought this was part of the deal. I never said this wouldn't happen." That was true, but I hated it.

"Today you said other things you never said," I said.

"I meant it today. I told you I love you." He made a sad sighing noise, perplexed. "Then I hurt your feelings."

"Is this it?" I asked. "It's always like this. You just go off and do it with whoever, and I just understand and get over it."

"Dennis and I just kind of naturally... it's like a habit," he said. "It's not that big of a deal." I shook my head: I don't buy that; it IS a big deal. "He was really sorry, by the way. He was embarrassed." I didn't care how Dennis felt and I shrugged. Then Joe made a sudden "Hmm," as though he'd just understood something. "It scares you," he said. I nodded, surprised. That was exactly it. I wasn't enraged or even hurt precisely; I was scared. "It doesn't mean I'm dropping you, you know," he said. "You're not losing me. It's just... "

"It feels like that," I said. "It feels like you're not paying attention, you're not concentrating. You're not putting your energy into really being with me. You just drift into things, and you forget all about me. Did you think about me at all when you were with Dennis today?"

"No. I didn't think about anything." He sounded almost irritated. "I didn't expect him to come back to the apartment. He came in and I was lying there, and it just happened. Like it's happened a million times with us. We're not lovers; we just... screw sometimes. It's always been like that." A wave of disapproval and fear was flowing from me and I knew Joe could feel it. "Actually, I guess I did think of you." He had just remembered this. "I was asleep when Dennis came in and when I heard him, before I woke up and knew who he was, I said 'Tiger.' He kidded me about it. I thought, This is the first time I've made it with anybody else since I first made it with Jim."

"The better part of three days," I said. "Wow."

"Don't be a prick. You asked me if I thought of you. I did."

"Thank you very much." I paused. "Well, at least Michael will be happy. He wants you to end up with Dennis."

"No." Joe sounded startled. "He just told me at lunch I should marry you. I wasn't expecting that, but he said it."

A feeling of gratitude and friendliness towards Michael came to me unbidden. It couldn't have been totally easy for him to encourage Joe to go forward with me. I knew he cared about Joe and he must have decided, even in spite of himself, that I was good for him.

"He likes you," Joe said. Then, honesty asserting itself, he amended that to, "Actually, he likes Tony, and he figures you must be a nice guy if you're Tony's best friend."

"Right," I said. "Sidekick of the straight vigilante. I'm so important. Thanks." Joe shrugged in exasperation.

"This isn't worth it," he said.

"Us going out?"

"Is that what you think?" He sounded uncertain and unhappy.

"What were you going to say?" I asked him quietly, backing down. I was learning not to escalate with Joe. "What's not worth it? Don't ask me what I think; just tell me what you were thinking." His face smoothed and he said,

"It's not worth making you upset like this. You're not the man I like being with when you're all threatened and scared like this." 'Threatened' made me sound pathetic and I resented it.

"My fault, naturally," I said. "Of course I should learn to behave better when you trick around."

"That's what I mean – all that tough sarcastic talk." He sighed. "I give up."

I thought he meant he was giving up on me, or on us. I wasn't able to make myself grieve. It was very comfortable on his chest, and if this was the last time, I didn't have the energy to end it. Maybe we'd stay together forever, even though we'd broken up, if I just didn't move.

"You're going to scare me into monogamy," he said at last. "I don't like this tension. I want it to be like on the beach today." This wasn't at all what I'd been bracing for. I raised my head just enough to look up at him for a moment. He put his hand on my head and pushed it back down. We lay for a few minutes without speaking. Several times Joe took sudden short breaths as though he were about to speak, but then didn't. I could hear him thinking. Then he had it.

"'Lay your sleeping head, my love, human on my faithless arm,'" he said. Slowly I began to smile, relaxing on him thankfully. "'Time and fevers...'" His voice trailed off: "'Da da da da...'" He forgot the words. "'... But to me the entirely beautiful.'" He was proud of the last tag and, finally, I put my arms around him and hugged him hard.

"'Grave the vision Venus sends,'" I said. "'Da da da da... Find the mortal world enough. Da da.'" He laughed; I felt the rattle right against my ear.

"You're my love," he said. The odd poetic phrase made me smile again. Then abruptly I sat up and pounded on his chest, rather hard, with both fists. He grimaced, looking wary.

"Don't think for a minute you can pull this cuddle-and-Auden thing on a regular basis," I said. "Quoting poetry to melt my heart. I only fall for that tired trick just once in a very *very* long while."

"So noted," he nodded. He was relieved that my pummeling his chest was meant in good humor. He reached down to pick up the beer and took a hit from it before holding it for me to sip from. "How long till dinner?" he asked.

"A couple of hours anyway. It's not even five yet."

"Are you going down or are they coming up?"

"We haven't discussed it. I was waiting to see what your plans were. Maybe they should come up; we haven't done dinner up here yet."

"I could make spaghetti," he said. "My mom's shortcut version." I nodded. There was plenty of time to let Rachel know, plenty of time to run out for supplies, plenty of time to call Gene and make arrangements for afterwards. "You sleepy?" Joe asked. "I could doze off here. I mean..." He broke off, embarrassed.

"You mean you were interrupted before," I said coldly. "You missed out on some of your Z-ration. There's no guarantee that won't happen here."

"That's a risk I'll just have to take, then," he said evenly, and closed his eyes.

Chapter 9 – Monday

The next morning Joe and I looked at the cupboard and found it dull. I said we should go downstairs and pester Rachel into making us something stylish for breakfast. We caught a glimpse of her and Tony through the glass door of the kitchen before we knocked. They were standing in the doorway from the kitchen into the living room, sipping coffee and looking through the house to the water. She had her head on his shoulder. Joe looked at me, eyebrows up.

"It's happening," I said. "Remember how they held hands coming back from the Strand the other night?"

"Yeah," he said. "That's nice." We knocked discreetly, they turned and saw us and came to the door smiling, and we stated our demand.

"The plagues of Egypt," she laughed. "Come on in."

"You boys have me badly outnumbered here," she said as we four sat sipping coffee on the porch after breakfast. It was quite true that the addition of Joe created some kind of critical mass on the male side of the equation. "Thank God Marie is coming; she can back me up if you all get out of hand. Although she'll have Walter and Ricardo with her too, come to think of it, won't she? Too bad Clare won't be coming."

"Tell us about their kids," Tony asked. Rachel smiled. He was showing a new friendly interest in children. So I told them about Jos and Hildie.

"And how's the little weasel?" he asked me. I smiled. I'd never quite known how Tony came to fasten this name on

Ricardo, but Ricardo loved it and in an odd way it suited him.

"He's the wonder of the age," I said. It wasn't easy for me to say how or what Ricardo was. When I first knew him, I simply thought he was the most beautiful boy I'd ever seen, and there were a few rough times when I thought I might be jealous of Walter for bagging him. Early on, though, I discovered to my own surprise that lust was really no part of what I felt for him. He inspired a strange cautious tenderness in me: Marie always said he was my child in an earlier incarnation.

"His business is going very well," I said, thinking that was the kind of thing one could say. "He opened up a florist shop two years ago," I explained to Rachel. "It's brought out this whole efficient magisterial side of him we'd never seen. He runs that place the way Imelda ran the Philippines: never a hair out of place, never raising his voice. He's a grown-up now, I guess, amazing as it seems."

"And he and Walter get along?" she asked. "I was happy when I heard Walter had found someone; he can be difficult, I know. Wonderful, of course, but difficult."

"Walter is just in awe of Ricardo," I said. "It's like being married to… I don't know: say St. Teresa of Avila had borne a child to Dionysios…"

"Is there anything special I should know about his diet – things he should or shouldn't have?" Rachel asked.

"He'll bring his juicer," I said. "He'll run it himself, and under no circumstances should you ask what he's doing or why. A single question and he'll subject us to hours of lectures on the medicinal properties of sprouts and beets. Otherwise he'll eat whatever we do – maybe a few anchovy pizzas and Twinkies thrown in."

"I'm looking forward to meeting him," she said. "Anton always smiles when he talks about Ricardo. He must be a lot of fun."

"Pretty boy, too" Joe said. I'd shown him pictures of some of the principal players. "Sexy."

"Unbelievable," I said. "Heartstopping. Though I don't think of him as sexy, exactly. Of course, it would be incest in a way: he's married to my best gay friend – so married. But it's also just the way he is. He puts out lots of affection, but he doesn't put out hotness. Part of it is, he just isn't looking. He and Walter don't even look at other..." Joe looked at the floor abruptly, and I stopped. I hadn't meant to make unflattering comparisons; I was just answering.

"You're going to love him," Tony told Rachel. Joe turned back to face me, though I didn't meet his eye. Tony looked at him and said,

"Big weekend coming up for you, isn't it, Joe? You're meeting the family." Joe took a moment before he returned Tony's look; then he just nodded and said,

"Pressure."

"Oh no, Joe," said Rachel. "I know Walter; he's very easy to make friends with. And I'll be meeting Marie and Ricardo myself, so you and I will be in it together. I'm sure they'll all like you just as much as we do." She thought a moment. "Maybe we should have a party while they're all here, and invite all your friends from Baltimore and California. Would that be fun? Gene and who else, Jim? And Michael and Bobby and... and Chris and... oh, I can't believe I'm forgetting his name, that nice young man I danced with the other evening." Now I was the one who looked down.

"That's Dennis," said Joe, reaching to pat my elbow. "Great old buddy of mine. Sure, that'd be super." Joe's pat was meant to reassure me, and I smiled at him a little weakly. Tony was looking at me closely. I had told him who Dennis was when we were in the water together a few days before and I knew he didn't approve of Joe's friendship with him. I tried not to look nervous. There was no point in avoiding Dennis or mentions of Dennis.

"Guess what?" Joe asked me.

"Uh – " I tried to guess.

"Time to go catch some rays," he said, standing up. Why ask Guess what? I shook my head and he started gathering up the plates and empty coffee mugs.

"I'll come with you," I said. As Joe stepped into the house just ahead of me, Tony put his hand up to stop me.

"What's all this with Dennis?" he asked.

"You're too sharp," I said, looking quickly to make sure Joe was out of earshot. I hesitated. "I think it's OK. I'll tell you about it later. You two want to join us?" They looked at each other and nodded.

"You go on ahead," said Rachel. "We'll catch up."

Joe and I found Dennis lying by himself under the red umbrella reading "People" magazine. He sat up very suddenly when Joe spoke his name, and his eyes darted for an instant before he greeted me with a simple Hey. He was wearing a bulky T-shirt and baggy shorts that came down past his knees.

It was a stylish enough combo, but almost matronly for Dennis, concealing more of him than anything he'd worn since I'd met him. It was unusual too to see him out of the sun, though when I asked him about it he reminded me that I'd commented on his burn two evenings before. Modestly dressed, and without his glossy cool, he was again what Rachel had called him, a nice young man, the one I'd seen for a moment as he danced with her. Joe squatted next to him and cracked his knuckles nervously, bouncing slightly on his toes. The pose suggested he was just stopping for a moment to say Hi and didn't mean to stay. Dennis too was visibly uneasy, hardly looking at Joe. The tension between them was palpable. They looked like kids confused by arbitrary adult expectations. I felt like some mean grown-up about to tell Dennis that he and Joe couldn't play together anymore.

"Where's Mother?" Joe asked. Michael hadn't come out today, Dennis answered; his family had dragged him off again. I tried for a moment to picture the interactions between fat bedizened Michael and his Eastern Shore relatives. Chris and Bobby, Dennis said, were in the water. Looking out over the blazing breakers, we could see them after a moment, tossing a beach ball over the heads of several entranced men who rocketed up out of the waves by turns to try to catch it. Chris was laughing, and once I'd identified him by sight I found I could pick his voice out of the jumble of sound. A muscular man, his chest-hair grey, slipped behind him and grabbed him around the waist, tossing him under the next wave. As they resurfaced, Chris was sputtering and laughing, and the man kissed him. Chris didn't seem to mind; the kiss lasted a few unhurried seconds. Evidently he was recovering from any disappointment he may have felt about Gene. The scene was distant and distinct, pristine almost, like a miniature perfectly captured in a paperweight. It had a fragility and prettiness one would be ashamed to smash. It was, in a sense, Joe's and Dennis' world.

"Hey Joe," I said. "You go play with the boys. We'll join you in a minute." Joe looked at me uncertainly, but went. When he was gone, Dennis turned to me and looked me frankly in the eye for the first time.

"So," he said.

"Yes," I said. "The first thing I want to say is that I'm fine and I don't blame anybody for what happened. Joe and I have talked about it and we're fine." He looked a little puzzled, but nodded and said, "Great." We sat for a minute and I wondered why I didn't feel completely relaxed. I'd made my little speech and I ought to feel relief and resolution. Maybe Dennis had expected me to say something else, or maybe there was something he meant to say himself and I'd cut him off. Glancing at his profile as he looked fixedly at the water, I seemed to see a little disappointment.

"So how are you?" I asked him. It seemed like a polite question, although I couldn't think of any reason he would be anything but OK – except, come to think of it, that now he would have to give up his spur-of-the-moment tumbles with Joe.

"I guess we won't be getting it on now," he said, looking at his knees.

"Joe told me he was willing to try monogamy," I said. "He intends not to pick up other men from now on." That seemed a little cold. "Of course you've been much more to him than that. I know you're close, and that won't change. I promise I'll do my best to make sure of that."

"That's nice," he said, smiling tightly, squinting or frowning around his eyes. "Joe and I are good buddies. I know that. I wasn't talking about Joe." He paused, watching my reaction, and said, "You're blushing." Now I looked down, and he reached to pat my leg. "It's OK, buddy," he said. "Don't worry about it." He paused again, and then added slyly, "Tiger." I laughed without looking up and he continued. "Joe called me that, did he tell you? He thought I was you when I first came in. He's got you on the brain."

"Joe," I said, shaking my head, not knowing what to say.

"He's a great guy," Dennis agreed. "He's wanted this for as long as I've known him. I'm not going to get in his way. I really hope he can swing it."

"'Swing it'?" I asked. "Meaning?"

"It's not his usual m.o.," he answered. "One guy. But if he says he's up for it, he'll give it the old college try, I guess. He wants you to like him."

I love him," I said. I looked up at him now, feeling shy.

"Oh, 'love'..." he said, considering it. He started to fidget. "Listen," he said, and stopped, biting his lower lip. "Listen," he repeated after a bit. "You've got to give Joe his turns at bat. Guy like that..." I took a long minute to wonder what he meant. Seeing my face, he explained. "He says you fuck him." I looked down again. "Which is great," he went on. "Which is normal. But Joe has got the greatest cock in the world. And he has to feel like a star, or he'll die."

238

"Has he complained to you?" I asked, feeling a hot pulse of embarrassment in my chest.

"No; he doesn't have to. I could tell yesterday. It wasn't great. His confidence is way down. He's lost his initiative. I was like: Dude!" He made a vague wide gesture with both hands. I smiled inside, but hoped Dennis didn't see it. Maybe Joe's heart wasn't in it now, with Dennis. "Joe's nightmare is you won't respect him. He may go along with stuff to make you happy, to keep your approval. He wants you to think he knows how to act, like he's good to you. But if you turn him into a boy toy, you're the loser. Joe is a lover."

I was touched by this, and I nodded despite my embarrassment. Joe was only a few yards away, in the surf, but I missed him. I wanted to show him that I did respect him, that to me he would always be a star. The undertow of failure he felt in his life in LA was something he must never feel in my arms.

Dennis looked out at the water, and said regretfully, "God, his cock." Then he turned to me. "What say we join the others, Tiger?" I smiled at him.

"Don't call me that, OK?" I said. Dennis could tell from my face that I wasn't putting him down, and he grinned back at me.

"You ARE in love, pal," he said. "OK." We got up and shed our T-shirts and pants and sunglasses.

As we headed down to the water, Dennis suddenly stopped and touched my elbow. I stopped too and faced him.

"I never said I'm sorry," he said to me. "I started it yesterday. I didn't know what your story was with Joe. I won't do that again." His sharp American face was glowing with the sun;

he was like a magazine cover, candid and good-natured.

"Thanks," I said, and patted his shoulder. "It never happened, OK?"

By late morning, we were all gathered around the umbrella. Gene and Patrick had joined us, and Chris was lounging nearby, looking in all directions but Gene's with conspicuous nonchalance. Bobby and Patrick were hitting it off and Bobby had taken to the Cybil name gleefully.

"Call me Vanna," he said, striking a pose and then laying his head for an instant on Patrick's shoulder. He kept flouncing and preening, tapping Patrick's forearm with his fingertips and calling him Sister. Patrick, the most elegant smoker I'd ever known, held his cigarette like the jutting bowsprit of a clipper ship and went along with the sister-talk, nodding and winking at Bobby from beneath his remarkable arched brows. Bobby didn't seem to notice – or perhaps he saw with crystal clarity – that Patrick could be ferociously manly when the occasion warranted. He was in his mid-fifties, and he put together a thriving decorating business back in the years when icy gay elegance was less respected than it had since become. He had won head-ramming contests with the stubbornest macho contractors and most intransigent socialites in Baltimore. Yet he showed every sign of enjoying Bobby's studied fey energy. If Bobby ever decided to do something other than wait tables, I thought, he might actually turn out something like Patrick. Patrick held a sharp focus on Bobby, both fond and calculating. I could tell he would strike sooner or later, translating sisterhood into something sweatier if possible. Bobby could do a great deal worse.

Joe and I meanwhile were enjoying something neither of us had much experience with: being in love among friends. He was sitting and reading his book. I had a hard time settling down in one spot. I kept wanting to touch him and tried at various times to sit beside him, to hold his hand, to lay my head in his lap, to embrace him. He smiled and called me a pest, and finally I quieted down, sitting beside him and sifting the hot dry sand through my fingers. I became fascinated with its feel in my hand and for a while I stopped even looking at Joe. In a way he was almost invisible to me. My mind was taken up with a kind of cloud or vapor called Lover that had formed in me over the years. Joe himself was blurred by this vision. He was a presence I was just learning to recognize and associate with certain kinds of shelter, warmth, and worry. I enjoyed being with him, yet felt shy and unused to him. He was sitting still and so he seemed more certain, more settled than me. Yet when I caught his eye I saw something like what I was feeling myself – something vague and archetypal in the eyes that looked past mine even as they met them. The others glanced at us occasionally and smiled with patient amusement.

Rachel and Tony were with us now; it was almost lunch-time. Gene had come over to sit with Joe and the Neubergs and me, tired of witnessing Patrick's slow seduction of Bobby and of absorbing Chris' pointed neglect. Gene and I agreed to take a walk and have lunch together. He said firmly that it would be good for Joe and me to take a break from each other and in my distracted infatuation I decided he was right. Joe agreed too, and Rachel insisted he join her and Tony at the house.

"We're going to poison his mind against you, Jimbo," Tony said. "We'll tell him about all your disgusting habits." Rachel swatted his arm and told him to hush.

As we were starting to stir, two men walked past us heading for a clear spot on the sand. At first glance it looked like a young man and his wasted and doddering grandfather. The young man was rigorously built up, toned to the verge of caricature, and wore very showy bikini trunks and some well-chosen gold around his neck. He had a moustache, in the style of the late Seventies, and on second glance it was hard to decide just how old he was. His precise handsome face was intent and respectful as he guided the old man by one elbow and slowed his own steps to match his shuffle. Over one shoulder he carried a large bag. Protruding from it I could see the usual beach stuff as well as a quantity of high-tech medical equipment. It wasn't clear to me why this exemplary muscle-queen would appear in public with such a very elderly friend or relative. I hated to think he was a hustler. It might be that he felt it would enhance his mystique to be seen with this old man: people would have to think he was kind and patient as well as hot.

Glancing at the old man, I was surprised to notice that he wore a gold chain around his neck that looked very similar to his younger friend's. He had practically no hair left, and what he had was as fair and fine as a child's. At its ends it still showed a lifeless brown color, as if it had grown out and faded after a bad tinting job. Incongruously, he too had a moustache, a rather pitiful vestige of masculinity in a face and body which had withered almost to nothing. His color was a sickly grey. I couldn't decide if the brilliant sun would be good for him or if it would just finish him off. His movements were frail and fussy. He gestured fretfully forward, and his massive companion hovered by him and pressed him gently in the direction he wanted to go. Two brash boys brushed roughly past them, not noticing them at first and then apologizing, with a politeness that belied their hard bar-boy looks, to the younger man. The old man just whinnied, apparently laughing appreciatively, and the young man nodded and smiled gravely, acknowledging the boys' apology with a look and then joining in his friend's laughter. They had moved several yards in several minutes.

Gene had been trying to place why he recognized the younger man without staring at him. After several sideways glances, he suddenly hissed to me,

"It's Steven; my God." He took my arm in a strong grip and squeezed it till I was about to ask him to stop. "That must be Al with him."

"Who are they?" I asked.

"Those two lovers from Washington," he said. "You know them; you met them at the last fundraiser at my house. Steven works on the Hill and you argued with him about the election." Now that he mentioned it, I did remember. Steven's generic clone face hadn't registered on my memory, but I recalled a confident conservative in a grey flannel suit who had dampened my initial attraction to him considerably by his ridiculous views on why we should all support Bush – something about Barbara lighting candles in the White House windows for, as Steven said, "AIDS victims." I wondered what he would say now on the same subject; since the election in November, every gay man in Washington had become a lifelong Democrat, though before it they were all Terry Dolan and Roy Cohn.

As the image of Steven reestablished itself in my mind, I recalled his lover too. Al had stood pertly beside him and said very little. He was almost as pumped up as Steven, gentler, quieter, maybe five years older, his face acne-scarred and not pretty, but pleasant and attractive. He held his glass primly and listened, flexing slightly, as Steven and I debated. He smiled politely at all my scores, and then nodded loyally at everything Steven said. Finally he said, in a high voice that didn't quite match the deliberate manliness of his appearance, "This is why we're not supposed to talk politics at parties." Steven immediately agreed and put his hand out to me with a practiced bluff friendliness. A few parting courtesies and Al guided Steven away with a gracious smile to me. In less than a year, that strong, thoughtful man had shrunk to a grasshopper, not five but fifty years older than his still-burgeoning lover. What did Aurora do when Tithonus finally got too old? Legend said she kept him in a little cage.

As Steven and Al settled on a towel, I saw Steven hook up a machine to Al's Hickman catheter. I forgave Steven all his politics in an instant, for the gentle solicitous look on his face and for the grief in his eyes that I could make out even at this distance, though he clearly tried to conceal it. We could just hear the pale chirpings of pleasure that Al made as he took in the familiar sights and sounds of the Rehoboth beach. I was sure he had insisted on Steven bringing him here, and imagined that Steven hoped it might do him some good, bring him some enjoyment at least. How many years had they come here together? This would be the last.

In whispers, the explanation of who these two were was passed around our group. I could hear Patrick say the single word "AIDS" to Bobby, who then whispered at length to Chris. Everyone gave his own variant on the AIDS look: weary, experienced, genuinely sorry, even with little smiles for the sweetness of the way Steven cared for Al and Al fitfully groped at vitality. Then we all looked away, one by one, and went back to packing our things up. Tony and Rachel, though, looked more stricken than the rest of us. When I told Tony, in answer to his question, that Al was about our age, he shook his head.

"I've never seen that," he said.

"Why would you have?" I said quietly, though inside I probably was thinking something like You jerk, or maybe even Fuck all straight people. "This has been our life for the past ten or twelve years," I went on, more sourly. "I guess we get used to it." He nodded unhappily and didn't say anything for a minute. Then he said,

"You're sure Ricardo's…"

"He's fine," I snapped. "T-cells to burn. He is absolutely fine and we're not going to talk about it." Tony didn't seem offended, but glanced again sadly at Steven and Al. Then he got up, and he and Rachel and Joe headed up the beach to the house.

"My hat," said Gene, "is off to you. THAT one!" He meant Joe. We were strolling along the beach towards the center of town. At first, the crowded families among which we picked our way didn't seem to notice us, intent on buying hotdogs and corralling children. Enjoying the confidential mood of our chat, Gene laced his arm through mine and hugged it close to his side. Two men in their forties, bellied and stringy-haired, glanced up at us without friendliness, and without a word said, without breaking stride, we started to wend our way up towards the boardwalk. It is considered neutral territory.

We found a little café on a side street and ordered our lunch. Our waiter, a standard boy with stiff hair, thickening some around the neck and waist, seemed to gawk for a moment at Gene. Then I realized he was just trying to recall the day's specials. He had a breezy confidence that we wanted to hear his little patter of jokes and opinions, and he cheerfully interrupted our conversation every time he returned to our table. He referred to his customers as clients. That baseless sense of entitlement tells its own story.

"A straight waiter," Gene laughed when we were free of him for a moment. "Imagine! I didn't know they still made them."

Gene and I didn't spend a lot of time alone together as a rule. He reigned as the undisputed monarch of gay Baltimore, and enjoying his friendship in public was so validating that I'd seldom really felt the need to press for private affirmation as well. We'd bump and giggle, as he put it, when our paths crossed, usually at meetings, parties, and bars, and over the years we had become close through those repeated low-impact contacts. Sitting across the table from him in the bright daylight, I saw certain things about him more clearly than usual: his hazel eyes, for instance. He was also a lot calmer than usual one on one. He even finished many of his sentences. I was getting glimpses of how he must have seemed to his many boyfriends and tricks over the years. His manner was open, affectionate, and flattering. I saw how it could be very seductive under the right circumstances. He gave me a kind of direct attention I wasn't used to and was quite aware I almost never gave anyone. His eye contact was constant without being intimidating; I could feel the contrast to my own restless glances around the room and out onto the street.

We talked fast and comfortably, catching each other up on Marie, Jock and Larry, and other mutual friends from home, and we traded impressions of people at the beach. Gene's initial fascination with Tony had been transferred just this morning to Rachel, whose elegance and poise – especially conspicuous when she was the only woman in a small swarm of highly-developed gay male personalities – impressed him greatly. He couldn't get over her hair: "Piss me OFF!" he said, each of several times he brought the conversation back to that topic. He tossed his head and made flicking hand motions at his shoulder, as though a great cloud of black curls might materialize on his head by mere force of will. I felt pretty sure I could guess the kind of wig he'd get this year for Hallowe'en.

When I asked him about Chris, the public Gene was suddenly back. "McManus," he said, "I'm serious: darling child. But HONestly!"

"Is it the distance thing?" I asked.

"Heavens NO!" he answered. "Only for this week in any case... but over-all, No. The very sweetest piece, of course; but the TEARS, my dear, and he said he wanted... and I said, Try that, I'll WRECK your life – wouldn't for worlds, you know, but he – and as I said, basically not." He paused. "And again, I just cherish... he's fine, though." I laughed. Apparently that was all the explanation I was going to get. Gene seemed to think he'd been perfectly lucid.

"Now Joe," he said. Some perversity in me thought it would be a little beat just to talk about being in love with Joe. I kind of wanted Gene to think I had as much glamorous man-trouble as he did. So I sighed and told him about Dennis.

"Dennis!" he said, making a low lustful whistle.

"Exactly," I said. "So imagine how I felt."

"But you and Joe seemed fine together this morning. All that billing and cooing."

"We talked," I said. "We worked it out."

"Everything's copacetic, then, I take it," he said. "No more hideous surprises."

"I think we're OK."

"Our next step," he said, "is to decide just exactly what you want out of this situation."

"I want Joe," I said.

"Do you want to move to LA?" he asked. "Does he want to move east? Do you intend to buy an airline?" Questions I'd asked myself often enough, and fair ones.

"I don't know," I said. "We'll think of something."

"Love will find a way?" He smiled and I shrugged. "Do you and Joe really talk the same talk?"

"I think so," I said. "We get our points across." I was remembering Joe quoting Auden when least expected, and the times I had surprised him into saying That's honest.

"You know what I think?" I could hear a bead-read

coming and braced myself. "This whole cross-country thing suits you. You thrive on impossibility. That's why you've been blowing off all the men who've wanted you in Baltimore all these years."

"Men you wouldn't touch with a barge pole yourself," I pointed out, thinking of the plain dull earnest men Gene often told me were hot for me, perfect for me: and for some reason – to prove my deep values, I think – I was supposed to settle for one of them. Then Gene would drift by an hour later with some astonishing demigod on his arm and ask me how I was coming along with whatever librarian or accountant he'd picked out as my future lover.

"Don't be so sure," he mused. "But you don't really want some glamor boy; you'd be bored to weeping in two weeks. You need someone more like yourself."

"Opposites attract, Gene," I said. "Whatever happened to desire? I'm not allowed to have that?"

"You desire plenty. You desire people you can't have. You desire Joe because he lives three thousand miles away. And it's what you liked about Peter: he wasn't available."

"That's not true," I said. I'd been hearing this whole Jim-can-only-love-someone-who's-not-available line for years, and I wasn't having any. "Peter told me over and over that he was available and wanted to get together. He just didn't get around to mentioning that he'd been seeing someone else for several weeks."

"Peter's a real nice guy," Gene said a little defensively. Gene bore the heavy burden of making sure all factions in gay Baltimore remained on speaking terms at least through the next fundraiser. Part Dag Hammarskjöld, part Elsa Maxwell, he was always pretty heavily invested in maintaining that anyone you might be mad at was basically a nice guy.

"Yeah yeah," I said, waving my hand. "That's a bill of goods we've all been sold. News-flash, Gene: Jim is a real nice guy, too, and he's done a lot more for gay Baltimore than Peter ever will in his whole sorry life, and he's sick and tired of all his friends saying how nice Peter is after Peter lied to him and strung him along for six weeks. It's not always a no-fault world, you know." Gene laughed and put his hands up to shield his face as though I'd been hurling rocks at him.

"OK OK!" he said. "But let's face it: you do go in for this romance thing." He started humming "The Impossible Dream."

"There's too little romance in this humdrum modern world," I said stiffly. He looked at me for a moment, and then smiled.

"I do like Joe," he said. "And you like each other. Maybe... and if so, I say: blessings on you both." The waiter came up at this point to sell us dessert – telling us, for all the world as if we cared, which ones he'd tried and liked that morning.

"How about you?" I asked Gene a short while later. "Are you ever going to settle down?"

"Notice how you've become a marriage counselor in two days?" he replied. Then he thought about it. "Who knows if I'll ever settle down?" Gene's best friend Jock had told me, years before, that when Gene first came out he wanted to find Mr. Right and cleave to him for life. I myself had known Richard, the ex-lover and dear friend whom Gene had lost to AIDS in the late Eighties. Gene's tireless conquests had to be read in the context of this disappointment and grief. Yet they were also part of the way he was: someone everyone wanted, someone with so much vitality he almost had to spread it around. "I don't need to have a husband, as long as I have..."

"What?" I asked.

"My life. My wonderful life. My boys and my business and... and my dear ones. Like Jocko, and Cybil, and – well, you know them all." He lifted his glass and clicked it against mine. "And one of the very dearest, more every time I see him."

"Who?"

"My McManus," he said. "We've been through a lot over the past seven or eight years, you know. It builds up bit by bit, and then you look around one day and you're friends."

I smiled. Gene's sentimentality was one of the things I'd always liked about him, but he'd seldom directed it this plainly at me. I knew he felt this way, but it was different to hear him say it. I looked at the table, using my fork to connect a few droplets of water that lay on the paper doily, and wondering how far I could presume on this closeness. There were memories that hurt, memories we shared. Gene generally did not like to talk about sad things. Yet if you couldn't talk about those things with someone, at least occasionally, then you weren't really friends.

"Gene," I asked, looking up, "do you remember the first time you came to my house?"

"The night your Robert died," he said, nodding. That was the night of my summer party in 1988. I'd gotten up my nerve to invite Gene, who was slightly out of my league at the time in social terms – he stood already at the very acme of Baltimore's gay A-List, but was starting to admit me into his circle because of our many mutual friends. I had been very flattered that he came. Luellen and Bob had left the party to go visit Robert, who was ailing and hadn't come. They found him dead of a freak coronary infarction, lying on his bed, the TV still on, and called me immediately. The other guests, including Gene, had helped me handle the first shock.

"Richard had gone just a few weeks before," I said.

"And Stuart... now was that before or after?"

"Stuart was just a few days before the party. Remember how Larry threw you out of the room because he wanted to talk about Stuart and you didn't?"

"Larry can be so macho," Gene smiled. "He and Stuart were very close. He took that one harder than most of us; and God knows we all loved Stuart plenty."

"And Garrett," I said; "I forget if you knew him."

"Oh God yes; what a dear man."

"I called him the Lay of the Century," I said.

"No!" he said, laughing, galvanized. "You really had... ? Well, as I've said before, your efficiency leaves me absolutely speechless."

"And my friend Chris, from grad school; I know you never met him. And... and Danny, and – no, actually, that's enough. I didn't mean to play this name game. It's too depressing." He looked at me gravely, and took a moment before he spoke.

"I heard Tony ask about our Ricky," he said. "He's well?" I could feel my eyes sting slightly, and I looked with a sudden lack of appetite at the puddle of ice cream on my plate.

252

"He's absolutely fine," I said. I felt safer airing this fear with Gene than with Tony; Gene would not say, I've never seen that. And with Walter, of course, I was locked into... not denial, really, but a fierce tigerish positive thinking that we conducted in tandem. "Life in him is... He's my baby, I say; Marie says. But Gene, it's – Ricardo: you know what I mean?" I was talking like Gene himself. He understood me, and nodded.

"How can you bear it? you wonder," he said. "Waiting. There's always one; one for each of us. The one we can't bear. 'Take me instead; take anyone but this one.' Ricardo's yours." He reached over the table and patted my hand. "He knows how much you love him, dear. He's a happy person, a lucky person. He has Walter, and you: he'll be fine. And believe me – you can't bear it till you have to bear it. Then you find out, Life truly goes on. I lost Richard, and I didn't die. Richard didn't want me to, and my dying would have done him no good. You live, you take care of him while you can, you remember him when he's gone. You never lose him, you know. Never. He cannot ever be lost." I had often guessed that Gene might actually be a source of comfort and wise counsel, but I'd never seen it.

"Did you ever cry when Richard died?" I remembered how tight Gene had been with his grief, how fearful of breaking. His friends had rallied around him in that stiff-upper-lip way that almost forbids genuine grieving. People always wanted Gene to be happy and charming, and he didn't always have room to be himself.

"Buckets," he said. "Alone. At home. In the shower, and when I arranged flowers. Those two places. Buckets." He wasn't smiling. It made me happy, in a sad way, to know that Gene wasn't just a good-looking networker after all. He had sorrowed and he had healed. He'd been there, and he'd come back. I met his eye, and for the first time in all our years of friendship felt truly close with him – felt that I knew him, that he had let me know him, that it was safe to let him know me. His eyes didn't flicker. There was no camp, no role-playing, no keeping of Baltimore's fragile gay peace. It was just Gene and Jim. Then he winked at me.

"Show me this fabulous studio of yours," he said. "I want to lord it over all the unfortunates who will not be received."

Gene's reaction to the studio surprised and disappointed me a little: he was polite, but he didn't rave. I guessed it was too trendy for him. He was like a lot of Baltimore gays in thinking that true class lay only in hunting prints, damask drapes, brass sconces, and old sleigh beds. When done right, it was genuinely wonderful. More often, it was simply cautious. None of my Baltimore-native friends understood why I put a contemporary fabric on two Empire gondola chairs I bought on Howard Street, and were unimpressed by my allusion to the Picasso/Toklas embroideries on the Louis XV side chairs I'd seen at the rare books library at Yale. They mostly disapproved of my decision to leave the concrete slab exposed when I took up the old carpeting in my living room: I told Jock that varnished concrete was very happening in SoHo, and he nodded and said, "I don't doubt it," as though no barbarism committed by Yankees could surprise him. At least Gene loved my big shiny white cotton bathrobe. He called it the best thing in Rehoboth. Then he asked for a beer and we went and sat on the balcony. The sun was a little too bright, though, even with the steady breeze, and after a few minutes we went in and I turned on the air conditioning and we settled on the sofa.

We talked a bit more of old friends who were gone. I think we may have talked more about Joe. By mid-afternoon, we were holding hands, enjoying our new easiness and closeness. There was a comfortable passionless satisfaction in having Gene's beautiful body seated right next to me. Hundreds, thousands of men had longed to be this close to him, yet even those who won his embrace may not have felt the warmth and comfort with him that I did.

"Our lives, McManus," he mused at one point. "Our crazy lives."

"We're still here," I said and smiled. "So many aren't."

"Why, do you think?"

"I don't know. Except it's good to be here. It's good to be alive. It's because life is a good thing that we wish they were still living. It's what we wish for others, so we should cherish it ourselves, since we're lucky enough to have it, for now."

"How about Steven and Al?" he asked. "Incredible, seeing them today. I have to speak to them if they're out tomorrow. We mustn't treat Al like an outcast."

"Yes," I nodded. "I think it was good to leave them alone today, though. Steven was at the breaking point; I could see it in his face. It was all he could do to go through with that walk across the sand." I paused. "That nice big strong man – just withered before our eyes."

"Steven'll miss him. How old do you think Steven is?" He laughed suddenly. "And WHEN is he going to lose that moustache?"

"I think he's about your age," I said, smiling. I remembered the shock waves that rocked Baltimore when Gene, bowing to fashion, shaved his own definitive clone moustache around 1987. "Al's mine, more or less."

"That's a long widowhood Steven's facing," Gene said.

"I don't know. In the grand scheme of things, thirty or forty or fifty years go by pretty quickly. It's nine years since I moved to Baltimore, and I still feel like the new kid in town. Time goes faster when there's less of it. Life is short. Al's just a short way ahead of us all on that road." Gene nodded.

Then we kissed.

Maybe ten minutes later, Tony knocked on the door. I hadn't heard him come up the stairs. Gene and I were seated sleepily, our arms around each other, half-reclining on the sofa. When Tony's knock came, I opened my eyes, instantly wide awake, and felt so completely innocent in Gene's embrace that I wasn't even embarrassed to see Tony peering quizzically at us through the glass door. I got up and let him in before I realized that my shirt was open, as was Gene's, and that at least I – I didn't venture to check Gene on this point – showed a profile in my shorts that wasn't entirely chaste. I started blushing; I could feel the tingle in my forehead. There was no telling what would have happened if Tony hadn't knocked and if Gene and I had awoken on our own. Tony was looking at me with frank wonder, and I felt foolish. I sensed that any attempt to explain would make me look guilty, like Scarlett when Archie and India caught her embracing Ashley.

"Hi, Tone," Gene called from the sofa, rubbing his eyes. Tony gave him a curt wave and kept looking at me.

"We've been reminiscing," I said. Tony nodded. He still hadn't said anything. Gene, betraying no discomfort, nevertheless picked up that he should go.

"Look at the time," he said. "Cybil will be frantic. I think he has the number here; if she calls, say I'm coming: on gossamer wings." He hugged me, some civilities were exchanged, and he was gone.

"I was going to ask you about Dennis," Tony said, "but now I guess I should ask you about Gene too." He sat at the table and looked at me appraisingly.

"Where are Joe and Rachel?" I asked. I went and sat next to him.

"They're bonding," Tony answered. "They cleaned up after lunch and now they've gone out on errands. Meanwhile you've gone out of your mind."

"No," I said. "You didn't take me in adultery, you know. Gene and I are old friends. Besides, we weren't having sex."

"If you're old friends, then there's no need to say you weren't having sex. My guess is, if I hadn't come along, you would have. If I'm wrong, tell me, but that's my guess."

"No. We were remembering; we were talking about friends who've died." I looked at my hands, clasped in front of me on the table. It occurred to me that bad actors did this to represent sincere soul-searching. I began to distrust myself slightly. Certainly it was unfair to use AIDS memories to cover my missteps. It was arguing in bad faith: it was like telling Tony, You couldn't possibly understand. He looked like a man

257

interrupted during an argument by a flag passing by; he would have to stop talking and doff his hat irritably, keeping a resentful silence until he could go back to what he was saying. But it was perfectly true that those unhappy shared memories had drawn Gene and me to touch. "That's what we were actually talking about, believe it or not."

"Oh, I believe you," Tony said. "You can talk about anything and still…"

"What's the meaning of that crack?" I said.

"I mean you can talk smoother tighter circles than anybody I've ever known," he said. "Slight risk of being bogus. Like you spend half your life waiting for Joe to come along, and then ten minutes later you do the one stupidest thing you could possibly do, and you talk yourself into believing you were actually being noble and sensitive." I was very stung by this, but I covered my fury and said,

"Being friends with Gene doesn't take anything away from what I feel about Joe. It's something different."

"Of course it is. But you need to set limits. I know a lot of beautiful women. Some of them I might even consider friends. But I don't sit on the sofa with my arms around them talking about super-private stuff like people we know who've died. That's just asking for trouble."

"You've found plenty of other ways to get in trouble with Rachel," I said, aware of being completely out of line; "very effective ways I might add."

"Said Jim McManus, court-appointed expert on how to treat women," Tony said angrily. "Famous for his love of women." I felt my face flush, but when I looked at Tony I was

258

surprised to see that he'd turned red also. He looked down at the table and said, "That wasn't fair, was it?"

"No," I said. I shuddered slightly at how angry we'd both gotten, and how quickly. "But I'm glad you said it. I hate it when you monopolize the high ground."

"Let's go back a step," he said. "Tell me about Dennis."

I told him.

"So in a way," he said, piecing it together in his mind, "maybe Joe and Dennis are like you and Gene. Old friends; and they really don't feel like there's anything wrong in..."

"That's obvious."

"So now there's a level playing field. You can't pull the moral superiority thing on Joe now. Maybe that's good." He sighed and looked at me, searching my face, not entirely happy. "You really like him, don't you?"

"Yes. And you don't?"

"You know I wouldn't have picked him for you. I don't like his background and I don't think he's half as smart as you are. But that's your business, not mine. He's a decent person. He's honest with you and he cares about you. I like the way he talks about you when you're not there; I just got to see that at lunch today. So I have to tell you this: don't screw it up. I'm only saying that because you're my best friend, and I've listened to your sad stories for years. So don't screw this one up, pal." He paused. "Or I'll just have to shoot you."

"Who would you have picked for me?" I asked, starting to smile again. He looked straight ahead out the side window, squinting his eyes in the bright light. He took a long time to answer.

"In a different world," he said finally, "I think we'd be lovers with the people we love the most. All this gay/straight business is nowhere. I mean, it's true; it's the way we are. But it shouldn't be that way." I was confused by this answer – in fact, it wasn't an answer.

"What are you saying?" I asked.

"I can't be totally fair to Joe, because part of me is jealous of him. You and I can't be together that way, but…"

"What about Rachel?" He looked surprised.

"Oh, Rachel and I would be together in any kind of world," he said. "That's a given. But I guess deep down inside I'm not totally crazy about somebody else taking up all your attention. Maybe I just wish…" He caught my eye and backed away from what he'd been about to say. "I just wish you could be with someone more like… me." He hadn't said, More like yourself. He clasped and unclasped his hands several times. "Do you have any clue what I'm talking about? I don't." He laughed.

"Yes," I said. "I don't know the word for it." I thought a moment. "In the Romance languages, the words for 'friend' and 'lover' are related – *amico, amante*… In English, we think of the two as being very different: Oh, we're just *friends*, we say, not *lovers*. But friendship is complicated. Even when love isn't really the issue – or… that kind of love, as we say – it's still a big deal. It takes some handling."

"Yeah," he said.

"But we're on the right track," I said. "Everybody's been telling me this week that you and I wouldn't be right together as lovers, even if it were possible." I stopped and smiled. "Joe told me that. I think he's on to something. But clearly he's jealous of you too, for what it's worth."

"Good," said Tony. I liked his admitting that this pleased him. "Are you going to tell him about Gene?"

"I guess I have to. I don't know what there is to tell, really."

"You have to tell him you're even. He won't feel so guilty about Dennis now. You can start off as equals."

"We are equals," I said.

"Then make sure he knows you believe that."

We heard footsteps on the gravel downstairs. I stood to look out the door, and saw Rachel and Joe going into the kitchen carrying packages brought from town.

"They're back," I said.

"Let's go down," Tony said. At the door he put one arm around my shoulder and squeezed me hard. "You're my guy," he said. He gave a little hum before releasing me, sounding almost frustrated by what we'd just tried to put words to.

"Thanks for yelling at me," I said.

"That's always been a two-way street," he said.

Joe and I had dinner alone upstairs and I told him about Gene. He seemed to understand. He said, "Cool!" appreciatively, as though I were bragging to him about some hot score, and commented on how sexy Gene was. I couldn't help thinking that it would have been easier if Joe, not Tony, had come upon Gene and me that afternoon. I said,

"But it wasn't right, really. Gene and I are good friends, and it was nice to be with him that way, but I'd just given you hell for doing the same thing with Dennis. I feel bad about that."

"It's not totally the same," he said. "Dennis and I really did it. And he's an old habit for me. You and Gene were doing something new. You were getting closer. It probably took you both by surprise. You can't be blamed for that."

"You're being very nice about this," I said. "I still don't mean for this kind of thing to happen again." He nodded.

"I understand that," he said.

"Tony says this means we're equals," I said.

"We were equals anyway."

It was past eleven and we were on the balcony looking at the fragments of moon scattered on the waves. Joe lay in the lounge chair, holding my hand on his armrest. He was starting to look sleepy. His big body was sprawled back carelessly, and no amount of cagey posing could have made him more attractive. He gave a sudden gasping kind of yawn and squeezed my hand.

"Bedtime," he said.

A few minutes later he came out of the bathroom as I was opening up the bed, and hugged me from behind. The strength in his arms took me by surprise; I could feel a slight unexpected tension in my body at the commanding pressure, an odd awareness that it would be very difficult for me to get away from him if I wanted to. Of course, I didn't want to, but my body tensed anyway.

He felt it. Immediately he let go, and turned me gently to face him.

"Hey, Tiger," he said, "it's me. Relax." I smiled and looked down.

"You're so strong," I said.

"I would never hurt you. You know that." I nodded. I was amazed at myself, how shy I suddenly felt with him, how exposed. I didn't even reach to touch him, but my tension started to ebb. He was licking my neck and kneading my back hard with his hands. His cock was rising against my leg, and I slipped one hand into his shorts to stroke it. It was smooth, silky, dry and fresh feeling, a simple shapely cylinder, a nice size in the hand. I remembered what Dennis had said about it, and wondered if I had ever let Joe see that I liked it too. My big project with Joe had been proving to myself that he would let me in, mentally and physically. Now my fingertips suddenly sent my brain a very plain message: Joe wanted in too. There was a new exultation as that message was received with complete clarity, and I put my arms around his shoulders. He pressed forward against me just slightly, until gravity took my weight off my feet. But I didn't fall backwards. He laid me down as gently as if I were eggshell. Then he was lying on me. His weight warmed me like the piles of leaves my brother and I used to heap on each other as children on shining fall days. I was doing nothing; my hands lay on either side of my head, and I wasn't even kissing him back as he strayed, with cherishing little murmurs, over my face and neck and chest. I couldn't imagine moving. I seemed turned to liquid. In a moment there would be nothing left of me but a puddle, one of those little pools of water left on the sodden sand by a retreating tide. There were strands of green seaweed caught in me and all I could do was soak in their beauty, their color paled to grey in the moonlight. They winked at me and I could hear a murmur of waves above me. Then I blinked my eyes and was awake again to Joe's lovemaking. I wondered what exactly I was feeling. It fluttered a little under my sternum, looking for a name. Joe was whispering to me, his breath wet and warm.

"But to me the entirely beautiful," he said, over and over. I realized what I felt. For the first time in my life, I felt beautiful.

Joe was away for a moment. Cool air prickled me everywhere he had been just before. He was laying my head on the pillow, lifting my legs onto the bed, pulling up a sheet with a sudden windy billow. Then he was next to me.

"Relax," he said. "It's Joe. I'm right here."

Chapter 10 – Tuesday into Wednesday morning

I dreamed about Angel that night. I hadn't dreamed of him in months, maybe years. We were in some large underground space like a shopping concourse, and I saw him a long time before he spoke to me. He was paying attention to everyone there but me. Then I was standing on the beach and could hear the flutter of his wings overhead. I looked up and saw him hovering over me, smiling at me. He didn't actually have angel wings; he was kept aloft by the whirring spinning of a huge disk of light behind his shoulders. He looked very much like himself, but he was bigger. Angel was a small man, and once I made the mistake, in a worshipful moment of ardor, of calling him Little One: I almost got frostbite from his reaction. He would have liked this dream, I think, in which he was as commanding as a seraph, the span of his rotor-wing vast and strong. I asked him why he hadn't called or written in so long.

He said, "But you know you come first with me."

I asked him if I'd see him again.

He said, "This is where I live." For some reason that answer reassured me and made me very happy.

Then I was flying with him. We looked down and saw Tony and Rachel in the yard of their house in Glencoe. I was visiting them and had gotten lost in town, unsure of how to find my way back before dark. Now Angel was being unusually nice to me, staying with me, helping me get there.

When I woke up I told Joe about this dream. Waking from dreams of Angel usually made me a little sad, but this morning I found that the feeling of safety and companionship from the dream didn't dissipate. It was hard to explain why the dream was so touching to me. I asked Joe what it was about.

"It's about me," he said complacently. "Angel equals love to you. He never came through for you in real life. But now love comes through for you, and you can fly. It takes you back to Tony too. Plus notice he's at home with Rachel; that means you've accepted their marriage in a new way, maybe like you want something like it for yourself." He had one arm behind his head and was rattling this off officiously. He was obviously enjoying himself in this new Delphic/Freudian role, explaining me to myself. The annoying thing was that he was completely and exactly right.

"What did you dream?" I asked him, sitting up on the edge of the bed.

"Don't remember," he said. Then he scrunched his forehead and pretended to recall. "Oh yeah," he said. "I dreamed I was dating this older guy who taught college. He was really squirrelly and hard to get along with, but I liked him. And the amazing thing was, he turned out to be a great lay."

"Are you always this cheerful in the morning?" I asked him. "It's really obnoxious." He lunged across the bed and grappled me around the waist.

"Help," I said listlessly, yawning in his face. "Police."

"No one can hear you," he said. "You're at my mercy." We rolled around for a minute. Then I laughed and got up and made coffee.

I was sitting alone on the front porch later that morning. Joe was showering, Tony was on the phone to the office, and

Rachel was upstairs in their bedroom, working. I had my laptop open but was having trouble concentrating. It was another spectacular day of bright white sunshine and thrilling breezes, a few high shreds of cloud in the glowing sky. I couldn't stop thinking about Joe. For several days it had made me happy just to see that he wasn't skittering away like all the other men I'd gone out with. Now he wasn't just consenting to my attentions; he was starting to pester me for them, to pay me his own with a new kind of amusement and ardor. I felt like getting a wholesome butch haircut and tying my shirttails in front and running across the sand singing "I'm in Love With a Wonderful Guy."

Tony came out of the house and sat next to me.

"So how's my guy today?" he asked.

"Determined to lead a better life," I said. "If you ever give me that disapproving look again, I'll shrivel up and die."

"Good," he said. "I'll be watching you. Remember that."

"Is it me, or is Rachel very cheerful these days?" I asked. She was singing "The Last Time I Saw Paris" to herself. The sound barely trailed down the stairs until she got to the last phrase: "No matter how they *change* her, I'll remember her that way." She gave it a little more voice and scooped some on the word "change." I could tell she'd heard Kiri do it. Rachel's singing voice was a bit husky and she was normally self-conscious about it when I was around, though Tony always claimed she sang a lot at home.

"Yeah," he said, shaking his head. "She's very psyched about you and Joe, you know."

"I doubt that's why she's singing," I said. I checked his face closely for a reaction, but there was none. "Did you tell her about Gene and me, by the way?"

"No. She respects you."

"Whoo!" I said, flinching.

"Just kidding," he said.

"So you two are OK now?" I asked.

"Yes. OK."

"Are you being cryptic for any good reason?"

"I'm not being cryptic at all. We're fine."

"Great," I said. "And the baby thing?"

"I think we've dropped it for now." I noticed I had a tiny reaction of disappointment. Without knowing it, I'd become attached to the idea of their having a child. So Joe was right. I'd accepted their marriage in a new way.

"So that takes some pressure off you, I guess," I said.

"Yeah. Well." He stretched his legs out and put his feet up on the railing. The sun was shining directly on all of him but his face, which was shaded by the overhang of the second floor. "It's still not clear how this affects our… " He meant their sex life. He made a vague gesture with one hand, to remind me that we'd talked about this before. "Anyway we're OK."

"It'll work out," I said. "You two are good together." I was remembering them holding hands, gazing out to sea together, Rachel's increasing happiness over the past few days. It didn't seem possible that Tony was still holding out on her, but I'd give myself a headache if I tried too hard to decide how I felt about that. I pushed the thought from my mind.

"Anton?" Rachel's voice sounded very close, but she was nowhere in sight. Tony and I looked at each other before he realized she must be calling down from one of the front windows upstairs. He put his feet down, stood, and hopped down the front steps, turning to smile up at her and shielding his eyes from the glare reflecting off the white bricks.

"What light from yonder window breaks?" he asked, and I heard her giggle. Rachel virtually never giggled, but when Tony wanted to be disarming he could be ruthlessly cute. It would be too much to expect even the greatest of ladies never to react to that.

"Why don't you and Jim decide what to do about lunch," she said. "I'll be busy up here for another hour or so. Maybe you two could be creative for me."

"Are you feeling creative, Jimbo?" he asked me, rubbing his hands together. I stepped down to join him and waved up at Rachel.

"Not since the dawn of the Renaissance has such creativity been loose in the world," I said. "I see a legend taking form."

"Good," she said. "Call me when you're ready to set up and I'll be down to help you." She pulled her head in, and in a moment we could heard the tapping of keys and Rachel humming the lead-in to "All the Things You Are."

Our creativity went as far as going to a deli and bringing back cold cuts and macaroni salad. Joe had come downstairs looking for me by the time we got back, and was in the living room reading.

"This guy wants to cut Hercules up, doesn't he?" he asked me, holding his book up.

"Yes," I said. "*Infatti... eccolo qui!*" I brandished the deli tray in his face and he said "Gag me" and laughed.

Rachel came down when she heard us come in. She asked me to help her set the table and assigned Tony to entertain Joe.

"How's the honeymoon going?" she asked me, as we stood at the kitchen island and got out the silver and placemats. I shrugged and she looked serious. "I don't mean to tease you about it. Maybe I'm putting words in your mouth."

"No no," I said. "I think 'honeymoon' is accurate. Ups and downs, of course, but mostly ups." I looked around. "Glasses? I forget in this huge kitchen." She pointed to a cupboard over the sinks. "I'm not used to it yet," I went on. "I haven't fallen in love in years. I'm not sure what to do or say."

"It's like riding a bicycle, isn't it? You never forget." Then she thought for a second and said, "What do I know? I haven't fallen in love since 1968." After a moment she started humming again.

"You songbird you," I said. "What's going on?" She made a face and stacked the dishes on a tray.

"You take that in," she said. "I'll get the mustard and stuff." Then as we stood across the dining room table from each other, she said, "It's a vicarious thing, maybe. It's been very good for me and Anton to see you and Joe get together. We've been together since we were sixteen. It's nice to see how grown-ups go about it."

"Like I'm such an expert on grown-up behavior," I said. "I'm glad you've been on hand to supervise developments. It's made it feel safer." She nodded.

"I guess there have been some tensions, too," she said as

she set the places on her side. "You and Anton have a complicated history. So do you and I in a way. I hope we haven't put you in too much of a fishbowl here." She spooned some mustard into a little bowl and rapped the spoon hard on the bowl's edge. "Anyway we're both really happy about what's happening, and I hope you know we're on your side." Years and years of single life had made me allergic to the too-frequent "we" married people used. I was aware of this habitual defensive reaction before it occurred to me that I apparently wasn't a single person anymore. Nevertheless I made a silent promise to myself never to talk as though Joe and I were one thing. She checked the table and decided it was done.

"Go get the others, will you?" she asked me. Then just before stepping through the swinging door back into the kitchen, she stopped and said, "I never would have made friends with Joe if you hadn't been here." What she was too gracious to say was that she didn't have any other friends who were waiters. It was quite true that gay society at its best was rather egalitarian. "I've really enjoyed that," she said. "He's... " I expected her to say He's sweet or He's nice or He's cute. "He's interesting," she said; "really kind of complicated." A brief shadow across her face made me wonder if she'd been talking to him about me, and she must have seen that I was about to ask her, because she quickly said, "I like him," and shouldered her way through the swinging door.

In the early afternoon, Chris and Gene stopped by on their way to the beach. We were all sitting on the porch when they came up the front steps. Gene stood leaning against one of the square brick columns and Chris sat on the railing beside him. Chris reached often to pat Gene's hand or shoulder but looked at him rather little. He was acting energetically easy and familiar with Gene, as though they'd been together a long time. His pale eyes, shining proudly, and those constant little pats and touches gave him away.

"We just had lunch at the Moon," he said. "We were going back to the beach to meet the others, and we just decided to drop in and see if anyone here wanted to come with us." We we we, I thought. Gene winked at me but I wasn't sure what he meant by it.

"You just ran into each other this morning?" I asked.

"No," said Chris. "Gene called me last night and we met out at the Renegade. It's near our place."

"I've seen where you're staying," I nodded. Maybe he hadn't heard that story.

Tony glanced at me, then spoke to Chris.

"Last night?" he said. "You didn't call our guys here? Oh, that's right. They wanted to stay in." He and Gene exchanged a quick look; Gene gave the hint of a smile and nodded almost imperceptibly, blinking slowly.

"And we just had to go out," he said. He reached out and rumpled Chris' fascinating black curls. "We've only got a few days of each other's fashionable company left." Chris smiled at the affectionate tone in Gene's voice and jumped down from the railing, eager to go.

"Anyone coming with?" he asked, but we put him off: we'd be down later maybe. "Whatever," he said, waving, bounding down the steps, looking even younger than he was. Gene leaned over me for a moment to whisper,

"Don't say I never did anything for you." It took me a second to realize that he meant he was covering for me, proving to Tony that there had been nothing illicit between him and me. I glanced down the walk at Chris, who waited for Gene with a beautiful little smile of impatience.

"The depth of your sacrifice is duly noted," I said, arching my eyebrows. Gene patted my shoulder, waved good-bye to the others, and left.

Joe and I strolled along the boardwalk before joining the group on the beach. Every hundred yards or so there are little timber shelters and benches, like quainted-up versions of urban bus stops. Joe pulled me into one of these and we sat without talking and watched the people go by for a while.

After a few minutes he shifted himself a little closer to me and said, "Come on, Tiger, be sociable." I put my arm around his shoulder.

"Who's your new boyfriend?" I asked him.

"You are," he said, and nuzzled my neck. I felt my heart race slightly with brazen enjoyment. Not everyone who passed by looked completely delighted with our public display, but I sincerely didn't care. One comment from one ignorant beach-squatting redneck, and I would stage a zap, a queer-in, a straight-bashing.

"Something has changed, hasn't it?" I said. "The first few days you weren't this lovey-dovey. I had to court you pretty hard. Now you're all over me."

"Should I stop?"

"No thank you. Just answer my question." He thought a moment and said,

"You scared me." I knew exactly what he meant. I had a small guilty reaction, as though my show of jealousy and hurt feelings over Dennis had been just an unfair manipulative ploy. That wasn't really true; it was just that I wasn't used to having my genuine reactions work out so much in my favor. Anyway I thought it would be tactful now to look surprised and confused. So he explained. "You could get away from me pretty fast," he said. "That thing with Dennis: you almost walked."

"But you even said yourself that *I* was scared," I said.

"You were," he nodded. "But one more scare like that and you were out of there. And that scared *me*. I didn't want you back out on the circuit: you'd get snapped up in a heartbeat."

"Why do you say that? I've been completely unmarketable for years."

"Guys have seen us together the past few days," Joe said. "We make a cute little couple, too, you know. The minute somebody who's been in a cute little couple shows up on the scene single again, guys go for him. It's a rule of nature. Nobody wants somebody that nobody wants; but if they know somebody else wanted him, then they do too." He hesitated, and then said something that apparently embarrassed him somewhat. "Like when I saw you dancing with Rachel last week. Suddenly I was all hot for you, because I thought you'd gotten married." I laughed, more at the idea of Rachel and me being married than at Joe's tawdry confession.

"Kind of a dreary picture you paint of bar values," I said.

"But I'm right," he said. "You're a lot hotter now than

you were a week ago, because you've been with me. I might not get a second chance with you." He leaned against me and then said, "Gene noticed, too."

"Oh, no," I said, "Gene wasn't being calculating like that. We just kind of spontaneously bonded." He cocked his head to one side skeptically.

"I don't know," he said. "You could have bonded like that five years ago: why yesterday? Gene's got a lot of experience. Guys like that can smell it when somebody's available." I found it fascinating and flattering that Joe believed this. I'd probably always been just attracted enough to Gene to wish he'd at least show an interest; then we could act on it or not, depending on what made the most sense. Joe was saying that this was exactly what had happened.

"I'm not available," I said. "He was imagining things."

"Good," he nodded. A few gay men walked past, and one of them, seeing my arm around Joe, blew us a kiss. The two young lesbians we'd seen dancing on the speakers at the Strand came running up behind them and they all squealed, hugging and kissing on both cheeks, and went on together. The girls were wearing big black wedgies, with ribbons laced around their ankles, identical to the ones my grandmother wore in pictures from the late Forties.

"What are we going to do?" I asked suddenly. He didn't look at me, but the slight tension in his shoulder told me he knew what I meant.

"You've got to come see me," he said. "I'll show you a great time in LA." I smiled. "Actually I could get you out there for free," he said. "I've got an old friend Rudy who's a travel agent and he could put you on his comp ticket list; then you could take standby anytime you wanted. I think you pay like a twenty-five dollar fee. He offered to list me, but it wasn't worth it just for the one or two times a year I come east. But you'll be coming more than that. I'll ask him as soon as I get back."

"Great," I said.

"Because I've already kind of seen your life," he said.

"Not really. This is Brigadoon. You've got to see my house and office and meet my dog and cat and go to church with me." I laughed. "I can't wait for Lydia Baldwin to meet you."

"I'll come," he nodded. Then he sighed. "It's not the easiest way to start off."

"Maybe we agree to a trial period; like maybe if we visit back and forth for a year and still feel the same way, then we talk about somebody moving."

"Like me, you mean," he said.

"Well..." I laughed. "Yes." It was hard to deal with someone who saw through my country-club dissimulations. "But we don't have to decide this minute. You can think about it as long as you want." He was looking at the water dreamily. I wondered if he'd picked this trick up from Rachel. "Meanwhile you get to show me a good time in LA." He snapped out of it with a grin.

"Meanwhile I get to show you a good time in Rehoboth," he said. There was some kind of lewd promise in his tone which made me smile and tighten my arm around his shoulder.

"What day is it today?" he suddenly asked.

"Tuesday," I said.

"Guess what?"

"You want to go find the others," I guessed.

"Well, yeah," he said, "but that's not what I meant." He gave me a guessing face with eyebrows up, but I couldn't think of anything. "It was a week ago tonight I saw you at the Renegade."

"That's right," I said. "A lot can happen in a week. Why didn't you speak to me?"

"You were in the middle of that crowd. All those queens wanting to talk to Rachel. I didn't want to compete with all that."

"Like you've ever been afraid of competition," I said. *"Gran divo che sei."*

"'*Divo*'?" he said, sitting up to look at me. "They say that for men? You always hear *diva* in English."

"No, they use both genders in Italian," I said, "depending on the person. Pavarotti's a *divo*; or Giannini. And that's what you are. You're my great big star." He smiled and leaned into me again. "Rachel knew you were there that night, you know," I said. "Did I tell you?"

"What do you mean? She saw me?"

"No. But on the drive home she said I was going to meet someone soon. She said she even thought he might have been there in the bar that night, but it wasn't any of the men we danced with or talked to."

"Wo!" he said, impressed. Now he would idolize Rachel even more, I reflected, tiresome as that would be.

"That's why she invited you to lunch the next day," I said. "I'm sure she knew you were the one."

"We didn't even know ourselves at that point."

"She's a goddess," I said.

We got up and walked along the boardwalk holding

hands, scanning the beach for Joe's party.

Poodle Beach was crowded and it took a minute to pick out Michael's distinctive red umbrella. We approached it from the back, and Joe crouched down to spring around it and surprise the other boys. They were a bit more surprised than he intended: in fact, they were total strangers. They were rather placid queens from Philadelphia, quite a bit older than me, and they did a lot of breast-clutching and cleavage-fanning at having this muscular young man suddenly leap on them. When we all finished shrieking and laughing, they pointed out Michael's party a few hundred feet further down the beach.

"When did you get this umbrella?" Joe asked them.

"Yesterday," they answered. "We saw your friend's and we just had to have one. We went to every shop on the boardwalk. Isn't it fabulous? It will be a sensation in Philly, I promise you."

"The sincerest form of flattery," I said as we walked away.

"Mother must be pitching a fit," Joe predicted darkly.

I told Michael what had happened, expecting him to laugh at the Philly queens' surprise, but he made a disgusted impatient gesture. He was actually mad that they had bought the same umbrella he had. "Still," he said after several moments of sputtering, "it can't be helped."

"Exactly," I said. "You have to take it as a tribute to your taste. Be grand about it." Michael finally smiled and nodded.

Joe was leaning back against me, cradled between my legs. I stroked his chest and belly with my hands and had to be careful not to start groping him. His hips pressed back against my shorts were beginning to have an effect on me.

"*Ti voglio un gran bene, sai*," I said. "*E ti voglio.*"

"*Grazie*," he said. He stirred as if he were going to turn around.

"You can't move," I said, grasping him firmly.

"Why not?" he asked.

"You're making me wet," I whispered. He shook his head and settled back into place.

"Such a tiger," he said.

Patrick was there again with Bobby. They were sitting side by side and it was hard to tell if they had connected yet or if it were some sort of mentorial bond forming. Gene and Chris were lying next to Joe and me, and I whispered, "Christopher, what's going on with those two?"

Chris said, "Who knows?" Then he propped himself up on one elbow and said, "My name's not Christopher, by the way. It's Christian." This was the first time Chris had actually initiated conversation with me, except to ask about Gene.

"Oh," I said. "Nice name. Are you... what's your last name?"

"Massoud," he told me. "It's Egyptian." That suddenly made sense of his tight black curls and dazzling pale eyes and the startling whiteness of his smile in his smooth olive face. I'd thought he might be Latino but hadn't been sure. "Egyptian men from Christian families are almost always named Christian," he explained, "first name or middle name. My real name is Claude Christian." He pronounced it beautifully, in French.

"Now I understand that cross you wear," I said. "It's from your family?"

"Yes," he said, "my grandfather gave it to me at my first Communion. It was his mother's."

"Do you speak French at home?" I asked.

"Some. French and Arabic. My parents are from Egypt, and they sent us to Arabic schools until we were in high school."

"So you're – trilingual, I guess," I said.

"I guess. *Oui*." He laughed. Gene and Joe laughed with him, their first participation in this little exchange. It was nice to be out in public with Joe and I hoped he didn't mind my talking with Chris. His presence gave me the freedom to have a pleasant friendly conversation with this nice interesting boy who previously had made me feel mostly frustration. I gave Joe a fond little pat and kissed his hair. He started to turn around again, then remembered.

"How are you tracking?" he asked me. I glanced down to check.

"Stay right where you are," I said.

"Hmm," he said. "I want to go in the water." He looked around for a moment and then seemed to resign himself to sitting still a few more minutes.

"Mother," he said, "can you pour me some water?" Michael had a brilliant red plastic quart-size water container from which he squirted water into his mouth and onto his face every so often, as though he were competing in a grueling bicycle race rather than lying fatly on a beach towel. He filled a paper cup from it and handed it to Joe. Joe took a sip and then handed it back to me over his shoulder. Just as I was reaching up to take it, he dropped it. It spilled down his back and my chest, and formed a small puddle between us before soaking through the towel. It was surprisingly cold and I said "Yow!" and pulled back from him, startled. The others reacted to my little cry, offering us napkins and calling Joe a clumsy idiot. He looked down over his shoulder and saw that the front of my trunks was wet through.

"Oops," he said, smiling, and got up. "Sorry I'm such an oaf." I hadn't understood till then what he was doing.

"Aren't you clever?" I said. I got up too and we headed down into the water.

After dinner Rachel asked Joe if he wanted to go dancing. Tony and I weren't invited. We looked at the movie listings in the paper and decided we could entertain ourselves without the two of them. So they tooled off in the rental car.

Joe took the keys. He looked like some kind of Southern California divinity at the wheel of the blue convertible. There was something perfectly photographable about him as he drove the sporty little car: the angle of his elbow when he reached up behind Rachel to look backwards in reverse, the way he drummed the fingers of his left hand on the car door as he pulled out, even the satisfied cock of his head as he laid a little modest rubber taking the corner out of the drive. It was a distinct part of his cuteness that he knew exactly how to look good while driving. It reminded me of the delightfully sexy way he slouched on the stool years before in New Haven as he watched music videos at the bar. There was a free meld between him and the ignoble joys of American pop culture. I could suddenly imagine him buying me rock CDs and telling me what ridiculous trendy tie to buy in some unimaginable West Hollywood boutique. I'd never planned to love a man like that.

Tony and I went to see a movie a friend of his in Chicago had recommended. Neither of us knew much about the plot in advance, though I knew I thought the leading man was cute. It turned out to be a romantic comedy about a bicoastal courtship.

"See?" Tony said as we walked home. "Things'll work out."

"I hope so," I said courteously, with a new sense that what happened between me and Joe was somehow private, not to be too freely aired even with Tony. "You're a mensch to take such an interest."

He made a small hiss of exasperation. I recognized it: it was the sound he always made to say I was acting like a clench-jawed WASP. He called me that once in college, and I told him I was Scottish-American and Scots could not be called Anglo-Saxon. He accused me of splitting hairs, and I said in that case there was no difference between Sephardic and Ashkenazy Jews as far as I was concerned and I didn't want to hear another word about it. So he took my point and for a while he took to calling me a WCP, White Celtic Protestant, and experimented with different more or less offensive-sounding ways of pronouncing it before developing this little hissing noise instead. There was a dismissive wave of the hand that went with it, which I could barely make out now in the dark.

"Don't be so polite," he said. "This is Doro you're talking to. Of course I take an interest."

We were walking along a tree-shaded street. As he said this, we stepped into a pool of moonlight where there was a gap in the trees, and I looked sideways at the pale whitish glow of his hair in the midnight monochrome. I had a surge of fondness for him. His loyalty towards me had lasted for decades now, and for him it was not sustained by any simple kind of carnality. I hated to admit to myself that I might not have cared so steadfastly for him over the years if he hadn't been so good-looking. But he had kept after me stubbornly without that motivation. He'd identified and understood, years before me, what we were just now getting to: real friendship. He had known that we weren't meant to be lovers, but that there was something between us that had to be kept up even when it became costly. He had even been willing to try it on my terms. Seeing him through the lens of love, I had read him as withholding, not delivering, letting me down. But through the lens of friendship, he had been remarkably constant, probably more than I had been. In that way, I could even compare him to Joe: he was the one who stayed, who let me know that he wanted to be with me.

I stopped walking, and he turned to see why. I just said, "That's right. You're my Doro. I forgot for a minute."

He nodded and said, "Exactly. That's more like it."

Back at the house we sat on the porch sipping Scotch and waiting for our dancing fools to get back. It was almost two when we heard them. The street was so quiet that the noise of two cars turning into it at the far end was almost brutal. I recognized Gene's Saturn pulling into the drive behind the blue convertible when Tony and I stepped around to the corner of the porch to see what the commotion was. Gene and Chris and

Patrick and Bobby got out, chattering happily, and everyone said good night to Rachel as she took the keys from Joe and stepped up to the back door. Tony and I went in through the house and met her as she was letting herself into the kitchen. The others were on the steps up to the studio, and Joe, seeing me in the kitchen, came back down and told me he'd invited the boys back for a last gasp before bed.

Rachel put her arm around his waist as he stood in the kitchen door and said to me, "Joe is such a dancer."

"So you two had fun?" I asked.

"The most," Joe said.

"We decided everything," Rachel said. "Joe will tell you." She reached up to put her hands on his shoulders and kissed him on both cheeks. "Good night, dear," she said. He smiled as though the anointed of the Lord had blessed him. Then Rachel turned to me and said, "You too." I asked if she and Tony didn't want to join us upstairs, but she said,

"No, we're boring old married people and you don't want us intruding on your chic bohemian party." Joe didn't know she was teasing and denied hotly that they were boring, adding the unnecessary detail that I was months older than either of them.

But Tony patted his shoulder and said, "No, thanks. We're through for tonight. You have a good time for us." So we all said good night again and they locked the door behind us and we went upstairs.

Gene and Chris were clinched in a corner of the sofa when we came in. Joe stepped into the kitchenette and came back with a sixpack of beer and a bag of tortilla chips which he set on the coffee table: a kind of stripped down hospitality that made me feel like a college boy again. Patrick asked if we didn't have anything soft, and Bobby immediately said he wanted a soda too. Chris made some exclamation of surprise.

"Who are you?" Joe asked Bobby with a laugh. Bobby looked embarrassed and glanced at Patrick.

"Just soda for me," he insisted. "Coke's fine; or whatever." Joe shrugged and went back to the refrigerator.

I went with him and said quietly, "You know we should never question anyone who says he doesn't want alcohol. It might be a touchy subject for him and we shouldn't put him on the spot about it."

He looked at me as if I were preaching at him and said, "But I know Bobby."

"You don't know Patrick," I said. "He may have an issue about it. Or maybe it's just late and he's had as much as he needs."

"Yeah," Joe said, getting two Cokes out of the plastic holder. "Let's drop it, OK?"

"OK," I said. We walked around the counter and stood with our backs to it, facing into the main area.

Bobby meanwhile had taken the large armchair and was slung back in it, half-reclining with his feet on the floor and his knees widely splayed. Patrick was perched on the arm. He had taken a supple pose, back straight and one foot caught gracefully under the opposite knee, and he looked very good – not just "for his age," but really. Again there was a cigarette in his hand, and he managed it with an elegance that didn't so much mimic Bette Davis as reflect the same understanding of class and glamor as hers. After several minutes of talk, Bobby reached for Patrick's hand. Chris looked over at me and put his eyebrows up: A-hah.

"How's Michael?" I asked Chris and Bobby. It occurred to me in looking around the room that three of Michael's four boys were with me. "Isn't he going to get lonely out there at the NoTell Motel?"

"Dennis is there tonight," Chris said quickly.

"And *moi*," Bobby said, fingertips to his breastbone. Patrick showed no reaction. Bobby however had seen me glance at Patrick and said, "He'll get me back there, won't you, Cybil?"

"If it's that or put up with your antics all night," Patrick said, "I'll *carry* you back." Bobby snapped his fingers and hooted. "Don't worry, hon," Patrick added, patting his hand. "I'll run you out there when the time comes."

"We agreed before we came east that at least one of us would stay with Mother every night," Chris explained to me. "Even if Mother brought someone home herself."

"It's no fun if you don't have someone there to brag to about it," Bobby explained.

"Does that happen?" I asked. I hadn't seen Michael try particularly hard to meet anyone, and wondered if maybe he was too caught up in living through his younger friends. There was a slight pause and they all looked a little ashamed. At some level they knew that Michael sacrificed part of his own sexuality for the privilege of watching them operate.

"It does," Joe said finally, "sometimes. I mean, it has happened." Rather seldom, I gathered. "Mother doesn't know about our agreement, by the way," he added.

"That was nice of you," I said. It actually did make me think better of the four younger men that they at least had this tact about their homely protector's feelings and pride.

"It takes planning some nights," Chris said. "And our numbers are down now, of course." He smiled suddenly, a brash dissy smile I didn't understand.

"'From four little maids take one away,'" Gene said, matching Chris' smile.

"But: silly US!" Bobby said, with a hands-up gesture of helplessness and surprise. "It just never ocCURred to us to pack bridesmaids' dresses. We were just planning to tramp around like the wild women we essentially are."

"Cupid's darts," Gene nodded. "Always a surprise – JUST as it should be... and me in exile here without so much as a *yard* of Kelly green: and I'm the matron of HONor! And how we're to get our hair to stay up in this salt sea air... Cybil – use ALL your skill, I beg of you." I hadn't grasped what they were talking about, though everyone else in the room, Joe included, was smiling. He threaded his arm through mine and then, with our elbows locked, raised his hand and took a sip of beer. Gene lifted his glass and made a gesture with the other hand as though he were striking it lightly with a fork. The others did the same and finally I got it: they were talking about our wedding. Joe kissed me, smiling tolerantly at my slowness.

"Can you waltz?" I asked him, setting our beers on the counter.

"You lead," he said, touching his forehead to mine. So I did. I was humming "The Merry Widow Waltz" and Bobby sat up straight and started sawing at an imaginary gypsy violin, until Patrick took his hand and pulled him up out of his chair to dance with him. After a moment Chris and Gene got up too, so that all six of us were quietly shuffling around the floor.

"So I'll dare the music," I sang, "while you hold me near..." Some of the others were humming along, and Patrick added his "La da da dum" in a deep sure voice. "... to convey what I can't say: I love you, dear," I sang. Chris did a series of spins under Gene's uplifted hand, and Bobby gave Patrick a deep curtsey. Despite their playfulness it was a rather touching moment and filled me with some kind of inchoate gay pride.

"An enchanted evening," Gene said. "No one gives better romance than the good doctor." His eyes fastened for an instant on Joe and he added quickly, "And our darling Joe, too." He patted Chris and said, "Get your wrap, dear. We must fly."

It took us two minutes to straighten up after they'd all gone. As he put the unopened cans back in the refrigerator, Joe said, "Don't lecture me, OK?"

"Did I lecture you?"

"Yeah. About Bobby not wanting to drink." I remembered.

"I didn't mean to lecture you," I said, "but I do think it's important not to pressure people."

"Well DUH." My face stung slightly at his heavy sarcasm. "You should have trusted me," he was saying. "I know Bobby doesn't have a problem with alcohol. You don't know anything about him."

"I was thinking of Patrick, though. He clearly didn't want to drink anymore, but he wouldn't want to think he was dragging Bobby onto the wagon against his will..."

"Bobby can answer for himself. You should have trusted me."

"So – what? I just don't say anything when I think you might be out of line?"

"I wasn't out of line." He was really irritated by this. He looked stubborn and offended.

"No, you weren't. You're right that you know Bobby way better than I do. But another time, I might disagree with you. That wouldn't necessarily mean I'm lecturing you."

"Look," he said, "obviously you're older than me and you know stuff. But I'm not some stupid idiot." He wasn't making sense and I saw that it wouldn't help to try to be rational.

"Divo," I said. "That's what you are." I had no idea how I was going to avoid ruffling him like this again in the future. There didn't seem to be any real moral to the story, but he did smile at being called Divo. "Come here, Deeve," I said. He let me put my arms around his waist and pull him to me. He was looking down, still resisting slightly, not completely over his feeling of insult. I realized that this was the first time we'd had words without my fearing it might be the end. I said, "I'll try to be careful. But you've got to believe: I would never put you down intentionally. Whatever I say or do that you don't like, at least you need to know I don't mean it as a put-down."

"That's fair," he said.

"You know what's cute?" I asked.

"I am." He was still sulking, but nicely.

"Yes. And the fact that you danced with me even though you were mad at me."

"Well, you're still my Tiger even when you're being a

jerk."

We were lying in bed a few minutes later. We had left our briefs and T-shirts on. It gave me a nice feeling of being comfortable together, of not having a point to prove about hotness and sex.

"So you had a good time at the Renegade?" I asked.

"It was fairly quiet," he said. "We talked a lot. Rachel's a good dancer." One more star in Rachel's crown, I thought. "Plus what did I tell you? I had probably five guys come up to me and ask where you were – like they were all set to hit on me if I said we'd broken up."

"At least five guys would probably have hit on you in any case," I said. He tucked his chin in a gesture meant to be modest.

"No," he said. "It's that couple thing I was telling you about. You'll see, the next time you're out without me."

"Do you really think it's wise to let me go out unchaperoned?" I asked. "Sex idol that I am?" Then I asked him what he and Rachel had talked about.

"You," he said. "She loves you." He laughed. "She told me she asked you once what translation of the *Divine Comedy* you recommended and you said, 'I don't know; I've never read it in English.' She loved that. She said, 'He's such a snob.' She was really bragging about you."

He rolled over so that he was lying face down, half on top of me. Most of his weight was on the mattress, but our chests and bellies touched closely. He shut his eyes. I understood that I was supposed to rub his back, and I slipped my hand under his shirt. I growled in his ear to be friendly and he gave a faint smile, showing the same freedom from passion as I felt.

"She was warning me, in a way," he said. "She wanted to be sure I knew how important you are." He was relaxing towards sleep and I could feel the soft swell of his stomach against mine as he breathed slowly. I noticed with something almost like pride that I wasn't holding my stomach in; it was OK to let Joe know where I was soft. Because I was getting sleepy too, I started to free-associate, and this touch reminded me of the feel of Rachel's body pressed against mine on the dance floor. Joe's touch was generally a strong one, with a press of muscle behind it. But here in bed his belly too was slack and tender, with the gentle pulse of life in his breathing.

"Let's have a baby," I said. He hummed a little laugh into my ear. After a long sleepy pause he said,

"Rachel's going to, I think." I tensed, suddenly much more awake.

"Did she tell you about that?" I was a little jealous that she'd shared that confidence with him. She and Tony and I had known each other for years, and still they had made a big deal of travelling across the country and staking out a two-week vacation just to talk to me about the issue.

"Tell me what? Am I right?"

"She's... they're considering it," I said. "I mean, they've discussed it. I thought maybe she'd told you." Joe shook his head.

"We didn't talk about it," he said. "I just got a feeling she was carrying. We were slow-dancing, and suddenly I sensed something."

"She wants to," I said. "But Tony's holding out on her.

It's what they've been arguing about. It's what you were picking up on with him being weird to her. I don't think she can be pregnant."

"Hmm," he said. "I guess I was wrong. It was just such a strong idea, for no reason."

"You and Rachel," I said. "I'm not going to let either of you go to the Renegade anymore. All these mystical insights you get there; too much for me." He nodded.

"They ought to have a child," he said.

"We could try to make one for them," I suggested. The lust implied in this comment was purely theoretical. I had a very strong longing to be with Joe just then, but neither of us had the shadow of an erection. His warm familiar scent was heightened with the Armani he'd slapped on to go dancing. That mix of earthiness and sophistication filled me with some lazy hunger that couldn't quite be expressed sexually. I squeezed my arms around him and he shifted his weight on me with a soft slow wriggle. He checked me with his hand to be sure I wasn't serious. Then he whispered,

"Not tonight, dear. I have a headache." I laughed at his little joke. He raised his head for a moment and said, "Let's open the windows. I think it's cool enough tonight." His voice was sleepy and I knew he meant that I should be the one to get up. I slipped out from under him and knelt on the bed to open the windows over it. Outside the air was just cooler than inside, and the sound of the surf came up strongly, a New Age lullaby. I got up to open windows across the room and felt a whisper of breeze begin to stir the inside air. "There you go," he said from the bed.

By the time I was lying next to him again, he was asleep.

Chapter 11 – Wednesday into Thursday morning

Sometime before sunrise it started to rain. I woke up in the dark feeling a chilly mist coming through the screens over the bed, and got up quickly to shut the windows. Joe didn't stir and the warmth of his body was welcoming when I slipped back into the bed. I felt an old childish sense of safety at lying in bed during a rain storm, and I burrowed under him as though I were pulling a down comforter over my head. I used the edge of the sheet to pat some of the dampness of the rain from his hair and face. His deep breaths seemed to be stoking a hot little furnace in him and I knew the sheet would be dry in a few minutes from the heat he was generating.

We hadn't gone to bed until after three, but by a little after nine I was wide awake. Part of me wanted to wake Joe up and force him into a mood of passion. The part that prevailed thought that he looked very happy in his sleep and that he needed the rest. This was an odd and tender thought, as though he were resting from heavy honest toil. In fact, of course, if he was tired it was only because he had partied into the wee hours and gotten me to do the same. It still gave me some cheap feeling of protective vigilance to get up quietly and shower without waking him. When I came out of the bathroom he still hadn't moved. The smell of coffee finally seemed to get through to him. He rolled over and opened his eyes to see me standing at the counter in my bathrobe pouring the first cup.

"Che ore sono?" he asked.

"Le dieci e un po'." I pointed at my coffee mug and asked, *"Ne vuoi?"*

"I heard a hooker say that once in Milan," he said. He rubbed his eyes with his fingertips in an incongruously refined gesture. I didn't know he'd ever been to Milan and almost asked him about it, but I said,

"I meant coffee you pig." He stretched and reached his hand out. I mixed milk and sugar in the cup as I had seen him do and took it over to him. He could smell the soap on my skin, and after his first sip of coffee he said,

"You're so clean and I'm so dirty."

"Never forget that," I said.

"Did it rain last night?" he asked, looking out at the slate sky. "I thought I dreamed it." He got up and took his coffee into the bathroom.

He came out twenty minutes later with a towel around his waist and said, "Happy anniversary."

"A week," I nodded. "Are we still having fun?"

"So far," he said, and fished a doughnut out of the fridge to dip in his coffee. "Cheers," he said. I was amazed.

"I've ruined you," I said with a rueful smile. "We're going to get fat together."

"You're not fat," he said generously. I had thought I was joking. In a moment now he would say he hoped he'd look as good as me when he got to be my age.

"I'm going to smack you," I said.

"What?" he asked, looking confused. "You're not fat!"

"Of course I'm not fat," I said, coming up behind his chair and hooking my arm around his neck like a wrestler.

"Touchy," he said when I released him. "Sheesh."

By the time we were dressed and ready to start the

day, the wind was blowing the sky clear, and Joe again said we should open the windows. The first gust from the front window scattered some papers I'd left lying on the table. Joe jumped to pick them up and asked me what order they went in, glancing at the top of each page and reading it aloud. By the time we had them rearranged we were talking about Ariosto. After a few minutes we heard a window sash being thrown up in the main house, and Rachel's voice was carried across to us by the wind.

"... and the livin' is easy," she sang. "Fish are jumpin'..." Her voice faded as she moved away from the window. Joe looked up and broke out in a grin.

"Get her!" he said. He put his head down again, looking for something he'd been about to comment on. But he was singing softly to himself now as he scanned the page: "Oh, your daddy's rich and your ma is good-lookin'."

Later in the morning he was sitting on the balcony reading an entertainment magazine I'd picked up for him in town. I was inside at the computer, glancing up occasionally to look with satisfaction at his shapely legs and feet propped on the railing. I was trying to decide which hero in the *Orlando furioso* might have looked like Joe. He wouldn't have fit Ariosto's view of male beauty – boys lovely as flowers, men graceful and cultured and deadly, draped in silks or glittering in damascened armor, their beards curled and scented. I felt a twinge of disloyalty in thinking that he was more like the members of the peasant rabble that the paladins periodically get to skewer and dismember *en masse*. But then I remembered Orlando himself: not beautiful to the poet, brawny and hairy-chested (these were not aesthetic traits for Ariosto, though he suppressed earlier traditions that had Orlando cross-eyed and stuttering as well), but endearing, forthright, stalwart, stupidly devoted in love, sexy in his own way. I smiled to myself. Orlando might not be Ariosto's idea of a pin-up, but he was certainly the star.

I heard Joe make a sudden sound of pleasure and surprise as he turned a page. His shoulder blocked my view of what he was looking at, but after a few seconds he got up and brought the magazine inside and spread it on the table in front of me.

"I didn't think this was coming out till next month," he said.

There was a cologne ad on one whole page, a full-face close-up of Joe. There was an expressionless girl with him, to the side of the picture, her face turned slightly away from the camera, one hand barely touching his shoulder. She had short lacquered black hair and an almost ferocious mask of make-up, like the sex-zombies who do back-up in Robert Palmer videos. You could just see a black spaghetti strap on her shoulder, and part of the collar of Joe's tuxedo shirt showed too.

Actually it took me a slow second to register what I was looking at. For one thing, Joe's hair had been slicked back and looked very dark, and his face had been generalized a bit in the retouching. He looked shiny and rich, all his bristliness smoothed away. For some reason too his eyes had been printed an easy generic blue. I was genuinely puzzled by that detail. Apparently there was a professional world out there where the judgement might be made that Joe's wonderful green eyes, his one feature I would unhesitatingly have called beautiful, would be more – what? more box-office? – if they were blue.

But that wasn't what threw me off in first seeing the ad. It was a picture designed to take your breath away, to fill you with longing: to be that man, to be like him, to be with him, to have him. The girl's face, you could almost think, was turned aside in frustration – she couldn't possess him, and she couldn't quite equal him either. You could imagine her drumming her fists on his unresponsive chest and then shaking her head, blinking back tears, and running off with a clatter of heels, dragging her stole. He seemed hardly to know her or to know she was there. He was looking at *you*, at the camera, smiling slightly to himself. You couldn't flatter yourself that he was looking at you in invitation. Rather he seemed just to be processing his own wonderfulness, taking in his own adorability, reveling in the slow-dawning awareness of his own inaccessible dreaminess. And yet the Joe I was falling in love with was exactly not that kind of eat-your-heart-out man. And just a moment before I had been thinking what I had thought all along, that he wasn't precisely handsome either.

"Deeve!" I said, and put my arm up around his waist as he stood beside me. "You're so famous." I was really thrilled with the picture. I hadn't realized that he ever got such high-profile work. He needed that for his ego as much as for his career. But I was also a little confused by the discrepancy between what I was seeing on the page and what I thought I knew about Joe. I tugged on the tails of his T-shirt and he crouched next to me. He was looking at his picture, smiling a shy little smile of satisfaction and hopefulness. He didn't look at me. "Look at how beautiful you are," I said, looking back at the magazine.

"You don't think it's kind of low-class?" he asked. I turned his face towards me and kissed him.

"It ravishes me," I said.

"That's not what I asked you." Joe knew that men wanted him, I remembered. "I just thought you'd rather I was doing... I don't know: Shakespeare in the Park."

"I think it's beautiful," I said. "I'm going to cut this out and keep it on my bedside table when I get home."

"No," he said, "I'll get you a real print of it." I'd clearly said the right thing, because he looked down quickly, embarrassed at how gratified he was.

"But what have they done with your eyes?" I asked. "Your sweet green eyes I love?" He shrugged, then said,

"Maybe they knew I'd be meeting a blue-eyed guy. It's like we're brothers or something."

"That," I said, "is perverted." He smiled.

"OK, not brothers," he said. "But together. Family or something."

"Or something," I agreed. I still needed to know: "What were you thinking of?" I asked him. I pointed to the heart-breaker in the picture and he understood.

"Giving attitude," he said. He gave me a smug smile as though he knew I hadn't quite trusted him to be aware of it. "It sells."

"That poor girl," I said.

"Who, Jenna? She can take care of herself, believe me. She's a bitch on wheels when she doesn't like the way the shoot is going. Plus in most of her shoots she's the star. She hated turning her head here. She made him shoot a roll with her full-face just in case, like she could talk him into changing his idea. She kept yelling, 'You're giving him the whole shot!' He was cool though. 'We're selling co-LOGNE here, Jenna! Hel-LO! This is JO-ey's shot.'"

"He calls you Joey?" He arched his eyebrows and smiled again, not saying anything. "I hate the son of a bitch," I said. He looked pleased and I made a note to myself that displays of jealousy worked with Joe, however much he claimed he didn't want to be tied down. I put my arm around his shoulder. I felt a warm pounding in my chest. I pulled him closer and laid his head against my heart.

"Wo!" he said. "Listen to that." He put his arms around my waist.

"That's how much Jimmy loves you," I said. "It hurts." I was smiling, but it did hurt. Every step I took forward with Joe meant giving up a little more freedom, relying a little less on the self-defenses which I knew worked and trusting a little more in his good will and honesty.

"No it doesn't," he said. He put one hand over my heart and rubbed. "It's just good aerobic exercise." He made his little humming noise a few times, looking for what to say. Then he said, "I won't let it hurt you." He took my hand and laid it to his chest. His heart wasn't racing; it had a deep steady beat that seemed to come up through the floor from the ground itself. It was a strong reassuring thump and I let his skin warm my hand for a moment without speaking.

"That's how much Joey loves you," he said.

There was a discreet knock just then and when we looked over to the glass door I was surprised to see Michael standing by himself at the top of the stairs. Joe stood up and went to let him in. They hugged and Joe offered Michael the last cup of coffee. Michael was wearing a beautiful blue batik robe and I assumed he was dressed for the beach under it, though the weather was still a little chancy-looking. He was carrying a large bag and the red umbrella, and put them down by the door. He said he'd slipped away from the boys back at the motel. I wondered what Dennis might be up to, to make Michael clear out like this; or maybe Bobby and Patrick were lounging annoyingly. Anyway Michael asked if he could use the studio as his base of operations for the day. Joe looked at me quickly in case I took this as an imposition.

"Jim may have to work," he said protectively. But I was in a generous mood, and I assured Michael he could come and go as he pleased, or crash on the sofa if necessary, without bothering me.

He took a seat across the table from me. I commented on his magnificent robe. Secretly I was thinking how much better it would look on me. Then it occurred to me that Michael had the right to dress beautifully and that it wasn't his fault he was awkward and funny-looking. Certainly there was no law, natural or social, forbidding ugly people to wear lovely clothes. It must be hard for someone like Michael to decide how to present himself, short of just swathing himself in a chador. An elderly queen I knew in Connecticut had worked in Hollywood in the Forties as a costume and dress designer. He never used the words "dress" or "gown"; dresses were always "creations" to him. And he told me once, "The creation must never overwhelm the woman. When a woman comes into a room and all you can see is the *creation*, that designer isn't doing his job." And he was talking about beautiful and glamorous women; it was even trickier for Michael. He had to find a way to choose and wear nice clothes without being swallowed up in them, and with the knowledge that he'd never exactly look good no matter what he wore.

"It's not really my color," he said, smiling modestly. "You'd look wonderful in this blue." What *was* his color, I wondered? I didn't think they made lounge wear in mouse brown or clay grey. "I just like it."

"It looks nice on you," I lied. I liked the fact that he would buy and wear something just because he liked it, without regard to how it looked on him. He'd come to some kind of separate peace about his looks and I gave him credit for that. "It lends you grandeur." He raised one hand in the Queen's wave.

"Good coffee," he said. Just then my eye fell on Joe's magazine and I passed it across the table to him. I was glad I'd thought to mention it before Joe had.

"Look what our star model is up to," I said. Michael took the magazine with a look of delighted recognition and clucked fondly over the picture, like a grandmother seeing her grandson's Cub Scout troop picture in a newspaper clipping sent by his parents. He should have been wearing reading glasses to complete the effect.

"Oh, *look* at how well this came out!" he crowed. He smiled up at Joe. "After all the hassles you told me about. That Jenna's a pistol from what Joseph has told me," he said to me confidingly.

"She can just get over herself," I said.

"Thank you very much," he said. He smiled and cleared

his throat and glanced back and forth between Joe and me.

"Hey Deeve," I said. "Why don't you show this to Rachel and Tony? They'll be thrilled."

"You think? OK." He took the magazine from Michael, who showed a pleasant reluctance to give it up, holding onto it for a lingering moment and looking at the picture with an approving shake of the head. "I'll be right back," Joe said to us, and left.

"The stories he told me about that shoot," Michael said when he was gone.

"That's a very nice gig to have gotten, though, isn't it?"

"Excellent," Michael nodded. "It was a big break for Joe: he's never had a real solo shot like that; on a big national campaign, anyway. An old... an old friend got it for him. The photographer's assistant, I think: recommended him. Of course, he was already on the agency's rolls, so he'd done the leg-work himself." I gathered that Michael meant that an old trick of Joe's had put in the good word for him.

"He's really excited about it," I said. "You should have seen his face when he showed it to me."

Michael gave a strange little smile, close and proud. There was warmth in it, and anxiety. It was the first time I'd ever seen any acknowledgement in his facial expression of the pain which I knew his affection for Joe entailed.

"Anything that seems like a break just tickles him," he said.

"'Seems like'?" I asked. "Isn't that a real break? A big ad like that?"

"You don't know the business," he said. "That's a new

product. Probably a hundred major new colognes get introduced every year; maybe two or three last. Now if this one takes
off, they may want to do more work with Joe – he could be
like a new Marlboro Man. But if it doesn't, or if they go with
another model, he could wait another ten years for his next big
solo shoot. Or not wait, more likely. He's tired of waiting."

"But he can get other work off this, can't he?"

"Anything can happen." He looked down and stirred his
cup, watching the eddying coffee as if it were an oracle.

"Do you really *want* him to make it?" I asked after a moment. It was an unexpectedly bold question. He seemed to take
it well. Perhaps it was exactly what he had been asking himself.

"Well of course I do," he said. "But I know how unlikely
it is. I've known lots of boys like... well, just look at the crew
I've brought along this week. They all..." His voice trailed off. I
think he meant to say something like, They all want it, and so
few of them get it.

"Are you afraid you'll lose him if he really takes off?" I
asked. "I don't think Joe's the type to drop people, if that's what
you're afraid of."

"I'm not a bit scared of that. I'm just scared of what Joe
will think of himself if he doesn't make it. It worries me." That
made sense to me. Michael looked up at me directly and made
a frank appeal. "Jim: he cares about you. You mustn't do anything to keep him back."

"I was thinking about that," I said. "Joe really has a decent portfolio, doesn't he? More than I knew. And you know,
there's a strong regional market in the Baltimore-Washington
area; it's not like he couldn't find things to do..."

Michael made a face. He was being too polite to say Puh-LEEZE but that was the clear implication of what he did with the corners of his mouth.

"Jim," he said. "Certain things can only happen in certain places. Regional markets are fine, but they're not New York; they're not Los Angeles. And Joe needs to be able to work this kind of opportunity. He *needs* to. You may not think it's the biggest deal, but to him it's important. No: vital." I wondered what I'd done to make Michael think I wouldn't be supportive of Joe's ambitions. But I had told Joe I expected him to be the one to move, if it came to that, and Joe himself had been afraid I'd think his cologne ad was low-class. I thought for a moment before I spoke.

"I think I'm getting that," I said. "He is really happy about this ad; I saw it. Happy in a way I haven't seen. Let me tell you this just once, so you won't worry: I'll truly try to do what's best for Joe. I think you know how I feel about him." Having said that, I realized I meant it. I'd signed a contract, in a way, and I felt another loss of power. Someone who cared for Joe had heard me promise I wouldn't stand in his way, and that might mean letting him stay in LA and go on without me. Michael looked, as I had expected, both pleased and saddened. It couldn't be pure joy for him to hear me say I loved Joe.

"Thank you," he said. I let what I had said sink in, not just for Michael but also for myself. But there was something left to say. I couldn't just set Joe free in an unconditional psycho-babble way. There was a limit I had the right to set, and I looked for the words for it.

"The only thing I won't let him do," I said, "is throw his

life away for something that we all know may never happen."

"Meaning?"

"There's the chance that he and I could be happy together, make some kind of odd-ball life together. I won't let this whole Hollywood dream wreck that." He sighed unevenly as if he were stifling a sudden pain. In a sense, it was the Hollywood dream, stringing Joe along with hopes and semi-breaks, that kept him in Michael's life. Yet he didn't want Joe to suffer failure, and it might be that I was to be Joe's shelter from that.

"Amen," he said. He put his hands up helplessly, as though he'd just given his blessing to a union he didn't understand and might disapprove. He looked as if he might say, Young people today! but he said, "A mother always wants her kids to be happy."

"Joe is happy with me," I said, "so far at least."

"Yes he is." There was a long pause, as if neither of us knew quite what to do or say now. We had both, in our own ways, given Joe up. There was no telling which one of us would finally be called upon to make the sacrifice he had just offered. Suddenly I smiled.

"What?" he asked me.

"I'm remembering Joe's face when he saw that ad," I said. He smiled too.

"I think I can picture it," he said. "I remember once we were watching TV at my place, and a beer ad he was in came on. A lot of kids on the beach, and beer cans splashing into ice water, and windsurfers... ?" I shook my head; I hadn't seen it. "Well really there were just one or two flashes of Joe; you know how fast they cross-cut these commercials nowadays. He was jumping up to hit a volleyball, and he was arm-wrestling – I forget. But to see his face when the ad came on: it was like he... believed."

"Not conceited, really," I said, nodding.

"Not at all. Just that he really believed he could do it. It almost makes him..."

"Shy," I said. He looked surprised, and then nodded, his jowls showing under his beard.

"Exactly," he said. He smiled with genuine pleasure. I think it reassured him that he and I had seen the same thing in Joe. So he said something very generous:

"Something else makes him shy." He tilted his head coquettishly. I didn't understand. "*You* make him shy," he explained.

The three of us went downstairs for lunch on the porch with Rachel and Tony. As we stood in the kitchen serving plates and putting things on trays, Rachel complimented Michael on his robe.

"Thank you," he said, nodding in my direction. "I get a lot of comments on it." She looked at him appraisingly for a moment. She was holding a plate in one hand, and suddenly put it down on the counter.

"Are you decent underneath?" she asked.

"I've got my trunks on," he said. Hardly decent, I observed to myself, except in the strictest legal definition of the term. Rachel said,

"May I suggest something?"

"Please," he said, intrigued. He gave Tony a nervous giggle. Rachel untied his belt, which he had cinched under his belly. Then he stood with his arms out and she retied the belt at his point of maximum girth, plumped and smoothed the knot expertly, and pulled some of the robe's fullness around from the back so that it hung evenly in stately fluted folds.

"There," she said. "Take a few steps."

"All right!" said Joe, clapping once or twice at the graceful swaying of the robe as Michael walked. He looked like some kind of Asiatic despot now, not so much fat as well-fed and languorous, with just a hint of some kind of barbaric virility. It was a look for sure. He acted flattered and pleased, but neither he nor Joe seemed to realize how out of character this whole conversation was for Rachel. I would have been only slightly more surprised if she'd suddenly had her hair bobbed and frosted.

She also made a big fuss over Joe and his picture. She'd gotten herself a copy of the magazine when she was downtown shopping for lunch, and by now she had the ad cut out and stuck to the refrigerator door with magnets. It was an odd touch: the only homey detail in a kitchen which looked like the dream of a sterile Martian design queen, yet at the same time not exactly the kind of picture most American households post on the fridge. "I've never known a star model before," she said.

"Christie Brinkley watch out," said Tony.

"Christie's a sweet-heart," Michael said. All of us but Joe looked startled, and Michael explained, with his unbecoming modest moue, "Billy has been into my shop twice for signings. She came too, the second time."

"Anton: let's move to Los Angeles," Rachel said. "These people are so much more glamorous than we are." I had to

308

smile to myself. Rachel was probably the only authentic Friend Of Hillary I would ever know, though you practically had to tie her down to get her to talk about it; she had debated William Bennett on national TV: at times, her glamor was pretty blinding. Yet here she was claiming to envy a fat name-dropping queen for knowing pop stars and supermodels. I caught Tony's eye, and his amused expression confirmed what I was thinking. She'd taken on a new kind of gaiety, giggling at Tony, singing and humming, reaccessorizing Michael, and now all but camping. Joe winked at me and I wondered why. He didn't know her well enough to be picking up on what I was thinking. Suddenly I shivered as I remembered how he'd said in bed the night before that he thought Rachel was pregnant. That couldn't be what Tony was thinking; his little smiles at Rachel's good humor were too untroubled for that.

Joe brushed my shoulder with his as he carried plates out to the porch, and whispered,

"What did I tell you?"

"Oh just stop," I said, following him out.

I was alone at the sink with Rachel after lunch. She had her hands in the soapy water and passed dishes to me to rinse and dry. She was humming "My Romance" to herself, and I started to sing along. She stopped humming immediately, as though she'd forgotten there was an expert in the room, but I made her continue. I did something I almost never did, not being much of a pop vocalist: I attempted simple back-up harmonies while she hummed the tune. It didn't sound terrible, and she smiled at me happily at the cadence.

"I love that song," I said. "Have you heard James Taylor do it?"

"Wonderful," she said with a nod. She had finished the last dish and she sloshed the water around the sink as it drained out. She rinsed her arms up to the elbow. I passed her the hand towel and she dried her hands and rolled her sleeves back down.

"So what's up?" I asked her.

"Nothing," she said, sounding a little defensive. "Can't a girl sing at her chores anymore?" I wanted to tell her what Joe had guessed, but it was impossibly intrusive. And if it wasn't true – and how could it be? – it would just make her sad to think about it. "I think it's just unwinding like this. I love my work, of course, but I love vacations too. That's all."

"Tony says you've more or less dropped Topic A," I said. Then I was embarrassed and said, "It's not my business, I know." She rolled her eyes.

"It IS your business, if you want it to be," she said. "Don't be so..."

"Such a clench-jawed WASP?"

"Precisely," she said, flicking the towel at me menacingly. "But I know you hate to be called an Anglo-Saxon."

"So?" I asked her. She looked out the kitchen window at the completely uninteresting street. She could have seen the ocean if she'd craned her neck to the left, but she didn't.

"To tell you the truth, I haven't thought about it in a couple of days," she said. "Strange, because I've had it on the brain for months. Maybe my mind just wanted to take a break from it." She thought for a moment and said, "No, that's not it. It's what you said the other day. Anton and I are fine together

310

either way. I think it took some time away like this for me really to see that. And it helped to have someone who knows us well point it out to me in plain English."

"Things change when you realize you're OK," I said. "It's funny how all the years I was miserable about being single, I didn't meet anyone. Then I got here and chilled out and decided I was fine, and Joe came along."

"They ought to charge us by the therapeutic hour for this house," Rachel said. "Look at all the breakthroughs we've been having." She laughed suddenly, a frivolous young laugh I hadn't heard from her in years. "Actually, I think they do." It reminded me of the way kids in college used to half-apologize, half-brag about spending their parents' money on Grateful Dead tickets or really good grass.

"I insist you come back here next summer," I said. "If I don't get to stay in that studio again, I'll die."

"Absolutely," she said. "Let's go tell Anton." We went back out to the porch and informed Tony of our decision.

That evening Gene summoned Joe and me for dinner at the house he and Patrick had taken. Michael was still with us and we took him along; Patrick and Gene greeted him ecstatically with socialite kisses to left and right. He had insisted on bringing a bottle of Johnny Walker Black and Patrick immediately decanted some into coffee cups for himself and Michael and me. Michael had also brought his beach bag and umbrella, planning to get a ride back to the guest house with Patrick. There was an old Aretha tape playing and Gene, dressed in army boots and a tank top and a swirling short black and yellow kilt, was doing do-wop steps all around the kitchen as he set things up. Bobby was there, following Patrick around and giggling and doing an occasional bump with Gene. At one point, professing curiosity, he lifted the hem of Gene's kilt and satisfied himself and the rest of us that Gene was wearing just what he should be underneath it.

Chris was missing. I asked Gene where he was, and he said,

"Off with some boy *du jour*."

"And that's OK?" I asked.

"That's just FINE," he said. He sounded slightly hot about it. It was not possible to keep up with Gene; one day, dating Chris was purely civic duty, and the next he was in a snit because Chris was elsewhere. Then again, Chris had seemed all aglow at being with Gene on the sand just the day before, and now had lit off after some other interest. A match, one might say. The whole atmosphere when we arrived was slightly manic, as though Gene and Patrick had been gearing up to party since long before we got there. Jock and Larry were expected down to spend the next week with them, but for now the house was half-empty and I sensed that they wanted a few more shrieks per inch to feel quite at home.

Dinner was a mix of splendor and squalor – very beach, Gene said. There were sumptuous steaks grilled in the back yard and served on unmatched plates around the picnic table. Asparagus and hollandaise; potato salad from an old-fashioned caterer in town; watermelon and fancy pastries for dessert. Beer was served in bottles for those who wanted it. Gene had brought his trademark black candles with him from Baltimore and stuck them in juice glasses. Patrick had made a centerpiece of driftwood and sea shells that I stared at for whole minutes, unable to decide if it was Shinto-shrine elegant or sailor's-Valentine tacky. Part of Patrick's glamor was that he could pull off tackiness – "pulling" things "off" was one of his favorite expressions – so asking him what he meant by it did no good.

"Isn't it fun?" he said, dragging languidly on his cigarette.

Joe sat across the table from me. He was wearing my blue Lyric Opera T-shirt. He'd taken a liking to it, I suspected because he knew Tony had given it to me and he wanted to stake some territory. I noticed, as I'd noticed before, that I liked to watch Joe eat. You didn't find yourself wondering whether he was hungry or not, whether he liked it or not: he was as intent as Ootch. At the same time, he showed curiously good manners, which I hadn't quite focused on before. He took small bites, laid his knife and fork down just so when he wasn't using them, dabbed his mouth scrupulously with a paper towel. For the first time, I was curious about his mother: watching him eat, I could almost see her shadow behind him and imagine the years of lectures on deportment she had lavished on her seven kids. He was visibly what one of my friends in Baltimore liked to call an NIB – a nice Italian boy. I looked down and smiled.

There was a fair amount of yakking about Joe's picture in the magazine. Michael continued to brag about it and pat Joe's arm, telling everyone what the photographer had said and what Jenna had said and what Joe had said, as though he'd been there. Bobby teased Joe about the whole thing as though it weren't such a big deal. I wondered if he wasn't just a little jealous despite his insistence that all he wanted to do himself was wait tables. He was clearly pleased for Joe and wasn't quite sure how to express that. Friends' successes were always hard to deal with, especially for young people who might not have had enough of their own yet. Patrick and Gene merely raved about Joe's beauty and coldness and claimed to be absolutely terrified of him. Joe acknowledged all these reactions with gruff nods of the head, little smiles, and raisings of his hand.

Then he said, "You know, tonight is our anniversary." He lifted his beer bottle and said, "One week with my Tiger."

Everyone exclaimed and made toasts and clapped their hands, and I leaned across Patrick's shells to kiss Joe.

Then Michael said, "There's another reason we should toast Joe, too."

Joe ducked his head and said, "No." He looked straight at Michael for a moment and Michael dropped the subject, whatever it was. That was another thing I had to remember to ask Joe about. I would have to start a new file on the laptop: ASKDIVO.DOC.

Bobby talked brightly about what a slut Chris was and Gene just laughed. Then Patrick bragged about what a slut Gene was, and we all laughed. Then Michael talked about Dennis, who he claimed was having a hard time. He seemed to mean that Dennis hadn't scored in a couple of days and we should all feel very sad for him.

"And YOU," Michael said to Joe, wagging his finger, "have got to make some time for him. He misses you."

"Hey," said Joe, "it's not like I've blown him off." He glanced at me. "Maybe tomorrow we can have lunch or something." Michael nodded.

"I'll tell him," he said. "Now you CALL him tomorrow morning, OK?" Then he looked around the table to explain. "Joe's life is just taking off, you know? With this big ad campaign, and – well, meeting Jim, of course. He can't just leave Dennis in the dust."

This was a little shocking: Michael had told me how uncertain he thought Joe's future was, and he must know, as I did, that Dennis wasn't worried about their friendship. Maybe Michael just needed something to scold Joe about. If so, it worked: Joe looked abashed, as if he'd been very thoughtless and full of himself. I wanted to reach across the table and smack Michael's fat bronzed face. Joe didn't need cutting down to size, just then at least. He needed to be able to enjoy all these breaks that Michael claimed to be excited about for him. I'd used up the last of my new-found good will towards Michael. I was glad our day with him was drawing to an end.

All the others were going out for a twirl and a nightcap after dinner, but I got Joe to agree to go back to the studio with me. As we were all saying good-night at the door to Gene and Patrick's house, Michael said to him, "Happy anniversary, baby. And happy... well, you know." Then he gave him a strongly puckered kiss, wet enough that I could actually see the sheen it left on Joe's lips.

"Thanks, Mom," Joe said.

It was barely one when we lay down. I had lit some candles and put them on the window sills by the bed. I thought we should indulge in a little smarmy romance for this anniversary that so much had been made of. Joe was still wearing my blue shirt and I loved the deep teal color it and the candle light brought out in his eyes. I tried to remember the things I was supposed to ask him about.

"When were you in Milan?" I asked him.

"With the Cats, on tour," he said – his undergraduate singing group. "I was still a straight boy then, remember? This hooker winked at me and said, *'Ne vuoi?'*"

"And Giuseppe replied... ?" I asked.

"*'No, grazie.'* There was another one who just walked up and down saying, *'Sono stanca, voglio andare a letto,'* over and over."

"So did you ever make it with a woman?" I asked.

"Oh yeah," he said. "Lots of times. I never paid for it, though." In spite of my PC convictions, I found this ex-hetero side of Joe alluring. I felt the ghost of Robert hovering lustfully over my shoulder.

"*Togliti la camicetta,*" I said, and helped him tug it off over his head. I started kissing him and slipped my hand down the back of his shorts. I meant to ask him something else, but I couldn't think of what it was.

"Guess what?" he said, pulling away. Guess what? I thought irritably.

"Nancy Reagan's having another sex-change operation," I said. He punched my arm and said,

"No. Guess."

"Uh – Michael Jackson's chimps are claiming he harassed them."

"Gross," he said, and punched my arm again, and then started stroking it. I looked into his eyes for a long second without blinking. I remembered what I'd wanted to ask him about: Michael saying "Happy..." and then breaking off.

"Today's your birthday," I guessed.

He gave me a smile like the one he'd given Rachel the night before: adoring.

"Yes," he said. "How'd you guess?"

"Because you're glowing," I said, feeling false and devious. "You have a birthday glow."

"You're really good," he said, impressed.

"Plus of course it makes sense that you're a Leo," I added. "Leos are all *divo*. So you're... you're thirty-four today. I always tell people to be careful when they're thirty-three because that's how old Jesus was when he was crucified. You made it safely to thirty-four; good. Now you're home free."

"Thank God," he said. He was laughing at my corny remarks. His expression changed suddenly as something else occurred to him. "Guess what?" he asked again.

"No," I said, and scowled.

"We haven't had sex since Monday."

"And we're extremely happy about this, right? We're going to brag to all our friends about it." He made a guttural sound of exasperation and shook his head.

"But we're more boyfriends than we were Monday," he insisted, "and we haven't had sex. That means there's more to it than that."

"I guess," I said. He was right: I hadn't felt any special need to screw just to prove we were together, and that was good in a way. And barely a week earlier, he'd questioned his own ability to stay celibate for twenty-four hours; it was good that he could go sex-free this long without losing interest in me.

But I also didn't want to sign onto some kind of understanding whereby the less sex we had, the deeper and more beautiful our relationship would be.

"Whoopee," I said. "Let's never have sex again. Then we'll be *really* happy."

"No, that's not what I mean. I just mean..."

"Don't tell me what you mean. Show me." He frowned and propped himself up on one elbow. He stroked my chest with his free hand, but didn't seem to know how to show me what he meant. He smiled and said,

"I can't believe you guessed it was my birthday."

"I am astonishing," I said. "And I love you."

He kissed me. He kissed me, as the saying went, passionately. By guessing it was his birthday and by not insisting on sex, I had pushed some intimacy button, scored some direct hit and obliterated his defenses. He pulled at the neck of my shirt without taking his mouth off mine; he wanted my shirt off, and we broke our kiss just long enough for it to hit the floor.

My hand was groping inside his shorts again. There was a steady rising and relaxing of muscle in an eager response to my fingers.

"Inside me," he murmured. "Tiger. Jimmy." I threw the sheet back and slipped his briefs down over his feet. I kissed his feet and spoke gently to them, to his ankles, to his knees: I remember that what I was saying made sense and was important. I had understood something critical about how and why I loved him, and there was a kind of stammering clarity as I explained it in new mismatched syllables to his legs. He was humming, understanding and agreeing. His hands stroked my hair as I came closer to his cock. I could explain to his cock only by kissing and licking, but that was enough.

Suddenly his humming stopped and he said very clearly, "Remind me I have to call home tomorrow. I have to check in with my parents; they'll call me for my birthday, but they don't know I'm east."

"I'll remember," I promised. I knew with perfect certainty that I would remember. The mood was not changed: I'd been telling him something important, and he'd told me something important, and we were still making love.

He reached up to the windowsill and handed me the tube and the little foil envelope. He wrapped his legs around my waist and I came into him slowly and without effort, like a ship slipping securely into its berth, his breath held and released a few times to signal me for the next push. His eyes were closed until we both felt that the fit was complete. Then he looked at me and pulled my mouth to his. I didn't think I would be quite limber enough to reach him, but I was melting into him and there was no resistance anywhere in me. Cradling him in my arms, rocking him, yet engulfed and nestled inside him and held by arms and legs stronger than mine, I felt a full dynamic of power and surrender, safety and adventure. He was whispering my name. I recognized it even with our tongues laced. There was a long time when I couldn't remember what his name was, though I knew *him* – I knew who he was. I think I was just saying, "Home."

I felt a strong gripping down at the base of myself and I knew that he was getting there; something was pumping into whatever was slick between us, and his eyes opened and his hands on my back were steely for a moment. I stopped to watch him, happy at the look of forgetfulness and imploring that crossed his face. From a great distance I knew I had to stop too; it was the right thing to do.

I relaxed my hands on his shoulders, but he said, "No. No. No." He rocked me from beneath and we went on together for a few more minutes, till there was nowhere left to go. There was an edge, and we went over it, and we disappeared, and we were still together.

Neither of us said Oh God.

Joe said, "I love you."

I said, "Joe."

Chapter 12 – Thursday

When I opened my eyes early the next morning, Joe was already wide awake, kneeling next to me, resting his head on his arms on the back of the sofa and looking at the sunrise. It was a showy one and he got me up to watch it with him. The two of us peering over the sill reminded me of children riding backwards in the back seat of a station wagon making faces at following drivers. I told Joe this and he started making faces at the sun.

"Let's go swimming," I said.

"It's barely five o'clock," he said. Then he said, "OK."

The water was coolish but the air was already thick. It was going to be a hot day, and this was probably our last chance to go in without being blasted on the hot sand. Joe skipped into the deeper water and gave a little whoop as the first wave went above the elastic in his trunks. He started frisking around in the water, bouncing and playing the way he was doing when I first saw him the week before. He looked just way too appealing and I suddenly suspected that he was putting on a show for me. Perhaps even that first morning, he had known I was there watching him. He'd admitted to noticing me dancing with Rachel the night before. He'd thought I might be married to her, and that had somehow alchemically made a fascination in his mind, a desire for my notice. I was sure I was right.

I sloshed in after him and grabbed him by the waist and asked him:

"You knew I was watching you last week, didn't you?

Before you came up and spoke to me."

He glanced away and said, "No, I didn't see you till I was coming out of the water."

I felt a chill of delight: he was lying, just this once, to hide how much he'd wanted my attention.

"*Che bugiardo che sei,*" I said, kissing his dripping face.

"*Non è una bugia,*" he insisted, and I let it go. We horsed around in the water for a few more minutes, and then Joe, looking up and down the deserted beach, said, "Let's take our trunks off." We went in near enough to sling them clear of the surf and onto dry sand. I felt implausibly wholesome and spontaneous riding the waves nude with this smiling merman next to me: a little like the coy Mr. Natural types in old Athletic Model Guild layouts, a little like the frolicking tritons in a big Rubens. The glowing light shone through the waves and glanced off them up onto Joe's animated face. I noticed the lines worn around his eyes by his persistent smile and remembered that I had thought they were a flaw a few days before. Now I suddenly embraced him in the water and licked them, for the sake of the smile that had traced them.

"I want to be your Tiger for the rest of my life," I said.

"Go for it," he said with a serious smile. Then naturally we were making out, standing naked in water up to our chests, our eyes closed, hopping together by instinct with each rising wave, as if we were slow-dancing, both leading, both following. The salt water on him seemed to enhance his scent and my hands strayed reverently up and down him, barely touching him, slick on his slick skin. When we opened our eyes, I could see that his eyes exactly matched the deep smoky green of the water around us.

"Huh," he said, looking at me closely.

"What?"

"Your eyes. They're the same color as the water – this grey-blue color. I mean, exactly." I was about to tell him what I'd just been thinking, but I was afraid he wouldn't believe me. I ran one fingertip along the bridge of his strong Roman nose.

"It's too big," he said, making a scrunchy face. He had the strange touchy vanity of people who knew others found them attractive and worried that the spell would be broken once a flaw was noticed. He was aware of not being a perfect commodity.

"You know what Diana Vreeland says," I said. "'A puny little nose is a *pretty* poor performance.'" He shook his head as though nothing I said or did could surprise him any more.

We'd been out in deeper water for several minutes when Joe said he was ready for breakfast and started to turn in to shore. Suddenly he stood, his feet barely touching bottom, and pointed. Rachel was standing on the sand waving at us.

"Uh-oh," he said, as if we were about to get scolded. Maybe he thought she'd disapprove of us swimming alone in the strong morning surf.

"What?" I said, and waved back at her.

"Tiger," he said, grabbing my shoulder to keep me from swimming in immediately, "we're nude." I'd forgotten.

"Oh yeah," I said.

Meanwhile we had been eased in slowly by the last few waves and by now were close enough to shore that Joe was crouching slightly to stay covered. Rachel had started wading in to join us.

I cupped my hands and called out, in a police-bullhorn voice, "Stay where you are." She seemed surprised and I explained, "We're not decent." I pointed at where we'd tossed our suits and she looked disoriented for a minute.

Then she shook her head and said, "Boys boys boys," and went to get them. She made a gesture as though she were going to throw them farther up the beach and Joe called "No!" and she laughed, pleased with herself.

Then she came back into the water and threw them out to us, and we scuttled into deeper water and put them on.

"I hate to break up this little naturalist outing you were having," she said when we were all in the water together. She looked extraordinary, paddling around in a gentle bobbing breast stroke, with her hair fanning out behind her like a vast waving net. When she stood, it lay hydrodynamically sleek against her head and formed Mucha tendrils over her shoulders. She closed her eyes and splashed water on her face and then blinked luxuriantly, her lashes long enough to keep the water out of her eyes without her hands rubbing them.

"Where's your boyfriend?" I asked her.

"I think it's one of his sleep-in mornings," she said. "He looks like a man who will never move again." I knew exactly the look she meant, from many chaste tender mornings of gazing at him in college. There was something about Tony at such times that made you think you'd rather die than wake him. I must have given a knowing look without knowing it; Rachel's eyes and mine met for a moment and then we both looked away.

"Hey Rachel," said Joe, "guess what?" I rolled my eyes but no one noticed. Rachel looked thoughtful and courteous and finally said, "What?" She was standing in waist-deep water skimming the surface with her hands to either side. Joe looked expectantly at me and I realized I was supposed to tell her something. For a scary moment I couldn't think of what it could be. She already knew we were in love, so that wasn't it. He couldn't possibly mean that I should tell her he thought she was pregnant. From the look on his face I knew that he would be hurt if I didn't think, very quickly, of what he wanted me to say. Then suddenly I remembered.

"Today is Divo's birthday," I said.

Rachel looked confused and said, "Divo?"

"Joe," I said, nodding at him. "My superstar."

"Joe!" she said. "Happy birthday!" She reached to give him a kiss on one cheek. Then she looked busy and practical and said, "Now we really have to get this party organized, don't we? What kind of cake do you want?" Joe made a deprecatory gesture and she waved her hand and said, "No, Joe, I insist. We're going to do this the way things should be done."

"We'll have Marie here by tonight," I pointed out. "No one orchestrates a kitchen like Marie."

"Good," Rachel said, nodding with the grim efficiency of a General Schwartzkopf. Any moment she would start meting out assignments, and I wasn't ready for that.

"Breakfast first," I said; "coffee. Then we lay our evil plans." Rachel took my hand and we all waded back in to shore. She laughed suddenly and said,

"No wonder you were in your birthday suits when I got

325

here."

"Ha ha," said Joe, and she shrugged.

She looked at him and said, "Divo. I like that. It suits you." He was scraping water off his arms and legs with his fingers and looked divine enough.

"No one calls me that except..." He nodded at me, and after a pause he finished: "... my Tiger." Rachel laughed out loud. I gathered she hadn't heard Joe's name for me, and she seemed to find it amusing in some way. I gave her a dirty look.

"No, dear," she said. "I'm not laughing at you. That is absolutely perfect." She smiled at Joe in a gossipy girl-friendly way and said, "A beautiful and dangerous animal. Yes. That's our Jim." I suspected I was being dished to my face and the sly smiles passing freely between them were infuriating.

"Do you and Tony have nicknames for each other?" Joe asked her. It surprised me that I had never thought to wonder that.

"No," she said. "Just 'Rachel' and 'Anton.' I mean, things like 'dear' and 'honey' don't count, do they? But I guess 'Anton' is almost a nickname, when you think of it; a private name, anyway. No one else calls him that. Even his mother calls him 'Tony.'" I felt myself about to blush, knowing what was coming, and quickly toweled my hair to hide my face.

"Jim calls him 'Doro,' you know," Rachel was saying. "Why do you call him that, Jim? Come out from under that towel." In twenty-three years, she had never asked me. Tony and I had talked about it the week before, but, while everything I said to one of them always seemed to filter back to me from the other, this single item had been left out of the loop. I still felt stupidly grateful that Tony still reserved at least this tiny corner of intimacy for me.

There was a Phil Donohue voice inside me that said it would be very good for me to tell her. I would be coming clean, breaking a decades-long silence, opening up something private that I had no real business keeping shut. It would be fair and faithful to Joe finally to let that secret go; it would honor my new warmth and candor with Rachel. There were three of us standing there, and two of us clearly agreed with Phil. But Jim said,

"I can't tell you."

Rachel smiled and shrugged.

"It's been so long, no wonder you've forgotten." She picked up her towel and I felt a strong relief that she'd taken my meaning to be that I'd forgotten. That was by far the easiest version for us all to live with. Unfortunately, a glance at Joe showed that he knew better.

He even asked me directly about it, a few minutes later, as we were showering together upstairs. Rachel was going to come up to join us for breakfast in half an hour. It was not yet seven o'clock and there was no chance Tony would be stirring yet if he was in one of his comas.

"So why *do* you call him 'Doro'?" he asked. He was soaping my back, so I didn't have to look him in the eye.

"I can't tell you," I said. He didn't say anything. He was projecting a surprising dose of disapproval through his fingers on my shoulders; it was as though I could hear him scowling.

"I love you," I said, in a baby-talk voice, to change the subject.

He turned me around very nicely and started licking the water running off my neck. I felt guilty for a second. Maybe I was manipulating Joe, going behind his back with this stubborn attachment to Tony and then working his sentimentality with cute play-voices. I wouldn't have been surprised, or even have thought he was being unfair, if he'd called me on it. He didn't seem to mind, though.

When Rachel knocked on the door a few minutes later, she had a sealed greeting card in her hand.

"I found this taped to your door," she said. It was a birthday card for Joe from Michael. It was a fairly standard jokey card with a fat drag queen brandishing a rolling pin and making some coarse remark. Michael had added a few whorish comments and a big red lipstick kiss, and signed it 'Mommie Dearest.' I read it over Joe's shoulder, but he slipped it into its envelope without showing it to Rachel, and gave a grumpy smile.

"How nice of him," Rachel said; I smiled and thought something less complimentary. "He must have just left it while you were in the shower," she was saying, "or you would have heard him. I wonder if he knocked, poor thing. Of course, he would assume you were still sleeping. Where's he gone, do you suppose?"

We stepped onto the front balcony but couldn't see him on the beach, where a few hardy types were beginning to spread towels and set up umbrellas. It struck me as almost furtive that he should be nowhere in sight, as though he were ashamed to let Joe or me see him.

Joe's reaction to the card helped me understand why Michael might have made himself scarce: he was a little put out by it.

"He doesn't know you know it's my birthday," he said. "As far as he knows, I haven't told you yet. This would have blown the secret."

"That's OK," I said, hoping to sound generous. "He can't help it if he dotes on you." He shook his head, still irritated, and slapped the envelope several times against the palm of his hand. I hoped I would remember, if the time ever came, that he didn't like having his instructions ignored.

At mid-morning we heard the stereo playing downstairs and knew that Tony was up and about. Rachel left us soon after. As the day drifted on, Joe went into town to meet Dennis for lunch, and Tony wandered up to the studio to talk. He had to go into town too, to fax something to his office in Chicago. I had never operated a fax machine and didn't usually recognize them when I saw them, whereas Tony had ferreted out, without my even noticing it, a commercial establishment in Rehoboth that would handle his vacation faxing for him. I was a little surprised that the phone in the master bedroom of the main house didn't have a fax machine built in – as the enormous TV seemed of a single piece with its attendant VCR, and the tub with its whirlpool.

Anyway I asked if I could tag along; then he could go with me to get a birthday present for Joe at Splash. I had seen a nice pleated-front linen tux shirt in their window the day before, and if they had it in green I was going to get it.

I didn't much care for the ferocious blond sales-twit who was leaning against the wall behind the counter looking at his nails when we stepped into the store. I came through the door first and he raised his head with an icy "Can I help you?" that would have done credit to a flight attendant on the eve of a strike – the typical bored and condescending service we gave and got in the modern so-called service economy. He telegraphed at me that he had recognized me as another gay man, one older than he, less buffed, more tired: he would use the dreary process of making a sale to me to underscore that hierarchy. Then he caught sight of Tony. The sudden whiteness of his smile was startling and false in his mahogany face. Clearly he thought Tony was too good for me, and a few moments in the store would help Tony see that too.

He could barely bestir himself to slouch listlessly from rack to rack in response to direct questions from me, but was roused to small fits of tooth-showing and hair-patting when Tony expressed an opinion.

"You guys are getting this for... ?" he asked when I pulled a Medium off the rack on its hanger. He squinted at Tony speculatively for a moment, and took the shirt from me rather briskly to flap it up against Tony's chest. It would clearly be too tight on him.

Tony shook his head and said, "His boyfriend," nodding at me.

"A-hah," the twit said, not immediately taking his hand off Tony's chest, where he was holding the shirt's shoulder. "Nice choice. And he's... ?" His head turned towards me, but his eyes were unfocused.

"My size, more or less," I said, irritated.

"More," Tony said. "Joe's a little chunkier than you are, Jimbo."

"Pumped up," I said quickly, in case the salesman thought that I was the type of loser who would have a pudgy boyfriend and that Tony just hung around me out of pity or good nature.

"This should be fine," he said, without checking the shirt on me. "It's cut big. You guys local?" he asked Tony.

"He's your Baltimore boy," Tony answered, nodding at me. "My wife and I are in from Chicago."

There was the merest flicker of a reaction in the blond's eyes, and for a sad second he looked at me, his gay brother, for confirmation of what Tony was telling him. The appeal and disappointment in his eyes, as if somehow I could make this not be true, should have touched me, but I just coldly thought Take a number, kid. It fascinated me that Tony had mentioned his wife just in time to forestall a come-on, though he'd shown no signs of understanding the salesman's attentions.

"You guys come back, now," the twit said to the tissue paper as he wrapped the shirt up and I signed the Visa slip. "And enjoy your stay in Rehoboth," he said to Tony with a thin hopeful smile, holding the bag out to him.

"Thanks," I said, reaching to take it.

"Nice guy," Tony said to me, as we walked out of the store.

"For a creep," I said.

Two young men were walking together on the opposite sidewalk with the pantherine prowling motion that some men got in settings where they felt completely in control – slung hips, heads forward, eyes darting and menacing: Start something, such men seemed to be saying, or, when gay, Eat your heart out. After a clueless moment of admiring their hotness I realized they were Joe and Dennis. I noticed with some concern that Tony had recognized them a second before me and had his hand up to wave. They loped easily across the street to say Hi, dodging cars, the predatory cruisers of a moment before suddenly transformed into smiling friendly young guys, flatteringly glad to see us.

"Off to lunch?" Tony asked.

"Yeah," said Dennis. "We got a brew at the Moon and we're just heading down to the Alley now." Brew; Moon; Alley; I had a moment's amusement at the thought that I was dating someone whose best friend talked like that. I was also glad to see that Dennis' eyes hadn't lost that frank appraising look – a kind of involuntary once-over I hadn't nearly gotten tired of yet. "You?" he asked us. Tony looked suddenly cunning and mysterious.

"Us?" he said. "Oh – nothing."

Joe laughed.

"What'd he get me?" he asked Tony. Then he saw the Splash bag in my hand and said, "Uh-oh. He's dressing me up."

"If it's Speedos," Dennis said, "he won't wear them."

"It's not Speedos," I said.

Dennis took me aside with a hand on my shoulder and said, "Show me."

We stood with our backs to Joe, and Tony made elaborate movements to distract him:

"Oh, look!" he said, and pointed at a tree across the street. I held the shopping bag by one handle so that it hung open, and Dennis pulled the tissue off the shirt. "Just my size!" he said happily, and then, satisfied with Joe's protests, he winked at me and said, "I like." He turned back to Joe and gave him a gentle punch in the chest. "Lunch time," he said.

Joe nodded and saluted at me and Tony.

"Later," he said to me, and made a little pucker, for some reason suddenly discreet about kissing in public. As they were walking away I heard Dennis say loudly, for my benefit,

"That present is way too glamorous for you, Joe." When I laughed, he called back over his shoulder, "Oh, did you hear that? See you guys."

Again I had that feeling of being immensely gratified by Dennis' flirting, and I wondered at the same time if I weren't maybe being deftly handled for some unknown purpose by this stylish and handsome young man – a subspecies whose motivations and strategies had always been obscure to me. Maybe Dennis being there had something to do with Joe not wanting to kiss me, though to be fair I hadn't moved to kiss him either; or maybe that was because Tony was there.

"I wonder what that was all about," I said lamely to Tony, as though there had been something awkward about our running into Joe and Dennis. He just shook his head and said,

"You and your boys."

By midafternoon I was back in the studio alone. I wrapped Joe's present in brown paper and drew funny pictures of us on it: him up on a pedestal with a big star-shaped spotlight shining on him, and me in a tiger suit operating the light and smiling at him.

The book Joe had been reading lay on the glass end-table by the sofa, the torn sheet of notebook paper he used as a bookmark no further back than it had been a couple of days before. On the bookmark Joe had written "indicative (?) + CHE + subjunctive" and "-ssi -ssi -sse -ssimo -ste -ssero," and "Divo" several times; he'd also written "*il mio Tigre*," sideways up the margin. I smiled and wished he were there, so I could tell him that *tigre* was feminine in Italian, though I could just imagine the obnoxious comments he would make about that.

I tried to do a little writing, but the heavy grey sky seemed to drag me down. Anyway I'd been up at five o'clock splashing around in the Atlantic and would be up late welcoming the arrivals from Washington. It seemed to make sense to lie down on the immense green sofa and, as Joe would say, Z.

For some reason I became irritated that he wasn't there. Something in the way Dennis had bantered with me clung to the back of my mind and I started practicing jealous tirades that I would hurl at Joe when it turned out that he'd cheated on me with Dennis again. Joe would apologize and be cute and appealing, and I'd be grand and cold, and eventually he'd get mad and stalk out and slam the door. Maybe I'd break something. That would prove I was every bit as passionate and spontaneous as an Italian – not prissy or repressive at all, really. Then when Walter arrived that evening and expressed disappointment at not meeting Joe, I would smile grimly and sing, "Ah, 'twas not to be" from *Candide*. At some point Joe would no doubt want to come back, and I would be cheerful and correct and say it wasn't possible: "I don't blame *you*, Joe; you've been great. I'm older and I should have known it couldn't work out." The whole thing was moving me by now and I recognized something almost like pleasure in the mere familiarity of the well-rehearsed scenes of renunciation. I was feeling sad and lonely and put-upon, and rather soon I was sleeping.

I dreamed I was looking for Joe in a busy subway corridor. There were co-workers of his in the crowd and with disappointment I realized that, even if I found him, we'd have to hang out with all these people and I wouldn't get to ask him about something. Then I walked down a long deserted service corridor and found his hotel room. He was in it, alone, and was eager to see me. We started making love, but his neck got longer and longer, like the stalk of a flower, and as I kissed him I had to be sure to hold his head carefully to avoid putting any pressure on it: it could snap if I weren't careful. I felt passionate and protective of his fragility and his dearness.

I awoke very suddenly, aware that I'd been out for some time. I must have been exhausted because I could tell instantly that I'd lain in exactly the same position since closing my eyes. I woke up because Joe was moving quietly past the sofa, on his way to sit on the balcony.

He heard me stir and said "Hey. Sorry. You were seriously snoozing. I didn't think you'd hear me."

"Was I snoring?" I asked him.

"In your case they should invent a whole new word for it," he said. "You were like, howling in your sleep. Like a train or something."

I felt the anxiety of the dream run off me like water. Joe was looking down at me, smiling and holding a coffee mug. He must have been in the studio for several minutes at least, but I hadn't heard him come in or make the coffee. The picture of him ghosting gently around the room without disturbing me was touching and I patted the sofa in front of me and he came and sat where he could rub my shoulder and call me Tiger.

"Do I wear you out?" he asked. "I got you up pretty early."

"You heard my loud shrieks of protest," I said. I rubbed my eyes, still feeling weighted down, but enjoying the feeling now.

"Tired Tiger," he said softly.

"Lie down for a minute," I said. "Then I'll get up and you can make me some coffee too."

"No," he said, "you're still beat. I can see it in your eyes." He stretched out on his side, facing me and pressing me against the back of the sofa. He managed to get an arm around and under me and seemed to think the whole point of the exercise was to warm me. He breathed quietly on my neck and face with his mouth open and started stroking my back with his free hand.

"You're going to make me snore again," I said.

"That's the master plan," he said.

"How's Dennis?" I asked suddenly. I knew they hadn't been fooling around. The memory of my little break-up scenario from a short while before now seemed kind of funny. I thought I should work on this tendency I had to spin out self-harrowing imaginings at the slightest pretext. Then, as I got sleepier, I wondered if maybe I hadn't actually kept the whole thing from happening, precisely by imagining it.

"He's fine," Joe said. He was murmuring now, because he wanted to put me back to sleep. "He said to tell you Hi." He paused and chuckled to himself. "He's still hot for you, I think."

"So are you going to let him have me?"

"Hell no," he said firmly, like a dumb kid in class who wanted to show he knew the right answer. Then he made his little hum, thinking about something. "He wouldn't do that to me, anyway," he said. Then as an afterthought, he added, "And neither would you, would you, Tiger?" He shook me and made a threatening growl.

"Mm-mm," I said: Uh-uh.

"Good," he said, and patted my head. By now the closeness of his body was beginning to make me sweat and I gave a little squirm to make him back away. He slipped off the sofa and knelt next to it, resting his chin on the arm where he could watch my face and continuing to rub my back.

"You're so cute," he said, like a child patting his panda. I was too sleepy to protest; in fact, I was so sleepy I actually enjoyed it. "Who's my Jimmy?" he asked me in a quiet sing-song. His voice had a cooing tone which instantly made me think of his mother. I knew this was how she'd talked to him when he was a child and she was tucking him in for the night. I wanted to be friends with her and to tell her I loved her son.

"Don't forget to call your parents today," I said, alert and competent for an instant. He nodded as though I were prattling, but didn't change his lulling voice.

"Who's your new boyfriend?" he asked. "Who's my love?" he asked before I could answer. "Who's my Tiger?"

"Stop!" I said, rallying my last particle of energy to say this one syllable rather clearly, and laughed. "You're being ridiculous," I said, slurring again.

"Who's my Tiger?" he asked again after a pause.

A long while later I opened my eyes. Joe had just picked up the phone receiver, and the gentle clicking noise sounded very sharp in the quiet room. He was seated at the kitchenette counter with his back to me. I could hear him punch in a long series of numbers and knew he was dialing his parents in Brooklyn and charging it to his number in LA. I wanted to speak up and tell him not to bother; I would pay for the call. But I was stalled by another thought which suddenly intrigued my logy mind. It occurred to me that I didn't know his address or number in California yet, that in a week I would know by heart the number he was dialing. By the time I'd smiled at that, his call had gone through.

Ciao Ma'a," he said. He pronounced "Ma" in a distinctly Italian way, nothing Appalachian about it, trailing the "a" into a long syllable that rose and fell as though he'd just left out the second "m" in "mama." "Yeah, thanks," he was saying. "I'm east, Ma. I'm in Rehoboth. I wasn't home for your call. That's why I'm calling you." He listened for a moment and said, "Michael and Dennis; some other guys I don't think you know... Yeah, it's been all right." I could barely hear a forceful little squeak from the phone and began to wonder if I could make out words, or the cadence of this woman's voice that I would get to know some day. I guessed from the boxy acoustic from the phone that her voice was rather deep. "Ma'a," Joe said, "you've got to get

Entertainment News this week. Just because, Ma. No, just get it, OK? *Entertainment News.*" He laughed.

Then "Say, Ma'a," he said gently. His voice was very ethnic when he spoke to her; not a Brooklyn accent, really, but the high hoarse caressing whine of an Italian street vendor. And the way he kept calling her by name summoned up his whole neighborhood somehow, the mothers calling up and down the street, the stickball games, the back fences, the front stoops, the corner grocery. She must have broken in, because he just hummed a few times now.

Then he started again. "Say, Ma'a," he repeated, with the patient tone of the good Italian son who will say "Say, Ma'a" quietly a hundred times until his mother listens. "There's somebody here I'm seeing. You need to meet him next time I'm out... No." He said "No" as in Italian, with no diphthong at all. "No, Baltimore. But I knew him before, at school, Ma'a. You'll like him. He's a professor, and Ma, guess what? He speaks Italian. He teaches Italian at the university in Baltimore."

I closed my eyes in case he was looking over at me.

"*No, Ma'a; sta a ddurmì.* Next time he'll say Hi. I made your spaghetti sauce for him and his friends... Well of course they did, Ma." I could hear her tinny laugh and felt a surge of affection for her, for him. Then there was a peremptory little bark. "Jim, Ma," he answered. "Jim McManus."

I heard a skeptical arch of words and imagined her saying, Jim McManus? What kind of a name is that? But "Yeah, Ma," he said, as though he were being catechized. "He's real nice to me. He gives me the real star treatment. He even calls me *Divo.* I like him, Ma." There was some kind of sketch of concession in the little squeak I heard: Well, I don't know, Joey; if you're sure this is what you want... I knew that, when all was said and done, she was going to love me as long as I was good to Joe.

"So, Ma – is Papi there?" Joe's father; I hadn't heard a word about him since the furor at Yale over Joe's coming out. I'd always pictured a stocky red-faced man stomping around yelling No son of mine...! How had all that shaken down since then? "Papi" sounded affectionate. Maybe Mr. Andreoli went to P-FLAG meetings now and marched in Gay Pride parades with a sandwich board I LOVE MY GAY SON and a button KISS ME I'M ITALIAN. Maybe he slammed his contractor-buddies against walls when they made homophobic jibes and said, My son is gay, OK? and so help me God, if you say one more word...

"No?" Joe said. "Oh – how's Zia? Well tell him I called, OK, Ma?" He hummed and laughed. "*Sì, Ma'a. Te vojo bene.* Yeah, I'll tell him. *Ciao.*"

He hung up and said, "You can open your eyes now. She says Hi."

"How'd you know I was awake?" I asked.

"You were being quiet," he said. "Get up. I'll make you some coffee."

I sat at the counter and he poured water into the coffee maker – "*il signor Caffè,*" as he called it. He had changed into his at-home costume, skimpy tank-top and baggy shorts. He looked domestic and intent, his rough face settling into odd lines, a gathering of skin on his neck suggesting where the double chin might start to show in a few years. Take him off stage, out of the magazines, out of the world of bars and parties where I'd first learned to desire him, and he was really no beauty. He might actually be something of a dullard, a Brooklyn boy whose *romanacci* parents would be suspicious of my by-the-book Tuscan Italian. I could imagine him looking like holy hell if he had a cold. It would take years to find out if all that bothered me.

"*Ecco a Lei, professore,*" he said, and poured coffee into a cup for me. I pointed at the top of the refrigerator behind him.

"*Ecco il tuo regalo,*" I said. "*Aprilo adesso.*"

He pulled it down and stood across the counter from me admiring the drawings on the paper. He carefully untaped it and stuck it to the refrigerator door, leaving the shirt still bundled in tissue. When he unwrapped it, it took him a few seconds to smile. He fingered the material and just said, "It's so fancy." I thought maybe it wasn't cool and he wouldn't wear it; it would take a while for me to know what he liked and what he didn't.

"Is it too dressy?" I asked. "We can take it back if you want. Maybe you don't really need a shirt like that." It wasn't really dressy at all – just a green linen shirt that no one would actually wear with black tie.

"No no," he said, "it's great. I would never have bought it." He was still looking at it coolly, almost professionally. He held it up to himself and checked his reflection in the side of the toaster, stretching his neck right and left, appraising himself dispassionately for the effect. "It's definitely my color," he said.

"'Don't you think I carry the color of your eyes well in my mind?'" I asked. He kept looking at himself for a moment.

Then his eyes flickered with confused recognition.

"Who says that?" he asked me.

"Rhett," I said, "when he buys Scarlett that Paris hat."

"Right," he said dubiously. "You're too much." He looked back at his reflection and suddenly grinned. "It's me," he said.

"Whew," I said. He turned and faced me with some funny look: vanity, awareness that he could pull off a new Uptown effect, and still his usual diffidence. The green linen, held to his chest, gave a sudden sparkle to his eyes, and all the good looks that I'd just been thinking I could live without were back in an instant. What's more, he knew it.

"You are so..." I said.

"So what?" he asked.

"So... lovely," I said. "So nice to look at."

"And be with," he added.

"And be with," I nodded.

"Thanks, Tiger," he said. He leaned across the counter and awkwardly hugged my head against his shoulder. "This is actually pretty cool," he said, releasing me. "You picked something I wouldn't even have looked at in the store." A new thought struck him and he asked, "When's your birthday?"

"You missed it," I said. "It's in late June."

"I'm going to find you something real smart," he said, almost threateningly. "Trust me." I laughed and he had better sense than to ask why. Then I looked at my watch.

"We should probably go downstairs soon and see if Rachel needs help with dinner," I said. "The family's coming tonight."

"So you finish your coffee and I'll put on my shoes," he

said.

"We could cuddle on the couch first," I offered.

"Yeah," he said.

As it happened, I went downstairs some time before Joe, who got involved in some strange compulsive cleaning in the kitchen which I thought maybe had to do with having heard his mother's voice on the phone. With his sponges and scouring pads and his faded old clothes, he reminded me of the shapeless Ukrainian drudges obsessively scrubbing their marble steps in my neighborhood in Baltimore. I was perfectly aware that in another mood I might have thought he looked cute, absorbed in this kind of honest housework. But I was ready to go join Tony and Rachel and he seemed to be introducing ridiculous delays.

"It doesn't matter when we go down," he said when I tried to hurry him. "They didn't tell us any special time."

He was right about that, but I was still restless and bored. I tried to help him for a few minutes, but he was in his own world, barely able even to answer when I asked what he wanted me to do. When he started sponging the inside of the perfectly clean refrigerator, I got irritated. I asked him point-blank if there were plastic covers on the furniture in his parents' living room, and he more or less threw me out of the studio. As I stomped down the iron steps, I suddenly smiled, remembering that twenty minutes before we'd been lying on the sofa whispering each other's names. I went back up to the door and called "I love you" into the studio.

"Get out of here," he yelled.

I let myself into the kitchen downstairs. The house was very still and as I stepped into the living room I saw Tony and Rachel lying on the leather couch, his arm around her, her head on his shoulder. They seemed to be sleeping, but he opened his eyes and smiled at me when I tiptoed in. He put his finger to his lips and at this protective gesture I had to smile too. It was a fairly comfortable thought for me by now that Rachel loved Tony; it was nice to be able to smile like this at being reminded that he loved her too. It made him seem very good and loyal. I sat down as quietly as I could, but the slight motion of Tony's arm when he shushed me seemed to have communicated something to Rachel. She stirred and said, "What?"

"Jimbo's here," Tony said.

"Oh," she said, and sat up, rubbing her eyes and twisting her hair back into the chignon that had slipped on Tony's shoulder.

"Don't get up," I said. "You look very peaceful."

"So peaceful," she said. "But we have to get organized, don't we? What time is it? Where's Joe?" She wasn't quite awake and looked around a little vaguely.

"He kicked me out," I said. She frowned. "He's having some kind of atavistic cleaning frenzy. The last time I saw him he was polishing the tops of the salt and pepper shakers."

Rachel smiled knowingly without looking at me. "He's just acting out. He's getting anxious," she said, as though it were perfectly self-evident.

"Anxious about what?" I asked, after a moment of trying to decide what she could think was so obvious. "Oh, about Walter and Ricardo and Marie coming tonight."

344

"Well, maybe," she said. "But I meant about leaving you in a couple of days. Aren't you getting kind of nervous too?"

"I wasn't till right this minute," I said. "Maybe you should just go back to sleep."

"Sorry," she smiled, swinging her feet down to the floor and slipping on her espadrilles. She put her hands out for me to help her up. "You'll be fine." I stood and pulled her up and she patted her hair. "Anton," she asked, "why don't you go up and tell Joe to stop whatever he's doing and come down here? Tell him I need him to help with dinner."

"A direct summons from Cyndi Lauper couldn't get him down here faster," I said. No one could accuse Rachel of being manipulative, I thought; when she intended that people should do something, she simply ordered them to do it. Tony didn't need to be told that she wanted to tell me something in private. He smiled and went out through the kitchen. I felt a touch of anxiety as I tried to think just what she had stored up to tell me, mixed with the obscure pleasure of knowing that the conversation for the next few moments would be all about me. Some of the mystique Rachel had for Joe was rubbing off on me; it was flattering to me to have her complete attention. She turned to me as Tony left the room, her black eyes perfectly alert now.

"Now, Jim," she said, "don't worry about how Joe's acting. It's to be expected, really. This will be your first separation and it will be hard on you both. You're older and you have to help Joe understand it. If he acts squirrelly the next couple of days, you at least try to stay calm. Don't rise to the bait."

"It's not like we really fought," I said. I didn't know where this advice was coming from.

"Of course not. Just don't. And when you're apart... well, be careful."

"'Careful'?"

"You're bound to have offers back in Baltimore now," she said. "People who've seen you here with Joe; whatever. Just people who pick up on your new glow." Exactly what Joe had said a few days earlier. "And you can't let your vanity make you give in. Joe would be crushed." I wondered if Tony had told her about Dennis and Gene after all, but her eyes were candid, without hidden message or secret knowledge. "Joe cares about you."

"Has he told you?"

"Well – yes, of course he has, indirectly. More than once. And I have eyes, you know. You mustn't hurt Joe. He may not always have the words to tell you what you have to do or not do. It will be up to you sometimes to be responsible."

"Why am I getting lectured?" I was a little stung that she seemed to be taking Joe's side in a conflict that hadn't even occurred yet. "Joe could hurt me too, you know; and I'm certainly not going to be randomly savage to him."

"I know," she said, patting my arm. "I don't mean to lecture you. Joe won't hurt you if he can help it; I promise you. He cares about you, just for being you. Who wouldn't?" She added this with a little smile, as though she'd remembered a useful courtesy phrase in a foreign language – JimSpeak, perhaps. "So you must must *must* be good to him." This was suddenly getting rather intense and I felt a little prickle in my face wondering when they'd spoken about me and what he could have said to her.

I asked her, and she said, "Completely confidential. I promised. He did ask me to... he said, To put in a good word for him – a few days ago. He was frightened by something you did, or something he did; I didn't really understand. But Jim: he – loves you. In his own way. And he's not tough, really, at all. When we first met I thought he was kind of tough – not really sensitive enough for you, I thought. Now I'm afraid he may be... too sensitive. You can be kind of overwhelming. Of course, you know I mean that as a compliment. But think of how you must seem to Joe, who wants your respect maybe even more than your... well, you understand." Her speech had become strangely disconnected, pressured, as if she might cry or laugh – Violetta, a little, just before *"Amami, Alfredo."*

She patted her hair again, a nervous gesture, not like her. For just an instant it grazed my mind that, modern woman though she was, she had still a tiny bit of embarrassment at this level of engagement in a gay love affair. She hadn't been able to say what she meant, that Joe didn't want me just to want him. And she was, after all, speaking to a friend who would have laid her husband any time he could have for over twenty years. "Don't tell him I've spoken to you, will you?" she asked me.

Suddenly she put her arms around me. "I'm so happy," she said, and I patted her back a little uncertainly. "Everything is going to be wonderful." She broke away and I was very touched to see her eyes shining, just short of tears.

"Thanks for..." I said, not knowing how to finish. "You know I'll be good to Joe. He knows it too. He told his mother just now on the phone: Yeah, Ma'a, he's real good to me. I was supposed to be asleep, but I heard it." She nodded, closing and sealing the subject.

"Come help me in the kitchen," she said briskly. "Anton and Joe will be down any second."

After dinner, the four of us squeezed onto the little balcony in my studio and mixed Campari into the last of the champagne Tony had popped at the table in honor of Joe's birthday. It was just starting to get dark when we heard the distinctive truck-like rumble of Marie's Saab Turbo at the end of the street; moments later the wheels crunched on the gravel behind the house. I jumped up, closely followed by Tony and Rachel. Joe didn't move at first. I looked back from the middle of the room and saw him gripping the arms of his deckchair and looking out over the water uncertainly. Before I could say anything, Tony went back and patted Joe on the shoulder.

"Come on, champ," he said.

Walter, Ricardo, and Marie were climbing out of the car by the time we got out to the landing.

"We made it," Marie called up to us. Ricardo was reaching back into the car for some flowers he'd brought Rachel. They were lavish, an immense bouquet wrapped in deep blue tissue scattered with foil stars. He rested them gently on the roof of the car as he heard us come out. There were lots of cordial waves and shouts of Hi over the top of the car, all three of the newcomers seeming to seek me rather firmly with their eyes; they did not want to stare at Joe.

I went down the steps quickly and hugged Walter first. *"Fra queste mura pie la regina di Spagna può sola penetrar,"* I said to him.

"O ciel!" said Ricardo, and Walter and I stared at him.

"Marriage has changed this boy," I said.

"You like my shirt?" Ricardo asked as he put his arms around me. Of course I did; I had bought it for him for his last birthday. It was a washed silk, deep purple, and in defiance of the heat he had it buttoned to the neck. A normal man would have sweated, but nature suspended its normal rules for Ricardo. I just caught Rachel's unbelieving stare at him before she tossed a quick smile over it. I was used to Ricardo now, his white simple smile, his black satin hair, his startling falconish profile. When we first met I wouldn't have believed that he could get handsomer, but he had. How old I felt when I first realized that my feelings for Ricardo were largely chaste and paternal, and that I harbored a variety of purely respectable hopes for his happiness and well-being despite the fact that his clear purpose on the planet was to evoke unbearable desire. Of course, Walter, who should know, had always insisted that Ricardo was "not hot."

By now Tony was reaching to hook his elbow around Ricardo's neck and was saying, "Come here, you little weasel," and Ricardo was hugging him and making a delighted whoop.

As I embraced Marie, I was aware that it seemed terribly long since I'd seen her and the others, though it was barely three weeks. They were from another world, I told myself; at Rehoboth I'd fallen back into old habits of having my emotional life revolve around Tony. As soon as that idea had occurred to me, though, a kind of halo formed around the familiar feeling about Tony: it was a new friendship with Rachel, and it was Joe.

I looked around for Joe and saw him hovering, hanging

back at the fringe of the little milling crowd. I put my hand out to him, but he didn't see; his eyes were clouded over a little, and mine weren't much better. I remembered the greetings when my grandparents pulled into our drive at Christmas when I was a child – my brother and sister and parents and I, all swarming around, the adults wanting us each to know without being told what we should carry for the grandparents and how much time we got to hug and kiss and talk to them before we all went inside, and the kids wishing we knew the single phrase – there must be one – that could tell them, in the instant each of us had their attention, everything we'd done in the months since we'd seen them, and that we'd missed them, and that we were glad they'd come.

Joe did eventually find his way over to me and stood beside me without speaking. We were all standing around in a loose circle, people chatting and handing bags out of the car, and I wasn't sure how or if to call the group to order. At the same time I was certain that everyone, especially Joe, expected me to say something formal to introduce him. Rachel and Marie had met somehow when I wasn't looking and were holding hands like old school friends. Rachel had one arm banked with Ricardo's flowers, an arrangement so shockingly opulent and tropical that she looked like a Madonna in a Latin street festival, one whose great glittering fan-shaped stiff velvet gown had somehow tipped upside down and now threatened to engulf her head in its swelling hem. She met my eye and smiled encouragingly, though I'd instinctively hoped she would take charge and present Joe for me; there might be some kind of normal formula that was slipping from my nervous mind and that she would know. All I could do was stand next to Joe touching his arm and smiling.

Thank God for Ricardo. He suddenly put down the large bag he'd slung over his shoulder and said, "*Ay,* you're Joe. I got so excited meeting Rachel I've heard so much about for so long... but honey," he said slyly, putting his arm through Joe's, "you've got no idea how much we love your new boyfriend here, and you've got to be careful he treats you right because he's a complete animal."

Joe looked guarded and in a way I was glad. People generally melted in the glow of Ricardo's charm and gorgeousness and it had become a cliché for me. I preferred it when they gave themselves the time to love him for his actual sweetness. Joe had his chin tucked, a defensive gesture I hadn't seen in several days, and it made me feel warmly nostalgic, as if we'd been married for twenty years and were looking at old pictures from the days of our courtship: Oh look, honey, remember that old shirt you used to wear? But he did muster the gumption to say,

"I know. I call him Tiger." Ricardo gave his arm a matronly pat and said,

"Exactly, dear. Get over here, baby."

Walter obeyed the call and gave Joe the full benefit of his most Episcopalian smile, the smile that reminded me sometimes, when I saw him through other people's eyes, that essentially he was a real gentleman, one who instinctively did the done thing, refined, polite, brought up in a four-chimney pre-Revolutionary brick house on the green of a sleepy old town in Massachusetts; no amount of dishy opera-queendom could change that.

"This really is a pleasure, Joe," Walter said, his hand out, man to man, but patting Joe's shoulder with his free hand to indicate that in the Nineties, among gay men, we could also be spontaneous. Marie came up too and said,

"My turn. I'm Marie and you're Joe." She kissed Joe on both cheeks and said, "There. Now I'm not going to say Jim has told me all about you because that will only make you nervous, and in fact he's been selfish and horrible about it and kept the whole thing terribly mysterious and so I'll have to find out all about you for myself. But he did make it pretty clear he's crazy about you and that's all I care about. BooBoo," she said, turning to me with one hand still on Joe's arm and giving him no chance to respond, "I love this man." Marie had become very We're Here We're Queer since she settled down with Clare, and I smiled at this display of old-time belle prattle and took it as its own kind of tribute to Joe.

"Well," said Rachel, "we don't really need to stand around in the driveway, do we? Let's get you people settled in. Joe, take Marie's bag, will you? My arms are full of these wonderful flowers." She was including Joe as one of the family, someone who could help her receive her guests, and the dogged promptness with which he did as she asked touched me. It meant a lot to him to have her good will; within a few hours, I hoped, he would feel that way about my other old friends too.

Walter hung back and walked into the house last with me, his arm around my waist. Joe had gone ahead of us with Marie's bag, and I couldn't help noticing with some ignoble proprietary pleasure that, though his huge T-shirt concealed most of his humpiness, his shorts caressed him superbly.

"Aren't you just the smartest thing?" Walter said to me.

"He's not usually such a lug," I said. "He's gotten all shy about meeting you."

"This is good. We don't want some brassy trashy piece for you. A little reserve; a little decorum; very *jeune fille*."

"Well," I said, bragging slightly, "I never said he wasn't trashy." Walter smiled.

"That bohunkus," he said, as we lingered at the door for a moment. The others, including a strenuously responsible-looking Joe, had gone upstairs. "Not since Fragonard's *Verrou...*"

I was astonished to feel myself blush.

"What?" he asked me. "I know; I'm badly out of line. He seems really very nice and I'm not going to be coarse about him."

"No," I said. There was so very much to say to Walter: Joe, Rachel; volumes and volumes about Tony – Walter had known that story as long as there had been a story to know. I felt a sudden pressure building, that there wasn't time to tell Walter what I was feeling and had been through.

"What?" he asked, touching my arm gently. My face was still hot, and I felt absurd. Like Rachel earlier in the evening, I was about to cry, about to laugh.

"I'm scared," I suddenly said. My throat was very tight.

"No," he said, "you're fine."

"I'm scared," I repeated. "Walter... :" I put my arms around him on impulse. I was starting to shake.

"Oh my God," he said, "Jimmy is in love." He laughed and hugged me. *"Amor, sublime amore,"* he sang, like a lullaby.

"Yes," I said. I was grateful; I hadn't known why I was

scared, but he had, and he'd been able to tell me. I could feel tears on my face, from the release of tension more than from sadness – in fact, I wasn't sad at all, really; I was happy.

"It is the single most frightening thing that will ever happen to you," he said, rocking me a little. "You remember me, don't you? Making the biggest fool of myself back in 1988?" Walter had run from Ricardo like a panicked rat in a maze, though anyone who knew him could see, not just that Ricardo was a treasure, but that he was the very treasure laid up from the foundations of the earth just for Walter. I'd finally had to take him aside and speak home truths through the distorting haze of my own jealousy and fear of abandonment, while we washed strawberries at my kitchen sink the night of my summer party that year. "But I survived, and so can you. I have complete faith in you. And it won't really hurt, will it, now? that Joe is one of the eleven sexiest boys we've ever seen, and clearly mad for you – enough to be virtually paralyzed with fear at meeting your perfectly inoffensive friends." Walter knew exactly how intimidating he could be and was being bad to make me smile. "Now we go inside. How are you doing? No one must see you've been weeping." He broke away and looked at me, smiling critically, from arm's length.

"*Di lagrime avea d'uopo,*" I said. "*Or son tranquilla; lo vedi? Ti sorrido.*" He used his thumb to dry my eyes, gently but firmly, as though he were applying make-up for a Noh performance.

"I think you promised me an Empire camp bed," he said, satisfied with my face and taking me through the door with his arm around my shoulder. "I want to make sure; Ms. Marie has no scruples at all, you know, and I'm not about to settle for some tedious sleigh bed that for all we know could be from Ethan Allen's American Collection. And that awful boy I married is completely capable of tossing our bags on some fold-out nightmare with plaid Polo fabric and paisley pillows: and I simply *won't* have some dreary hetero preppie telling me how to mix and match. I'm an OGM and I *know* how to accessorize, thank you very much." Walter fell in love with the phrase "openly gay man" when the press took to it in the late Eighties as if it were an entirely new category of being. It amused him no end, especially when he could apply it to people who had been out activists since before Harry Hay.

"You haven't seen this house," I said. "Believe me, you're in a win-win situation here. And I did give strict orders about the camp bed; Rachel knows."

"Is it me," he asked, "or is she getting more beautiful? Didn't she use to be just a pretty girl with wavy hair?" We were on the steps by now and he swung around to whisper this down to me over his shoulder.

"You used to be a skinny blond kid with glasses," I said. "Now you're an ambassador of glamor."

"True," he said, turning around again and continuing up the stairs. "And you're bagging Italo sex-idols on your vacation from being pursued by ardent undergraduate lacrosse players. I just love being a grown-up."

"Baby," Ricardo was calling from down the hall. "In here." We found him sitting on the camp bed; Joe must be in Marie's room, where I could hear Rachel talking about towels. "Is this bed big enough?"

"*Perfecto,*" Walter said. "We'll pretend I'm Napoleon and

you're Czar Alexander." Ricardo laughed, a tolerant good-humored laugh with a faint lubricious undertone; I'd heard it many times over the years when Walter made references Ricardo didn't quite get. Sometimes he'd ask for an explanation, sometimes not, but he had learned to believe with absolute confidence that the allusion was always meant to be flattering. Now he cocked his head and took a guess.

"And you can conquer me," he said.

"And burn Moscow around your ears," Walter said; "and you'll still adore me, though you may be ashamed to admit it."

"Well," said Ricardo, "I've been ashamed of you as long as I can remember." He turned to me. "Joe's nice," he said. "Maybe tomorrow he won't be so nervous. And that Rachel!"

"Promise me you won't try to do her hair," Walter said.

"Oh, no," he answered very seriously. "She's very classy; she doesn't want done hair. Just like she is is perfect. I kind of wish I'd just brought her yellow roses now."

"No, she loves what you brought," I said. "I could tell. She never would have picked them, and that's fun for her."

"Good." He got up and took my hand. "Let's go find Joe. I'm going to make him like me, you'll see. When I'm through with him he'll like us all so much he won't be able to stand it."

I was impressed that Ricardo had noticed Joe's slight holding back; he was used to making easy devastation among all those he met and didn't usually have any need to be modest about it.

"Don't smother the poor guy," I said.

Ricardo hesitated.

"I know what you mean, honey," he said. "I'll be very

smooth. This is important."

Walter cuffed Ricardo's sleeve and said,

"*Entonces, mi amor*, we know the quality of your detective work." Walter had picked up a fair amount of Spanish since he'd been with Ricardo and nurtured a delusion that he could dazzle me with facile little tags like this. What did dazzle me was the way this lethal WASP charmed Ricardo's family. Walter swore, when they got back from his first visit to San Juan, that Ricardo's mother insisted he call her Mamita by dinner time the first day. I categorically refused to believe it until I met her myself when she came to Washington and I heard her call Walter *hijito* and *querido*, with fond pats on the cheek and commands to eat more. It would probably be needless to describe the ravages Ricardo caused in Massachusetts, the elaborate ritualized unbendings of Walter's stately parents, the efficient smiles and sibilant cooings of the doting Yankee aunts who plied Ricardo with Boston baked beans on one night (to make him feel part of the family) and plantains and roast pork the next (to make him feel at home – having walked to the town library in their sensible shoes and L.L. Bean parkas to research the recipes).

"You had thirty seconds with Joe on the stairs," Walter was asking Ricardo: "your honest opinion."

"Oh, Jimmy's going to marry him, of course."

"You think?" I asked.

"Definitely." He gave the taut little nod which always accompanied his firmest pronouncements. Ricardo had bought fairly heavily into Walter's and my reliance on his intuition and was by now completely autocratic in his judgements of people; he was also invariably right. "Joe's made up his mind." I laughed.

"You talk as though I hadn't," I said.

"You're like Walter. You're going to give him a hard time."

"Don't worry about our Jim," Walter said. "I'll vouch for him. But you think Joe's intentions are honorable?"

"Yeah. He's gonzo over Jim. And he's the stubborn type."

"That settles it, young James," Walter said, turning to me. "Charo has spoken. There's nothing left to do now but drop by Tiffany's and pick a silver pattern."

"Just don't screw it up, honey," Ricardo said, patting my arm. "He likes you so much."

"I have just about had it with all my so-called friends telling me to be nice to Joe," I said. I was hissing slightly because I didn't want my voice to carry down the hall. "To my knowledge the Vatican has not yet officially canonized the man and for your information he has been more than his share of churlish this week. Why aren't you all telling him to be nice to *me*, for God's sake?"

"That's probably what his friends have been doing," Walter said. "It's their job."

"Come to think of it," I said, backing down and smiling, "they have. He has a fat old gay duenna named Michael who ordered him to marry me a few days ago."

"You see?" Ricardo said. "So we can hassle you all we want." I laughed, but he could see I was feeling a little needled. "Now honey," he crooned annoyingly, "you know it's just because we love you."

"Thanks so very much," I said grudgingly, as the three of us crowded out the door and down the hall to join the others.

"You and the Neubergs are going to get along famously. Reading me is their new hobby."

Joe was standing nearest the door with Tony beside him, while Rachel and Marie bustled around the bed and closet. It was a very retro gender scene; any moment the two women would swap recipes, and Joe and Tony would start puffing on cigars and talking about sports. Joe turned without smiling when he heard us come in. I put my arms around him from behind and breathed "Yo Divo" in his ear. I noticed that, as I said it, I wasn't feeling especially lovey; I said it just to be supportive. Maybe this was the kind of daily maintenance that kept relationships going after the first glow. Old married people always said it wasn't the romance that lasted, but the loyalty and companionship, and I'd never really understood how that would work. Joe leaned back against me now and hugged my arms without relaxing.

"How are you doing?" I whispered.

"Good," he said, still not smiling. I think it gave him courage that I was hugging him in front of the others.

"Relax," I said. "Remember when I met your friends last week? I lived."

"That's right," he said, and I felt him soften a bit. After a moment he stepped away from me and said, "Ricardo, let me show you where to plug in your blender."

"It's not a blender, darling," Ricardo said, as though Joe had accused him of shopping at Caldor's. "It's a high-tech juicer."

"Sorry," Joe said. "Let me show you."

"OK." Ricardo took Joe's arm and looked across at me. "Jim," he said, "you should dress Joe in green – just look at his eyes." Joe laughed.

"He does," he said. "It's all he talks about."

"Well good," Ricardo said. He spoke in the intense confiding tone of some great society beauty who wanted to make it very clear to everyone within earshot that she'd taken a sweet pretty artless country girl under her patronage, promising to take her by the rue des Capucines to meet her dressmaker and to give her a letter to Alexandre. It hadn't occurred to Ricardo, before whom the most odious closeted Capitol Hill lobbyists routinely swooned with desire, that Joe was idolized, fawned over and lusted after in his own right. Joe seemed to enjoy this novel form of attention, like a movie star receiving a friendly welcome from a grand dowager who had never seen one of his movies and didn't know he was famous. He smiled shyly and let Ricardo fuss over him and pluck at his sleeve. "Now show me where to plug in," Ricardo said over his shoulder as they left the room, elaborately conspiratorial. "And I can tell you all about Jim. Oh Joe... !" He rolled his eyes in warning.

"Scare me," Joe said, and they disappeared down the hall.

Rachel caught my eye from across the room and nodded once. "Let's all go downstairs," she said. "There's some food left if any of you travelers are hungry. We'll try to find a CD that's not too twinkly."

"I've got some Jessye Norman in the car if you decide you need it," said Marie, "and some Monteverdi." Since Clare came on the scene, Marie had become the gay world's greatest proponent of early music and tossed around terms like "chiff" and "white tone" and "terraced dynamics" like a veteran madrigal singer; she even claimed to like Gesualdo. Her infatuation with Jessye, whom Clare considered the Enemy, was years older and involved some kind of erotic fantasy I'd never allowed myself to think too much about.

As I started down the stairs with her and Rachel, I heard Walter behind us saying to Tony, "So, Jim tells me you've been doing just spectacularly well." Tony said something genial like "Can't complain. You look great." Ricardo's chatter drifted to us from the kitchen, punctuated from time to time by Joe's little hum. From the sound of it, he was amused, relaxing at last, though clearly unable like most of us to get a word in edgewise with Ricardo when he was on a tear. My life, I thought, and smiled.

Chapter 13 – Friday into Saturday morning

Over night the heat broke and when I opened the door to step out onto the balcony that morning there was a wonderful cool wind blowing. I stood there for a few minutes and let it blow around inside my robe, rustling away the sense of the sweaty sticky night which even the air conditioning hadn't made pleasant. Joe was being a pain and I was glad to leave him showering inside.

We'd been up rather late; the Washington group wanted to see the studio, and we talked for a long time after Tony and Rachel went back to the main house. Ricardo had discovered Joe's picture taped to the fridge downstairs and it had made a big impression. All three of the newcomers made a point in their differing ways of raving about it. Joe was not completely comfortable with Walter and Marie, though he did seem to be warming up to Ricardo fairly well. He was gruff when Walter praised him and resisted Marie's kindly-meant flirting just as gravely as if she hadn't been safely lesbian and married. He didn't say much after they left and fell asleep next to me with the barest of good-night grunts.

When I woke up in the morning he was still sleeping with his back to me. I slipped one arm over him and kissed the back of his neck. He stirred and made a grumpy sound. I hoped he was joking because I was feeling rather frisky. I pressed myself against him very slowly and, I hoped he would think, gently and respectfully.

"No," he said, and shrugged hard to get my hand off his

shoulder. "Always want to fuck me." His eyes were closed and he sounded more than half-asleep as well as seriously irritated. I rolled over and left him alone, not very happily. I was waiting for him to repent and make some timid approach to me, but he didn't.

I awoke again several minutes later when he made a sudden lurch and sat up.

"Wo," he said, as though he'd startled himself.

"What?" I said.

"Nothing."

"You feeling better?"

"What do you mean?" He looked at me without friendliness.

"You were a terrible grouch a while ago," I said.

"You were being a horny bastard," he said. "I wasn't put on this planet for you to play with whenever you want." I gaped for a moment and then said,

"I assure you the outrage will not recur." I sat up too, my back to him, and reached for my robe.

"You sound like Walter," he said irritably.

"Indeed? And this is to be construed as a bad thing?"

"Cut it out," he said. "It's not even what you say; it's that goddamn tone of voice. Like you're both so smart."

"We *are* smart," I said, and stood up. "'Yo Joe; how ya doin'?' You prefer that? I can do that if it makes you feel more at home."

"OK, now you're being insulting."

"And you're insulting one of my best friends," I said, "someone who's been on my side consistently since 1970; but apparently I should ditch him the second you deign to grace my life?" He closed his eyes and shook his head hard with disgust, as if he were trying to clear a nasty dream out of his mind.

"You're out of control," he said. "Anyway I've decided I'm going to hang out with Michael today."

"Yesterday we were mad at Mother," I said.

"Don't call him that," he snapped. Then he went on in a bogus reasonable pleasant tone of voice. "Anyway – maybe I'll see you guys for dinner. You'll want to spend the day with your friends. Plus we're all coming for the party tonight." I was turning cold. Joe was free to do anything he wanted, of course, and I couldn't force him to like my friends. On the other hand, he hadn't given them the breath of a chance and I thought he owed me at least that.

"Joe!" I said, exasperated. "You know I want you to get to know these people. How can you run off and spend the day with people you're going to be spending all your free time with again anyway, come Monday?"

"I'm sure you and Walter are going to want to dissect me. You can't do that with me sitting there like a rock. I'm sure he'll appreciate the chance. He'll be very – witty." He said the last word in a prissy British accent. It was fortunate that my breath was taken away by his spitefulness, because if I could have I would have screamed at him. Then I remembered Rachel: she had said everything would be wonderful, and Joe wouldn't hurt me if he could help it. I stepped back to the bed and put my hands on his shoulders.

"Leave me alone," he said, as though I were groping him crudely.

"Divo, please," I said. I held my hands up in front of his face as if to show him I carried no weapon. Then I put them back on his shoulders as tenderly as I knew how. I couldn't think what to say.

"There's no point in it," he said after a second. "They're not going to like me."

"They already do," I said.

"That's so condescending." He was looking down. "Plus how am I supposed to take you home to Brooklyn? What are you going to think?" He left a long silence, as though imagining horrors: awkward pauses, frozen smiles, bad grammar. "My parents may not be high-class and they don't have a lot of education, but they're good people. They're very simple people." He said this very fervently, like a right-wing politician bringing himself to the verge of tears by descanting on family values. It might reflect a little shame at his own escape from Brooklyn, his Ivy League BA; it might even explain a little of his chronic underachieving since college. In any case it was a defense he'd rehearsed many times, I was sure. In his mind I'd already been rude and snobby to his parents and he was doing the righteous thing by standing up for them. He looked up defiantly, meaning to be a stalwart revolutionary, but when he met my eyes his gaze faltered. Apparently I didn't look like the phantasm of aristocratic hauteur and privilege that he'd been arguing with in his mind. I must have looked frightened.

"I'll love them," I said. "I'll thank them for making you. I don't care where they went to school or *if* they went to school."

"You think you mean that." He looked at his hands and then suddenly lay back, staring at the ceiling and drumming his fists stiffly on the mattress. "This isn't going to work."

I sat next to him and patted his stomach. I still didn't know what to say. His nerves were clearly shot and there was a real danger that anything I said would make them worse. I kept patting him without talking, until he laid his hand on mine.

"Tiger," he said sadly.

I decided to put my faith in a higher power.

"Let me tell you something Rachel told me yesterday," I said. I could feel him tense slightly; he was afraid she'd sold out whatever confidence he'd placed in her, which I suddenly hoped had been simply to tell her how much he loved me.

"OK," he said suspiciously.

"She told me this would be a hard time for us." I had almost said 'a hard time for you,' and sent up a quick prayer of thanks that I'd caught myself. "There are some major stressors here: you meet my friends, which let's face it makes you nervous – you know it took me some time to warm up to..." He squirmed in protest and I quickly said, "But the point is I *did* warm up to them. And you are going to love my friends too. Remember the first couple of days you didn't like Tony? But..." I checked in my recent memory for proof that Joe actually had grown fond of Tony and wasn't sure, so I didn't press the point. "And then in a couple of days, you're going back to LA and we don't know how long till we see each other again." He didn't respond, but he felt less tense under my hand. "That's enough to make anybody nervous."

Still he didn't say anything and I leaned back on one elbow beside him.

"Joe," I said, "help me out here. I'm trying, but I need

help." His eyes were soft now, unsure. I tried to kiss him but he turned aside slightly without changing his expression, thinking deeply.

"I'm going to take a shower," he said. "You make the coffee."

"Are you going to stick around and play with us here? Please give yourself a chance to like these people. All they want is to love you." He still didn't look at me. "For what it's worth, Ricardo is positive we're getting married," I said. Still looking at the ceiling, he at least smiled slightly at this and nodded.

"He's a nice guy," he said. "Real genuine."

"So?" I asked. "Stick around this morning. Please. You can run off with Michael for lunch, for the afternoon. I want you here for the morning." Since he didn't answer, I put my face next to his and said "I love you" in a wheedling bimbo-voice.

"Oh please," he said, and rolled away from me. He stood up, and finally looked at me. He didn't seem as angry or withdrawn as before. "I'm going to take a shower. I'll think about it." I got up and followed him to the bathroom door.

"I just spilled my guts and swallowed my pride: and you're going to think about it," I said. "Where's my big pay-off?"

"This is it," he said. "I'll think about it. Now I'm closing the door." He smiled and made a feint to close the door in my face, since I hadn't moved. At least he was starting to tease a little. "Come on," he said; I stood there. "God you're stubborn."

"Promise," I said.

"No. But I'll kiss you if you'll let me close the door."

He leaned forward with his lips puckered ridiculously and I admit I smiled. But I didn't want a silly kiss; I just wanted him not to do this disappearing act. I put my arms around him, my face to his shoulder, and squeezed him fairly hard, trying to press a concession out of him.

"Hey," he said. "OK; that's enough. *Basta*, Tiger. *Cazzo, che testa dura.*" He pushed me away, using his strength gently, and closed the door. There was still a pressure in my chest, fear that something was really wrong, that our lives couldn't be made to mesh. I wanted him to give me a reassurance, and he wouldn't. I went and set up the coffee machine, and while it was brewing I stepped out onto the balcony. The ocean breeze gave my spirits the first real lift they'd had all morning.

Maybe ten minutes later he came out of the bathroom and I went back inside to see what he'd decided. He was standing naked at the foot of the bed toweling his hair, and laughed when he saw me:

"God you look terrible," he said.

"Well you've been hogging the bathroom," I said. "All my beauty aids are in there." I looked in the long mirror on the outside of the bathroom door and saw that my hair was standing straight up from the pillow and the salt breeze. "Eek!" I said. "*Road*-kill!"

He laughed again. His eyes were clear now and he seemed more like himself.

"You crack me up," he said. "You really are pretty funny, the way you talk and all." He reworded that, to show that he didn't mean I was ridiculous. "I mean, you're actually amusing."

I felt a chill on the back of my neck; that last phrase sounded like something Walter or I would say. It would probably be impolitic to point that out to Joe just now.

As the immense white towel flicked around him, giving flashes of his wonderful nakedness, I felt a sudden passion to touch him.

"Lie down a minute," I said. "You're dry enough. I must worship your body this moment or go mad." He laughed again and threw his head back. Then he obligingly flopped face-down on the rumpled sheets.

"Rub my back," he said. "And no funny business." He laid his head on his crossed arms and closed his eyes. I sat next to him and started stroking his back, loving the familiar feel of its soft strong curves. I had one of those lacerating lover's insights, when all the strength and beauty of the beloved seemed the frailest membrane cast over his tender core of fears and sorrows. Inside this massive longed-for man's body was a person who truly feared that I wouldn't respect him.

"Joe," I whispered, "I love you so much." He nodded. "So what's the verdict, by the way?" I asked.

"You got me for the morning," he said.

"I've got you for life," I said, and shook him firmly with both hands on his shoulders.

"I guess," he said provokingly. On impulse I smacked his butt and he made a sudden warning sound like a quack, "Aa aa": Watch it. I moved my hand up again to his back and just said,

"I can't help lusting after you when all your loveliness is arrayed like this in full view."

"I know," he said, and opened his eyes to smile at me. "I love working your nerves." Then he rolled over and sat up. "No nookie this morning, though," he said. "I'm too hyper. After the party tonight maybe I'll make it up to you."

We've been around this block before, I thought tiredly. Then I remembered the making up and didn't mind so much. He went over to his duffle bag and fished out some shorts and a shirt. He looked at me and said, "You've got to wash up and comb your hair or I'll be embarrassed to be your new boyfriend." As I stepped obediently towards the bathroom door, he came up behind me and put his arms around me. He was still naked and it felt very sweet and homey to have him pressed to me through the silky cotton of my robe; it also felt, of course, as Gene would say, right hot.

"OK," he said. "For the record, I love you too. I'm calming down now, see? I can do this."

As soon as we were both ready we went looking for the others in the kitchen downstairs. The door stood open and as we came down the iron stairs we could hear Rachel and Ricardo talking inside. Against all my instructions, she was apparently asking him about his juicer. He said something about nutrition, and she made a grave hum of agreement. She had written two or three widely-quoted articles on nutrition in public-school lunch programs, but she didn't mention this to Ricardo. He was listing fruits and vegetables according to some scheme I didn't understand.

"Good," she said; "I think I've got all of that down. And you'll let me surprise you?"

"Oh honey!" he said, one of his strongest terms of assent. As I opened the screen door, I saw them standing at the central island counter, their heads together over the machine; she had a slip of paper and a pen and had been taking notes. They looked up and said Hi.

"The others are on the porch with the bagels and things," Rachel said. "There's plenty for you two."

"I've been telling her about my diet," Ricardo said. He put his hand on Joe's arm and said confidingly, "I'm HIV-positive, you know."

"Jim told me."

"So I pay a lot of attention to what I eat." I resisted the temptation to mention his predilection for Fritos and Diet Coke.

"Well whatever you're doing," Rachel said, "it's obviously working. Good for you."

"It's been eight years," Ricardo said proudly. "I got a bad transfusion in eighty-five, after I was in this accident in San Juan," he explained to Joe. "It was just before they identified the virus and started screening blood. Can you believe it? And the ironic thing is, I'd always been real careful; the first guy I ever made it with was from New York and he told me all about safe sex."

"Drag," Joe said.

"I'm OK, though," Ricardo said, nodding to acknowledge Joe's laconic sympathy.

"You do AZT?" Joe asked.

"No way." Ricardo was very heated about anti-virals and I always felt a rising panic when the subject came up. I lived down the street from Johns Hopkins Hospital, and of course Luellen was the head physician's assistant on Osler 8. The high-tech approach to AIDS was a familiar one to me and I'd always wished Ricardo would give AZT a chance. He said he'd rather drink arsenic, and, as he always reminded me, it was his body. Luellen swore to me that his holistic take on the disease had some real medical legitimacy and that I should just be as supportive of his decisions as I could. Eight asymptomatic years did seem like a good argument in his favor. I could always feel the tense bracing inside myself, though, when I thought of him, as if from day to day the word might come that some infection had presented and the quick or slow decline had begun. It was as though all his preciousness and goodness hung by a single strand of cobweb. Walter said to me once, with a poise which impressed and moved me very much, that all life was that tenuous: it could be snuffed out in an instant and we had to learn to cherish every second of it, sick or not. HIV had forced him and Ricardo to live up to that insight. Perhaps if I were a Zen master instead of a Presbyterian elder I could live that way too.

Rachel's face, I was glad to see, was drawn rather close; she too felt some distress at Ricardo's dismissal of Western medicine's best offer, but she smiled.

"Let's go outside," she said, "before they forget we're here."

Tony was entertaining Marie and Walter on the porch, pouring second cups of coffee and passing the plate of bagels around. The men were still in their robes, but Marie had already put on her bathing suit, a smart racing number with black and grey stripes. She was very dedicated about swimming rapid compulsive laps on her lunch breaks and still had the figure of a college girl. She was wearing a short red kimono with a pattern of asparagus stalks in white, but had let it fall open to show the suit.

"Good morning, boys," she said as Joe and I stepped out onto the porch. "Did you sleep well? I love my futon."

Joe glanced at me and said,

"Not really. I was being a jerk."

"No!" said Marie, as if they were settling in for a jokey gossip. "About what?" He hesitated.

"I wasn't very nice to my Tiger here." I smiled and looked down. It really wasn't necessary for him to do this kind of public penance. Everyone else on the porch seemed to speak at once, to reassure him.

"I'm sure it wasn't that bad, Joe," said Tony;

"Well he can be terribly irritating," said Walter;

"I don't believe you," said Ricardo.

Somehow Marie and Rachel spoke in exact unison:

"No, Joe, you have to be nice to him." Marie added, "Our BooBoo is very sensitive." Rachel looked at her and said,

"'BooBoo'? I'm learning so much about Jim this summer."

"I'm trying," Joe said to them. "I think I'm learning." His voice was still serious and humble.

"No, come on, Joe," I said, "it's OK now. We're still friends." I took his hand and kissed it.

"Who wants to go swimming?" Marie said. "We didn't come here to sit on the porch and eat bagels."

"Speak for yourself," I said, sitting down.

"We'll come," Joe said – speaking for me, I noticed. "Just give us a minute." He sat on the floor by my chair and spread cream cheese on a bagel and held it out for me to take a bite.

"Stoke that mighty engine," Walter said, looking at my

waist.

"He looks good, doesn't he?" Joe said, looking Walter frankly in the eye.

"He always looks good," said Ricardo.

"I love this old shirt on him," Joe said. He'd made me put on his fetish-shirt from the Lyric Opera. "It makes his eyes look so blue."

"That's so condescending," I said. Joe turned quickly to contradict me, and then realized I was quoting him. He let his breath out and smiled.

"Yeah," he said, getting my point. He started chomping on an unsliced bagel with nothing on it, making muscles stand out in his temples.

"Say, Jimbo," said Tony, "where'd you get that old shirt, anyway?" He smiled at Joe, a smile which Joe apparently took as a challenge.

"I know you gave it to him," he said a little grudgingly; "he told me."

"Oh, that's right," Tony said innocently. "I did, didn't I?"

"Hurry up," Joe said to me, standing. "Let's go hop in our suits and we can go out with Marie." He took an apple off the table and did that butch thing of tossing it a few inches in the air and catching it with a hard downward swipe of the same hand, making a loud smack. As he stood and tugged on my sleeve to hurry me, I saw Marie take an orange and start to juggle it in high tosses without looking either at it or at her hands, making a point of chatting with Tony the whole time.

"I'll wait for you right here," she called to us over her shoulder as we left the porch.

It was a beautiful morning by now and we ran into a dozen or more people we knew as we crossed the sand. Marie commented on how there were more women on the gay beach than the summer before, and I pointed out my pet young lesbian, the one who'd been dancing on the speakers at the Strand. She was holding hands with her girlfriend and chatting with two long-hair boys on the next towel. Two or three unlikable men with the standard big pecs came up and tried to hit on Joe, on the chance that he was holding my hand only because I was his older brother or former landlord or because he felt sorry for me. Marie was delighted to run into several Baltimoreans she hadn't seen since her move to Washington, and introduced me to one or two people she had met there.

I spotted the red umbrella and sent Joe over to make his lunch plans while Marie and I settled on a spot near the water.

"Any news from Clare?" I asked her.

"She called two nights ago. They're having the greatest time; they took the kids to the zoo and Jos tried to teach the toucan '*O magnum mysterium*.'" It was gracious of Josquin, who at five was mostly involved in playing soccer with a foam ball and molding detailed miniature aliens out of Play-Doh, to make this concession to his mother's sensibilities. "Pedro says Hi, by the way; Clare too." Pedro, the kids' father, was a Mexican violist with enormous brown eyes who had said very nice things about my singing during his visit east the summer before. Clare played her lute and I did a couple of Dowland songs and we all had a minor bonding over the issues of *gruppetto* turns on or before the beat and the *appoggiatura* from above or below. "Of course she's all curious about Joe and I told her I'd bring back a full report."

"Joe," I said, sighing.

"You didn't really fight last night, did you?"

"Kind of; this morning, mostly. He more or less accused me of being an élitist snob. But then he got over it. He's wound up so tight about meeting you all."

"Like we're so scary."

"He was nervous about Tony and Rachel too when he first met them," I said. "And now he's crazy about them." Again, for the sake of literal accuracy, I added, "About Rachel, anyway. I think Tony is too Man for him."

"No, it's just that he's too Your man for him." I looked confused and she said, "I mean, Joe is jealous of Tony. He knows you used to be in love with him."

"That's what Rachel said the first time she met him."

"That Rachel!" Marie exhaled hard with a little shooshing sound. "She is just – so – *beau*tiful." She paused and made a kind of respectful serious face, as if to show that she wasn't being rudely libidinous. "I think I want her to be my mommy," she said.

"Joe just frankly worships her," I said. "It's really funny sometimes. If you ever want to get Joe to do anything, just tell him it's what Rachel would do."

"Well, I'd call her a fairly wholesome role-model, wouldn't you?" She looked out over the water, shielding her eyes, maybe trying to recognize people she knew. It was a practical sensible scan she was conducting, not one of Rachel's oracular readings. Then she turned to me and said, "I think I like Joe. At first glance I just thought, Uh-oh, here goes Jim chasing after another hot muscle-boy who probably doesn't think about anything but sex and disco. And that's fun, of course, but it's not where you want to end up – and to be fair it's obviously not really Joe either. I do think he's being too weird about me and Walter. But I really liked the way he took the blame for your fight on the porch. He was very direct: like, There it is, I screwed up."

"Honesty," I said. "That's his word for it. He believes in being honest. I actually think he's taught me a fair amount about that in the past ten days."

"You've always been honest."

"Not always with the men I've dated. I've been really self-protective as a rule, kind of crabby and pushy and uncomfortable. With Joe, we work things out. We yell and then we're over it."

"*You* yell?"

"Well, not literally. I feel like it sometimes. I mean I say what I really think. Then we deal with it." I thought. "He's fairly literal; I wonder if he's smart sometimes. But he's got very good sense, especially about people-things."

"He's been kind of off about us, though – I mean, me and Walter."

"He's coming around."

"You just have to get him better trained before he meets your mother. If he sulks at her I'll beat him up." I loved the fact that she was taking my side, admitting some faults in Joe. If for some reason Joe and I didn't work things out, she and I would still be friends. Once I'd let that feeling sink in securely, I could think about being fair to Joe.

"I know Joe is being a little strange," I said, "but I got the biggest talking-to from Rachel yesterday about how it's inevitable, with him being nervous about fitting in with my friends, and about him and me trying to work out a cross-country thing, and she told me I'd have to be big about it. I guess I want you to do that too. You're being really nice to him and I want you to keep it up for a while longer. He'll catch on; he's trying."

"Just as long as you see he's being weird," she said, and put her head on my shoulder. She considered for a long moment and said, "I like the way you talk about him."

A few minutes later he came back from Michael's umbrella and said to me, "The guys all say Hi." He remained standing in front of Marie and me and asked, "You want to go right in?" I looked at her.

"I'm up for it," I said.

"Let's go," she said, and put her book and kimono and glasses in a careful pile.

The water was still very warm from the day before but the fresh breeze made it pleasant. Joe and Marie left me alone several times as they tore off on aggressive laps just beyond the breakers. Marie was swimming very hard and generally got back to me an arm or two ahead of Joe. Once I looked over at them as they reached their farthest point and saw them both stop and tread water for a minute. Joe could just touch bottom in the trough of each wave, and Marie put a hand on his shoulder to steady herself while she bobbed. He said something and she responded with what I call her girl-laugh, a flattering confiding giggle with her chin tilted up. I saw him smile with surprise; he hadn't been sure she'd enjoy whatever he'd said. She's seriously vamping, I thought. She suddenly dropped her hand from his shoulder and started swimming back, and he dove after her. His arms were flailing furiously and he swam up to me and grabbed my arm a second before she did. Apparently I was the finish line.

"Beat you," he said, as the two of them stood up and gasped, spraying me with the drops of water that dripped from their lips as they exhaled.

"You're pretty fast," she said generously.

"My aqua-jocks," I said.

"Marie," Joe said, "you body-surf?"

"Yeah," she said. "Gene and I always have contests. You know Gene, don't you?" He looked thoughtful for a second and then, as he felt a wave rising behind him, made a lightning motion that surprised us, hurtling himself into the mounting crest and starting a quick plunge towards shore.

"Oh you *cheat*er!" Marie yelled, and went after him. By the time I'd hopped over the wave and cleared my eyes, the two of them were flopping prone in a boiling sandy foam an incredible distance in from me. She scrambled to her feet and pulled him up, both of them shaking the water from their faces and laughing.

"Beat you!" he crowed.

"Yeah you *cheat*er," she said, sounding exactly like a fifth-grader. "That's *one* for you." They came splashing out to me and pestered me to be score-keeper. Before I knew it, they'd shot off again on a mad careen into shore.

After lunch Walter and Ricardo came upstairs with me to hang out. Rachel and Marie had gone for a walk on the beach.

They seemed to enjoy each other quite a bit and talked freely about all the rest of us. As the only women in the group, they had clearly taken it upon themselves to figure out what was to become of all of us and how we should feel about it. Meanwhile Michael and his boys had swung by to get Joe and roistered off into town with him. Patrick was with them, staying quietly on the fringe of the group with his cigarette cocked and one eyebrow raised, keeping a steady focus on Bobby. Apparently they were going to meet Gene in town too. I was a little confused by this and couldn't quite decipher Chris' proud smile when he mentioned it. He looked fairly breathtaking in a billowing white pirate shirt which I very much feared came from International Male; open almost to the waist, it set off his taut olive skin ruthlessly. "*Claude Christian*," I said when I first saw him, and he kissed me demurely on both cheeks without touching me with his hands. This dazzled Ricardo, who pretended to be jealous and said I always had the prettiest boys kissing me. When Walter casually and decently mentioned how cute Chris was after they'd all left, Ricardo elbowed him firmly in the ribs and told him to cool it.

He took the huge chair by the sofa while Walter and I sat at the table and talked about Tony and Rachel, whom Walter hadn't seen in several years. Ricardo was leafing through *Entertainment News*, from which Joe's picture had already been cut, and suddenly broke into our conversation:

"Oh look, Jim," he said, "it's your favorite singer. 'The greatest Rossini singer of the century.'" He held the magazine up to show me her picture and I swore. He laughed, deeply proud of himself for knowing how to get to me.

"Admit she's good," Walter said to me, smiling at Ricardo's amusement.

"Of course she's good!" I sputtered. "I like her just fine. It's just this whole publicity machine – the Greatest Singer of the Millennium, after three or four successful débuts, as though the public had forgotten anything that happened before 1989. I mean – excuse me – Conchita Supervia was (am I correctly informed?) a singer of this century, was she not? and not too awfully shoddy in Rossini, I believe? And Berganza, my... no, let's not just talk about ME: the adored idol of *millions* of superb purist fanatics – an artist of which century, please? And still short of sixty, thank you, with a rather respectable discography. I was in a store the other day and asked the boylet behind the counter if they had any of her CDs, and he said 'Who?' and I said – 'No, she's a BIG star; no, a major diva in Europe' (every bit as big as Sutherland, my most *exquis* French friends assure me) – 'Mozart, Rossini, *Carmen*, art song': and this... this child asked me, 'You're sure you don't mean Sessilia Bar-TO-li?' Nonono. The Superstar Flavor of the Month; the March of Time – I've had it." By this point Ricardo was sliding out of his chair laughing. "It's not funny, Ricardo," I said.

"*Ay*," he said, gripping the arms of the chair and kicking.

"Come on," I said. "Put yourself in my position." Ricardo laughed and lay back in the chair, his head barely reaching to its back now, and threw his legs up in the air. Walter and I looked down on him frostily.

"Do you remember," I asked Walter, "when Ricardo was a sweet unspoiled young man and we all just loved him so?"

"I assure you," he answered, "he's the biggest bitch in the

gay world now."

"'Sessilia Bar-TO-li'!" Ricardo said between shrieks. Walter and I were both laughing now.

"You know," Walter said, "when we were married, Charo didn't know a cabaletta from a Cuisinart. Now he purses his lips and passes austere judgements on the so-called Three Tenors for taking too much *rubato* in *'Nessun dorma.'*"

"No," Ricardo gasped," for making it a trio to begin with." He wiped his eyes. "And for singing it in the Baths. Who do they think they are: Steber?" He started laughing again.

"See what I mean?" Walter was watching Ricardo with a little smile of delighted wonder. He got that smile every now and then, as if he'd never noticed before how cute Ricardo was. I'd have called it a honeymoon smile except that I'd been seeing it more and more often as the years passed. "The iciest opera-queen in the world. The other day I asked him how he liked Norman in the *'Demoiselle élue'* and he shrugged and sneered and said, 'All that... AR-tistry!' My blood ran cold."

"Ricardo," I said, "I'm going to want you to give Joe some lessons, OK?"

"Oh, we've already started. Last night, when he was in the kitchen with me plugging in the juicer? he asked me how I handled all the stuff you two talk about. I told him he should just decide if he actually liked any of it himself, and if he didn't he should blow it off, but if he did, he shouldn't talk himself out of it just to be stubborn and prove a point."

"Good for you, baby," Walter said.

"That's exactly the way he handles the books," I said. "Maybe there's hope for us." Ricardo waved his hand at me, dismissing all my fears with a gesture.

"Oh honey," he said.

By late afternoon Joe was back. He seemed relaxed and breezy and asked me about my day. I stood next to him at the bathroom sink as he shaved for dinner. He fussed for a minute to rinse all the stray whiskers down the drain. I realized I hadn't seen one left in the basin any of the days he'd stayed with me.

"You're so neat," I said. "I love your mother." He smiled as he dried his face and rubbed his Armani cream over his chin. "What's the latest with Gene and Chris?" I asked him. He shrugged.

"They were all up in each other at lunch," he said. "I think they went off together. We'll see tonight."

"And the rest of you all came to the beach after lunch?" I asked. "We didn't see you."

"No. Dennis and Michael and I went... " He stepped back from the sink and, looking at me obliquely in the mirror, raised his eyebrows to create a little suspense. "Guess what?" he asked.

"You bought me a diamond ring," I said. "But I've foolishly neglected to give you my measurements. How did you know what size?"

"Have you ever seen a diamond too big?" he laughed. "But I did get you something – for the party." He slipped past me into the dining area and pulled a flat little package out of the pocket of his jacket, which was slung over one of the chairs. He tossed it at me like a frisbee and I caught it, not very jockishly, by clutching it to my stomach. It was a CD of Italian opera choruses.

"How great," I said. "I don't have this." I started pounding the wall by the bathroom door with one fist and sang, *"Chi del gitano i giorni abbella?"*

"What's *'gitano'?*" he asked me.

Later we were sitting on the balcony watching the water. It was around happy hour and the beach was clearing out. The shadow of the house was lengthening by now and reached far down the sand. Soon it would be time to rendezvous downstairs for dinner. I'd lost track of everyone's whereabouts, except that Ricardo had insisted he needed what he redundantly called his beauty sleep. He normally slept as much as the pandas in the National Zoo and then would get up in a frenzy of vitality that exhausted everyone who knew him.

"So how are we doing?" I asked Joe.

"Fine," he said. "Dennis and Michael read me the riot act."

"About?"

"You. They said I had to be nicer to you." He watched the waves and looked serious. "We're really different, you know. It'll be hard."

"We've both done hard things before."

"You got that right." He gave a common-sense nod.

"Rachel and Marie said you had to be nice to me, too." He nodded again. After thinking for a second he chuckled and said,

"Marie is so competitive."

"It's cute the way our friends are ganging up on us," I said. "Rachel and Tony have been very stern with me. Tony said he'd have to shoot me if I screwed things up with you."

"He said that?" He seemed gratified. "I thought he didn't like me." He didn't speak for a minute and hummed once or twice. I knew something was percolating and let him think. "You know what scares me?" he asked. "It felt good to be mad at you. It was like, if you were being a jerk I didn't have to go any further with you. I could blow you off and go back to LA with a clean slate. I liked that." He paused. "But that's fucked up."

"It's human nature, I think. I fantasized breaking up with you yesterday because I pictured you going off with Dennis again. Why did I think that? It makes no sense, and it didn't make me happy. But it was a comfortable thought in a way. I know how to do that – breaking up, having things not work out. I don't know how to do this." He reached and took my hand.

"I like you when you're like this," he said. "I'm going to miss you."

"Not for long," I said.

"Hey!" he protested.

"No; I mean I'm going to come visit you before school starts." He laughed.

"Get me," he said. "Always thinking the worst."

We sat without talking for a long time. Eventually the beach was almost completely deserted, as people drifted off to dinner or happy hour. With the shade and the breeze it was getting almost chilly. We saw one lone swimmer, a woman with short hair who was far enough out to make me a little nervous. She had a firm stroke and turned occasionally to float on her back when she might be tiring. Her opulent figure seemed incongruous with the sleek efficient helmet of her black hair. From time to time she dove for a long moment and then shot out of the water, bringing her hands down to each side like a ballerina as she emerged. Her black suit glistened when the slanting sunlight touched her. She would tread water at times and splash handfuls of sea in her face. When she could touch bottom she would raise her cupped hands and let the water run luxuriantly down her arms. I liked her and wished she would come closer in to shore. In another minute or two I might have to go down onto the beach and call to her. The undercurrent was stronger in the evening, and I could already notice that she was getting sucked back a little into the deeper water each time she put her feet down.

"Is she OK?" I asked Joe finally.

"I think so," he said. "She seems to know what she's doing. It's quite a show."

"It's not a show," I said. "It's just her and the ocean."

"My God," he said, after watching her another minute or two. She had been some distance to our left when we first saw her; she had been swept past us by now and was far enough off to the right that he had to lean forward a bit to see around me.

"What?"

"It's Rachel," he said.

"No. Look at her hair."

"Watch her." He squinted as the reddening sun glinted off the water. "Good. She's coming in." As I watched, the woman began to ride waves, staying on the surface to avoid the current until she could stand securely.

"It's not Rachel," I said. "It looks nothing like her." I was squinting too. When the highest waves were coming just above her breasts, she braced herself and put her hands to the nape of her neck. She fumbled with something and released a long tight-twisted rope of hair, then leaned back into the water and shook her head. When she stood, her hair had soaked itself free of the compact coil and spread across her shoulders like a broad wimple.

"So I was wrong," I said.

Rachel came slowly towards shore, her steps staggered by incoming waves that broke around her legs. She was shaking slightly, from the chill or from fatigue. Yet she lingered in the water, stopping every couple of steps, stroking the surface of the foam as if it were a favorite cat. When she was in surf only up to her knees, she turned her back to shore and reached down to scoop up handfuls of water, rising and spreading her arms to scatter them in the air. She did this three or four times and then simply stood still, facing the deep water, and raised her hands far over her head, reaching widely to each side.

A few minutes later we saw her come up the wooden steps from the sand to the boardwalk. She was walking a little wearily and kept a firm grasp on the handrail on her way up the stairs. As she approached the house, we could hear the front door open. She looked up and smiled, not at us; she probably couldn't see us, with the sun's glare behind us.

"Hello, dear," she said.

"I've been keeping an eye on you from our window." It was Tony's voice, from the front porch.

"Thank you," she said. "I know." A moment later, we

heard them go in the front door.

Around nine that evening Joe and I dressed for the party. He looked through the closet for something I could wear to be a credit to him before his California friends and didn't pretend to be very optimistic. I'd brought an Armani Exchange seersucker shirt with blue and white pinstripes and he thought that was probably the best we could do for this particular evening.

"Chris worked there last summer," he said, "so at least he'll recognize it. He's big on labels." The idea of playing label-chicken with someone who wore pirate shirts from International Male was abhorrent, but I didn't say a word. Joe put on his new green shirt and a pair of tightly pressed chinos and looked… well, very good. We went down to the main house and, finding no one downstairs yet, wandered up to the second floor. In Walter's and Ricardo's room there was the usual flurry as Ricardo got ready. In another place and time, he would have been one of those great ladies of the court, the one of whom everyone said that she was as gracious and kind as she was lovely, except those few who had seen her drive her tiring-maids to weeping fifteen minutes before the ball. He was standing by the bed in a black silk shirt and Walter was reaching into the closet to get him a pair of pants. I was glad we'd gotten there in time to see his bare legs.

"Not those," he said, stamping his foot impatiently. "The other white ones." Walter just looked dumb and obedient and flicked through the hanging clothes to find the other pair of white pants.

"This belt?" he asked, holding up a black web belt with

a brass buckle. Ricardo made a noise in the back of his throat, as if fifteen Frenchmen had decided to say "r" at the same time. He rolled his eyes at Joe and went over to look for himself. He found a black belt studded with silver and turquoise medallions and held it up in Walter's face as if he were explaining some very simple principle of physics to him for the twelfth or thirteenth time.

"*This* belt," he said with murderous calm. "I'm going to wear my *boots*, Walter." Ricardo had taken madly to two-stepping a couple of years ago and had a pair of pewter-trimmed black cowboy boots that were his pride. His real achievement, in my eyes, was that he had succeeded in getting Walter to go dancing with him on a weekly basis. When I wanted to annoy Walter now, I just called him Clem or Tex.

"Oh," Walter said, all trace of amusement scrupulously scrubbed out of his voice. "That'll look nice." He turned to Joe and said, "A lot of people think it's all fun and games being married to a great beauty. It's hell."

"You two look pretty," Ricardo said as an afterthought, sitting on the bed to pull his boots on.

Marie came to stand in the open door and knocked on the jamb. "Are you all decent?" she asked. "How do I look?" She'd put on some sheer blue tights she bought with me in Rome one summer – her sausage-casings, she called them – and a billowy grey cotton shirt like a tunic. Hanging loose with no belt, it gave a very sexy suggestion that you could just run your hands up inside it from here to there with no obstacle of any kind.

"Oh honey," Ricardo said. "But no jewelry? Don't you

think a big necklace?"

"I don't know," Marie said uncertainly. "I was going to ask you." Marie, who needed no help accessorizing, had always been very polite about deferring to Ricardo on the subject.

"Let's ask Rachel," Ricardo said, turning to check his back in the full-length mirror. "Maybe she brought something." The two of them went across the hall and knocked at the master bedroom door. Walter looked at Joe and me with a fresh smile, as if he hadn't really had a chance to see us yet.

"Oh Joe," he said, "yes. The new shirt: Scarlett Andreoli. Eye lak ze emerald."

The three of us were downstairs doing last-minute arrangements when the others came down. Marie had succumbed to Ricardo and taken one of Rachel's gypsy-glamor necklaces. Tony, in a deep blue broadcloth shirt, had put what a hairdresser friend of mine called "product" in his hair and slicked it back a little. He looked fresh, glossy, and appetizing. Luckily all the smart gays who would be coming knew his story and I didn't have to worry too much that any of them would actually knock him to the floor and try to have him.

Rachel was wearing a rust-red caftan of a luxurious nappy cotton, crusted with gold embroidery at the neck and cuffs and hem. It was broad and rustly and trailed after her down the stairs. The neck opened in a straight cut down from the throat, and gave fleeting glimpses of deep cleavage as she moved. It was a barbarous imperial gown – what a nomad princess might make of a fabric traded from Byzantium; the winding shroud of a Scythian queen or a Visigoth chieftain's wife. Did Roxanne wear this dress the night she met Alexander, or the Empress

Zoe when she poisoned the Captain of the Sacred Guard? Rachel had it now. She had her hair up, a little bigger and fancier than usual, with casual little curls in front of her ears, and she wore clinking garnet-bead earrings.

"What do you think?" Ricardo asked the rest of us, as though we might decide she should dash upstairs and change: Oh no, Rachel – your blue denim smock is so lovely...

"Wow," Joe said. He sounded exactly like a boy in a Fifties film when the knock-about girl with freckles he'd asked to the prom came floating down the stairs looking like a lady.

"Thank you, Joe," she said, nodding a little grandly. She was just a tiny bit nervous, afraid we'd see that she was proud of how she looked. I'd never seen Rachel betray a moment's vanity. It was touching to see that she actually did appreciate and enjoy the effect of her beauty, maybe not just when she made the occasional spectacular toilette with the big entrance down the long stairway. Maybe every day, in the simple black swimsuit, in the sea-blue shirt-dress, in the wide jeans-skirt, she knew it and worked it. It was a little like thinking, Maybe she's a regular person. She put a hand on Tony's arm and said, "Check the bar, Anton. I'll look at... I'll check in the kitchen. Jim, keep Joe out here."

There was a lot of music that night. Bobby sat at the piano and picked out "Chopsticks," annoying everyone, and then surprised those of us who didn't know him well by breaking into some fairly inventive jazz variations on it. Patrick stood behind him and watched his fingers for all the world as if he played himself and were picking up some technical tricks from a fellow-artist. Bobby segued into a generalized Latin filler and said, without looking up from the keys, "Come on, Mother."

Michael, who was talking to Tony at the time, put one hand to his throat and said, "No you don't," and Joe said "Come on" and Chris said "Come on" and Dennis said "Come on" and Michael finally went over to the piano, walking with an exaggerated rocking at the waist to show his reluctance, and put his drink down. Suddenly he threw both arms in the air and flung his head back. Bobby knew his cue, and started pounding out a melody I almost recognized.

"No!" Walter said, laughing, getting it. I didn't, until Michael sang, "Don't cry for me..." He stopped for an instant and put his face in his hands.

"Come on!" his boys chorused. Gene started clapping in rhythm to make him sing. Joe made woofing noises and rotated his fist next to his face.

"Honestly," Michael said, laughing, shaking his head, and continued.

During the ovation Ricardo came and stood next to me, nodding and smiling without looking at me.

"You two have to do a song," he said discreetly, like an ambassadress whispering to her husband at the reception Don't forget to invite the Austrian Cultural Attaché to the *Schubertabend* next week. He meant me and Walter.

"No," I said.

"I'll tell Walter," he said, ignoring me. "Wait here." A few moments later, red-faced, sure I was about to make a permanent fool of myself in front of Tony, Rachel, Joe, and all his peers, I stood with one hand on the piano and stared at the floor smiling while Walter plunked out the introduction to "Diamonds Are a Girl's Best Friend." It went fairly well once it was started. There was encouraging laughter from around the room and I decided that being shy about it was just part of the incongruous charm of the moment. "But stiff back or stiff knees, You stand straight at Tiffany's!" was my best reading and I saw Michael laugh into his hand, a good sign. I took some courage from Walter's collaboration; he turned to sing the refrain over his shoulder with me and cracked me up by interpolating little snatches of opera arias in the right hand between phrases. People were clapping and no one cared if I dropped a few words or, as I did once, turned and drummed my fists on the piano, face down, at the absurdity of it all.

"What a ham," Tony said when it was over, and Joe said, "I'm going to start calling *you* Divo."

Around midnight there was a sudden scramble and the lights went out. Everyone seemed prepared for this except Joe and me. We were sitting on the couch talking to Marie and she suddenly, on a signal from someone I hadn't seen, stood up and started singing "Happy birthday." Walter and Bobby slid onto the piano bench and played, Walter providing crashing classical chords and Bobby a tuneless jazz filigree at the top of the keyboard. Their key had nothing to do with what Marie was singing, though they couldn't be blamed for that: Marie never really sang in any one key anyway. Through the archway from the dining room we could see a glow and then Rachel came in carrying the blazing cake. She had it lifted up and seemed like a priestess of some kind, with her caftan hanging from her outstretched arms in heavy symmetrical folds.

"When did you have time to make this?" Joe asked after he'd blown out the candles and cut the cake.

"When you were out this afternoon," she said. "I hate to say it, but it's a very easy recipe." That might almost have been true, her persistent *sprezzatura* notwithstanding. It was a very good sponge cake made in an angel's-food pan, with some kind of liqueur soaked into the top of it and a dusting of powdered sugar.

"It's easy for a really good cook," Marie said. "Classic cooking is the easiest to mess up."

"It's good," Joe said. I smiled at his plain speaking; I'd been about to say something fancy – Attic simplicity perhaps, or *La nudité ne convient qu'aux déesses.*

"Sing a song, birthday boy," Dennis said a while later.

"No," Joe said. There'd been a lot of No followed by shocking performances that evening. No one was going to let him get away with No. Finally he stood and asked Walter if he knew "Broadway."

"I know the tune," Walter said. "I can wing it. What key?"

"It starts in G," Joe said, "but it goes up a half-step every verse."

"Fine, Joe," Walter said, a martyr. "Just drive me mad for no reason."

"We could just stay in..."

"No, no. We modulate. Just as you wish." Walter ran his hands up and down the keyboard clunkily, trying out arpeggios in the keys he would need. He cracked his knuckles and cleared his throat. "Begin."

I hadn't heard Joe sing full-voice since Yale days. The first note hit me like a shell. His voice was not just brassy. It was enveloping, a chromium cage, an incitement to riot. The acoustic of pop vocalism had always been a complete mystery to me. Joe's voice came out of someplace, but I had no sympathetic sense of how it worked in his larynx or head resonators. He just opened his mouth and the sound was already behind us, whooshing out to sea. His eyes were focused out the window, over the water, following his voice rather than projecting it. Certainly he was not with us. At his first modulation, Walter dropped a note or two before he found his footing. Joe didn't falter; Walter could have dropped out altogether and Joe would have scaled the same fearless rungs, spiraling up verse by verse to his blinding high B-flat with the same steady certainty with which he'd scoured the sink the day before. His head up, his eyes shining, he sang and listened to himself at the same time, smiling, believing. Walter played louder with each verse, goosing with the left hand, lifting the floor to follow the voice that sprang above it.

"I won't quit till I'm a star," Joe sang, a song about his very deepest self that had no reference of any kind to me. He would have sung this song, just this way, if he'd never known me, if I'd never been born. By a strong physical effort I restrained myself from jumping up and grabbing him. I wanted to remind him that I was there. I wanted to be deep inside him, not in sex necessarily – though admittedly he had never been more attractive. I just wanted him to know me; I just wanted him to let me touch him. You made me love you, I thought, star-struck. I could picture him being shatteringly famous and me, a shy anonymous fan, adoring him from a small town in Iowa, his magnetism the only flash of power and glory in my life.

He didn't trail off at the end, the way you heard the song on the radio. He finished the last verse and then added the words "Oh hey" on an octave skip that took him back up to his highest note. The note was absolutely uniform: no bloom of any kind, just a blank stunning wall, immobile and majestic, a rock formation you could stand in front of and gawk at for hours. His face was set in an unchanging smile that didn't give any clue as to how the note was placed or produced. It was almost as if he were lip-synching to a blast from a synthesizer. It seemed to last a very long time. I went on a whole mental journey about lust and unattainability and despair and exaltation while Joe held the note, and I wasn't really safely back when he cut it off with a toss of his head. It was like the moment after the bagpipes stop; you instinctively checked to see if your heart was still beating.

After a few instants of silence, Walter, white-faced, turned around on the bench and said, "Joe." Then the others clapped.

The guests didn't stay terribly late; by one-thirty the only people left in the house were the ones who would sleep there. It was a fun party over-all, but rather sedate by Joe's standards I thought. I was a little worried that, if it hadn't been for me and my elderly friends, he would have wanted to party down till dawn. He did well, all things considered. When he wasn't with me he seemed to put some effort into being charming with Marie and Walter. He also chaperoned Rachel around the room and made sure Chris and Dennis and Bobby talked politely when she was within earshot. At one point he perched on the arm of the sofa while she and Gene were talking, listening protectively as if Gene might say something uncalled-for from one moment to the next, and poised to break in if he had to.

Another time I saw him gravely mediate a conversation between Tony and Michael. Ricardo came up to me while I was watching this exchange across the room and said,

"He's so responsible. He's making sure everyone behaves. He just raised his eyebrows at Bobby when he was doing Vanna and Rachel came by." This seemed to amuse Ricardo considerably. He had decided Rachel was cool.

Once the visitors were out of the house, Marie and I started ferrying dishes to the dishwasher and putting things in the refrigerator.

"Let's do the bare minimum tonight," Rachel said. "Things that will spoil. Tomorrow's our last full day here and I want to get up early and make the most of it. The dishes can wait." She looked a little hollow-eyed and I realized she was tired. It occured to me that gliding through life in a cloud of glory must be wearying. She stood and watched us carry dishes for a moment before she made herself start helping.

"No, Rachel," Marie said. "You go upstairs. We'll just do five minutes' worth. You've been working like... much too hard." I smiled: she'd been about to say, Working like a lesbian. Rachel nodded and blinked. She kissed everyone good-night and then went up the stairs, lifting the hem of her dress with both hands. Midway up, she stopped and turned. She dropped her skirts and stood in a Whistler caryatid pose, arms at her sides, the heavy folds of her caftan draping in stately waves around her on the stairs.

"Anton?" she said. Tony was standing with me across the room, gathering up glasses and holding several by their stems. His eyes met hers, and I could almost hear his attention rush towards her. There was nothing left of the blankness with which he'd looked at her ten days earlier. He was suddenly with her in his mind. Sunlight reflecting on the waves: the water invisible without the light, and without the water, nothing for the light to reflect off of. He put the glasses down on the coffee table, quickly and gently, without looking at them, and went to join her. She reached her right hand out to him and gathered her skirts back up in her left. They went upstairs together.

We were in the studio and Joe was humming "Broadway" to himself as he hung up his new shirt. He smoothed it carefully, though he nodded when I said, "Linen is supposed to get a little rumpled."

I felt a stark new excitement at having him to myself now, the man who had sung so – so hard. I was shy of him and just followed him around and waited to see what came next. He was still rapt in his song and smiled privately as he moved around the studio without speaking. Every time our paths crossed he would smile at me, pat my arm, or lift his chin in greeting, but he didn't say anything to interrupt the tune he was humming. He hung up his pants and closed me out of the bathroom for a few minutes. I heard him humming as the toilet flushed and water splashed in the sink; he was still humming when he opened the door and I could see him rubbing cream into his face. He stood by the sink and brushed his teeth while I washed. He was in a haze of abstract good will. He smiled at me and looked past me at the same time.

"What?" I asked. He shrugged and rinsed his mouth out and went to open up the bed without answering.

I turned out the lights and laid my robe over the back of a chair. Joe was lying down now, his shorts tossed aside. He was on his back and had one hand to his cock, which was flopped to one side. He looked at me and was suddenly wistful.

"Here," he said, and patted the bed next to him. "I want to touch you."

"You've already touched me more than you know," I said, clambering across the mattress.

"Yeah yeah," he said, nodding as if he were seeing through a hackneyed line. I was going to say, No, I mean it, but he put his arm around my neck and pulled me to kiss him, one of those Let's-not-talk kisses. Suddenly he stopped and said, "I know. You love me." I nodded as much as I could with his elbow locked on my neck. He sighed deeply, sounding very tired. "You do crack me up," he said. He laughed to himself, free-associating, a million miles away, hunting all over the dark ceiling for the spot across the ocean where he'd aimed his song of stardom. "I can't fuck right now," he said. "I'm beat. I'm sorry. I know I said I would." I shook my head: That's OK; don't worry about it, Joe.

"I've got a job for you tonight," he said. "You up for a job?" I nodded. "Keep your arms around me every single minute till morning," he said. I nodded. I could barely breathe. It was as though everything I'd ever wanted was simply to hold him. He was not just consenting to it; he was commissioning me to do the very thing I most wanted and needed to do. "Because I'm jumping off a cliff for you. You've got be there to catch me."

He released me and worked himself down in the bed till his head was on my chest. He burrowed his face in my neck and hummed a little on his next few exhalations. With my free hand I grabbed the edge of the top sheet and whisked it over him, tucking it carefully around his neck. Within a couple of minutes I was pretty sure he was sleeping, but just in case he could still hear, I stroked his curls away from his ear and whispered,

"Jump."

Chapter 14 – Saturday

For several years before and after Tony's marriage I had a recurring dream, or perhaps it would be more accurate to say I had a series of dreams, always different in their details but sharing the same basic plot. In the dreams, I was always sad about some actual love affair in my life at that time. I would dream that Tony was with me, sorry that I was sad and anxious to do something to show his concern. He tried different ways to distract me, he tried to make me laugh, he hugged me. By the end of every dream, he offered to make love with me, only because he wanted to make me happier. Usually Tony and I were the only people in these dreams. The last time I remembered having one, maybe five years after he and Rachel were married, she was in it too. He and I were talking on a hillside overlooking a lake. Down by the shore there was a yacht club with a marina. Rachel was standing by one of the boats. She looked up and waved at us on the hill. She knew what Tony was offering me and she was OK with it. I never actually dreamed of sex with Tony, but the dreams always left me a deep feeling of comfort. I would wake up and think that there was someone good a thousand miles away who cared about me and was worried for me and would sacrifice something for my happiness.

That night as I slept with Joe's head on my shoulder, I had a version of this old dream. Joe was away and Tony came to me and asked, "Are we still pals?" His face and hair were a mask and helmet of pure gold; only his eyes, a brilliant cobalt enamel color with almost no white showing, let me be sure he was Tony and not an idol. Under the lustrous metallic surface he was still my best friend, warm and kind and loving. He was as beautiful as anything in creation and my heart went to him with an almost painful surging motion like a wave heavily churning sand along the beach.

"Do you still want to make love?" I asked him. He was cradling something in one arm. He laid it on my shoulder as if he were passing a sleeping baby to me. It was some kind of young animal, maybe a hippogriff; someday it would be mythic and mighty, but for now it had the large pleading needful eyes of a puppy. It nuzzled me. Against my will I loved it. I could feel my freedom drain away as I held this beast and I saw Tony step back to look at us with a generous approving smile. He had entrusted a uniquely precious creature to my love and keeping, and now he had to go home. I didn't want him to leave, and obviously we wouldn't be having sex now. Yet as he went I was still happy. I held my new charge lovingly in my arms, and I was proud that Tony had chosen me as its guardian. There was a glow of security that came from knowing that Tony had come to find me and commission me in this way, and even when he was gone we were not parted.

Joe's rough morning breathing woke me around nine o'clock. Apparently neither of us had moved since we fell asleep. The sun had been up for hours and the studio was brilliant with its light. The windowpanes broke it into large irregular geometric patches of bleached brightness on the walls and ceiling. Joe's arm across my chest was gleaming with sweat and his breath was hot. I gave him a shake and he opened his eyes.

"My arm's asleep," I said. He hunched himself up off the mattress enough for me to slip my arm out from under him and then huddled close again. He had one hand to my heart.

"Remember," he said. I knew that he meant I was to keep my arm around him. I pressed tightly against him even though we were both slick from each other's body heat. His cock was hard against my leg and I reached down to stroke it, recognizing the damp sweetish smell on my hand when I brought it back up. He raised one leg slightly and my cock slid in between his thighs without a touch from either of us. His was nestled between our stomachs. We began to sway together, the slightest movement. The dense soft muscles of his crotch made an embrace that was secure and familiar. We didn't kiss; our lips were laid to one another and touched more or less closely only as our bodies moved. Neither of us said a word. There was no big build-up of pressure. At some point I could tell I was done, almost as if I'd slept through it. Then I felt a quick warm pulse against my stomach, though Joe showed no signs of climax, no gripping hands, no facial contractions. Neither of us moved.

Several minutes later, I roused myself enough to say, "See? I've had my arms around you every single minute."

He stretched comfortably, lolling like a lion cub. He braced one leg against the mattress and leaned back. His back was arched and he reached with one arm, fist clenched, far off the edge of the bed. Then he relaxed all at once and flopped next to me.

"Good morning," he said. *"Buon giorno."*

I ran my fingers up and down his torso. The hair on his belly was sticky and he winced and made a laughing little groan when my fingers caught in it. He scratched his scalp with both hands and sat up.

"Rush Limbaugh would go gay in a heartbeat if he could see you now," I said. I sat up next to him and played with his hair. "Look. I never noticed this."

"What?" he asked. A small shiver went up and down my arms.

"There are highlights in your hair when you're in direct sunlight like this." He nodded and made a modest little humphing sound. "Little strands of... of gold," I said.

Walter rapped on the glass door as we were having coffee.

"How's life in the garret?" he called to me when Joe opened the door. "*Sacrifichiam la sedia!* Good morning, Joseph." I was standing in the kitchenette. I heard Joe close the door behind Walter, who turned around and said to him, "*Bravo*, by the way. Last night. Really extraordinary." It was the businesslike tone in which he always paid his most serious compliments. Joe may not quite have understood this, but I heard him say "Thanks" and could picture the guarded nod that went with it.

"Where's the devil-child?" I asked when I saw that Walter was alone.

"Still asleep," he answered. He walked over to the counter, took one of the stools, and propped his elbows to lean across and talk to me. "Those Greek-key borders on the sheets," he said; "the Empire bed... the whole thing is absurdly photogenic. I thought I was trapped in a *toile de Jouy* scene of the sleeping Cupid." He reached indolently to accept the coffee mug I was offering him. For years now he'd shown this curious detachment about Ricardo's good looks and sexiness. The scene he was evoking in my mind was one from which I didn't think I would have been physically able to tear myself. Yet here he was, preferring coffee in the company of friends to the chance to shower burning kisses on the face of his sleeping beauty. "Anyway he'll be up soon. He was fairly wired last night; he can't wait to get out on the beach."

I looked at the wall clock. It was almost ten.

"Shaking him does no good," Walter explained. "He reproaches you for it later. I resorted to strategy and opened the blinds. He made resentful noises and put a pillow over his face, but I know the sun will get to him within a few minutes."

"You two have been together... ?" Joe asked.

"Five and a half years," Walter said.

"He seems like a great guy." Walter shrugged; he didn't like to be cornered into sentimental admissions.

"He's a doll," I said quickly, knowing Joe would think all my friends were weirdly indifferent to their dazzling life-partners. He might start to wonder if I would be the same way.

There was another knock on the door. I stepped around to see who it was. Ricardo was waiting on the landing in his robe, a very short white wrap-around bordered in black. He was holding it closed by hugging himself, as though it were bitterly cold out and he were a waif. He had a sleepy look on his face which I knew was also pure pretense.

"I thought you'd be up here," he said to Walter when I let him in. He ran a hand through his hair, which slipped back into place on his forehead like the wing of a brooding Hollywood raven. He gave a false stagey yawn and smiled. Deep down inside, I thought, he really does know just how lovely he is. Walter reached out from his stool and Ricardo went to stand between his knees, letting Walter hug and kiss him with a little show of sleepy reluctance.

"How's my sweet little one?" Walter asked. In certain moods Walter and Ricardo were capable of reverting to the most nauseous baby/lover-talk. Joe met my eye and smiled at me. Ricardo squirmed and shrugged as if he weren't sure how he was; clearly what he wanted was for Walter to squeeze him a little harder, and Walter did.

"Come back down and get ready," Ricardo said. "Jim and Joe are busy and I want to go out on the beach." There was some pouty display about this little speech. Maybe Ricardo thought Walter had been neglecting him by coming up to see us without him. His mind could be fairly mysterious.

"No," Joe said, "let us come with you." Ricardo gave him a very sharp look, wide awake.

"Meet us in our room in twenty minutes," he said. Somehow Joe had apparently said exactly what Ricardo intended for him to say. Walter stood and said,

"Lead the way, Small Dyke." Once soon after they met, Ricardo let slip that he thought cuddling was the best part of sex. Ever since, Walter had claimed that Ricardo was really a lesbian. He turned to us and said, "Well, we'll leave you two to do whatever it is that young boys in love do."

"Too late," Joe said; "we just did."

"Joe!" I said, wanting to blush but secretly pleased. Walter raised one eyebrow in tribute and said nothing, raising his arm so that Ricardo could slip under it while he held the door. Twenty minutes later we went downstairs to meet them.

It was a perfect day on the beach. There was a high cool wind coming off the water and the sounds of the surf came up to us in gusts and buffets. We joined the throng on the gay beach, saying Hi to people we knew. Every one of the dozens of Washington gays we saw seemed to know or recognize Ricardo and he began to swagger slightly without knowing it. Several decorative men ran up to pay their respects and, if Ricardo was engaged, they'd give a moment's vague friendly attention to Walter. When I asked Walter how he knew these men, he'd smile and say, "Why, he's a cousin of Oriane's!" Though Walter ostensibly was bragging about Ricardo's broad social connections when he said this, it was obvious to me that he also took an unadmitted personal pleasure in knowing all the luminaries of the public gay life of DC, run on a star system more ruthless than that of Thirties Hollywood. He might at times pretend even to be a little bored with all of this sycophantic attention to Ricardo, but his quick recall of these guys' names, the suitability of his polite questions to them, and his contented little nods and smiles as he conversed with them all gave him away.

Ricardo was wearing his black and white robe over his black bikini trunks. The wind blew it open all at once and he gave a flattered and scandalized laugh, as if the wind had paid him a very forward but very sincere compliment. He tried to clasp the lapels of the robe and hold it closed, but couldn't catch the fabric which streamed like a white flame behind him.

Walter reached with the deferential gentleness of a valet

to take the robe off Ricardo's shoulders.

"We're going in anyway as soon as we find a spot to leave our stuff," he said. He tried to fold the flapping robe, but the wind was too strong and he ended up just rolling it into a loose ball.

Ricardo seemed not to notice the ripple of attention that went through the crowd when his robe came off. He watched Walter closely to be sure he wasn't creasing the kimono as he held it under his arm. I hadn't seen this much of Ricardo since our last trip to the beach two or three years earlier. He was bigger than I remembered. He'd been working out all along as part of his HIV-regimen – he said – and apparently now, as he approached thirty, it was starting to take in a new way. He was strong and shapely and burnished, like the allegorical Barye nudes that frame the Washington Monument in Baltimore, the lazy-dreaming faces of youths on the sleek majestic bodies of laboring men. The only sign he gave of hearing the low buzz of commentary from the men on the beach was a slight heightening of his color.

Sticking upright in the sand a few yards away were round dowels supporting the upper halves of two female mannequins. The dummies were wearing sunglasses, with pastel and leopard chiffon scarves tied over their elaborate wigs, one copper-red and one high-gloss black. Complex trailing drapes in lamé and taffeta beat in the wind all around their bikini tops. They represented some fairly serious drag fantasies and I smiled, semi-tolerantly, at the effort involved. Suddenly at Ricardo's unveiling, a piercing wolf whistle came from one of them. We all turned in surprise.

"Get over here, you big stud," the mannequin called in a high man's voice. "We're Leena and Loretta the Lesbo Sisters and we're going to rock your gay world." There was a wary silence from our little group.

"Somebody must have mounted speakers in their bodies," Joe said. "Somebody's got a mic and is talking into it." We glanced around nervously. Dozens of smiling faces were looking up at us, waiting for Ricardo's reaction, or maybe for Walter's. There was no mic in sight.

Ricardo laughed. Again, it was a flattered exuberant laugh, like Marilyn when the *paparazzi* crowded around her and she'd pout and flounce and blow kisses like a good sport.

"Which one is Leena?" he asked, lifting his chin to call.

"Which one do you want to be Leena?" There was another whistle. "Get over here and let us lick that chest."

"Honey," he called, "you don't want me. I'm just an old married lady." He put his arm through Walter's and smiled.

"Why don't you dump the troll and come play with your sisters?" the dummy suggested. Ricardo gave a complacently virtuous look and patted Walter's arm.

"No. Way." He pronounced the two words with heavy and equal emphasis. The dummies emitted at least two shrill laughs.

"We'll just be over here waiting," one of them said.

"I told you I'm married," Ricardo said loudly, explaining to the crowd. "And anyway I'm positive. So get over it."

"We're positive you're hot," Leena or Loretta said.

"Somebody's not getting the message," Joe said, walking over towards the dummies and looking truculent. "The man said No way."

"Scary muscle man!" the dummy warbled.

"If he were half as butch as he thinks he is," the other one said, "he'd be dangerous."

"Come over and *give* us the message... or the massage!" the first one said. "Ha!"

Walter looked at me and said, "The wit of the witless."

"Joe," I said, "don't bother." I reached for his elbow but he was a few inches too far from me. I could imagine him decking dummies and getting into an undignified tangle of chiffon.

"It's Joe!" one of the Lesbo Sisters said to the other. "Volleyball-Joe from LA! My beating heart."

"My throbbing..."

"Oh stop! We're Lesbian Ladies anyway – remember? We only go for pussy."

"On a *stick*, Sis!"

Several men around us were following all this and laughing. A few looked disgusted in that DC-gay respectability-mongering way that almost made me side with the Sisters. But it wasn't my favorite kind of humor. It was the usual slutty brazen thing that drag queens did from deep cover and then claimed to be brave. The invisible mic and the suspicion that practically any of the men in sight might be operating it were a little uncanny.

"Let's go," I said. "This scene is nowhere." We struck out for another part of the beach. A trail of uninteresting drag invective from the Sisters followed us for a few moments and a collective groan went up as the crowd saw Ricardo walk away.

"Be good, boys," he called over his shoulder.

We found a clear place some distance away. Joe and Ricardo went immediately into the water. Walter and I could see heads turning and fingers pointing as the two of them slipped and stumbled on the loose sand on their way in.

"This is to be our destiny, apparently," Walter said. "To squire our absurdly hot boyfriends through mobs of unprincipled drag queens who will resort to the fiercest stratagems to lure them from us."

"Are you feeling very brave?" I asked.

"The sacred name of duty will sustain me."

We sat for a while and enjoyed the wind and sun. Walter was very fair but always did well with the sun; he would take on a healthy rosy color and start to gleam a bit.

"So how's Ricardo?" I asked him.

"He's fine. I think the Whitman-Walker Clinic wants to make him its poster-boy. He's their pet holistic case." He smiled. "Last week they sent him to do an outreach-talk on prevention to Latino teens. Apparently he did very well with these inner-city kids."

"They got him?"

"They absolutely got him. He was so full of himself afterwards I wasn't sure I could take his word for it, but the Clinic called the next day to see if they could schedule some more speaking engagements for him."

"He looks awfully well."

"He is." Walter kept his eyes unswervingly on the horizon – a clench-jawed WASP, I thought with a smile. God knew he had reason to clench his jaw where Ricardo was concerned. Every day a gift: even I clung to that, but Walter had to live by it. There was a longish silence. "I suppose I should tell you," he said after a few moments.

"What?" I tensed. Maybe there was some news about T-cells. He sighed.

"About love," he said, and smiled. "I'm your big grown-up old roomie. It's clearly advice time." He thought for a minute and said, "I don't know what to say."

"Tony and Rachel have been giving me advice all week. They're rooting fairly heavily for Joe."

"It's not a contest, you know. If Joe wins, you win."

"He will. He's the stubborn type, Ricardo said."

"Ricardo was talking about himself, I think," Walter answered, smiling. "Remember how he hounded me? He sees himself in Joe. It takes a bold young man to take either of us on, Jimmy."

He looked at me, his forearms resting on his knees. He looked very mature, very manly – Walter, who had always been such a model of style and sophistication to me, and now looked like someone's dad or a kindly older neighbor.

"These guys are hard," he said. "These Joes and Ricardos. These sweet attractive men who make us wonder if they really do want to be with us. Let's face it; attractive men have been mostly bad news for us over the years. They've used our fear of abandonment against us like an Uzi. The old I-can-always-get-a-date-whereas-who-wants-you? line. The old I-can-walk-at-any-moment-leaving-you-crabbed-and-lonely ordure. We got into some heavy defensive habits, and who could blame us? Then one day a cute boy comes along and knocks at your gates and claims that if you don't drop everything and love him without reservation you'll be hurting his feelings. You'll come off as un-nurturing. You'll lose the sympathy of all sensitive people for being so mean to someone so sweet who cares about you so much."

"Thank you," I said. "Rachel has been laying that one on with a trowel. Meanwhile Joe scared me rigid with a little..."

"Dalliance? A minor lapse or transgression?" I nodded and told him about Dennis. Then I was seized with an attack of honesty and told him about Gene too. He hooted. He had known Gene for years now and always wagered we would get horizontal sooner or later.

"So how does monogamy work?" I suddenly asked. Walter raised his eyebrows and sighed, seeming not to know. So I went on. "Think about it. I suddenly have the chance to be with this sort of dream-date of a man. He says he cares about me; no, he proves it. We get close, we have great sex, we fight, we make up, we work on issues: there's hope, in other words; there's something developing. Then I find my eye roving within two days. An old friend like Gene... or Dennis himself, for God's sake. I flirt with him with Joe standing right there. I always thought I was the sensitive romantic type. Now it turns out I'm just a horrid gay tomcat."

"It's been a fairly rich diet for you here these two weeks," Walter started, feeling his way, still unsure he had advice to give. "Being here with Tony, for one thing. Obviously you two are closer than you've been in years. I saw that last night. You love Tony. Things are very charged."

"I think we've finally kind of come to a separate peace with all that."

"Yes, of course. But my point remains." He considered something. "Tony's monogamous, isn't he?"

"Yes. There are some tensions there too, but that's not one of them."

"So that's one good model for you." He nodded and hummed, sounding almost like Joe while he thought. "It's not difficult for me and Ricardo for some reason."

"Do you still have sex?"

"Oh honey!" he said, catching Ricardo's voice exactly. I laughed. "Yes, actually; more than in years. I mean, we always did, but there's some kind of renaissance going on in the last year or so."

"He's getting more magnificent," I said.

"Yes, he is." Walter nodded as if we were discussing a curatorial project, a restoration effort on an ancient fresco, the discovery of a new Vermeer. "He is truly beautiful." He inhaled deeply all at once and again turned to look me in the eye. He squinted slightly from the sun and the soft strands of his hair were almost white with the light as they blew in his face.

"That has nothing to do with sex," he said. "He's more... he gets more – more *dear* with time. He becomes more himself with time, and his self is beautiful, so in a beautiful body it blooms; it springs. It radiates. And when we make out it's his self that I have to be dealing with: handling his feelings, showing him my love, taking his. You can't notice the old fantasy lust-triggers when you're doing that. The rules change when you – when you truly want to hold someone."

He paused. My throat was dry. Apparently I was still a romantic at heart. Walter too: his voice was getting a little uneven. He was thinking of holding Ricardo. A change in his face told me it was not a purely joyous thought all of a sudden.

"The other night…" he said, and stopped.

"What?"

"Just a crazy thought for no reason," he said apologetically. "The other night I suddenly imagined what it would be like… what it will be like."

"What? When?"

"When we make love when he's – not…" He bit his lip and breathed deeply. His New England ancestors seemed to crowd around his head for a moment to give him the right sober parlorish words for what he meant to say. "When he's not as lovely." When he's sick, he meant. He waited a moment and then took another step into the future. "And when he's – not here." I put my hand on his arm.

"What will it be like?"

"It will be just fine, as long as he's here," he said, nodding firmly. "I don't care how he looks. I just have to be able to touch him; to hold him. That's all sex really is. It's not beauty that drives sex. It's that you want to be with that person; you want inside the mystery of that man."

"Ricardo is a mystery," I agreed. He smiled bleakly.

"Jimmy," he said. "He is just so… dear. So extremely good. He's so brave and so loving and generous. I know you know him, but sometimes I think no one really sees him but me. What am I going to…?" He put his hand to his eyes, not to wipe tears, but as if to rub away a tired thought. "No; that's not for today. Not for a – a long, long time."

"Gene said…" I hesitated. Gene was not any kind of

emotional authority for Walter, who raised his eyebrows wearily at me as if I'd mentioned "Melrose Place" in the middle of *Les Enfants du Paradis*. "We got fairly deep the other day," I said. "He said, 'He cannot ever be lost.'"

"You were talking about Ricardo?"

"As a matter of fact, yes; we had been. But he was talking about his own... losses, I guess, when he said that. There's more to Gene than we always remember." Walter tried to show a decent respect for this unlikely theory of mine, but after a moment he asked,

"Your point?" I waited. I wasn't sure I had the standing to say this; besides, it was something Walter already knew.

"You and Ricardo will always be together," I said. He drew his brows in and nodded gravely.

"That's true," he said. His tight smile told me that, though he had been telling himself the same thing twenty times a day for years, there was still a grey pleasure in hearing someone else say it. "And anyway, that's another day's problem. It's OK for now." He shook his head briskly and I pressed my hand on his elbow.

"Anyway, we're supposed to be talking about you and Joe, you clever thing," he said, back to our topic. He sighed and sat up a little, rousing himself from his momentary sadness. "Joe," he repeated, and made a courteous panting face, just to underscore that he had noticed and given me credit for Joe's great hotness. "Monogamy... The good news is, you know, monogamy is easy. Whatever we used to get from stalking and banging cute guys is so little and so boring compared to being with somebody. And the other is just so much *work*... hunting, cruising, picking up, blowing off – getting blown off; the phone numbers, the awful dates and greasy food, the – the answering machines. Too much trouble for gentlemen our age." He paused. "I like Joe. You two will be fine. This is major and I'm very happy about it."

"Thank you," I said.

Obedient to some unspoken cue, Joe and Ricardo came into view now, walking up the beach along the very edge of the water looking for us. They'd vanished fairly rapidly when they first went in, moving south with the current. We waved when we saw them and they started up towards us. Several times we saw them nod, wink, wave, or salute to men who called out to them – friends or wannabes. Walter suddenly gave a little sound like a sigh or a gasp.

"God," he said, "I love him so much." He was watching Ricardo walk towards us. This was unusual for Walter and I pressed my hand hard to his elbow and flipped into an automatic reassurance tone I used for visiting old church ladies in nursing homes. Strangely, though, I found myself saying exactly what I meant.

"Of course you do," I said. "And he knows it. You make him feel very safe and very happy." He nodded.

"Now we get into a fierce competition to see which of us can have the most adorable marriage," he said.

"You're on," I said.

After dinner that night we all sat in the living room of the big house and talked. The wind was still very strong and it had been a little too chilly on the porch when we tried to settle there. Tony was wearing a red and black rugby shirt from our college. He looked – damn his hide – perfectly natural and hunky in it. Anytime I tried to wear sporty clothes, it made a grotesque pretentious effect and I felt I might as well have put on a hoop skirt or gaucho pants – or both, why not? Walter started humming our alma mater when he first saw Tony at dinner and the three of us were the only ones who got it and laughed.

In a lull in the after-dinner talk, Rachel looked under the lid of the piano bench and found some old sheet music and song albums. "Look, Jim," she said; "I'm sure you know some of these old songs. Oh, there's even some Handel. Come sing something for us." She started rolling chords and making tinkling baroquish sounds. I looked over her shoulder and pointed at one song in the table of contents. "Let me check the key," I said. It was fine and we started.

"*Non lo dirò col labbro*," I sang, "*che tanto ardir non ha.*" She stopped and said,

"Look at these lovely old Victorian words. Let's try it in English." Then, before I could start, she said, "Oh, no; it won't work. I mean, you're... you shouldn't sing it that way. With Joe here." She gave the slightest blush. What she meant was that I was an OGM and the English words were hetero, "Did you not hear my lady go down the garden singing?" I'd never thought, in all my years of activism and concertizing, to change the words of an old love song to make them gender-appropriate. I smiled.

"OK," I said. I glanced through the text, made a mental note or two, and then we started again.

"'Did you not hear my lover... ?'" It was a sweet easy

tune and, using a Victorian text, I didn't even bother to put in trills or ornaments of any kind. I found myself singing it in a full ardent style, in awful taste but loving it, like Domingo scooping and womping his way through Baroque music, caring only to sell the melody by making the voice as sumptuous as possible. I felt that I wanted to move and impress Joe deeply, though I didn't look at him. I could hear little supportive hums of agreement from Rachel as I shifted words: "'... for he is twice as fair... Though I am nothing to him...'" I was singing to someone. I wasn't sure who he was. He was some phantom from past years – someone who wasn't Joe or even Angel or anyone I could put a name to; someone who touched me and possibly hurt me, someone I felt the sweetness of longing for whether or not I could ever be with him. I knew I was singing well. The room was still and reverberant and I could barely see Marie twirling her wine glass slowly by the stem, her head down, as if entranced.

"'... Rivaling the glitt'ring sunshine with a glory of golden hair.'" The song was over and there was an instant before anyone clapped, during which I was still with whoever it was I'd been singing to. That "glory" in the last line was suddenly exactly right for him – the glow, the backlighting that made a halo around him in my mind. Oh Son of God, I remembered, Life-giver, joyful in Thine appearing... With an odd wrenching sense of disloyalty I reminded myself that my new lover was in the room with my other friends. I made myself look at Joe and smile, and saw that he was giving me a gentle steady attention, admiring what I'd done, hoping rather than assuming that it had anything to do with him. In the moment that it took me to look at Joe I could feel the man in the glow slip away from me, and I recognized a faint old regret at his going. I saw both Rachel and Walter glance at Tony. There was a floor lamp by the end of the sofa where he sat. Its dim light shone in his hair. I remembered my dream, in which he had seemed all made of gold.

"That was lovely," Rachel said, and patted my arm as she got up from the bench. She barely met my eye, but she smiled.

"Why don't you play something else?" I asked her. "That partita you were playing the other day." She shrugged.

"No," she said. "Not tonight." She went and sat by Tony.

Marie suggested we all go out dancing. The Neubergs begged off, and Joe gallantly said that Michael and his boys would be devastated by their absence. He and I went to the studio to change and then went to Walter's and Ricardo's room. The whole household was gathered there helping Ricardo dress. Rachel was holding up a pink knit cotton shirt she'd found in his drawer.

"This one?" she asked. He nodded and took it from her. He peeled his T-shirt off and splashed Grey Flannel on his chest before pulling on the pink shirt. Any number of men that night would go home and dream of being that lucky shirt, perhaps awakening in a disappointed sweat. Marie meanwhile had asked for Ricardo's help in fastening her necklace and he stopped, one shoe still off, and did the clasp for her with the admiring focus of an appraiser studying a Lalique brooch. Tony and Walter were seated on the bed talking. Tony kept one eye on the hubbub, which I supposed was an unfamiliar sight to him.

For the first time since we came through the door, Ricardo looked at Joe, and he gave a small Tsk of disapproval.

"Honey," he said, "you don't want people to think you're a lesbian." He caught himself and said, "Sorry, Marie. I forget sometimes because you're so glamorous." He sailed over to Joe and turned the collar of his crisp red cotton shirt firmly down. Joe had had it turned up for that natty jaunty look: Ricardo was quite right that sleek neat lesbians loved to wear their shirts that way. I froze. Granted, Ricardo was an expert on looking good, but Joe was nobody's fashion fool – a model, for God's sake, with pissy A-list West Coast gays making fools of themselves over him on a daily basis. Ricardo's gesture suggested a hierarchy of authority that I was pretty sure Joe wouldn't go for. I braced myself.

"Whatever you say, Ricky," Joe said mildly. He caught my eye to be sure I saw and understood that he was being good. He looked back at Ricardo, suddenly soft-eyed. "You're a honey," he murmured.

I almost didn't register the crowd at the Strand that night. There was a terrible press of people and everyone seemed to be having a good time. Marie got swept up in a crowd of Washington friends and I didn't see her for a half-hour at a time. Joe ran around with his LA friends, most of whom I saw only in passing. Chris was dancing on a speaker with Gene, who was shirtless and shining with sweat. Chris blew me a kiss and again I was able to bask in how much this impressed Ricardo. I didn't see Dennis and Michael at all once they'd come over to collect Joe, though I did literally bump into Bobby on the dance floor when Walter and I ventured out onto it.

"You GO!" he said to me, and squatted down low to do a couple of quick thrusts with me before whirling off into the mob. I didn't have time to ask him if Patrick was there. Patrick did surprisingly well in discos, mixing a few soft-shoe steps with a hint of tango and looking like a gay Balanchine on a spree.

Amidst all this gaiety I felt like an automaton. Joe and I were going to be separated the next day and that thought, which had still been rather abstract even the day before when we'd been fighting, was suddenly dreadful and stark. All around me I saw people who were having fun because they and their lovers were not going to be parted. None of them had continents just poised to hurl themselves between them – continents that had taken centuries to explore but that now, thanks to the unasked-for technologies of the late twentieth century, could toss themselves in your way as easily and maddeningly as a caddish boss standing in the aisle in your place of business to make unwelcome advances.

Walter and I tired of dancing and went looking for Ricardo. We saw him at a distance, standing at the bar sipping some orange-ish cocktail and talking to a mousy younger man with lanky hair and a small chin.

"*Un cousin d'Oriane?*" I asked.

"*Jamais couché avec,*" said Walter, shaking his head. "A new worshipper at the shrine, I take it." He rolled his eyes, pretending to regret Ricardo's insane popularity, in which I knew for a fact he took a deep pride. The boy was wearing a little

422

lime green bell-bottomed pants suit with a few sequins on it, something Sonny and/or Cher might have worn in the Sixties.

"Baby," Ricardo said, taking Walter's arm as we walked up, "this is Lonnie. This is Walter, my lover, and Jim our best friend." He gave a big emphatic nudge to each name, as though they were difficult words in a foreign language. "You guys remember Lonnie?" He smiled with his eyebrows up. Apparently Lonnie was some very dear old friend we were just suddenly blanking on for no reason. "*Leena*, from the *beach* this morning!" He pressed his arm around Lonnie's shoulder with a great show of comradeship.

"Oh, right," I said vaguely, hoping to suggest to the boy that I barely recalled his stupid jokes.

"Indeed," Walter said.

"And my lesbo sister is around here somewhere," Lonnie said, gesturing languidly over his shoulder. His voice was nervous trying to disguise itself as jaded. He looked barely old enough to be in the bar. I hated his outfit. It was his attempt at dressing like a boy while still being campy and flashy and fabulous. If we'd asked, he probably would have called it a unisex statement. It wasn't hard to imagine that he'd be much more comfortable in a hugely bubble-skirted off-the-shoulder hot red mini-dress and spike heels, clothes no woman I knew would wear even on Mardi Gras. I felt a little sorry for him and this irritated me deeply. I still resented all his cowardly trollopy talk on the beach and didn't think he had any right to my sympathy now. I certainly didn't want him schmoozing his way into Ricardo's circle.

He glanced at Walter with a small dose of fear and

dislike. He had been enjoying Ricardo's attention and perhaps hoped that it would be good for him at least to be seen with him. Maybe they could build up to one of those screamy kissy friendships that plain little drag queens sometimes concocted with notorious beauties.

"Have you seen Joe?" I asked Ricardo.

"Joe from LA?" Lonnie asked.

"Yes," I said. "He's my lover." I wondered why I'd felt the pitiless urge to tell him that.

"He's over there dancing with some super-hot blond," Lonnie said maliciously.

"Oh, yeah; Dennis," Ricardo said. "I did see them on the floor a few minutes ago. They're old friends," he explained to Lonnie.

"I'm going to go find him and check out," I said. "My work here is finished."

"We should head back too, my young love," Walter said. "You don't want to spend the morning sleeping and miss the beach scene tomorrow. *Vamos.*"

Lonnie pulled on Ricardo's belt-loop and whispered something to him.

"Yeah, honey; we'll see you tomorrow," Ricardo said. "But be nice. I told you I'm married." This was actually fairly kind; it implied that Lonnie might have been next in line for Ricardo's love if only he'd been single.

"Lighten up," Lonnie said.

I went and found Joe and Dennis on the dance floor. Dennis grabbed me with a smile and said "Jim sandwich!" and we all did a little dance with me squeezed between the two of them. After a minute I put my mouth to Joe's ear and managed to make him hear me.

"Let's go back," I said. "I miss you."

Walter and Ricardo were waiting for us near the door. They had talked to Marie and she was going to get a ride home with some of her DC crowd. We got our jackets from the checkroom and went out onto the blustering street. There was a wild scream from the floor just as we stepped outside: the crowd recognized the intro to the hit song of the season from what to me was an imperceptible shift in the numbing drumbeat.

"How can they tell?" I asked. "It's just poom-poom-poom."

"Are you serious?" Joe asked, incredulous. "They recognize the song."

"Oh right," I said. "It's actually poom-POOM-poom. Super-galactic difference."

"Don't start," he said. He was nice enough to take my hand even though he clearly thought I was being an awful curmudgeon.

"Come on, honey," Ricardo said to me. "You remember when we heard Kraus in concert? You knew the encore was 'Nessun dorma' before the poor pianist finished rolling the first chord. You smiled and leaned back and went, Hmm." Walter and I laughed.

"OK," I said. "True enough."

"Whoo," Walter said and snapped his fingers. "Terrible read."

"Exactly," said Joe.

It wasn't much past one when we got back to the house. Walter and Ricardo left us at the kitchen door and Joe and I went upstairs alone. Only two or three minutes later there was a knock at the door.

"They must have forgotten something up here today," Joe said from the bathroom. He had already undressed and was washing up. I went to the door and was surprised to see Tony and Rachel standing there. She was huddled in a long blue-green robe I hadn't seen. He was right behind her to shield her from the wind.

"We heard Ricardo and Walter come in and they said you'd just gotten back too," Rachel said as they stepped inside. "We've been waiting up for you." Joe stepped out of the bathroom wearing my robe. He looked solemn. "Hello, Joe." She sounded a little shy. "I hope you don't mind us coming up like this."

"What's up?" he asked, as if he were bracing for bad news of some kind.

"Everything's OK?" I asked. I looked back and forth from Rachel to Tony. They both looked a little odd, thrown off, not sure how to answer. Tony put a hand up reassuringly: OK, yes.

"Can we sit down?" Rachel asked. She was still wrapping her robe around herself tightly, with her hands under her arms. She went and sat in the large chair and Tony stood behind it, his hands on her shoulders. I was getting a bit spooked and I went to sit opposite them on the sofa. Joe took his usual spot in the corner next to me.

"Go ahead," Tony said to Rachel. She suddenly laughed

at our faces.

"Now that we've scared you both to death," she said. She looked down at her hands and then made herself look up. Tony was staring over our heads at the room's reflection in the window or, for all I could tell, at the black ocean beyond. Rachel held my eye for a long moment, unsure if I would be happy or not at what she was about to say.

"Apparently I'm pregnant," she said at last, making it sound a bit indefinite, perhaps in case I would find that comforting.

I sensed that Joe was smiling next to me, and he shifted excitedly in his seat as if he might jump up and hug someone. I glanced up at Tony and saw that he was smiling very slightly and that his eyes were still distant and vague. I looked at Rachel again and saw in her face a blend of concern and triumph. My mind was stalled, trying to do a calculation back to the time a week or so before when I'd started to notice Tony thawing towards her.

"I knew it," Joe said, before I could speak. Rachel looked at him, startled.

"You did? But we just found out tonight."

"One of those little home-kits," Tony said, still not looking at anyone.

"I could tell the other night when you and I were dancing. I told Jim, didn't I, Jim?"

"He did," I agreed, apologizing slightly to them for having a psychic boyfriend. "I told him I didn't think..." I stopped myself from saying, I didn't think it was possible; that might imply too intimate a knowledge of their sex-life.

"How amazing," Rachel said, cocking her head gravely. "Anyway, we wanted you to know right away. You've been... " She was looking at me, and made a point now of looking at Joe for a moment. "You've *both* been so – so kind."

"So... " I tried to think of words for my questions and for the emotions without names I was just starting to feel. "I guess I – don't know how those tests work. I mean, how long... ?"

"Just over a month," Rachel answered quickly. "It's way too early to tell anyone, of course. Anything could happen and you're supposed to wait two or three months. I was just a little bit – late and I thought I'd... " She smiled ruefully. "Where's all my maternal instinct? Some women can tell the moment it happens. I have to use this awful little over-the-counter device that looks like a thermometer... " She stopped and shrugged, and then bit her lip. "You're happy, aren't you, Jim?"

Just over a month, I was thinking. That meant that... I'd asked Tony, Never? and he'd said, Practically never. The whole time we'd been talking on the beach, the whole time Rachel had been looking out to sea, this had already happened.

"Oh honey!" I said quickly. "Of course I am." I spoke first; then I saw that the feeling was already formed; I actually was happy. "I'm just kind of stunned. This is wonderful. It's... it's what you've wanted. Doro?" I asked.

He didn't look down, still smiling his secret smile.

"It's pretty cool," he said, sounding much as he did twenty-odd years earlier when something unexpected and energizing came along – a pick-up game of touch football, an answer to his letter to Nixon, Tom Rush tickets. Only his blank eyes showed that this was something new and confusing for him. "I'm... " I imagined that he meant to say something like, I'm happy, or, I'm up for this. For some reason he was shy about it. Maybe he would tell me if we had a chance to talk alone. His hands were still on Rachel's shoulders and she reached up to pat one.

"So that's our news," she said, starting to stir. "We should let you two settle down. We all have lots to do tomorrow, don't we? We just wanted to be sure you heard right away."

"Are you going to tell the others?" I asked.

"Not yet," she said seriously. "We'll call them in a couple of months if everything goes well. I'd appreciate it if... "

"Of course," Joe said, looking steadfast. He made a gesture he'd learned from Gene, moving his fingers from one side of his mouth to the other as if he were zipping it shut. He got up too as Tony and Rachel started to drift towards the door, and pulled me to my feet. "I am just so psyched," he said. "I knew it!"

We all stood at the door for a minute to say good-night. Rachel put her hands on my shoulders to kiss me and say, "Thank you." I felt a slight thrill along my arms as I hugged her, a current running through her that I hadn't felt before.

While she said good-night to Joe, I stood by Tony and said,

"You're good?" He just nodded shyly.

"I'm proud of you, Doro," I said. "You always do the right thing." He wagged his head stiffly from side to side to shrug off the compliment, though he looked gratified. "You're going to be the world's greatest dad."

"Thanks," he said. I could feel him withdraw into another life that was taking form in his mind. There was a perceptible fear in the center of my chest that Tony was going away. It felt like the old pattern of Tony withdrawing. I was eighteen again for a second, and in love with him, and part of me chilled at the knowledge that he would spend his life with Rachel and not with me. But then, there had been decades now to prove that he would be there somehow anyway. I trusted Tony now and I knew that the universe had a corner of safety in it which was Tony's loyalty to me. By that same token he would be a great dad.

After they left I found myself wandering aimlessly around the studio while Joe opened the bed and lay down.

"Come on," he reminded me after a few minutes. "You're still dressed."

"Maybe I'll just sit up a while," I said.

"No you won't. Go wash your face and brush your teeth and then get in this bed." His firm instructions cut through my distracted thoughts and I followed them.

"I can't get over it," he said to himself, still psyched about Rachel's news. I was lying with my head on his shoulder. A few windows were open and it was pleasant to feel the slight chill in the air. You could almost convince yourself it was cold; we huddled as if we were stranded in an Alpine storm.

"How are you doing?" he asked. He'd just noticed that I wasn't exultant. "You're happy, aren't you?"

"Yes, I am. It's great news."

"It always takes you a while to figure out how you feel. Nice feelings, I mean; when you're bummed, it hits you that second." I nodded at this surprising little analysis. "You still love Tony," he said, half to himself, after a minute.

"Kind of," I said. "I can still be happy about this, though."

"Sure you can." He thought for a while and said, "It's hard loving straight guys. If you really love somebody, you love the way he is. Maybe you used to be in love with the idea of what Tony would be like if he were into guys, into you. But Tony loves Rachel. So now you're finally learning how to love Tony the way he is; how to love the Tony who's married to Rachel. That's a change for you. It's something new. That's hard."

"Thank you Dr. M. Scott Peck," I said.

"Say I'm right."

"You're right," I said. He *was* right and there was no point in denying it.

"Just like I'm getting used to loving a man who's always going to have to wait a week to see that he's happy."

"Ouch," I said, and laughed in spite of myself.

"Tiger," he said. "Guess what?"

"You once tricked with Gloria Swanson," I said.

"I'm coming with you," he said. "To Baltimore. I called Rudy today. My travel agent friend. He's going to fix my ticket so I can fly back to LA next week. This way I can see your house and scope out the town for a few days – see how things could work if I move there next year. Plus I can meet the dog and cat."

"I'll introduce you to my mother if you promise to behave," I said.

"I'll be good." He stroked my head in silence for a minute. "So how long do I really have to wait for a reaction here?" he asked finally.

I took a deep breath and lurched up to lie on top of him. I kissed his face dozens of times in a row without stopping. He laughed and groaned as if I were crushing him.

"Zero lag-time," I said. "I know I'm happy now."

Chapter 15 – Sunday

"What are we all going to wish we'd said after we've gone our separate ways today?" Rachel asked. The whole house party was seated around the dining room table for breakfast, she and Tony presiding from opposite ends like mommy and daddy. We were starting to have pauses in the conversation. It felt a little like waiting around the last few minutes at the airport with friends or relatives about to catch a plane.

"Tell them about your dream," Ricardo prompted Walter with a smug smile.

"Appalling," Walter said; "I blame it on the surf. The persistent lulling music of the waves, when we're used to screeching tires and Yo! and sirens like normal people... Enough to give anyone nightmares." Tony and Rachel looked concerned; everyone else smiled. I was glad to see that even Joe had picked up on Walter's tone of voice, whereas looking at Tony's face I was afraid for a moment that he'd ask Walter if he was OK talking about it.

"I dreamed we were at the Met to see *Faust*. Willie Nelson was listed to star..."

"As Faust?" Marie asked bravely. "No," she said, grasping quickly to hold the floor before he could answer her. "No, he was the Devil, of course! How AW-ful." She waved her napkin as though she could swat the dreadful image away. Ricardo gave a self-satisfied laugh, glad to be in on an in-joke.

"Marguerite!" Walter whooped. "The braids! *C'est la fille d'un roi...* " He sang through his nose in a nail-scraping twang and simpered disgustingly. He held an imaginary braid in one hand and an imaginary mirror in the other and did something with his shoulders to suggest he was twirling.

"And you found this in some way alarming," I said. "You who have three separate recordings of *Adriana* with Olivero – two of them live! I thought nothing could frighten you anymore." There was uncertain laughter from around the table, and then Tony cleared his throat and asked if everyone was set for their trips home.

"Guess what?" Joe asked the group. I looked down at my napkin and smiled. No one could guess. He told them he was going back to Baltimore with me for a week.

"Yea!" Ricardo said. He turned to Walter as if they'd disagreed hotly on the subject and said, "I *told* you."

"So you're already thinking of moving?" Tony asked.

"No, it's too soon to talk about that," I said quickly, not wanting Joe to feel too pressured.

"It is?" Joe asked me. He apparently couldn't decide what I meant by that, so he answered Tony, "Who knows? I just want to check the place out."

"Well, Jimbo," Tony said, "if Joe ends up moving east, where do you think you'll put him? Your house is on the small side for two people, isn't it?"

"I don't have a whole lot of stuff," Joe said.

"Don't be silly, Tony," Walter said; "there's Jimmy's study upstairs that's got practically nothing but books in it, and that big walk-in closet in there he never uses."

"That's true," Tony said.

"And the powder room at the foot of the stairs," Marie said, gesturing with her coffee spoon as if we were looking at blueprints spread on the table. "I'll bet you could even get a shower stall in there if you had to, BooBoo. We can call that contractor-friend of Patrick's."

"Joe won't need his own room anyway," Ricardo said archly. Joe looked back and forth as this conversation went on around him. Clearly everyone else at the table already knew my house inside-out, including Tony, who'd started the whole thing. He seemed a little intimidated and appealed to Rachel.

"You've been there, haven't you?" he asked her.

"Oh, yes; two or three times," she answered. "It's really a great little house, and it's not all that tiny, really. Marie's right about the shower; if you had two showers it would... My sister always says the secret of a happy marriage is separate bathrooms. Come to think of it, you two have only had one shower here and you've been OK; but this is vacation – it doesn't really count, does it?"

She looked serious, considering all the factors.

"See what you think, Joe," she said finally. "I think it'll be fine if that's what you decide to do."

There was time for a bit of surf before final packing. Rachel had already given orders about stripping beds, laundering sheets and towels, and doing last-minute cleaning in preparation for the owners' return. We all cleared dishes and then the group scattered to get ready for the beach. Rachel and I were at the sink alone again for a moment after the others had gone upstairs. She glanced at the door over her shoulder to be sure no one was within earshot.

"Anton and I were talking last night," she said. "Names."

She handed me a platter to dry. "Of course if it's a boy we'll name him Jacob, for Anton's father."

"I love that name," I said. "He was such a nice man." She nodded respectfully, though I recalled that, incredibly, there had been some tension between them. Tony's parents loved and approved of Rachel; it would have been virtually impossible not to. But there was some sort of archetypal structure in place that dictated a certain amount of bickering between in-laws. Tony's father was just Old World enough to find it confusing, almost insulting, that Rachel persisted in pursuing a high-profile career even though Tony made, as Mr. Neuberg genteelly put it, "plenty money for the both of them." He may have had some agenda about their childlessness too, as though this were Rachel's fault, as though she'd persuaded Tony to put off starting a family. One or two remarks, which I barely recalled now, might be taken in retrospect to imply this, though his smile softened the reproach. No one had discussed the issue with me in those years, and I certainly hadn't raised it. Anyway, her father-in-law's tacit criticisms had gotten to Rachel to some extent. I could remember some sputtering, a sense of Rachel ruffled and resentful, Rachel wondering if maybe Tony himself didn't feel the same way. She was younger then, with her way to make in the world and a lingering late-adolescent fear that adults did not truly respect her, and she had not yet taken on the high sheen of perfect tact and effortless achievement that was her trademark now. I had been acutely jealous of Rachel in those years and it touched me now, looking back, to see that even so I had observed her and watched her and, probably more than I knew at the time, cared about her.

"Jacob is the same name as James, you know," I said. She gave me a look that was a bit more fascinated than I thought necessary.

"No, I didn't know that. Oh, like Jacques; of course, it makes sense if you think about it." She lined the juice glasses up in the upper rack of the dishwasher and slid it in.

"What are we going to do with the left-over food?" I asked.

"It's fine; we can just leave it for the owners. They're coming back on Tuesday. You might bring anything you don't want to take with you down here from the studio before we leave."

"I refuse to leave them this bottle of Piper-Heidsieck."

"I'll bet Anton will let you take that home as a party-favor," she said. "You can christen Joe with it." She gave a short relaxed vacation-laugh, but then knit her brows again, back to my comment about the names. "That's interesting about Jacob and James, because Anton wants to call the baby Jim, whatever we actually name him. If it's a boy, I mean."

"He said that?" I asked, startled.

"Would I say he did if he didn't?" She wrung the dish-cloth out hard and looked mildly provoked with me. I smiled. It was the first time I'd ever heard that tone in Rachel's voice, that fond touchy nagging: the stereotyped Jewish mother. So this is real, I thought. She relented and leaned her head to one side. "I should have let Anton tell you that, shouldn't I? It was his idea." I felt myself blushing and looked down.

"He's..." I wasn't sure what I meant to say.

"He loves you; you know that," Rachel said. She sounded

437

brisk and sensible, like the frontier woman in the plain calico dress and starched apron in an old Western, explaining to one of her laconic slouching big-footed menfolk what he and his brother were feeling but couldn't find the words for. "This is something he wants to do for you." I was touched, both at Tony's decision and at Rachel's blurting it out to me. When she forgot diplomatic procedures, it meant that her feelings were directly engaged. She must have been happy enough at the idea of carrying a little Jim that she couldn't wait to tell me. I looked up at her for a moment and then asked,

"What will you name her if she's a girl?" She considered.

"I'd love to have a little girl," she said, glancing vaguely out the window. "She'd be named for my aunt, I guess – my Aunt Sarah, my mother's sister. She was much older than my mother, and she died last year. Sarah, or something with an 'S' anyway."

"I like 'Sarah,'" I said.

"So do I. But to tell you the truth, I'm positive it will be a boy." She smiled. "Listen to me; I'm talking as though it had happened already. Anton called my gynecologist this morning – I'm going in to see him tomorrow. I'm not even going to tell my mother until I've been to the doctor's, just in case. I'm forty: the baby may not be right; I could – miscarry, or…"

"'Rachel wouldn't miscarry on a bet,'" I quoted, over her head I think. She considered briefly.

"You're right," she said. "Everything will be fine. I'm sure." She was sure, and so I was sure. There was a serenity in the room that made me as certain as if little Jacob/Jimmy were already sleeping in a bassinet upstairs. She put the orange juice pitcher in the refrigerator and glanced around the kitchen to satisfy herself everything was in order. She was moving to the door, to go up and dress for the beach. She stopped suddenly in the doorway and turned around, leaning against the door frame with her arms crossed. "Come to the bris?" she asked, a little shyly.

"Where else would I be?"

"You missed our wedding, you know." Now she looked down at the floor. In a way I was surprised that she remembered that. I'd always imagined that the wedding was so much not about me, so much a matter of my being eclipsed and out-flanked and proven not to be important, that no one would have noticed my absence.

"That was then," I said.

"We... I was sorry you weren't there. It's always sad to think of someone being unhappy when you're so happy yourself. And it worried Anton."

"You called from the reception, do you remember? That was... thoughtful." I'd pictured Rachel in her big white dress, bustling around the reception hall in that bridal haze of self-important generosity, churning out radiance like an industrial by-product, and saying, after attending to thirty or forty more pressing networking matters, Oh, Tony, let's not forget to call Jim.

"Of course I remember," she said. "Anton insisted. We'd just gotten out of the reception line, and he dragged me over to the phone before we even danced or ate or anything. I didn't want to; I thought maybe you'd rather not talk to... to me. But you were very sweet." What I'd been, I thought, was frozen and polite. I'd said the right things, purely by rote: Hey; *mazel tov*. Sometimes that's enough, I guess. "Anton was very relieved after we spoke to you. You let him be happy."

"What kind of creep would do anything to keep Tony from being happy?" I asked.

"Exactly." She smiled. "You see? You were able to act on that even when you were – troubled. When you were hurt. You've always had a very generous heart."

"I think you're giving me too much credit," I said. She pursed her lips as though she were seriously weighing whether or not I deserved her good opinion.

"I don't think so." She straightened up and looked over her shoulder, about to go.

"This is going to be a great little kid," I said. She bit her lower lip and smiled privately. I went on, "Joe is so excited you'd think it was all his doing." She laughed and I said, "Well, you know what I mean."

"Did he really tell you he thought I was pregnant?"

"Yes. When you came home from the Renegade that night. He told me he thought you were 'carrying.'" She shook her head once in tribute.

"He's a wonder." Now at last she turned to leave the room. "Time to go get ready," she said. "We're all so lucky, aren't we?"

Not long after, our whole little household was on the beach. I was surprised at how crowded it was. With our own vacation in its last hours, I imagined that the whole world would be packing and saying good-byes. It was only Sunday morning though, after all, and most people at Rehoboth didn't have far to go to get home – a few hours by car at most, to Philly or DC or Baltimore. There was a lot of picturesqueness that morning: volley ball, attitude, children screeching, hot dog vendors. In another generation, a genre painter would have set up an easel and happily launched a whole career. Perhaps someday, just a simple snapshot of Rehoboth Beach in the Nineties would look as evocative as Boudin's ladies, their tiny purposeful feet showing unexpected and prosaic beneath their swaying truncated crinolines, like the clappers of decorative dinner bells oddly suspended over the reflective sand.

The whole scene seemed more and more distant to me. I'd already had a minor flashback while tossing books in a bag in a first stab at packing. I found my house keys at the bottom of the tote. I'd tossed them there when I first arrived, figuring I had no reason to carry them at Rehoboth. I fished them out now and restrung them in place next to my car key. My hand had barely gotten used to the lightness of the two single keys, for the studio and the car, that I'd been carrying for two weeks. I instantly recognized the weight of the reassembled key chain as the weight of real life, a weight that brought my house in Baltimore back to me as if from another planet. I would be there in a few hours now. It was hard to say just where I thought I was, but the beach, as I looked out the studio windows, seemed prodigiously far from my regular life. In a funny way the water seemed like the Pacific to me. It gave me the same feeling of far far far that I always got when I visited San Francisco or Los Angeles and had to keep reminding myself as I looked out over the ocean that north was right and south was left.

That was just it, actually: deep down inside I thought I was in California, where Joe lived. This vacation world of the beach was more his than mine. It was as if I'd courted and stalked him down canyons and across boulevards and around palm trees, and was now about to return with him to my daily life. I had a slight panic at how drastic the transplantation was. Maybe he wouldn't take to the climate, or the journey itself would be too much for our new relationship, fragile as a tropical plant whose transparent leaves the slightest jolt in the car might shiver off.

He himself seemed quiet and vague and showed some impatience with my fitful gestures towards packing.

"There's time," he said. "After the beach. It'll only take you fifteen minutes." I started to pack the laptop in its zip-up case and he said, "Come on; they're waiting."

"How about your stuff?" I asked. "Out at the guest house?"

"There's time," he repeated. "Michael doesn't have to check out till four. They've got a night flight."

"A night flight to California?"

"It's cheaper. Plus with the time change they'll still get in by one a.m.. Come on." He came and put his hand on mine to make me stop stacking papers on the table.

"I'm nervous," I said.

"No you're not," he said, as if he could tell.

"I want you to like my life," I said.

"I'll probably like it OK."

"Yeah," I said, brushing off this tepid affirmation. He gave me a maddening innocent look. I didn't want to give him the chance to say, I just can't say anything right with you today, can I? so I said, "Let's go."

He put some effort into mingling with Walter and Ricardo once we were sitting on the sand. Rachel and Marie sat together and I sat with Tony. There was a subtle but urgent sense of deadline between us. Anything we still needed to say would have to be said this morning: by nightfall we'd be in different time zones, back to our longstanding routines of affectionate but sporadic contact. Some kind of man-to-man moment was required to mark the change in our lives brought about by Rachel's pregnancy. The expectations were not entirely clear. On the one hand was a scenario written for us generations earlier, cigars and loosened neckties and arms around shoulders. This made me nervous; it was a male rite in which I might stupidly say the wrong thing or omit some gesture fraught with a symbolism that only straight men understood. Then for years after I'd torment myself with the thought that any of Tony's interchangeable racquetball partners could have done better, on a moment's notice in the locker room, than I, supposedly his best friend, had done with ample time to prepare. But on the other hand I knew that there was no atavistic pattern for the kind of talk we were supposed to have. All those men in the grey suits and wingtips in the Fifties, who had fought in the War and come home to stake territorial claims in the suburbs, who took commuter trains into the city to work, who drove their families to church in station wagons and flipped hamburgers on grills and, though never caring if they themselves were in shape or not, were fully conversant with the strenuous masculine cults of sport – none of those men had ever had to have this kind of talk. How the gay man and the straight man who love each other talk about things like pregnancy, jealousy, and reintegration: there was no manual yet.

Tony was looking up and down the beach, checking the crowd. At one point, I noticed his eye resting on Ricardo, who sat several yards in front of us flanked by Joe and Walter. He was slapping lotion on his gleaming shoulders and asked Joe to rub it down his back. Joe's face was slightly cramped and inscrutable as he stroked Ricardo, and I wondered if he wasn't experiencing some of the detached amazement with which I myself had noticed, years before now, that the touch of Ricardo's perfect body stirred no lust in friends who liked him.

A gust of wind brought their voices up to us clearly for a second, and we heard Ricardo laugh and say,

"Oh, I'd leave him for *George*, of course." Walter made a huffy gesture, folding his arms and hunching his shoulders for a moment to mime jealous disgust. This time he didn't say, as he sometimes did, *"Vil cortigiana."* Ricardo had nursed a well-publicized crush on George Stephanopoulos since the early days of the Administration and Walter played along by claiming to believe that they met in secret with harsh orgiastic cries on moonless nights on the Mall. He occasionally embroidered the fantasy with the participation of strapping Secret Service agents and/or the Vice President – I'd suggested to Walter more than once that he consider just frankly making a career as a pornographer. This infatuation with Boy George was the only celebrity crush Ricardo had ever admitted to – not counting k.d. lang, whom he called the most beautiful boy in the world. This last was a bit of vanity on his part, since she resembled

444

him somewhat facially: if k.d. ever coupled with a sentimental matador or an Aztec prince or an Egyptian falcon-god, she might hope to bring forth something more or less like Ricardo.

"He's... " Tony said, still looking at Ricardo's back. I checked his face for the cautious protective smile that often crossed the faces of people who were fond of Ricardo when they thought about his HIV-status. That wasn't what I saw in Tony's face; I wasn't sure what I did see. He looked slightly puzzled. "He's really a looker," he said after a moment.

It wasn't his word; it sounded archival, like something brought back on tape from the field by an ethno-dialectologist in the Twenties. I was almost as intrigued as if he'd said "gairl" or "Injah" or had called someone a "lamb." It occurred to me that Tony very seldom had any reason to comment on the good looks of other men. I'd heard him say things like You look good, or Great tie! or He looked tired. Once he'd even said "He's a great-looking guy," referring to a lawyer-friend of his, but when I met the man I realized that Tony meant he was a snappy dresser with a nice smile and a good personality: he looked like a dapper Wally Shawn. I'd never heard Tony praise another man's good looks. For Ricardo, to his own surprise, he found he wanted to say something, and he had to rummage for a word in the lexicon of some past generation. "He's really a looker": maybe he pulled that up out of an old movie script, I thought, or maybe an older friend of his mother's used to say it about – who? the milkman? another friend's husband? the infant Tony himself?

"He's an act of God," I nodded.

Maybe an hour or so later, it was time to go back inside. We'd all been in the water and were mostly dry by now. I'd made a half-hearted effort to find a keepsake shell, though I'd never, in all the times I had been to Rehoboth, found anything more than the chalky pounded-down fragments of clam and conch shells and a few weary papery blushes of crab shell. Sitting on the sand for the last time, I sifted the hot powder through my fingers. The tide was far enough out that I had to dig several inches down before the sand got even a little cold and wet. I was already warm from the powerful sunlight, but I still liked the luxuriant heat of the sand. It was a nice feeling to end the summer on, warmth to store up now before fall and winter came.

As we all gathered up our things, Tony met my eye and said, "Go for a drive?" He turned to Rachel and said, "We have time?"

"We'll be fine if we leave by two," she said. "Go ahead." A few minutes later he and I climbed into the convertible and went tooling off up the street away from the water.

"Turn left," I said when we got to the main street. "We haven't been down this way." The road led away from town, through a residential neighborhood. The houses looked less and less beachy, some not even having porches or big windows, and their yards were unnaturally neat and bright, with grass, shrubs and flowers forced to grow cheerily in the sandy soil. I remembered that people actually lived here. The mystic set-apart retreat in which I had come to terms with Tony and Rachel and Joe was the very place where other people's lives proceeded on daily schedule. Their key chains were their usual work-a-day weight; the little spaniel running in the yard we passed had not been left in a neighbor's keeping, but could scratch at the screen door and be let in by its own people. People in all these houses were going grocery shopping, waiting for plumbers, putting off mowing the grass. *"Mon Dieu,"* I hummed to myself, *"la vie est là, simple et tranquille."*

"You're quiet," Tony said after we'd driven a few blocks. I thought for a moment to see why I was feeling uncomfortable. It didn't occur to me at first that he might be a little uneasy too.

"I'm going to miss you," I said. "I've gotten back into the habit of seeing you every day now. We haven't seen each other this many days in a row since 1974."

"You know the cliché about old friends. You and I always pick up right where we left off." I nodded, but it *was* just a cliché and Tony knew it.

"This was different, though," I said. "We put some things right. I met someone. You saved your marriage. You're going to be a father."

"So dramatic," he said, smiling mildly. It wasn't quite a put-down because his smile had fondness and patience in it, but I still found myself thinking, Rachel wouldn't have said that; she would have said I was right. He had his elbow on the door and was driving with one hand. The wind ruffled his curls and he squinted in each patch of sunlight we passed through on the shady street. He had the look of easy competence which some men got at the wheel, as though he were effortlessly negotiating a thrill-strewn stunt course at high speed instead of gliding at 25 mph down a quiet street in a coastal resort. Gentle and sensitive, yes: he was also what he had always been, madly butch. Competence wasn't something he acquired or practiced;

it was just the way he was. I remembered the first time I went out driving with my mother and older sister, my learner's permit still smoking-hot in my back pocket. We'd gone a half block from the house and I hadn't hit anything, so the sense in the car was that I was doing very well. Though I kept my face calm I felt that my nerves must be sticking out an inch and a half all over my body. But my sister pretended not to notice; to be nice she said in mock-exasperation from the back seat, "I think boys are *born* knowing how to drive." I remembered it, perhaps, because that very gratifying moment of pure male privilege and entitlement remained a rarity in my life. But for Tony that was reality; he'd always breathed that air. That was perhaps the essence of what he called, in his cockier moments, his Tony-magic.

"I'm not being 'dramatic,'" I said, and rolled my eyes – perhaps a bit dramatically. It was wasted on him because he was looking ahead. "I'm right."

"Yeah," he said. He made a serious brooding motion with his lips and eyebrows. "Yeah, it's been good to hash some stuff out. And it's good to move on."

"That's true." He was suggesting that we didn't have to get real heavy; we'd been through all that. That was fine with me. I was aware of something I seldom felt with Tony any more. I found him a little intimidating, a regular guy, one of the big kids, somebody who might stop liking me if I forgot myself and said or did something faggy. I looked at the passing houses, mad at myself for wondering if there was a correct manly way to do so: maybe I wasn't looking bored enough, or – worse – my attempts at macho indifference might read as a pose of queenly languor. I asked myself irritably why I was nervous with Tony in the first place. He never seemed to mind the way I was. I was learning not to second-guess Joe; maybe eventually, after another twenty-three years, I would be able to accomplish the same with Tony.

"So just think," I said, "another eight months and you may have a little Jimmy on your hands." He smiled.

"Rachel told you," he said. I sensed that he was relieved. He was the man of the Nineties and the sweetest guy in the world, but for all that he still liked to rely sometimes on his wife to tell people about his feelings.

"That's the nicest thing you've ever done for me," I said.

"Hey – you're my guy." He cleared his throat, not quite happy with that response; it was too much a pre-Rehoboth formula. We'd been spilling our guts for two weeks and he wanted to show some respect for that. "I want him to be like you," he said after a moment. "I really do. You've got to be around when he's coming up."

"Count on it," I said, smiling. "You're sure he's going to be a boy, I guess."

"I hope so. Rachel says she's sure."

"Well: Rachel has spoken." He nodded. "Sure to be the cutest little boy who ever lived," I said. "And the smartest and best and sweetest."

"Since *I* was a kid, anyway," he said, and I laughed out loud. He looked over at me, pleased with himself. I remembered a story he'd told me when we were in college. When he was a tiny child his mother used to chant praises to him while she dressed him in the morning. Then when his brother was born Tony went to stay for a couple of days with his grand-mother. She didn't know the routine, so while she was putting his clothes on him the first day he had to fill in the missing dialogue himself: Beautiful Tony, handsome boy, such a good little man. I don't imagine that even his grandmother could have found this sunny prattling child more appealing than I did when I heard the story, nineteen years old and wildly in love with the happy humpy energetic young man he'd turned into. I pictured clearly the stocky-legged child, bright curls framing his stubborn certain smiling pretty face, reminding his grandmother courteously but insistently of a necessary bit of baby etiquette; and surely her heart swelled and she clasped him and laughed and kissed him and he wondered contentedly why such a simple explanation could trigger so passionate and delightful a response. I found the story so cute that it was phys-ically painful. It felt almost dangerous, as though Fate might be jealous of a child who had ever been so adorable. There was also a suppressed envy that Tony as a little boy had been so sure of himself. I'd been a nervous owlish child who spent most of his time observing the intriguing and perverse world of adults, trying to figure out what was expected of him. But by loving Tony I'd had a faint hope that I could garner for myself some of his confidence and joy in himself. By being his friend, I would get to be OK too.

We'd come out of the shade by now and he was shining in the sun. The squint was perfect; it made even Dennis' crinkly blond wholesomeness seem stagey and conniving. Suddenly it hit me. Tony's sexiness was back. Rachel's pregnancy had shown me, among other things, that he was a man who was having sex again. No more slack napping on deck-chairs for him. It was precisely the suspension of Tony's charisma that had made all the breakthroughs and insights of the past two weeks possible, including the whole process of falling in love with Joe. Joe had told me I'd have to learn to love the Tony who was straight, the Tony who was married to Rachel. It had seemed rather easy when he said it, but now with Tony's bright light rekindled it wasn't easy at all.

Yet at the same time, once I'd admitted to myself that Tony still had his hold on my nerves, I relaxed. We'd handled dicier situations in the past, and we were still fine together. Now he was going to be a father, a man with a baseball mitt, a man who could help with homework, a man who set rules on car keys and curfews and imparted the facts of life. His sexiness was now connected with his reliability and integrity, his basic goodness. For years, there had always been a threat in his attractiveness: that he was about to escape, that he would suddenly be gone, off on some cheerful footloose carefree boyish project. This summer he'd been proving, to Rachel and to me, that he was someone who would stay.

"Uncle Jim," he said to me, trying it out. "That'll work."

"Oh, I'm good at that. You've seen me with my nephew. I've got that whole routine down to an art form."

"This is going to be great," he said. He glanced at his watch and said, "Time to head back." He did a neat little U-turn, first swerving right to give himself room; it was probably the sportiest thing that had happened on that street in years. On the ride back I noticed myself enjoying the smartness of the blue car, its quiet smooth ride and zippy lines. It was typical of

Tony that, perhaps even without conscious thought, he would rent a car that was not just practical and potent but actually dashing. He'd probably said nothing more than, "A convertible would be great," and the rental clerk on the other end of the line had picked up the vibration of a sexy man with money and a modest swashbuckling streak. The few times I'd ever rented cars myself they turned out to be maroon Horizons or beige Cavaliers – just right for the podgy academic. I patted the outside of the car door as once I might have dreamed of patting Tony's body.

"You know," he said, bringing me out of a short reverie I hadn't even realized I'd lapsed into, "I used to think we were close."

I immediately understood what he meant. I smiled and said, "Me too."

He glanced over at me to be sure of my smile and then said,

"I guess we were. But there's more to it now. It's almost like we were just keeping the door open all those years, so all this could happen now. It's been a fairly incredible couple of weeks, when you think about it." I jabbed his upper arm with my fingertips.

"Twenty minutes ago I said the same thing and you said I was being 'dramatic,'" I said.

"So I'm slow," he said. Suddenly he nodded in agreement with himself and said, "You remember the stairs up to High Street?" I remembered. To get to campus from our dorm senior year, we had to walk up a long outdoor staircase. When we walked up together, I invariably had to wait for him at the top. I was always wired at that age, given to sudden scurrying bursts of motion, prone from one minute to the next to feel an urgent need to be elsewhere which I usually expressed with the sudden announcement, "I'm bored." I wasn't just high-strung, really. I was carrying the claustrophobic load of a serious closet-ed love which required me to cover every spontaneous impulse, and which vented itself in these manic bursts of energy. Part of Tony's deep-down bodily well-being, on the other hand, was a refusal to be hurried. After quietly racing up the stairs by twos and threes, I'd look down from the top and see him pulling himself up with a firm tug on the handrail for each step. He seemed to enjoy using his thick body as a counterweight for his arms, rocking backwards slightly and tugging at the rail to haul himself up, making a little work-out out of the simple process of climbing fifty steps. This indolence on the part of someone who, in another mood, could dash headlong into a scrimmage or suddenly offer to race me to the corner, struck me as irritating and charming. Our friends picked up on Tony's slowness as just one instance of our general disparateness: "Jim's here," they'd say; "I guess Tony'll be showing up in five or ten minutes." I took a special delight in our differences and sometimes boasted, naïve young lover that I was, "We're nothing alike," to show how well I knew him, and as if that proved that the affection between us was authentic and had cost us both something. But Rachel had said we were really very much alike in some ways, and Joe had been teasing me just the night before for exactly what Tony was now admitting to: being slow to understand my feelings.

"I remember," I said.

"The thing is..." he said. Again, I understood instantly. I wasn't nervous now.

"The thing is," I finished for him, "we both always got to the top." He nodded sagely, Joseph Campbell trapped in the body of a Britches model. "Doro," I said, "you make me laugh."

"You love that," he said smugly.

"That's true," I agreed.

"It's all part of my job," he said.

By the time we got back to the house, Ricardo was in the driveway loading bags into Marie's car. Marie came out the back door with a big lunch bag which she stowed in the shade under the dashboard. She also handed Ricardo her cosmetics case; he slipped it in next to her bag and closed the trunk. She had on a big loose shirt over her tank top and shorts and her sunglasses were pushed up on the top of her head. She looked like the goddess of beach. She gave us a wave as we pulled in next to her car and said,

"Just in time. We're leaving in a few minutes." I had a brief disorienting fear that if we'd been away just a little longer we might have gotten back to find that they'd all left without us.

"You missed Gene and Patrick," she said. "They were by a few minutes ago to say Good-bye."

"Well, I'll see them at home," I said.

"I think they wanted to say Good-bye to Tony," Ricardo said. "Hi, Tony."

"Hey, Weasel," Tony said.

"Where's Joe?" I asked.

"He's out front with Rachel," Ricardo said. "He's so macho." I didn't understand what Ricardo meant by this until I saw that Joe was carrying the porch furniture inside and sliding it into the large closet under the stairs under Rachel's supervision. The two of them fussed a little fitting the last folding chair into place. Finally the paneled door clicked neatly shut and they brushed their hands off and looked at each other with a comradely smile.

"Hi," Joe said to me.

"Did you miss me?" I asked.

"Yeah," he said; "I've had nothing else on my mind all morning." Rachel laughed and patted my arm.

"He's been miserable, Jim," she said.

"How are things upstairs?" I asked him.

"My stuff is all done," he said. "I brought the food down and I packed most of your stuff. There's just a few things left to throw in the bag. Go take a look. It'll take you two minutes."

He was right. As I glanced around the studio by myself, I saw that he had left very little for me to do. I could imagine him in something like the mood that had come over him a few days earlier in his housecleaning fit, blowing through the studio with stern efficiency, proving to me even in my absence that he was right about how easy it would be to pack everything up. It was strange to think that a life that had been so dense and absorbing for two weeks could be thrown into bags so swiftly. I folded the last of my clothes and tossed them into the big duffle bag. I knocked all my bathroom things into the black rubber toiletries kit Marie had bought me the year before. Joe had left his Armani in the shower stall by mistake and with a faint fetishistic thrill I packed it with my Aramis and Guerlain *Impériale*. The sheets and towels were already in the laundry downstairs; Joe had already packed the bathrobe, which Rachel said was a gift to me.

So there was really nothing to do but admire the wonderful light as it drenched the plain white walls and picked out the brilliant colors of the grouting on the counter. I sat for a moment on the slick green sofa. I felt lonely for Joe, who always sat next to me in the corner there. It was a luxurious self-indulgence to miss him, knowing he was thirty steps away downstairs. I looked out at the busy crowds on the beach and felt nostalgic, as if they and their happiness were part of a world from which I was now cut off forever. The studio itself felt like home now and I was distinctly sorry to be going. At the same time, it had the stale and unreal feeling of a place which one is about to leave, so that even if somehow it had become possible or necessary for Joe and me to stay there after all, it would have felt like an anticlimax, a backwater from the sweep of real life. It was too quiet; with the windows secured and the sun beating in, it was too warm. Checking the electric switches and the latch on the bathroom skylight one last time, I picked up my bags and let myself out.

I found Marie in her room stacking the laundered linens in the closet.

"You'll drive safely?" I asked.

"If I play my cards right," she said, "I won't drive at all. Ricardo loves driving my car."

"Watch out," I said, "he's got a heavy foot. There are speed traps all through Delaware."

"I know," she said. "He's a teenager at heart. But all I have to do is tell him to be careful; he loves showing how responsible he can be." She closed the closet door and glanced around the room to be sure it was all as it should be. "So Joe's going back with you," she said. I nodded. "That'll be pretty great. He can get his feet wet in your real life. You can bring him to DC, if you want. Maybe you two could go out and then spend the night at our house; or with Walter and Ricardo, I guess."

"I'll ask him. That could be fun." There was some kind of ringing endorsement that hadn't been made yet and I wasn't sure if I should press her for it. Her purse was still on the dresser and I handed it to her.

"No, I wasn't forgetting it," she said. She took a brush out of it and ran it through her hair, watching herself in the mirror. "Wait till Clare hears him sing," she said suddenly, giggling to herself. "She'll be *horr*ified." That was true; Clare loathed pop music almost as much as Wagner and Verismo, and her efforts to be polite about it were among the most amusing things about her.

"So what's your final verdict?" I asked her. She shook her hair out and put the brush back in her purse.

"There's no final verdict yet," she said. "I feel like I've barely met him." She smiled. "He was fun in the water yesterday," she said. "He's such a boy." She saw from my face that I wasn't satisfied yet with what she was saying.

"I want to like him," she said. "If he's nice to you, if he's right for you, I'm sure I will like him. He's nervous with you still, and that makes me nervous."

"I don't think he's really all that nervous with me any-more," I said. "He speaks his mind."

"Sometimes he'll have to keep his thoughts to himself," she said darkly. "There's such a thing as too much honesty in a relationship. You two are different. He has to let you be the way you are."

"You think he's trying to make me into a surfer/waiter?"

"I don't want you to make yourself into one just to be nice and make him love you," she said. "And those creepy bar-boys he hangs out with... he wants you to like them." I nodded, afraid to admit for the moment that to some extent I already did like them. "I don't want to be awful about this," she said. "I just want the best for you. I don't want you to settle for some silly boy just because you're afraid of being alone." I shook my head.

"He's not some silly boy," I said. "I love Joe."

"Good," she said quickly. Her encouraging tone sug-gested that she was humoring me and wasn't positive yet. "I've never heard you say you loved someone, you know that? In all the years we've known each other. That means things will work out. I'm sure I'll like him." She patted my arm and kissed my cheek. "It's good he's coming to Baltimore. It'll give us all a chance to get to know each other better." She slung her purse over her shoulder and said, "Time to go downstairs and say Good-bye."

It was only a few minutes later that Joe and I were in my car on our way to the guest house to get the rest of his stuff. The farewells at the main house had been almost surreally quick, as if a massive late-Romantic symphony had ended with a few bars of *pizzicato* and a ping of the triangle. Ricardo's attention was already focused on the prospect of driving Marie's Turbo and he hustled her and Walter into the car with a kind of distracted wave to Joe and me.

"See you this week," he called from the driver's seat, and turned the key with a smile at the motor's deep heavy roar. Walter shrugged at us and slipped in behind Ricardo, and Marie blew kisses and settled in to give orders from the front passenger seat.

The Neubergs and Joe and I, left standing in the driveway, waved as the car lurched into the street; it wasn't clear that any of the three travelers was looking at us anymore. Then we looked uncertainly at each other on the gravel. It was one of those times when you exchanged simple smiling little tags of talk, clasped and unclasped your hands, cleared your throat: time to go. I may have had some minor expectations of drama, but they were left unfulfilled. Once we'd loaded our two cars we felt at loose ends. When Tony asked if anyone wanted some ice tea or a last walk on the beach, it sounded so aimless that we all decided we might as well just hit the road.

I said, "Call me tonight so I know you made it home," and Rachel said, "Say good-bye to Michael and the others for us," and we locked up the house and hugged and kissed and drove away.

The apartment at the guest house was all awhirl. It was something like being backstage at a drag show: there seemed to be dozens of men bustling about, deeply excited about essentially unimportant things.

"Where's my black TANK-top?" Bobby was screaming as he answered our knock, and when Dennis fished it out of his own bag a minute later and asked "Is this it?" it was so completely generic that I wondered how they could tell whose it was.

Chris had a camera and was taking shots like a fashion photographer, coaxing and coaching the other three boys as they spun around the apartment packing and cleaning and whacking each other with bits of beach wear. He knelt by a table or stood on the sofa or leaned through doorways to get angles.

"Good," he'd say every so often with a curt professional nod after a click of the shutter. This was the Chris who did video art in LA, I gathered – I hadn't seen him like this. I wondered what the artistic concept was: who would want to see pictures of these people packing and posing? The old artistic adage, I supposed – work with what you know. I hadn't the energy for the conversation we might have had on the subject.

"Claude Christian," I asked him instead, as he backed me to the door and made me come through it again, "did you see Gene on his way out of town?"

"Whatever," he said vaguely, squinting through the view finder. "Yeah," he said after a moment of fiddling with knobs and lenses; "he was by." He reached with a gesture of perfect elegance into the breast pocket of his loose red silk shirt, and with the tips of two fingers pulled out a slip of paper. "His address and number," he said, and smiled imperialistically as he dropped it back into his pocket. "Like we're ever going to see each other again." He smiled again, to himself. I couldn't tell if it was a smile of regret or vanity. Who was the conqueror there, I wondered, and who the ravaged province? I'd never imagined that any mere boy of flesh and blood could smile like that over Gene.

"I know he really likes you a lot," I said, feeling some need to say something warm and loyal – though I wasn't sure loyal to whom.

"He's super," Chris said complacently, and turned to take pictures of Bobby sitting on his suitcase.

Michael was seated in a big torn armchair sipping a gin and tonic. He smiled benevolently at the furor and made a knowing gesture for my benefit.

"Would either of you like a delicious cocktail?" he asked me and Joe.

Joe glanced at his watch and said "No, thanks" with a studious grown-up look. He and Dennis went into a bedroom to hunt for some of their stuff. I could hear them laughing over the radio music.

"Word," Dennis said at one point: it was an LA expression I'd learned from Joe a few days before, a generalized term of good feeling when there was nothing particular to say.

Michael lounged up out of his chair and walked me into the kitchen area.

"A Coke at least," he said. He took the rindy stub of lemon that was left on the refrigerator door shelf and squeezed it hard into an old Flintstones glass with some ice and some foamy Coke. The glass was very much of a piece with the fading tackiness of the guest house. The only surprise was that none of these Los Angeles men had thought to stash it in his bag: doubtless it would be considered a collectible, if not absolutely an antiquity, on the Coast.

Michael touched my glass with his and said,

"It's been great meeting you, Jim." His voice was self-consciously mature, the voice of a show-biz magnate who can clinch a deal in such a way as to have it said of him later by all who were there, He's a great guy. I nodded without saying anything. I shared his undifferentiated friendly feelings, though the obvious calculation he'd put into choosing his words made me a little uncomfortable.

"I guess I'll be out to visit soon," I said after a pause. He nodded.

"You can see the store," he said, as though he were offering me tickets to a Chandler Pavilion gala. Then he met my eye, firmly, as if on cue from a director in a family-market TV drama.

"Be *good* to him," he said.

I had a dangerous impulse to laugh. Michael's plain bronzed face was not made for drama. It wasn't fair that emotional honesty and sincerity should be more becoming to handsome people than to ugly, but it was true. Michael looked like a dog, a baboon, a Ferengi trying to impersonate Jimmy Stewart. Inconsequently I thought how glad I was that Clinton had been elected: I was so thoroughly sick of watching withered-lip head-shaking turkey-neck presidents pontificating on values, and whether or not you entirely trusted Bill at least you could watch him on TV without gagging.

In the moment that these thoughts were scurrying through my mind I heard Joe's voice in the next room saying "Hey, man" to Dennis. There was a tiny flicker in Michael's eyes, as by instinct he was about to turn to where his boys were talking before he remembered he had to look forthright and resolute by keeping his eye contact with me. In spite of myself I was touched. This is someone who genuinely likes Joe, I thought; he's saying something he has a right to say.

Notwithstanding this moment of moral grandeur I was unable to hold Michael's eye any longer, and looking at the floor to keep him from seeing my smile I said,

"Of course I will."

Dennis and Joe came out of the bedroom together and put down their two bags. Suddenly there was that same feeling we'd had in the driveway at the big house, everyone standing on one foot and then the other, starting sentences, interrupting each other, nodding and smiling.

"We'd better split," Joe said after a few moments. "You guys know your way back to the airport?" He laughed at himself, and added, "Like I *do*, right?"

"There's a limo," Michael said. He had the brisk tone of the responsible adult who would handle the logistics and let the boys stay busy with being hot and fabulous. "My folks couldn't get away this time." He gestured apologetically, hands apart.

"Say Hey to them for me," said Joe.

Michael suddenly went soft-eyed and said "Aw" and put his arms out for a hug. Then for a moment everyone was saying good-bye. Each of the boys was more or less charming to me and I decided I would have to admit to Marie that I liked them. Chris said "See you" and hugged me hard with one elbow locked around my neck. He was not wearing any fragrance and his skin had a clean substantial scent, oily and bread-like. I could imagine how it must be heightened in moments of passion and found it a very appetizing thought. I promised myself to give Gene the hardest time about it, he who had claimed to carry on with Chris only to prove my innocence to Tony.

"Come soon," Bobby said. "We'll make the *biggest* fuss over you. Mother, show him what he's WON!" He twirled once, arms up, and smiled like a girl in a tooth paste commercial. Michael made some gesture towards Joe and then giggled into one hand. "Best love to Cybil," Bobby said as an afterthought.

"You'll call him, won't you?" I asked. I had a sentimental fear that these callous West Coast kids had harrowed the tender feelings of all gay Baltimore: what if I got home to find Gene and Patrick and God only knew how many others plunged into the deepest despondency over svelte footloose Californians? Bobby laughed and swatted the air with one hand and said, "Oh sure." I couldn't tell, through the determined irony of his standard stance, if that meant he surely would or surely wouldn't. I thought I'd seen some kind of nice connection between him and Patrick. That might just be my own need to believe that something could work between men from opposite coasts; maybe neither Patrick and Bobby nor Gene and Chris had ever expected or wanted anything more than a pleasant vacation affair.

I had a slight moment of panic when Dennis put his hand out to me and said, "Hey, guy." He looked exceptionally cute, even for him; I think he was energized by the prospect of returning to Los Angeles, where life was real and absorbing. I felt a little guilty, as if I'd stolen Joe from him. It struck me that he didn't move to hug or kiss me: didn't LA people do that all the time, on any pretext? But he just said, "Have fun. I guess we'll see you soon, right?"

"Right," I said. In the corner of my eye I saw Michael standing with Joe, holding his hand and swinging it, stiff-armed. Joe came and did a moment's shadow-punching and hugging with Dennis. Then suddenly we were down the stairs waving up at the others on the porch, and then they closed the door.

Joe took my keys to open the trunk and toss in his bag.

"You want to drive?" I asked.

"You want me to?" He looked diffident. I wasn't sure if he wanted to or not.

"I'll start," I said.

"Careful shifting into third," he reminded me, handing my keys back to me. I didn't understand at first.

"Do you remember everything I say?" I asked him when it registered. He got into the passenger seat. "Maybe you can take over at the Bridge," I told him. "I get squirrelly about it sometimes."

"There's a bridge?" he asked. I was as surprised as if he'd said to a Roman, Oh, there's an amphitheatre? It reminded me that Joe was taking a big gamble here, entering a world whose best-known landmarks were new to him.

"So that's Rehoboth," Joe said as we rolled the windows down and I turned the key in the ignition. "When Michael suggested it, I said, 'Where?'"

"What if you hadn't come?" I said. It was one of those brush-with-destiny moments, like when it occurred to you that your parents very nearly married other people.

"You would have picked up some other boy on the beach," Joe said. "Shame on you."

There was a fairly long silence after we pulled out onto the highway. I felt I should be making charming small talk but couldn't think of anything to say. I found I wasn't quite sure that Joe was coming with me freely. Maybe I'd somehow sulked or threatened or guilt-tripped him into doing something that might not be right for him. I was spiriting him away from his usual stylish companions and the throbbing Nineties show-biz epicenter of LA to try to cram him into my sequestered academic life in a provincial eastern city. I was getting something I wanted, but I couldn't be positive that I'd gotten it fairly. I also couldn't ask him about it. He would have to deny it, and the conversation would make me sound petulant, not content with getting Joe but also cornering him into additional affirmations. Every time I glanced at Joe for the first few miles he was looking out his window and drumming his fingers on his leg.

Traffic was picking up as people started to check out of their hotels and head home. We had to stop at the last light on the way out of town. I suddenly felt the pull of the open road ahead of us and was frustrated that we had to wait at the light. When it finally turned green I did an impatient little hotrod acceleration. A large family van which had been stopped next to us at the light was suddenly way behind us and I heard Joe give a little hum of appreciation.

"*Drive* that Camry," he said. He shifted in his seat to face me half way, so that when I looked over at him now he was wedged against the car door, the way he always sat in the corner of the sofa. He looked amused.

"What?" I asked, about to be irritated.

"Look at you," he said, nodding.

"What?"

"My Mario Andretti," he said. I laughed and felt silly, as though he'd told me I looked good for my age. "You look kind of hot," he said a moment later.

"It's warm," I said. I hoped I wasn't sweating, because I didn't want to look flushed and elderly; besides, I was liking the fresh air from the open windows. "Should I turn on the AC?"

He reached over and rubbed my forehead with his hand, looking at his palm to satisfy himself it wasn't damp. "That's not what I meant," he said.

"What?"

"You look hot. You're…"

"Oh," I said, and smiled.

"I could go for a guy like you," he said. His voice had a practiced tone, teasing and flirtatious. I wondered for a moment if I could tell if he meant it or not. Maybe he was just working me in a nice way; maybe this was just the way he'd string me along and keep me happy over the years as I got older and odder. Then I decided it didn't matter.

"Should I pull over?" I asked him. "We could hop in the back seat this very second."

"Wo Tiger," he said, making a polite lustful face.

The miles were going by easily now. We spoke, as Italians said, of the more and the less; much of the time we didn't speak at all. We stopped briefly to poke around a photogenic little town with a clapboard Gothic church and a dusty antiques store. Joe described it rather patronizingly as "very east." We stopped again for burgers a few miles before the Bridge. By the time we were approaching it, the sun was starting to set and there were some postcard streaks of color on the Bay.

"This is where I get nervous sometimes," I said. It was by way of being a Baltimore tradition to get acrophobic while driving across the Bay Bridge. I never used to have any problems driving over bridges until some old-time Baltimorean friends told me about their own sudden gripping terrors at hanging hundreds of feet over the crabs on the road to or from the beach. It would hit me about one out of every three or four times I drove across; I couldn't tell yet if this would be one of them. "It's a difficult bit of road."

Joe looked at me for a second and seemed to decide I was fine. He turned back to look at the road. The Bridge swept up before us with its great pair of humped steel arches and beyond them the long curving roadways that seemed to skim the surface of the water for miles after the roller-coaster descent from the crest. The water was lighting up now as the sun slanted farther, as if sheets of red and yellow glass had been laid across it and glittered beneath the Bridge. The clumps of trees that crowded down to the sandy shore on the far side were a brooding velvety green over black shadows, as dark as the clustering *ginestra* along an Italian highway.

"It's beautiful," Joe said.

FINIS

Author's Note

Two works by the Italian novelist Cesare Pavese underlie this book: *La spiaggia* (*The Beach*), first published in serial form in the journal *"Lettere d'oggi"* in 1941 and then in its present form by Einaudi in 1956; and *Dialoghi con Leucò* (*Dialogues with Leucò*), Einaudi 1953. In the first book, a high school teacher describes his vacation at the beach with his best friend Doro, who is married to Clelia. He also becomes reacquainted with a former student, Berti. Despite an apparent coolness between Doro and Clelia, at the end of the book they discover that she is pregnant. The narrator and Berti then return to the city together. This is the book which Jim, in *Dialogues on the Beach,* tosses aside near the beginning of Chapter 4. *Dialoghi con Leucò,* a neo-Fraserian series of dialogues among characters from classical mythology, suggested some of the over-all imagery of *Dialogues on the Beach* – the use of elemental and/or archetypal references for the four main characters (water and the sea for Rachel, the sun for Tony, green growing things for Joe, and the beach itself, as an intermediate or liminal space, for the narrator Jim). This is the book which Joe starts reading in Chapter 5 of *Dialogues on the Beach.* There is no explicit gay content in either of Pavese's books.